IN THE WEEDS

BOOKS BY B.K. BORISON

✳

Lovelight Farms
In the Weeds
Mixed Signals

IN THE WEEDS

❊ ❊ ❊

B.K. BORISON

PAN BOOKS

First published 2022 by B.K. Borison

First published in the US 2023 by Berkley
an imprint of Penguin Random House LLC

First published in the UK 2023 by Pan Books
an imprint of Pan Macmillan
The Smithson, 6 Briset Street, London EC1M 5NR
EU representative: Macmillan Publishers Ireland Ltd, 1st Floor,
The Liffey Trust Centre, 117–126 Sheriff Street Upper,
Dublin 1, D01 YC43
Associated companies throughout the world
www.panmacmillan.com

ISBN 978-1-0350-2883-2

3 5 7 9 8 6 4

A CIP catalogue record for this book is available from the British Library.

Printed and bound by CPI Group (UK) Ltd, Croydon, CR0 4YY

Book design by Alison Cnockaert

Visit **www.panmacmillan.com** to read more about all our books
and to buy them. You will also find features, author interviews and
news of any author events, and you can sign up for e-newsletters
so that you're always first to hear about our new releases.

For everyone looking for their happy.
I hope you know how brave you are.

IN THE WEEDS

PROLOGUE

BECKETT

August

SHE'S SITTING AT the bar when I walk in, summer heat thick and oppressive at my back. My shirt clings to my skin, and her eyes cling everywhere else—a smile curling at the corners of her mouth.

Long legs in cutoff shorts. Straight black hair to her waist. Full lips painted red. She turns in her stool as the door snaps shut and looks right at me like I've kept her waiting. A tilt to her brow like she's pissed about it too.

"Sorry," I tell her as I slip onto the stool next to her, not quite knowing why I'm apologizing or how I got over to this seat to begin with. I'm caught halfway between doing and wanting, the humidity from outside lingering.

Her eyelashes flutter like she's amused, and a thick press of syrupy heat curls in the space between us. "For what?"

I . . . have no idea. I rub the heel of my hand against my jaw and busy myself with the drink menu, an inexplicable rush of embarrassment burning at my cheeks. I've never claimed to possess an ounce of charm, but I'm usually better than this.

I nod toward her half-empty glass.

"What're you drinking?" I ask. She rolls her lips to hide her smile and tips her glass back and forth.

"Tequila."

I must wince, because she laughs, her chin tilting up but her dark eyes staying right on me. "What? Not a fan?"

I shake my head, and she lowers the glass on the bar top between us, then turns it around and around in her pretty hands. One eyebrow arches high on her forehead. "Maybe you just haven't had the right kind."

"Maybe," I agree. I stop the movement of her hands with my fingers over hers and bring the glass to my lips. I make sure to set my mouth on the cherry red lipstick mark she left behind.

Smoke. Lime. A bite of salt.

I drop the glass back to the bar and lick my bottom lip.

"Not bad," I grit out.

She grins at me, her dark eyes like a thumbnail scratching at the line of my jaw. "Not bad at all."

SHE HAS A scar at the top of her thigh.

I don't know if she realizes it, but she wiggles every time I pass my thumb over it, her leg digging into my hip where she's draped over me. Her skin smells like lemons and rosemary, and I tuck my nose into the space below her ear where it's strongest, drag my face down until I can press a kiss to the smooth line of her throat.

She hums.

I can't stop tracing my palms over her skin, feeling her softness against me. Her fingers tangle in my hair and I press my face harder into her neck with a groan. She huffs a laugh against my collarbone.

Two damn nights together, and I officially don't even recognize myself. Evie is like a tide rolling in and clipping me at my ankles. A low, forceful tug. A blissful inevitability.

I drag my thumb over the scar again, slower this time, and her nose digs into my shoulder.

"I don't usually do this sort of thing."

I glance at the table tipped over in the corner, the coffeemaker that somehow managed to stay upright during our very enthusiastic entrance to the room. The ceramic dish holding the creamers isn't anywhere I can see, but the little disposable plastic containers are scattered across the carpet like fallen stars. Dots of white against navy blue.

I smooth my palm down her back and stretch my fingers wide, trying to see how much of her skin I can cover at once. She's warm under my touch, her skin a deep, flawless brown. Like a bottle of whiskey on the highest shelf, afternoon light dancing through.

I shift beneath her and grunt when her thigh grazes something interesting. "Nearly destroy a hotel room?"

She rocks her forehead back and forth against my neck with a laugh, and it slips down over my shoulders to sit heavy in the center of my chest. She leans up on one arm and rests her chin in the palm of her hand.

"No." She reaches behind my ear and plucks a feather from my hair, glancing at the half-torn pillow shoved haphazardly under my head. I'm surprised I didn't rip the sheets clean off the bed that second time—when she scratched her nails down my back, wrapped her long legs high around my hips, and set her teeth against my collarbone. She sighs low and slow, eyes searching mine, a bemused grin tilting her lips when I wrap a lock of her hair around my finger and tug. I had my whole fist in it about twenty minutes ago, and she looks amused that I've settled for a strand now.

"I don't usually get distracted on work trips," she explains.

Neither do I. I don't usually get distracted at all. While a one-night stand is my relationship of choice, I wasn't planning on one this trip. The Northeastern Organic Farmer's Conference isn't a hotbed of seduction. Or it hasn't been, typically.

Our shared glass of tequila turned into a shot on the bar top in front of me. That shot turned into Evie ordering the rest of the bottle. And that bottle turned into me licking a line of salt from the inside of her wrist, her knee pressed to mine beneath the bar. We stumbled back to the tiny hotel on the hill and fell into bed like we were made for it.

It turns out I don't mind tequila so much when I taste it on her.

Now we're here, tangled up and naked for the second night in a row. I told myself I wouldn't return to the bar, wouldn't go looking for her. But I couldn't stop thinking about her. Her skin pressed to mine. The low, husky moan when I slipped my hand between her legs. Her dark hair spread across stark white pillows.

As soon as the last speaker finished at my conference, I wandered right to that dive like she was singing a damn siren's song. And there she was, sitting on the same stool at the same bar, that same grin lighting up every inch of her face.

I trace my knuckles down her arm, mesmerized by the path of goose bumps that rise in the wake of my touch.

"Do you regret it?" I sit up, gently urging her to follow. She does, long legs rearranging around my hips. "The distraction," I clarify.

The sweat has hardly dried on my skin, but I want her again. I get an itch in my palms every time I look at her. I want to taste the soft skin just under her ear, feel her body tremble and roll above mine. I want to press my hand to those two divots at the base of her spine and feel her skin burn like an inferno as she moves against me.

She smiles and bites at her bottom lip like she knows where my mind has drifted off to, tracing the line of ink that curls over my shoulder. She taps there once and I get a glance of us in the mirror above the dresser, twisted white sheets and skin that shines like spun gold, my arm banded low around her waist. Never in my life have I wanted to take a picture of myself, but the urge strikes hot and fierce now, her bare skin touching mine. Her face in my neck and the swell of her ass just barely visible.

I nose beneath her chin and press a single, lingering kiss to the skin above her fluttering pulse—a wordless encouragement to answer the question.

"No. Turns out you're a fine distraction, Beck. The best kind, really." Her answer is a whisper, a secret in the dark. She pauses and then says, "Do you regret it?"

No, I don't regret it. Much as I probably should. I smile and drag my teeth up the line of her throat, nip at her earlobe, and tug once. I watch in the mirror as her whole body shivers, her hips rolling down into mine.

"I like your kind of distraction," I tell her as I catch her waist with my hands. I guide her into a smooth rhythm above me until we're both panting, her nails scratching through my hair.

"Did you—" She hums and lifts up on her knees, maneuvering us with her hand on my chest until my back is pressed to the headboard. She's bossy when she wants to be, and I like that she tells me exactly what she wants, how she wants it. The rasp of her voice in my ear last night had me shuddering against her, hands clenching at her hips as I worked to follow every single instruction she laid out.

Make it slower.

Harder.

Like that, yes. Right there.

My head hits the wood with a dull thump, and she settles in my lap, rearranging the sheets until it's skin on skin, a low moan of want heavy on my tongue. She mumbles something under her breath and then hiccups a sigh, another sound I chase with my lips on hers. She pulls back and looks down at me through heavy eyes. "Did you want more?"

The question has me huffing a laugh. I look at her and all I seem to do is want. I lean up until I can catch her mouth in a kiss and lick deep, my hand slipping from the back of her head to curl around her jaw. I hold her there until her hands turn into fists in my hair, body shifting impatiently above mine.

I can be bossy too.

"I want more," I tell her—another confession—my hand slipping down between us to brush the soft skin just below her belly button. "I want everything."

I WAKE TO a low roll of thunder, rain drumming against thick glass. A cool breeze sweeps in through the cracked window, and I twist beneath the sheets with a groan, my hand searching for sleep-warmed skin. Last I remember, Evie muttered something about room service, snuggled farther into the blankets, and fell asleep with both hands wrapped around my arm. It was . . . nice. Different but nice.

I lean up on my elbows and glance at the empty spot next to me. I'm surprised I didn't hear her moving around the room—didn't feel her slip from the bed. I don't usually sleep so soundly.

My gaze trips to the bathroom, the door half-cracked, a used towel slung over the back of it. It's possible she stepped out to grab coffee, but I don't see her suitcase, and the nightstand is glaringly bare. I scan the rest of the room. The only signs that she was here at all are a half-empty glass of water on the dresser and a crumpled receipt on the desk.

I collapse face-first into my pillow.

This, at least, is a familiar feeling. Waking up alone.

"Stupid," I tell myself. I sigh and dig the heel of my palm into my forehead.

I know better.

I have things I'm supposed to be doing here, and none of them are getting distracted by a gorgeous woman with legs for miles.

I flip onto my back and watch storm clouds gather outside the window. I just need to remember what those things are.

EVELYN

November

Well.

I was not expecting that.

I pace back and forth in my room at Inglewild's only bed-and-breakfast, watching my shadow follow along the floral wallpaper. Jenny, the owner, must have visited my room while I was at the farm, because I came back to candlelight and cookies, everything soft and romantic.

I frown at an ivory candle and debate my options.

I was in a similar bed-and-breakfast that weekend in Maine. There were flowers on the windowsill and a man with art on his skin pinning me to the bed, his lips against my neck and his throaty laugh in my ear. The same man I just ran into at the farm where he apparently works and that I was sent to evaluate.

Was not. Expecting. That.

Cookies tempt me from the shiny pewter tray in the corner. I snag one and swipe at my phone.

Josie answers on the third ring. "Did you get there okay?"

"We have a problem," I say around a mouthful of dark chocolate and peanut butter.

"Uh-oh." Her voice turns serious over the sound of paperwork being shuffled on the other end, the clink of a mug being set on a saucer. I check the time. It's still late afternoon in Portland. She's probably on her eighth cup of coffee. "Did Sway book you one of those escape room things again?"

Two months ago, my representation team thought it would make for quality content if I was locked in a room for forty-five minutes by myself. No preparation or warning. Thank god I'm not claustrophobic.

"No. Thanks for the reminder though." Josie laughs, and I collapse on the edge of the bed, eyeing the tray of cookies. "I got to the farm today."

"And? You were excited about this one."

I *was* excited about this one. I *am* excited about this one. A Christmas tree farm just off the Eastern Shore of Maryland, owned and operated by a woman named Stella. Her story is lovely and romantic, and the small glimpse I got of the farm today was nothing short of magical. I just wasn't expecting her head farmer to be the same man I had my first—and only—one-night stand with three months ago.

He had wandered into that dive bar with messy hair, a white T-shirt with the sleeves slightly rolled, and eyes like sea glass. He took one look at me, and I felt my stomach drop all the way to my toes.

"Beckett is here."

"Who?"

"You know," I drop my voice, *"Beckett."*

I hear the fumbling of a mug and a string of creative curse words. "Maine Beckett? Hot, tattooed Beckett?" She sucks in a breath through her teeth, and when she speaks again, her voice is three octaves higher. "Out of the ordinary, Evie is finally cutting loose, one-night stand *Beckett*?"

I give in and grab another cookie. "That's him."

Wrapped up on her couch like a burrito, I told Josie about Beckett after one too many glasses of sauvignon blanc. I couldn't figure out why I was still thinking about him months later. It was supposed to be fun and fleeting. A harmless night. No strings.

Not something to relive in marquee performances every other night in my fever dreams.

Josie laughs, a sharp cackle that has me pulling the phone away from my ear.

I roll my eyes. "Thank you very much for your support."

"Sorry, sorry," she says with a snicker. She tries to sober herself, but another chuckle slips through. "What are the odds? Is he visiting?"

"No, he works here. He manages the farm operations." He runs the place with the owner, Stella, and the woman who heads the bakery, Layla.

That sets her off into another fit of giggles. I debate hurling the phone right out the window. "Guess that explains why he was so good with his hands, huh?"

"I'm going to fire you."

I never said anything to Josie about his hands, but I remember them in explicit detail now. How his palm covered the entire expanse of my thigh. How, when he flexed his fingers and lifted, his biceps did something delicious. He was demanding with them, guiding me into the perfect position. The press of his thumb behind my ear. The delicate lines of a constellation trailing from his wrist to his elbow.

"You'll never fire me," Josie says. "How would you have any fun at all?"

Josie's been my self-appointed personal assistant since we turned eighteen and I decided to start my own YouTube channel. Her role and title have been formalized since my social media explosion, but her job as my best friend remains her top priority. I can always count on her to tell me how it is.

It's both the best and worst thing about her.

"Okay, let's recap. You slept with a smoking-hot stranger in August. You left without a word, and now, in November, you've run into him again while judging his farm for a social media contest." She makes an amused sound that I do not reciprocate. "Really though. What are the odds?"

"I have no idea."

"What are you going to do?"

"Again. I have no idea."

I pick at a loose thread at the edge of the quilt. I can't leave. What would I tell my corporate sponsors? *Sorry, I can't do this trip because I slept with one of the employees three months ago.* They've been agreeable in meetings, but I don't see that going over well.

And more than that, I'm not in the habit of running from my problems. Beckett was a choice I made. A choice I have zero regrets about, despite the memories of that night sticking to me like glue. I was telling him the truth when I told him he made a fine distraction. For once, I was blissfully out of my head. I laughed. I had fun.

I felt like myself.

But I'm here to do my job. Stella deserves that. Lovelight Farms is everything she described in her application and more. She deserves to be a finalist for this competition, and she deserves the recognition. All I need is a second to pull myself together. Get over the shock of seeing him again and move forward.

"The plan is . . ." I have no plan. I look around the room for inspiration. I guess the plan is to finish the rest of these cookies. Find a bottle of wine from . . . somewhere.

There's a knock at my door and I blow out a breath. I stare at the peephole with a sliver of apprehension. I don't need to guess as to who is on the other side.

"Oh my god, did I just hear a knock?" Josie is beside herself. "Is it him?"

I lift myself from the edge of the bed and smooth my palm over my hair. Of course it's him. "I've gotta go, Josie."

"Switch me to FaceTime," she demands. "Never mind, I'll do it. Evie, I swear to god, if you hang—"

I end the call before she has a chance to finish her threat, and I toss my phone on the table. It immediately rings with an incoming video call and I ignore it, adding a pillow on top for good measure.

I take my time on my walk to the door and hesitate with my hand above the knob. When he walked into the bakery earlier today, I felt that same swoop, low in my belly. Just like the first time. It was like cracking open a memory to take another look. Flannel instead of a white T-shirt. Backward baseball cap with a tiny embroidered tree.

Wide, surprised eyes.

I swing open the door like I'm ripping off a bandage and find

Beckett with his arms braced against the frame, hands curled around the edges like he's physically holding himself back. His fingers flex, and I get an immediate flashback of those hands wrapped tight around my thighs instead, Beckett on his knees in front of me, a single lock of dark blond hair plastered to his forehead.

I swallow.

"Hey," I whisper. I can barely look at him, and I sound like I swallowed six sheets of sandpaper. *Way to keep it together, Evie.*

I clear my throat.

He blinks at me, his gaze lingering and lazy, tripping from the top of my head to the drape of my sweater across my shoulder. His tongue licks at his bottom lip, and I feel like maybe I should grab the edge of the frame too. Cling to the brass door knocker for dear life.

I don't know what made me bring Beckett to my hotel with me that hazy summer night all those months ago. I'd never been remotely interested in a casual hookup before. I just—

I saw him walk in, and I wanted him.

Good to know his effect on me hasn't dimmed at all.

"Hey," he whispers back. He exhales through his nose and pushes off the doorframe, glancing once over his shoulder at the empty hallway behind him. I get a good look at the strong line of his jaw and have to clear my throat again. "Can I come in for a second?"

I nod and take a step back, letting him pass through the narrow doorway. All my hazy memories have apparently done the sheer size of him an injustice. He looks too big standing in the middle of the room with his hands in his pockets, pretending to study the painting of the pond hanging above the desk. I click the door shut and try not to think of the last time we were in a space just like this.

Gauzy white curtains. Tangled sheets. A warm hand splayed between my shoulder blades. His voice in my ear, telling me how good I felt. To *take it.*

I shake my head and lean against the dresser, legs crossed at the ankles. I am doing myself no favors. "You wanted to talk?"

He nods, still distracted by that painting. He glances at me from the corner of his eye. "Social media influencer, huh?"

I don't like the tone of his voice, the faint accusation I hear there. I hadn't offered my job, but neither had he. The both of us were focused on . . . other things during our time together. He didn't recognize me when I walked into the bar, and that had been a nice change. Refreshing.

Cheesy as it sounds, men typically don't want to be with me for me. Usually when I'm approached by men, there's something in it for them—a picture on one of my channels, a product plug. Once, a guy asked if I was up for a sex tape.

So when Beckett walked into that tiny bar with his inked arms and his gaze passing over me with appreciation instead of calculation, I took a chance. I took something for *myself*.

A lot of good that did me.

"Farmer, huh?" I mimic his cool indifference and watch the way his lips turn down at the corners, hands clenching into fists at his side.

"I'm just surprised, is all," he says, still with that slightly sarcastic tone. As if he can't believe he even needs to have this conversation with me. As if me being someone who works in social media is the most vile, repulsive thing he could possibly think of. He sniffs and rubs his knuckles against his jaw. "I didn't expect to see you again."

Clearly, I also didn't expect to see him, given that I ran from the bakehouse at the farm this afternoon like the place was on fire. Doesn't mean I'm going to be a jerk about it though.

He watches me carefully, eyes narrowed. I wish the cookie tray were closer. "Did you know?" he asks.

"Did I know what?"

"Did you know I work here?"

I frown and tilt my chin up. Does he think I did this on purpose? Came to his place of work to . . . what? Harass him? Embarrass him? "Absolutely not," I say firmly. "I didn't think I'd ever see you again either."

He smiles and it's not nice at all. "Well, you made that abundantly clear, Evie."

I blink at him.

"Sorry," he tells me, his voice gruff. He is not sorry at all. "You probably prefer Evelyn."

Something in my chest pulls tight at the sharp edge of his words. He sounds frustrated, uncomfortable. He's holding himself too still in the corner by the desk, a hard look in his eyes. I don't know why it hurts for him to call me Evelyn, only that it does.

But none of that matters. It doesn't matter that he's looking at me like I'm something stuck to the bottom of his shoe.

It doesn't change a single thing between us. Not what happened before and not what's happening now.

It's just . . . I had been Evie with him.

That had been nice.

The silence swells between us until it feels like there's a weight pressing on my shoulders. Beckett doesn't look like he's in any hurry to fill it. He tugs his hat from his head with a grumbled curse and drags his palm back and forth over the nape of his neck. Into his hair until half of it is sticking up.

"Listen, I didn't—" He tilts his head and looks at the ceiling, twisting his neck to the side in a tense stretch. He sighs and straightens, leveling me with a look that somehow channels both irritation and exasperation at the same time. I have no idea what to do with it. I have no idea what to do with any of it. This version of him is so very different from the man with the soft words and careful touches—his laugh a quiet, husky thing in the dark.

"I'm sorry. This isn't why I came here." He clenches his jaw so tight it's a wonder he's able to say anything at all. "I came here because— because I want to ask you to stay."

I can't quite stop the sound that trips out of my mouth. If that's him trying to convince me to stay, I'd hate to see what it looks like when he wants me to go. "Your pitch could use some work."

"Evelyn."

"I'm serious."

His frown deepens. "This contest means a lot to Stella. It means a lot to me too. Our farm needs your help, and I'd like for you to give us a fair shot at it."

Another painful pluck at my chest. "You think I wouldn't?"

"You did run from me earlier," he points out, the barest hint of a smirk curling at the corner of his mouth. I hate that it sends a lick of heat straight down my spine. "I mean, you literally ran from the bakery when you saw me."

I look down at my feet. Not my finest moment. But I didn't know what else to do. "I know."

A different kind of silence settles in the space between us.

"I'd like some reassurance," he says, voice quiet. I watch his feet as he shifts his weight. "That you'll stay."

"And what would that be?" I ask in his general direction. When he doesn't say anything in return, I release a breath and look up at him. He's still frowning, a little line between his eyebrows deepening. "For you to be reassured?"

I could write him a haiku. Bake him a cake and sign it in buttercream frosting. I know he's hesitant because of the way I left things, but it was a one-night—okay, a two-night—stand. A single weekend together.

I don't owe him anything.

His eyes flash a shade darker. For the first time since he's entered the room, he fixes his gaze intently on mine. Something twists and pulls between us. I feel it as sure as a touch against my arm. The small of my back.

"A promise," he says.

"Would you like me to take a blood oath?"

He makes an unamused sound.

I roll my eyes. "I'm here to do a job, Beckett. I wouldn't let anything get in the way of that. Stella deserves my best. I have no intentions of phoning it in."

I've never done anything but my best. He might think my job is ridiculous, but I know what my influence can do for people. I can bring business to this farm—customers, attention, a cannonball of social activity.

"So you promise?"

I nod, suddenly tired down to my very bones. I want the rest of that cookie tray and the bed, in that order.

I want my ghost of one-night stands past to find the nearest exit.

"I promise. I'll be there tomorrow. We can start over."

"You won't leave?" he asks, and I'm reminded of a hazy gray morning, a storm rolling in off the coast. His arm stretched out beneath the pillows, the bare skin of his back and the dip of his spine. The gentle snick of the door as it closed behind me, my suitcase at my feet.

I take a deep breath in through my nose and push it out just as slowly. It's not his fault that he doesn't believe me. Apparently, Beckett is the type to hold on to a grudge.

I grab another cookie from the tray. "I'll stay."

1

BECKETT

March

"DO YOU PLAN *on coming back to bed?*"

Her voice is raspy with sleep, and she has a hickey at the base of her throat, a deep purple bruise that I can't stop staring at. She stretches her arms above her head, and the sheet slips half an inch, the swell of her breasts rising from beneath. I want to catch that sheet in my teeth and drag it down until she's bare beneath me. I want a hundred other things too.

I shake my head from where I'm perched on the desk in the corner of the room and take another sip of coffee instead.

Restraint, I tell myself. Have some goddamn restraint.

She smirks at me.

"Oh, I get it." She drops her hands back down, one twisting through her hair, the other slipping beneath the sheets. One eyebrow arches high in invitation. "You like to watch."

I'm pretty sure I'd like just about anything with Evie. I want all that black silky hair wrapped around my fist, that smiling mouth at my neck. Last night she spent twenty-two minutes tracing the tattoo across my bicep with her mouth, and I want that too. I want to return the favor with the freckles on the inside of her wrist and the marks at her hips.

I push off the desk and set my cup to the side. I step toward the bed and watch the movement of her hand. She swipes it low across her stomach, a wicked smile on her pretty face. I plant my knee on the bed and find her ankle, her bare foot dangling off the edge.

"I love to watch," I tell her as I grip her thigh and make room for my body between her long legs. I drop a kiss to the inside of her knee, and her whole body shivers. I drop another kiss just above it. *"But I like to touch more."*

A finger digs into my ribcage as I'm violently yanked from my favorite daydream.

"Are you paying attention?"

My knee jolts and my boot catches on the chair in front of me, sending Becky Gardener rocking precariously to the side. She curls her hands around the edges with a white-knuckled grip and shoots me a look over her shoulder. I fix my attention on my boots and mumble an apology.

"I'm paying attention," I tell Stella, and swat her hand away.

Kind of. Not really. There are too many people in this room. All of the business owners in town are sandwiched together in the conference space at the rec hall, an old room that I'm pretty sure is used to store Easter decorations, if the slightly terrifying six-foot bunny in the rear corner is any indication. It smells like stale coffee and hairspray, and the ladies from the salon haven't stopped cackling since they stepped through the door. It's like sitting cross-legged in the middle of a parade while the drumline marches around me. All of the sound pulls my shoulders tight, an itch of discomfort pricking at my neck.

And I keep making eye contact with that bunny.

I don't usually come to these types of things, but Stella had insisted. *You wanted to be a partner,* she said. *This is what partners do.*

I thought being a partner meant I could buy the fancy fertilizer without checking with anyone, not attending meetings that serve absolutely no purpose. There's a reason I chose a job where I spend seventy-five percent of my day outside.

Alone. In the quiet.

I struggle with talking to people. Struggle with coming up with the right words in the right sequence at the right moment. Every single time I go into town, I feel like everyone is looking right at me. Some of that is in my head, I know, but some of it is—some of it is Cindy Croswell pretending to fall in the aisle at the pharmacy just so I have to help her up again. Or Becky Gardener from the school asking me if I can host a field trip while eyeing me up like I'm a rare steak with a side of potatoes. I've got no idea what goes on half the time I'm in town, but I feel like people lose their damn minds.

"You're not paying attention," Layla chimes in from my right, legs crossed and hand rummaging around in the giant bowl of popcorn she brought with her. Layla runs the bakery at the farm, while Stella holds down the tourism and marketing sides of things. Since Inglewild is the size of a postage stamp and Stella has a bone-deep urge to make Lovelight Farms a *cornerstone of the community*, we're now expected to be involved in a lot of town business.

I don't even know what this meeting is about.

"Where did the popcorn come from?" I deflect.

I glance at the gargantuan bag stuffed under Layla's chair. I know for a fact there's some brownies and half a box of crackers in there. She says the Inglewild bimonthly small business owner's meeting is a drag without a snack, and I'm inclined to agree. Not that she's offered to share.

Layla circles one finger right in front of my face and ignores my question. "You have that moony look on your face. You're thinking about Evelyn."

"Am not." I sigh and roll my shoulders, desperate to relieve the tension that sits between them. "I was thinking about the pepper crop," I lie.

I'm distracted. I've been that way since two hazy nights in August. Sweat-slicked skin. Hair like midnight. Evie St. James had smelled like sea salt and tasted like citrus.

I haven't had my head on straight since.

Layla rolls her eyes and crams another handful of popcorn into her mouth. "Okay, sure. Whatever you say."

Stella reaches across me and snatches the bowl out of Layla's hands. "They're getting ready to start. If we could pretend to be professional, that would be great."

I raise both eyebrows. "For the town meeting?"

"Yes, for the town meeting. The one in which we are currently in attendance."

"Ah, yes. Always very professional."

At the last town meeting, Pete Crawford tried to filibuster Georgie Simmons during a vote on new parking restrictions in front of the co-op. He had reenacted *Speed*, complete with props and voices.

Stella levels me with a look and turns back to the front of the room with the bowl in the crook of her arm. Layla shimmies closer and rests her chin on my shoulder. I sigh and look up at the heavy wooden beams that cut across the ceiling and pray for patience. There's a deflated balloon stuck up there, probably left over from the Valentine's Day event the town had last month. A speed-dating thing, I think. My sisters had tried to make me go, and I locked myself in my house and turned off my phone. I stare at the balloon and frown. A faded red heart, deflated and stuck, string wrapped around and around.

"Have you talked to her since she left?" Layla asks.

A couple of times. A bland text sent in the middle of the night after one too many beers. A generic response. A picture from her of an open field, somewhere out there in the world, a line of text that said, Not as nice as your farm but still pretty nice. I had fumbled my phone into the dirt when that message came through, my thumb tracing back and forth over her words like it was her skin instead.

A social media influencer. An important one, apparently. I'm still trying to wrap my head around that. Over a million followers. I looked her up one night when the silence of my house felt suffocating, my thumb tapping at the screen of my phone. I checked her account and couldn't stop staring at that little number at the top.

I never checked her account again.

I've had one-night stands before. Plenty of them. But I can't get Evie out of my head. Thinking about her is like a hunger in the hollow of my stomach, a buzzing just under my skin. We spent two nights together in Bar Harbor. I shouldn't—I don't know why I still see her when I close my eyes.

Twisted up in bedsheets. Hair in my face. That half smile that drove me crazy.

"I was thinking about peppers," I say again, determined to hold on to this lie. It's best not to give Layla an inch. She'll take a mile and the shirt off your back for the trouble of it. I grew up with three sisters. I can sense the inquisition like a wind change.

"Your face does not say you're thinking about peppers. It says you're thinking about Evelyn."

"Stop looking at my face."

"Stop making the face you're making, and I'll stop looking at it." I sigh.

"I just think it's a shame, is all." Layla reaches across me and grabs another handful of popcorn, and a kernel lands in my lap. I flick it off and hit Becky Gardener right in the back of the head. *Christ*. I wince and sink farther in my chair. "You two seemed to hit it off."

What we seemed to do is circle each other like two skittish kittens. After I went to visit her at the bed-and-breakfast, I promised I'd give her a wide berth to do her job. It had been harder than I expected, keeping that promise. Seeing her standing among the rows and rows of trees on the farm, a smile on her face, her hands passing over the branches—well, it was like taking a baseball bat to the face. Repeatedly. But the contest meant everything to Stella, and I wasn't about to ruin our chances with a . . . with a . . .

A crush? A flirtation?

I don't even know what.

All I know is that it was a challenge for me to be around her. I couldn't stop thinking about my body curled around hers. The way the skin just below her ear tasted. How it felt to have all that hair brush against my jaw, my shoulders, the tops of my thighs. I found myself wanting to make her laugh, wanting to talk to her.

I can count on one hand the number of people I *want* to talk to.

But we figured it out, settled into a routine while she was here. Cordial conversation and polite nods. A single slice of shared zucchini bread on a quiet afternoon—plenty of space between us. That same electric current that tugged us together at a dive bar in Maine knit slowly back together into a thin thread of connection.

And then she left. Again.

And unfortunately for me, I still haven't figured out how to stop thinking about her.

"What kind of peppers?"

I shake my head once, trying to pry loose an image of Evelyn standing in between two towering oak trees on the edge of the property, her face in profile and tilted toward the sky. The sun had painted her in shimmering golds, leaves fluttering lightly around her. I clear my throat and adjust my position in the folding chair, my knee knocking sideways into Layla's. I'm way too big for these chairs, and there are too many damn people in this room. "What?"

"What type of peppers are you planting? I haven't seen any markers for peppers out in the field."

The back of my neck goes hot. "You never go out in the fields."

"I'm in the fields every day."

She walks through the fields, sure, on the way to the bakehouse, situated smack-dab in the middle of them. But she never finds herself in the produce crop. Not unless she needs something. I scratch at my jaw, frustrated. I'd bet my savings she finds something she needs out there tomorrow morning.

"Bell," I manage between clenched teeth.

Shit, now I need to go out and plant bell peppers.

Layla hums, eyes alight with mischief. "What color?"

"What?"

"What color *bell pepper*"—she puts an annoying emphasis on the words—"have you planted?"

"He planted red bell peppers in the southeast fields in two rows next to the zucchini. Which you will get absolutely none of if you do not pay attention," Stella snaps.

Layla and I both glance at her in shock. It's not like Stella to get aggravated. Not to mention that is . . . not a true statement. And we both know it.

Some of the steel melts out of her shoulders and she slumps, handing Layla her popcorn bowl. "Sorry. I'm stressed."

"Clearly," Layla says with a laugh, hand back to rummaging around in her snacks. Her eyes find mine and hold, narrowing until all I can see is a glimpse of hazel. She still has some jelly in her hair from baking earlier today. Strawberry, by the looks of it. She points her finger right between my eyebrows and taps me there once. "Don't think I'm going to forget about this."

I swat her hand away. She could persist on this topic for the next six months for all I care. It'll just sound like background noise.

I turn my attention to Stella and wedge my boot against hers. She stops the nervous tapping of her foot and grimaces. "Sorry."

"Nothing to apologize over." I shrug and scan the edges of the room. "Luka not coming?"

If Luka were here, he'd smooth his hand between her shoulder blades, and she'd melt like butter. They were like that before they got together, and it took them a stupidly long time to see what was right in front of them. I didn't win the townwide betting pool, but it was close. Gus over at the fire station hasn't shut up about it, going as far as making a plaque to hang above the ambulance bay at the firehouse. It says INGLEWILD'S TOP MATCHMAKER, like he had anything to do with Luka and Stella orbiting each other for close to a decade. I slip down farther in my seat and try to rearrange my legs so I actually fit in this damn chair.

"He's on his way," she says, eyes darting to the door and holding like she can make him appear by sheer force of will. A hand pushes tangled black curls off her face. "But he's running late."

"He'll be here," I assure her. Pretty sure Luka wouldn't miss this for anything. Even if his tiny Italian mother and all her ferocious sisters were blocking the door. If he said he'd come, he'll be here.

"Hey." I lower my voice and lean closer, conscious of Layla still snacking away on my right. She's started tossing pieces up in the air and catching them in her mouth. Accurate every time. "I didn't plant any bell peppers."

That seems to relax Stella a bit, a coy smile turning the corners of her lips. "I know that."

"Why'd you lie, then?"

"Because you looked like you needed an out. And I know a thing or two about having to sort through feelings before you can share them with everyone else." The door to the rec hall creaks open and Luka steps inside, eyes searching. His hair is sticking in every direction, the edge of his shirt half tucked into his jeans. He looks like he ran straight here from the Delaware border. Stella breathes out a sigh and a grin pulls her mouth wide. An answering smile blooms on Luka's face the second he finds her in the crowd. Watching them together is like shoving a cupcake directly into my face.

"Plus—" Stella's eyes don't blink away from Luka as he tries to climb his way through rows of people to get to the empty seat next to her. He knocks over a folding chair and almost sends Cindy Croswell to the ground with it. "I've been wanting bell peppers on the farm for ages."

"Ah, okay. There it is."

"Luka makes really good stuffed peppers." She chuckles as Luka slips into the space next to her. His hand immediately sneaks under her hair, and her shoulders do a little shimmy as she leans into him. I avert my eyes to the front of the room, where Sheriff Jones is getting ready at the wooden podium, but I don't miss the low murmuring between them, the way Stella folds her body into his. How Luka's foot hooks in the bottom of her chair to pull her a little bit closer.

Not for the first time, I'm jealous. I've never had that with another person. Never been able to slide into someone's space and press my fingertips to their skin, watch them lean farther into me.

I think of my thumb against a full bottom lip, red as a cherry, and shift in my seat. The metal squeaks ominously beneath me.

I'd really love to stop thinking about Evelyn.

Layla leans around me, her bowl digging into my ribcage. "The maintenance closet is available if you two want to get a room."

I snort a laugh. Stella groans. Luka bends forward and scoops his hand into the popcorn bowl.

"Does it have a lock?"

Layla cackles loud enough to attract attention from the front of the room. Some of the salon ladies stop their conversation to give us looks, and Alex from the bookstore raises his coffee in greeting. I notice Deputy Caleb Alvarez standing just behind the sheriff, a smile twitching on his lips, his gaze fixed on Layla.

I catch Stella's eye and she grins.

"All right, let's get this show on the road." Sheriff Dane Jones clears his throat and then clears it again, the chatter in the room quieting as everyone settles in for the meeting. "First order of business. Ms. Beatrice, the police department would appreciate it if you stopped trying to tow the cars in front of the café on your own. You don't have the equipment for it, and using your vehicle as a battering ram has resulted in a few complaints."

"She tried to kill me," Sam Montez shouts from the back of the room, his hat falling off sideways as he jumps from his chair. "I was out of my car for a minute—two, tops—and she tried to kill me!"

I hide my smile behind my fist. Sam has a bad habit of double-parking. Not usually a problem on our small-town roads, but annoying all the same. I can just barely make out the top of Ms. Beatrice's head at the end of the front row, her gray hair pulled into a messy bun. She mutters something that I don't quite catch. Dane frowns, and Caleb practically swallows his tongue.

"Well, there's no need for that kind of language. If someone is blocking the loading dock, you can give me or Caleb a ring."

She mumbles something else, and Shirley from the salon gasps. Dane pinches the bridge of his nose between thumb and forefinger. "Bea, what have I told you about making threats of physical violence in front of a police officer? Sam, sit down."

Sam drops down in his seat and scoops up his hat. Luka reaches across me for another handful of popcorn from Layla's bowl.

"You undersold this meeting, La La."

"They're not usually this colorful," Stella tells him, accepting a piece of offered popcorn.

"Yes, they are," Layla and I reply in unison.

"Next up—" Dane glances down at the stack of papers on the podium and lets out a muffled groan. He glances at Caleb with a pleading expression. Caleb shrugs and Dane turns back to the room. "Ms. Beatrice, if you could kindly remove the WANTED posters from the window of the shop, that would be great."

This time, I'm not the only one who has to stifle a laugh. The room breaks out into a low murmur and Caleb has to completely turn around to hide his grin, his back facing the audience and his shoulders shaking. Ms. Beatrice has been putting up WANTED signs in her windows for months now, ever since she caught two tourists in the bathroom using the sink in new and creative ways.

Dane tilts his head to listen to whatever Ms. Beatrice has to say on the matter. "I agree public indecency is a crime, but again, just give me or Caleb a call." He holds up his hand to cut off her response and glances down at the podium, eager to move the conversation along. But whatever he sees has him folding up the whole stack of paperwork with a grunt. "All right, Beatrice, clearly you and I need to have a side conversation. We'll table the"—he flips over the paper and glances at it again—"other seven things for another time."

"Do you think someone complained about how she refuses to buy almond milk?" Layla whispers out of the corner of her mouth. She did buy it, actually. She just put it in a canister that says HIPSTER JUICE on the side.

"Probably something about Karen and the latte incident," I reply. I rarely come into town during the afternoons, but I happened to be walking by the day Ms. Beatrice refused to serve Karen Wilkes on account of her being rude to the waitstaff. A latte somehow found its way all over Karen's faux fur bomber jacket. Can't say I blame her for that one.

"All right." Dane's voice booms over the room and everyone settles again. "Next up. The pizza shop is, uh . . ." He hesitates, rubbing his fingertips over his mustache and down his chin. He taps there once and glances around the room. "Matty would like you all to know there's a special this month. Half the profits on Wednesdays go to the elementary school to fund their science trips."

Stella's hand shoots into the air. Dane looks like he wants to walk out the door and keep walking. "Yes, Stella?"

"Is this an appropriate time to share that I think you two are the cutest couple I've ever seen in my life and express my congratulations that you've finally moved in together?"

"I like the wreath you put on your door," Mabel Brewster adds from somewhere in the middle of the room. "And the birdbath in the front yard. Didn't know you had such an eye for gardening, Sheriff."

The rest of the room bursts into a series of comments and questions on the sheriff's love life.

"Did you see them at the farmers market? I swear I've never seen Dane Jones smile so much."

"Do you mean he smiled once? Because I think that's the standing record."

"They were holding *hands*. He bought Matty *flowers*."

"Where is Matty? You can't keep him locked up just because you two are an item now."

I sink farther into my chair, the hum of sound rising up and over me. It's like a buzz in the back of my head, a ringing in my ears. I press my thumb deep into my palm and try to focus there instead.

Dane looks about ready to burst at the front of the room, his cheeks a flaming red above his beard, hands fussing with the hat tucked under his arm.

I nudge Stella with my elbow. "You're not worried this is going to turn on you?"

"What do you mean?"

I gesture between her and Luka. "When are you two moving in together?"

"Oh"—she waves her hand, unconcerned—"as soon as we can figure out how to add more space. I don't think Luka is ready for me in my full messy glory quite yet."

Stella lives in a cottage on the opposite side of the farm, a tiny house filled to the brim with old magazines and half-empty coffee mugs. It looks like an eighty-year-old woman with a hoarding problem lives there, Luka's interference be damned. I once heard them arguing about kitchen towels with gnomes on them. Stella didn't want to throw them away because, apparently, they're a conversation piece.

"We'll move in together when we can add a bedroom or two so he has someplace to cry when I don't fold his T-shirts exactly right." She shrugs, jostling Luka's arm around her shoulders. He pinches her lightly without even looking, and her smile spreads into a grin. "I'm happy to share that with anyone who asks. All of this—Dane needs to know we love him. We love *them*. He told me once he didn't think he was enough for Matty. He was afraid to take the chance." She leans into Luka, her temple against his chin. "He deserves to know he's got the town rooting for him. That we're glad he's happy."

That's all well and good, but Dane looks like he's about to melt into the floor.

"Even if it derails the rest of this meeting?"

She grins. Luka shouts something about matching china patterns. There's an answering cheer throughout the small room and Dane presses his fist to his forehead. "Especially then."

I lean back in my seat with a chuckle and cross my arms over my chest, pull my baseball cap low over my eyes, and stretch my legs out as much as I'm able. Best just to wait these things out, in my experience.

I close my eyes, breathe in deep, and think about peppers.

2

EVELYN

"UH, HEY." A *throat clears somewhere above me, a rough rumble. "You waiting on someone?"*

I glance up from my phone to the tall figure leaning at the edge of the table, a frown tugging his lips down. I don't think I've seen him smile once since I got here—on the limited occasions I have seen him, of course. I think he's been hiding in one of the barns every time I'm touring the grounds.

It makes me sad.

A little annoyed too.

"I'm not." I push the empty seat across from me back with my boot. A silent invitation.

He waits a beat and then folds his body into the small seat across from me. I watch him over the rim of my coffee mug. Elbows on the table, hunched shoulders. His body curls forward as he stares at the table like it holds the secrets to the universe. Minutes pass, and he doesn't say a word.

"So . . ." I drop my chin in my hand and take a noisy sip of my coffee. I keep my voice light and bright, markedly different from the awkward tension that's twisting in my gut. My mom says I'm impervious to the moods of others. That I could brighten even the darkest storm cloud.

With Beckett, I feel like we're both the storm cloud. Together, we're a monsoon.

"How is your day going?"

He glances up at me, a bite of zucchini bread perfectly poised on the end of his fork. "Hm?"

"Your day," I repeat. If he wanted to sit in silence, he could have gone to any of the empty tables lined against the wall. Instead he sat down here with me. "How is it going?"

"Oh"—he shifts in his seat and traces the edge of his porcelain plate with his thumb—"it's fine," he mumbles. Blue-green eyes peek up at me and then dart down again. Another awkward pause, the silence stretching a moment too long. I can't believe this man walked right up to me in a bar and put his body next to mine. Leaned into my space until I could smell the summer rain on his skin and asked me what I was drinking. "Yours?"

"Fine." I want to fling his plate across the bakehouse, if only to get a reaction out of him. I wait for him to say something else, and when he doesn't, I sigh. "Stella is taking me on a tour through the fields later."

He makes a vaguely interested sound.

"It really is beautiful here."

Another sound under his breath.

All right, fine.

I collapse back in my seat and cross my arms over my chest, busying myself with looking out the floor-to-ceiling window to my left. From this angle I can see a couple of kids weaving in and out of the trees—a tiny squirrel hiding in the brush, digging a hole in the dirt. The bakehouse is hidden in one of the fields, a surprise for visitors to stumble upon when they're out hunting for the perfect tree. Inside, condensation gathers at the bottom of the windows, a perfect frame of gray-white. Tree branches brush at the windows. It feels like I'm in one of those vintage Christmas cards, and I bet it's damn near magical when it snows.

"You know, I was walking past the strawberry fields earlier."

I dart my gaze back to Beckett, still staring at that stupid plate. "Yeah? I didn't know you had strawberry fields here."

He ignores me, a bob in his throat as he swallows tightly. Stoic. Insulated. A million miles away.

"I heard some of them crying, I think."

"What?"

"The strawberries," he explains. "I heard some of them crying."

I blink at him. "I have no idea what you're talking about."

"It's because—" a small smile curls at the edge of his mouth, right at the corner. It tugs at his bottom lip as he shifts in his seat and I remember, viscerally, what that smile feels like tucked in the place between my shoulder and neck. He looks up at me through his lashes, and it's the moment after a storm when the sun decides to peek out from behind the heavy clouds—rain still dripping from the edges of the roof, the trees, the mailbox on the corner. "It's because their parents were in a jam, I think."

It takes me a second to understand.

A joke.

Beckett just made a joke.

A really stupid one too.

A surprised laugh bursts out of me, bright and loud. Several people turn to look.

But I'm too busy staring at Beckett, the grin on his face wide and unrestrained. A little bit wild. A lot bit beautiful.

I press my fist to my lips, delighted by his shining eyes. He ducks his head down and takes another bite of his zucchini bread.

"That was a dumb joke," I tell him.

"Yeah." His smile settles into something soft. Something I've felt before with the palm of my hand in the dead of night. "Yeah, it was."

I'm pulled out of my daydream with a sharp kick to my shin.

I jump in my seat, my knee hitting the underside of the wooden table that stretches the length of the room. Josie gives me a look from her place across from me, both eyebrows raised high. I haven't been able to keep my thoughts from drifting since I sat down at this meeting, and given the bruise forming on my leg, she's noticed.

"How do you feel about dance?"

My agent of the day, Kirstyn, taps her pen against a pale pink notepad. Peony pink. The-sky-right-before-the-sun-hits-the-water pink. Sway doesn't believe in assigning one specific agent to a client. Instead, I have a rotating fleet of young, attractive, and trendy consultants at my beck and call. Kirstyn and her severe cloud of perfume has me yearning for Derrick and his fluorescent nail polish. Shelly and her oversized blanket scarves.

Kirstyn pinches her lips together in annoyance. "Did you hear what I said?"

Josie's teeth clamp down on her bottom lip, and she widens both her eyes. *Well*, that looks says. *Did you?*

I did not. I was too busy remembering a quiet November afternoon in a sun-filled bakery. I wonder what Beckett would think of a place like this. I imagine him here, overwhelmed and confused, squinting at the chalkboard placards on the outside of each work space. Glaring at the mason jars in the open kitchen. Scowling at the fresh cucumber water and complimentary warm hand towels.

I shake my head.

"I'm sorry." I clear my throat and curl my hands around my teacup. "Could you repeat what you said?"

Kirstyn flicks her shining blond hair behind her shoulder. She's wearing oversized glasses with a thin, gold wire frame. A collection of bangles dance down her wrist. She lifts the mint green teakettle off the tray in the center of the table and offers it to me. I shake my head.

"Dance," she says, placing the kettle back down with a small pout. "You know, like those challenges you see everywhere?"

She gestures to her phone faceup next to the tray—a cohesive stream of dancing influencers. I try to picture myself there, wedged in between all that content. I can't even begin to imagine it and I feel a twist of anxiety. I'm pretty sure the last time I did any sort of choreographed movement, I was thirteen in my parents' basement, singing to Backstreet Boys at the top of my lungs with Josie, using an umbrella as a microphone stand.

"I know the challenges," I offer, with no small amount of hesitation. I can see where this is going.

This isn't where you're supposed to be, a voice in the back of my mind whispers. It's been getting louder and louder, that voice, a steady trickle of doubt. But if I'm not supposed to be here, where am I supposed to be? What am I supposed to be doing? I've spent my entire life curating this platform, building this audience.

I blink away from the phone and look out the window at the bustling sidewalk below, distracting myself with the people on the street. I watch as everyone moves past one another without looking up—a mindless, endless drive forward. A gust of wind tunnels down the sidewalk and lifts the edge of a bright red scarf. For a second, the woman clinging to it looks like she's flying, her hand grasping at the ends. She manages to catch it just as she stumbles past a tiny empanada shop—a bright pink building with string lights across the top, sandwiched between a national box store and a glossy bank. A small woman with olive skin laughs in the window and snaps her towel at someone on the other side of the counter. A smile kicks up the corner of my mouth. I can hear her joy from here.

"Evie," I feel Josie's boot under the table, nudging against mine. "You okay?"

"I'm sorry," I repeat. I shake my head and force my attention back to Kirstyn. I'm all over the place today. I need a strong coffee and a six-day nap. "I'm here. I'm listening. Explain to me what you're looking for."

"We think you should add some choreography to your videos," Kirstyn repeats slowly, enunciating each word. I would hazard a guess that I won't be seeing Kirstyn again after today. "Sway believes movement and dance would make your content more approachable."

Josie slowly turns her head to look at Kirstyn. If looks could kill, I'm pretty sure Kirstyn would be a pile of ash. Movement and dance. I tap a fingernail against the lip of my cup.

"What do you suggest?"

The light pinching of her lips turns into a tightening between her eyebrows. "Dance," she repeats, the first hint of frustration spilling out of her lightly lined lips. "Movement—"

I wave my hand. "Yes, movement will make my content more approachable. But as I am sure you are aware, my content is largely aspirational. Travel focused." I frown. "Do you think I should do 'Yah Trick Yah' in the aisle of a small-town bookstore?"

Josie snorts. My sarcasm goes sailing right over Kirstyn's head.

"That's amazing," she tells me, greedy hands reaching for her laptop. She begins to frantically type, her hot pink nails dancing across the keyboard. "What an incredible idea. I can't believe we didn't think of that."

A dull headache pounds at the base of my skull. "That wasn't—" I sigh and look back out the window, down toward the empanada shop. The woman laughing in the window is gone now. "I was joking."

"Oh, well"—Kirstyn doesn't look up from her computer—"it's a good idea. Maybe you can workshop it on your next trip."

Josie widens her eyes at me. *Workshop it*, she mouths. She mimes a dance move from the early nineties I'm pretty sure we *workshopped* during our Backstreet Boys routine.

I don't dignify the suggestion with a response, and attempt to change the subject. I am weary down to my very bones. "Where is my next trip?"

Half of me hopes Kirstyn tells me my next trip is home, to the tiny and mostly bare apartment I rent here in the Bay Area. I don't know why I signed a lease to begin with. I think I've spent a total of six nights there over the past three months. But I had been yearning for some roots and an apartment seemed the logical answer.

"Oh, right. Here we go."

I began my partnership with Sway because I wanted to help more people, tell more stories, access more communities with small businesses trying to get their names out. Like Peter in Spokane, a retired veteran with a grilled cheese food truck and—no lie—the best tomato soup I've ever had. Eliza and her dress shop in Sacramento, recycling fast fashion into sustainable pieces. Stella at Lovelight Farms, working so hard to create a whimsical winter wonderland. The people I visit have everything they need to make an impact. I just . . . help them along. Give them a boost.

Account management was starting to be a little too much for Josie and me to handle. We were spending more time on the administrative side of things instead of the creative bit of it. My partnership with Sway was supposed to make all of this easier. But honestly, it's been one headache after another.

"This is your next trip," Kirstyn announces with all the flair I've come to expect from Sway.

A blank screen hums its arrival as it drops from the ceiling. It winks awake with a burst of color, loud and heavy bass drum filling the space. Josie jumps in her seat, scrambling to keep her teacup from flipping over.

Bejeweled bodies dance with their arms in the air. A woman with fur boots to her thighs and a bright purple sequined bodysuit swings from a vine across—I squint at the screen—a bright red pool of Jell-O.

"Holy crap," Josie whispers.

My headache deepens.

"Why are you showing me Burning Man?"

"It's not Burning Man. It's the Okeechobee Music and Arts Festival," Kirstyn tells me, almost bubbling over with excitement. The bracelets on her wrist make a tinkling noise that I feel in my teeth. "It's a newer festival, and Sway thinks this will be a good fit for your brand evolution."

Sway thinks. I pinch the bridge of my nose.

"My brand evolution."

"Yes."

"Is it run by a small business?" I'm distracted by the half-naked bodies thrusting and rolling on the screen, and the strobe lights are making my headache worse. I glance through the industrial glass window to the rest of the office, where employees are set up in a coworking space. A guy sitting at the corner in a beret bobs his head to the music. A woman with hot pink tips looks like she's humming under her breath. Everyone is completely unperturbed by the three-woman rave happening in conference room two. "Does it have an interesting story?"

Maybe I'm missing something.

"You'll be sponsored by CoverGirl," she tells me. The screen changes to a video I did about a month ago, a clip from one of my accounts of me holding up a bright orange tube of mascara, a gust of wind blowing my hair over my face. I think you see the actual product in use for less than a second. The tiny number in the lower right corner is highlighted. Over four million views. I wince.

I had agonized over this piece, iffy about such heavy-handed product placement. Most of my income is derived from sponsorship, sure, but it lives on my blog in ad spaces. In a place where people expect it to be. But Sway had been insistent that it could be a strong experiment for more branded content, and I was tired, distracted. I caved and posted a stupid video of myself promoting mascara.

And look at me now. A CoverGirl sponsorship.

I should be overjoyed.

Why am I not overjoyed?

Because this isn't where you're supposed to be.

I shouldn't be panicking about partnerships and promotions and music festivals. I've spent all of this time creating content and breaking off pieces of myself for public consumption, and what do I have to show for it? An empty apartment and millions of strangers following my every move.

I'm so tired.

"I think I need to take a break." The words slip from my mouth with a sigh, quiet but gaining strength as they settle in the space between the three of us. I roll my shoulders back and take a deep breath. I lift my chin. "I'm going to take a break."

Josie does a tiny fist pump on her side of the table.

"I'll book you a spa package at your hotel in Okeechobee," Kirstyn says. Something tells me Okeechobee is not known for their spas. "Oh! If you wanted to extend your trip and start in Miami, I bet we could snag you a couple of club sponsorships."

I shake my head and nudge my teacup back to the ornate porcelain saucer. I absolutely do not want to go clubbing in Miami. "No, I mean I'm going to take a break. From all of . . . this."

Kirstyn blinks up at me from behind her screen. I can see the dancing bodies from Okeechobee reflected in her oversized lenses. It's disorienting, like something from *Alice in Wonderland*. She gapes at me, hands held perfectly still just above the keyboard. "Like a hiatus?"

"Sure." That's a fine word for it. I have plenty in my savings account to support a mini vacation, bolstered by years of meticulous financial planning. An influencer's income is hardly stable, and I've always been afraid of the attention slipping away as quickly as it arrived. Social media is a fickle thing.

Maybe some time away is exactly what I need. Space to refocus, realign.

I turn and look over my shoulder through the big windows to the empanada shop below. I start gathering my things.

Some space to eat empanadas.

"But you'll keep posting, right?" There's a thin thread of unease in Kirstyn's voice as she slides from her chair, trailing me to the open door. Josie waits for me at the entrance to the room, quiet pride in her big brown eyes. She's been ready to leave since we got here. I'm not even sure she packed her laptop. She bounces on her feet, curly hair bouncing with her.

Kirstyn follows us, hanging on to the edge of the industrial glass window like she's about to leap from a plane. "You won't, like, go completely dark?"

I shrug. "I haven't really thought about it yet." But now that she's mentioned it, completely ignoring my social media channels for a couple of weeks sounds amazing. I shrug on my jacket and curl my hands in the sleeves. "Do I have any sponsorship things I'm on contract for?"

She practically sprints to the table, flipping through her pink notebook. "No." Her face falls in dismay. "No, nothing you're obligated to post. But we've got some interest from Ray-Ban, if you want—"

"That's all right, thank you." I try to smooth the edges of my quick refusal. "Listen, Kirstyn. I'm thankful for the work you did on this pitch, but I think it's best if I take a step back right now. Go into planning mode for a couple of weeks."

Her face blanches. "Weeks?"

I need to figure out what I'm doing, why everything suddenly feels like shrugging on a sweater that's way too small. I keep waiting for this feeling to go away, but it's not. It's only getting worse.

"I'll keep you updated, okay? Check in. Feel free to keep sending me options, but"—I glance at the screen, the strobe lights, and the face paint—"this doesn't feel right. I'm looking for something different than this."

Kirstyn nods. "We can do that. We can support something different. I'll have options in your inbox tonight."

I start backing my way to the elevator. Josie is already aggressively jamming the button with her thumb. "I won't look at them tonight, so take your time. I'm serious about the break."

She follows me like a baby lamb. Some of the people at the collection of tables in the center of the room are half standing from their seats, watching our progress. There's a woman at the front with blunt-cut bangs, her teeth sawing her bottom lip. A man behind her in a short-sleeved button-down stands, his palm against his forehead. I feel like I've just flipped a table and drop-kicked one of their mothers. All of their faces are stricken, concerned. I give them a wave and what I hope is a reassuring smile. They stare blankly back.

"Always a pleasure, guys!" Josie waves over her shoulder, not bothering to turn from the elevator. The doors slide open, and Kirstyn follows us, right to the edge of the sliding doors.

"Your followers will miss you," she tells me as I slip into the small space, green fern wallpaper wrapped floor to ceiling. There's a gold-framed mirror on the ceiling and white shag carpet on the floor. It is the most ridiculous elevator I have ever been in. "Everyone is going to wonder where you went."

It's not the warning she thinks it is. If anything, it makes me want to drop my phone right down this elevator shaft. They'll wonder, and then they'll find someone new to follow. Another account. Another collection of reels and posts and . . . dances. The elevator doors begin to close. I give her a reassuring smile.

"We'll talk soon."

❧ ❧

THE EMPANADAS, AS it turns out, are incredible.

"I thought her face was going to melt right off," Josie says around a mouthful of spinach and cheese. She does something grotesque with her palms pressed tight to her cheeks—an attempt, I think, to illustrate her face melting. It's difficult to tell exactly what she's going for. I snort into another bite of flaky, buttery goodness. "She was genuinely shocked you don't want to start wearing body paint."

"It was weird, right? I don't think they understand—" *me*, I almost say. An unfair comment considering I don't understand myself these days. "I don't think they get the type of content I'm looking for."

"Obviously. I'm proud of you for saying something. I've only been waiting the past six months for it to happen." She pokes around in the empty basket between us. "We need more empanadas."

The lady behind the counter laughs when I slip out of the small booth and wander up for a third round.

"You're still hungry?" Her laugh is loud and boisterous, just as magical as I thought.

"Give her a croqueta," an older woman sitting at the edge of the counter says, half hidden behind a giant plant, her long gray hair wrapped in a bright purple silk scarf. She's been eating tres leches since we sat down, a tiny cup of Cuban coffee on the counter in front of her. "Jamon."

"I'll have two." I smile at the woman and glance at the handwritten menu board. "And a pastelito." I glance back at Josie and she holds up two fingers. "Actually, let's do two of those."

I consider a coffee, but I'm pretty sure I'll be bouncing off the walls if it's as strong as it smells. I slip back into the cozy booth in the corner and pick at what's left of my empanada, pulling my phone from my pocket and placing it flat on the tabletop. I glance down at my lock screen, a picture of my parents with their arms around each other in front of the tiny boutique store they own on the outskirts of Portland. Beaming smiles. ST. JAMES SUNDRY STORE handpainted on the window.

I don't know how I got from there to here.

"I love that picture," Josie says with a smile. "They look so happy."

"They do." I smile, looking at my mother's face. "They are." We have the same smile, the same scrunch in our noses when we laugh. I wonder what she's doing right now. If she's restocking the candy she keeps in a small basket at the back of the store for the kids who manage to find it, or if she's washing the windows with the same ratty bright pink towel she's always had. A pang of homesickness hits me right in the chest.

"Evie."

"Hm?" I blink up from my phone and look at my friend, at the face of the person who knows me better than anyone. She tilts her head and gives me a soft smile.

"What's going on? You feel like—you feel like you're half here. Stuck in your head somewhere." I drop my chin and press two fingers above my eyebrow as Josie rushes to explain. "Not in a bad way, necessarily. You seem distracted, I guess."

This break feels less like an idea and more like a necessity. I wake up every morning with a hollow feeling in my chest, an anxious pounding that gets worse the longer I lie in an unfamiliar bed staring at an unfamiliar room. I spend more time in hotels than at the small apartment I rent. I check my social accounts, and I feel ballooning pressure in my chest. I feel like a liar. A fake.

"I've got no idea what I'm doing." I sigh.

Josie frowns. "That has never once been true."

"It's been true more than you think," I mutter. I've gotten excellent at pretending everything is okay.

I poke around our empty basket, fingering the edge of the greasy paper that's crinkled at the bottom. I pick up a crumb with my finger and lick it off. "I'm just going through the motions."

Smiling for the camera. Adding pithy captions. Making my life seem like it's one big wonderful adventure when really I'm stuck in my head. I've become obsessed with numbers, how posts are performing. I'm more interested in the aesthetic of a story than the actual story part of it. On my last trip, I forgot the name of the town I was in. Twice.

"How long have you felt like this?"

It's settled in slowly, like a fog rolling in off the water. Everything lately has felt . . . off . . . and I don't know why. I thought the blogging would be a stepping stone to something bigger, not the basis for the rest of my career. Now, though, I have everything I've ever wanted from a job. I'm successful, sought after.

And terribly lonely.

I feel disconnected, I guess. Muted. Far away from anything that feels real. The guilt kicks in and I avert my gaze to the tabletop.

Poor social media influencer, sad she has too many followers and not enough friends. I feel like an impostor. Like the worst kind of fraud.

"I'm lying to everyone. I post this content and I'm just—Josie, I'm just pretending."

"Pretending what?"

Everything, I think. *Everything, all the time.*

The owner of the empanada shop makes her way over to our table, a plateful of fried deliciousness in her hands. She sets it on the edge and shouts over her shoulder in Spanish, another loud, cackling laugh echoing through the space. My heart lifts. A little bit of real-life magic.

"I don't want to post content," I say to Josie, still distracted.

She pops a pastelito in her mouth. "Then don't."

"I'm tired of traveling."

"Take a break."

"I don't want to lose everything I've worked for."

"You won't."

"I feel like I've forgotten how to be happy," I whisper, my most secret thought. The one that slips through my head like a wisp of smoke when I'm flat on my back and staring up at the ceiling of whichever hotel I'm staying in for the night, unable to sleep. Mind racing. Thoughts buzzing.

"Did this ever make you feel good?" Josie asks. "Before you exploded into internet stardom, I mean. Were you happy making videos?"

I was. Some of the very best memories I have are from wandering around with my dad's old camera. I'd spend my Saturdays sitting on a bench at the farmers market, just listening to people talk. I lost some of that, I think. Somewhere along the way.

Josie reaches for a croqueta and studies me. "I think this is a good thing for you. Most people go through this. You want to take a step back and evaluate if this is still the right fit. I champion some self-reflection." She raises her croqueta in a little toast, knocks it against my forehead once. "Do you, baby girl."

"You don't think I'm being ridiculous?"

"I think you are being forty-five percent ridiculous. And that is primarily attributed to the way you're talking about yourself. Nothing you have has happened by accident. You work hard and move at the speed of light. I think that's the crux of your problem. You've been bebopping all around and haven't found roots to dig in. Your cute little body is exhausted. Your brain too."

I reach for a croqueta and take a bite, salty flavor bursting on my tongue. "I'm happy when I'm eating these," I mumble around a mouthful.

Josie grins. "Well, we could send you on a food tour." She leans back in the booth with a satisfied sigh. She pats her belly once and twists her lips in thought. "Seriously though, when was the last time you felt like you weren't doing a job? Where is the last place you felt happy?"

It comes to me instantly. Leaves beneath my boots. A cloudless sky as blue as a mountain lake. Dirt roads and a big red barn by the road. Rows and rows of trees, pine needles in my hair.

A stupid joke about strawberries on a sunny afternoon. A plate of zucchini bread on the table.

I feel myself settle, my shoulders rolling back with the first deep breath I've taken in what feels like months. "I think I know."

She nods, a satisfied glint in her eye. "Then let's start there."

3

BECKETT

"CAN I JUST say—" Jeremy Roughman leans up against the back of the tractor, sunlight beginning to wink over the horizon. I hear his voice, and it's a challenge for me not to turn around and go right back to my cabin on the edge of the property. "—I'm real excited you decided to bring me on as an apprentice."

I did not decide to bring him on as an apprentice. Sheriff Jones cornered me in the paper products aisle of the pharmacy and lightly threatened me with crosswalk duty for the elementary school until I agreed to take him on. Apparently, Jeremy can't keep himself out of trouble for more than thirty-seven seconds, and if Ms. Beatrice catches him making out with another girl in her alleyway, she's likely to do something that results in jail time.

"I know his parents would be appreciative," Dane had said, and I almost flung my body into the paper towel shelf. "He just needs a little direction."

So here we are, giving direction. Dawn crawls across the sky in bright pink and burnished gold, a brilliant brushstroke of cloud through the center of it. I can still feel the bite of winter this early in the morning, and I'm grateful for my thermal shirt and the cat curled up against my neck, dozing with her chin on my shoulder.

I glance up at Barney, perched on the driver's seat of the tractor—

his old wide-brim hat pulled low over his eyes. He smirks at me around a mouthful of donut.

"Real excited, boss," he says. He shoves fried dough and powdered sugar into his mouth. "Could hardly sleep last night on account of it."

I roll my eyes and reach for the shovel propped up against the tire. For all his needling, Barney makes my job easier. He's a walking encyclopedia of crops and soil, plant-eating diseases, and . . . the 1990 Baltimore Orioles roster. I've got no use for the last bit, but the rest of it comes in handy. I've been working with him ever since I took over my dad's shift at the produce farm almost two decades ago. When Stella recruited me and I gave my notice, he gave his too. Patted me on the back and told me he couldn't let me screw up a whole new farm by myself.

I hand the shovel to Jeremy, and he grips it between thumb and forefinger, holding it away from his letterman jacket. I didn't even realize they still hand those things out, but Inglewild has always felt a little frozen in time. Prancer echoes a plaintive meow right into my ear, and I rub my knuckles over her soft head.

"We're gonna chisel today," I tell Jeremy.

"Dude, I can't chisel something with a shovel." Jeremy tries to hand it to me. "I thought I'd, like . . . advise on placement or something. Give you a fresh perspective on the aesthetics of the place."

I summon my patience. "The aesthetics of the place?"

He flips his hair back and tips his chin up. "Isn't that why you brought me in?"

I did not . . . bring him in. I was conned in front of the paper towels. I fold my arms over my chest and lean against the side of the tractor. Prancer takes the opportunity to hop from my shoulder to the top of the cab, settling into the divot next to the seat. She likes to ride with Barney in the mornings and wander home when she's ready.

I do my best to ignore Barney shaking with silent laughter atop the tractor.

"What do you know about farming, Jeremy?"

He combs his hand through his hair and squints at the horizon. "I know a bit."

"Let's hear it, then."

"Well," he shuffles his feet, puts his hands in his jacket pockets only to pull them out again. "Obviously, you plant things."

"Obviously."

"And nourish them."

"Sure."

"I actually have some ideas about your growth patterns. How do you feel about canna—"

"Do not finish that sentence," I growl. I've heard enough weed jokes to last a lifetime. I jerk my head to the back of the tractor. "Maybe we can talk about growth patterns next week." Barney makes a choking noise. "In the meantime, we have a tradition. The newest member of the crew is on rock duty. You're going to follow after Barney and scoop rocks out of the topsoil, toss them in that bucket on the side. It'll make it easier for us to disc and then plant in the next week or so."

I was on rock duty every summer for four years at Parson's Produce. Did it myself here when it was just Barney and me getting the fields ready. It'll be a nice change not to do it this time. I glance at Jeremy's shoes.

Brand new Nikes, pristine white.

A twinge of guilt pulls at my gut. It's not exactly his fault he didn't know what to expect. I remember my first day at the farm, when I was a kid, too skinny and out of my element, stumbling to keep up with everyone around me. It was like trying to jump into a dance midway through without hearing the damn music. I remember laughter when my feet slipped in the dirt behind the tractor, the sun beating down on my neck and blistering my skin.

"You got a hat, kid?"

He shakes his head, still staring at the shovel in his hand. I dig into one of the packs slung over the seat and pull out an old baseball cap, faded and ripped on one side. I toss it to him. It hits him in the chest and then falls to the dirt. He looks at it like he'd rather die than put it on his perfectly styled hair.

I shrug my shoulders and Barney snorts a laugh, hitting the ignition and putting the tractor into gear. "You seeing your pop tonight for dinner?" Barney shouts over the rumble of the engine.

I nod. We have family dinners every Tuesday night, a tradition for as long as I can remember.

"Tell him I say hello. And he owes me one hundred and forty-seven dollars after our last poker night."

I roll my eyes and wave him off. Barney and my dad have been playing poker together every Saturday night for about as long as we've been having family dinners. Pretty sure neither of them has ever settled the debt between them.

Jeremy stares mournfully at me as Barney starts the slow trek toward the edge of the west fields, the wheels of the tractor bumping along. It's slow work but important, and we'll spend the next couple weeks getting the fields ready for the shipment of saplings from the north. The trees we plant won't be ready for at least five years, but that's the nature of a tree farm.

It's all about patience.

"Where are you going?" Jeremy yells across the field, stopping to scoop the hat from the ground. If he doesn't get himself moving, he'll be shoveling rocks until next week.

"To take a look at the aesthetics," I shout back.

THERE'S PLENTY TO occupy myself with while the fieldwork gets underway. Stella and I decided after our first season that we wouldn't rely solely on Christmas trees to see us through the year. In the off-season, we experiment with several different crops. Pumpkins in the fall. Berries in the summer.

Bell peppers, apparently, in the spring.

Salvatore meets me near the barn as I make my way over to the produce fields, a sunny grin on his weathered face. He claps me once on the shoulder and guides me toward the massive sliding doors instead of the fields.

"Got a little hiccup," he tells me, that grin still stretched across his face. Last summer we had a rainstorm that turned all of the fields into gaping mud pits. Two steps off the tractor and he had slipped and covered himself head to toe in thick sludge. He had smiled so wide I could only see the white of his teeth through the dirt. I'm half convinced his face got stuck that way. I've never seen someone smile so much in my damn life.

"I don't know how many hiccups I can handle this season, Sal."

"Bah." He gives me a sly look as we slip into the barn. "I think you'll like this one."

Susie, one of the farmhands who helps with collection, offers a wave from the far corner of the open space. Half of the barn is used for visiting Santa during the holiday season, the other half for storage. She's set up right by the divider in the middle, her arms cradling . . . something.

"Did you find more kittens?" I ask. Last fall, Stella discovered a whole family of cats tucked behind one of the giant wooden nutcrackers. All four of them live with me now, a tiny army of soft fur and obstinate opinions about the quality of my sheets. I wake up every morning with at least one of them curled up on my chest, purring away.

"Better," Sal tells me. As I get closer, I see a tiny puff of yellow. Susie opens up the towel she's holding, and tucked inside is a duckling, hardly bigger than the palm of my hand, a streak of dark fluff right on top of its head. It gazes up at me and lets out the tiniest little squeak, its wings ruffling slightly at the disruption to its cocoon.

"Ah, shit." The damn thing is cute as hell. "You think it was abandoned?"

"Looks that way." Sal rocks back on his heels. "Haven't seen any trace of Mom."

I don't know much about ducks, but I'd assume ducklings can't survive long without their mom close by. I stare down at the little guy and rub my knuckles against my jaw. "I'll take him into town. Swing by Dr. Colson's and see what can be done."

I hold out my hands for the bundle. I try to avoid town if I can help it, but I've got to place an order at the hardware store anyway. Christopher, the owner, refuses to do anything over the phone and won't answer if I call too many times. I can drop this little guy off at the vet, place the order, and be back before lunch.

The duckling squeaks up in my general direction, its bill nudging once at the back of my hand. I stroke my finger over the top of its head, its downy fuzz impossibly soft.

I try to gather the threads of my restraint as we gaze at each other. Naturally, my brain has already started making plans. We have some chicken wire in the greenhouse. I could loop it around the edges of the kitchen. Make a fence.

I sigh as I watch the little guy doze in the safety of my hands. I can't adopt another animal. I don't know the first thing about ducks.

You didn't know the first thing about cats either. That didn't stop you.

The duckling makes a small squeak and nuzzles farther down in my hand. I sigh.

I will not adopt another animal.

I hear the click of a camera and look up to see Sal and his damn smile angling his phone at me. I frown and he clicks again, a chuckle under his breath.

"What the hell are you doing?"

"Stella's calendar idea," he tells me with a laugh. Stella has been pushing the idea for close to a year now of a farm calendar featuring only pictures of Luka and me out in the fields, an attempt to try to boost profits. Needless to say, I am not on board with it. "You've kind of got a Snow White vibe going on, my friend."

I head out the door without another word.

≫ · ≪

"WELL"—DR. COLSON holds the duckling in the palm of his hand, nudging his glasses up his nose with his knuckles—"it's a duckling, all right."

I shift on my feet and fight the urge to roll my eyes. I am pushing my capacity for socialization today, and it's not even noon. I still have dinner with my family tonight, and my sisters aren't exactly known for their calm and quiet demeanors.

"Sure is," I manage instead, clenching my teeth when Dr. Colson peers up at me from above his glasses. He swivels on his chair and places the duck carefully back into the cardboard box I bundled him up in. The little guy quacks and waddles closer to me, settling down in a corner and mouthing at my hand with his tiny bill.

Do not name him, I tell myself. If I give him a name, I'll bring him home, and I'm not sure a pack of kittens and a baby duck would make good roommates. *Don't you dare give him a name.*

"I'll make some calls and see if there is a rescue nearby that will take him in, but ducks are tricky. He'll have to be accepted by a new mother."

I breathe in deep through my nose. "And if he isn't?"

"If he isn't, I'm afraid the little guy won't make it. Not unless someone adopts him as a pet."

He gives me a significant look.

Fuck. "Is that a possibility? To have him as a pet?"

Dr. Colson nods. "With the proper care and attention, absolutely. It'll be time-consuming at first, but ducks can make great pets." He looks up at me with a sly grin. "Farms are a great environment."

"Not sure farms with a family of bloodthirsty cats are a great environment," I grumble. Prancer brought me three mice last weekend. She lined them up in front of my door like a sacrificial offering. It was both disgusting and endearing.

"Remind me to send you one of those Toks all the kids are sharing," Dr. Colson says. He stands with a wince and claps me on the back. His knees have been bothering him since he turned sixty. "Sheila at the front is always showing me new ones. I think there's a whole account dedicated to cats and ducks."

I wouldn't know. I have no interest in social media.

I haven't looked Evelyn up again, not since that first time. Not even after she posted her now-viral video of Luka and Stella pretending to love each other while also desperately pretending not to love each other. Luka had been so pleased by his internet celebrity, he walked around autographing everything within reach for weeks. The third time he signed a potato with a Sharpie, I snapped the marker in half right in front of his face.

"I can't adopt a duck," I say. Maybe if I vocalize my intentions, they'll manifest. My sister Nessa has told me that no less than seventy-five times. I sigh. "You'll keep him here for a bit? Give me a call when you hear from the rescue?"

Dr. Colson nods. The duck lets out a quack. I pinch the bridge of my nose.

I cannot adopt this duck.

"ARE YOU ADOPTING a duck?"

"Fuck," I curse under my breath as my sister Nova pops up in my window. I'm only slightly late to family dinner at my parents' house, but I guess she decided to wait out front for me to arrive. She hops up on the sidebar and loops her arm through my open window before I even manage to slow my truck to a stop. At five foot nothing and wearing her standard head-to-toe black, it's a wonder I didn't run her right over.

She pokes me once in the cheek as I shift into Park. I swat her hand away and grab the pie from the passenger seat.

"How do you know about the duck?"

Do not name the duck. You will not name the duck.

"The phone tree."

The Inglewild phone tree is only supposed to be used in cases of emergency, but in the last six months, it's turned into a town gossip distribution chain. Two weeks ago, Alex Alvarez from the bookstore called to tell me Sheriff Jones and Matty were seen picking out tulip bulbs at the greenhouse for their back garden. When I asked him why the fuck he was calling me about tulip bulbs, he muttered "phone tree" and hung up.

I did not continue the phone tree that day. I haven't had a single phone call since. I'm assuming I've been removed.

"Is he adopting a duck?" Harper shouts from the door, hanging over the banister on the front porch, a dish towel slung over her shoulder and a wooden spoon in her hand. I climb out of my truck with a sigh, careful not to send Nova flying off the door.

"I'm not adopting a duck." I sling my arm over Nova's shoulder and ruffle her hair as we walk up the ramp that leads to the porch. Some of the boards creak under my boots, and I pause, considering. I reach out and push at the handrail, the wood wobbling slightly under my grip.

"I'll help you fix it this week, if you want," Nova tells me, urging me forward and gently guiding me toward the house. She probably knows I'm about three seconds away from getting the toolbox out of my truck and reconstructing the whole thing. Guilt pricks at me. It's been too long since I've asked my parents if they need anything.

"Stop," Harper admonishes as soon as we step onto the porch. She smacks me once with her spoon. Of all my sisters, she's the one who looks most like me. Dark blond hair, blue-green eyes, an almost permanent frown. She's two years younger, but she might as well be my twin. "You're beating yourself up before you even enter the house. That must be a new record."

"No. Remember Christmas Eve two years ago? He forgot the stick of butter Mom asked him to bring, and he almost took out the mailbox heading to the grocery store. He didn't even make it out of the driver's seat before he started beating himself up."

"Or when he forgot about Nessa's dance recital. I thought he was going to sink through the floor." Harper's lips curl up at the edges, and her gaze cuts to me. "You didn't even miss it. You just got the date wrong. You were feeling guilty about *potentially* missing something."

They dissolve into a fit of giggles, and I push through them into the house. It doesn't bode well for me that the teasing has already started. I can usually count on Nova to be on my side, but not tonight, apparently.

Garlic and rosemary drift down the hallway from the kitchen as I toe off my boots. Fresh-baked bread and a hint of honey. I can hear the low murmur of my mom and Nessa chatting, my dad wheeling backward in his chair to poke his head around the corner as Nova and Harper follow me in.

"You adopting a duck?" he calls.

I roll my eyes and shrug out of my jacket. I contemplate returning to my truck and asking my mom to bring dinner out to me. She probably would. Nova loops her hand around my wrist before I can turn for the door and tugs me down the hallway into the kitchen, directing me to the island in the center. Her grip is scary strong for someone so small. She manhandles me until my arm is exposed under the light, the cuff of my sleeve rolled up so she can see the ink that decorates every inch of my skin.

"Can I get a drink first?" I beg.

"No."

She doesn't bother looking up as she traces one of the vines that starts at my elbow and curls down over my wrist. She added some flower buds to it about two weeks ago, and they're almost fully healed.

"They look good," she tells me, flipping my wrist and poking around at my skin with almost clinical detachment. She started tattooing me when she was sixteen and decided she wanted to be an artist. She apprenticed at a shop down the coast, but no one would let a teenager practice on their skin. So I volunteered. Every tattoo on my arms is by her, an interesting progression from my left arm to my right. Now that she's one of the most sought-after artists on the East Coast, she's been going back over her work, adding detail and cleaning up old missteps.

"I want to fix this one," she tells me, poking at a tiny oak leaf on the inside of my wrist. The edges are slightly blurred from too much pressure from the gun, a wobble in the crisp lines. I pull my arm out of her grip and roll my cuff down.

"Nope." I like that one. It was one of the first she ever did, and she had been so fucking proud when she pressed that cool wipe over my skin, cleaning away excess ink. It's a good memory, and I don't want to change it. "You can harass me into other changes after pie."

"And you can come say hello to your mother," my mom says over her shoulder, stirring something that smells like cinnamon and honey. I wander over to the stove and press a kiss to the back of her head.

"Hi, Mom." I reach for a sliver of roast carrot from the pan, enjoying the sharp crunch and answering sweetness.

"These from the farm?" I ask. I already know the answer. The carrots are from the farm, and the bread is from Nessa, and the music is a playlist Harper made over the summer, and the delicate bouquet of wildflowers drawn on the back of her arm is by Nova. My dad whittled the spoon she's using, and this whole kitchen is filled to the brim with pieces of my family. The love between my parents and for all of us, mixing together with thyme and butter and pie until all the tension I usually feel in a roomful of people is back in the hallway, shoved in the pocket of my coat. I'll pick it back up later, I'm sure, but for now I'm settled.

I'm home.

Food is served and conversation dissolves within minutes into a spirited discussion of some dating show, the volume of my sisters' and dad's voices rising until they're all yelling over one another.

When my dad first had his accident, he sat in the dark of his bedroom all day every day, caught in a depression that was almost as crippling as the fall that paralyzed him from the waist down. Nessa started sitting in the room with him, right at the edge of the bed. She'd turn on some show about housewives behaving badly, and he'd pretend not to be interested.

Now they have weekly viewings.

Harper glances at me from across the table as Nessa shrieks something about chardonnay. "Do you want your earmuffs?"

I nod, grateful she offered and I didn't have to ask. She tugs open a drawer in the china cabinet behind her and pulls out a fluffy pair of pink earmuffs. I thought Nessa had been making fun of me when she bought them for me three years ago, but she had been insistent that they would help.

I've always struggled with noise. It sets my teeth on edge, makes me feel like needles are pricking at my skin. The earmuffs buffer the sound without wiping it out completely. I can still hear what's going on around me without an overwhelming wave of tension.

And they never fail to make my mom smile.

I slip them over my head, and my chest loosens a bit, as I'm able to participate now that the noise has been dulled. Nessa has an exhibition coming up in June, her biggest one yet. And apparently Nova has been talking to Stella's brother, Charlie, about a tattoo of a scorpion on his ass.

I level a glare at her. "Why are you texting Charlie about his ass?"

Nova shrugs, unbothered. "I'm not. He's texting me about his ass."

"All right. Why is he texting you about his ass?"

"Because he wants a scorpion on it. I don't know."

Harper keeps to herself throughout dinner, unusually quiet, rearranging her food around and around on her plate. I make a mental note to dig into that later just as my dad launches into his weekly dramatic retelling of the failed wheat crop of 1976. I spear a carrot on my plate, and my mind begins to drift.

I picture Evelyn sitting at the table in the straight-backed chair with the flowers carved into the arms, right next to Nessa. I picture her smile and her glowing skin and the way her thumb smooths over her bottom lip when she's thinking about what she wants to say, eyes glinting with mischief. Would she laugh at my dad's stupid jokes? Would she dance with Nessa around the kitchen during cleanup? I can't stop picturing her in all the places I am.

"Beck?" my dad calls. "You all right?"

I nod. I've got no idea what's going on in my head lately. A whole lot of nonsense. I need to sleep more or something. I fork a bite of potatoes into my mouth.

"M'fine," I say.

My dad gives me a skeptical glance and continues to shoot me an entire spectrum's worth of concerned looks throughout the rest of dinner. I manage to deflect until the end of the night, when I'm overfull from pie and trying to balance three containers of leftovers. I shrug on my jacket in the hallway, and he corners me, his movements eerily quiet despite his wheelchair.

"Beckett."

"Jesus." My whole body topples sideways, my elbow landing against the antique clock my mom bought when I was six. One of the containers goes tumbling to the floor. "You need a bell. You scared the shit out of me, Dad."

"Paralyzed or not, I always got the jump on you kids." He scoops up the Tupperware and balances it on his lap. "Come on—I'll follow you out."

I nod in agreement and he squeezes my arm once, a wordless reminder of his dinner question. He's likely seeing me to my car in an effort to interrogate me further. My mom and sisters know the futility of trying to get me to talk at the dinner table. Where they prefer brash interrogation, my dad has a subtler approach.

We head out to the front porch and down the ramp, and I frown when I notice the way his wheelchair jumps over the rickety boards.

His hand holds one of the wheels steady while he pivots. He shouldn't have to maneuver his way up and down this thing.

"I'll swing by next week and fix it," I tell him.

He peers over his shoulder at me, his eyes reflecting the light from above the garage. "Fix what?"

"The ramp." I kick at a board that's sticking up half an inch, edging at the back of his wheelchair. "It's falling apart."

"Pshaw." He waves his hand. "It's only like that because I bet your mom I could get up and down in less than thirty seconds. This thing wasn't built for that kind of torque." He gives me a look and releases his grip on the wheels, letting his chair coast down the last foot of the ramp. He slips onto the driveway with a soft sound. "Plus, I've got arms, don't I?"

"You do."

"Good. Then leave my ramp alone. It suits me fine." He squints up at me, his face screwed up in the same look he always gets when he's trying to work out a puzzle. Pinched brows, scrunched nose, a downward tilt to his lips. He used to make that same face when Harper would lie to him about her plans for the night, later shimmying out her window and sneaking down the road to the bonfire parties instead of studying in her room.

"You doing all right, kiddo?"

I open the passenger side of the truck, and a tiny felt mouse falls to the driveway. Half of me expects Cupid or Vixen to come tumbling out after it. Of all of the cats, those two cause the most trouble. Stella found them pawing through a box of Triscuits in one of her kitchen cabinets two weeks ago.

"I'm good," I tell him, placing the Tupperware on the floorboard. I tuck the mouse in my pocket and lean up against the truck. "What's going on? Everything okay with you?"

He nods, swallows hard, and then tilts his head back to look up at the sky. I follow his gaze and glance up, my eyes immediately landing on Pleiades, a cluster of stars shaped like a question mark. Everything is illuminated tonight, not a cloud in sight. Clear enough that you can see the slight differentiation in color. Pale blue. Crisp white. Bright and shining yellow.

"You wouldn't shut up about the stars when you were a kid." My dad laughs, neck still craned back and face turned up. I ignore the stars and look at him instead, watching the way his hands curl around the arms of his chair. "You wanted to go to that space camp. Do you remember?"

I do. I saw the commercial and immediately started saving the money I earned around town. I devoured anything and everything about astronauts. I launched a one-man campaign to have a space-themed week during STEM units at the elementary school, and I made Nova and Nessa build a spaceship out of old garbage cans in the backyard. I wanted one of those patches they handed out with JUNIOR ASTRONAUT stitched on it. I wanted to eat space ice cream.

Stupid stuff. Kid stuff.

But as I got older, I started to look at what I had to study. I took out books from the library on engineering, math—goddamn biological science. School stopped being boring and became a path instead. A challenge.

But I never made it to that camp, and I never took a single class on engineering. My dad fell off a ladder while repairing some roof shingles at the produce farm. One of the rails had buckled, and the ladder listed to the left, sending my dad to the ground from a fifty-foot height. A freak accident.

I remember the exact pair of shoes I was wearing when my mom got the call. Red converse with both sets of laces undone, one half off my foot as I sat at the kitchen table and tried to do my English homework. The phone rang twice, and my mom answered with a cup of coffee in her hand, the receiver wedged between her shoulder and ear. I remember the small noise she made. A sharp intake of breath. A quiet "Where is he?" Shattered glass on the kitchen floor.

"What's this about, Dad?"

He heaves a deep breath and rubs his palms over his knees. "I just"—he swallows around the rest of his sentence and turns from the stars to look at me—"I guess I just want to know if you're happy."

" 'Course I'm happy," I reply. He studies me, looking for the flinch in my words. "What do I have to be unhappy about?"

I love working at Lovelight. I love my cabin on the edge of the grounds and the brisk early mornings when it's just me and my breath and the sun crawling up from behind the horizon. Cotton candy skies and the leaves on the trees rustling as sun beams urge them awake. I like the stillness, the quiet. Layla in her bakery, the smell of fresh-baked bread twisting through the towering oaks. Stella in her office, paperwork everywhere and a drawer full of pine tree air fresheners she thinks no one knows about. Sal with baskets looped over his arms and Barney on the tractor. Every single person that finds their way there down the narrow dirt road and around the bend. Through the arches and up the gravel driveway. The big red barn by the road and the rows and rows of trees, waiting for a home.

It is exactly where I'm supposed to be. My hands in the dirt and my feet on the ground. I've never doubted that for a second.

Rooted.

"I feel like I made a choice for you, is all. You were fifteen years old, and I—"

I push off the truck and grab his shoulder the way he's always grabbed mine. I shake him once. "It was my choice," I tell him.

He puts his hand over mine. Squeezes tight. "You're sure?"

"I'm sure."

4

EVELYN

"GOD, EVELYN. I'M so sorry."

On the verge of tears, Jenny stands behind the small desk at Inglewild's bed-and-breakfast with a big fluffy robe wrapped tight around her thin frame. She had been locking up for the night when I pulled up to the curb in my rental and, and she hurried to let me in, robe and all.

"It's just—you did such a good job for us the last time you were here. We've been booked solid since. And there's a kite festival at the beach this weekend and—"

I've sent her into a tailspin. She flips open the paper ledger and sorts through the pages like it'll say something different than the computer sitting on the corner of her little desk. She swallows and glances up at me before continuing to flip back and forth. It's bad enough that I've held her up after-hours. Now I'm about to give her a nervous breakdown too.

I reach over and catch her hand in mine, keeping her fingers from ripping the pages out of the book. "Jenny. It's all right."

It's not like I booked this trip in advance. Or put any thought into it other than—

I was happy standing in that field with my boots sinking into the mud, and maybe I should go back and see if I can find my happy again.

A stupid idea. A whimsical one. One that seemed brilliant after six empanadas and Josie fist-pumping across the table while I booked my ticket. I pull back my hand and tug my hair into a ponytail. I feel greasy and gross from the plane trip, my shirt clinging to the small of my back. I stare at the ledger mournfully. Damn. I had been looking forward to a long soak in the giant clawfoot bathtubs Jenny has in every suite.

"It's all right," I repeat, and try to convince myself of the same. I'll just find somewhere else to stay. No problem. "Can you recommend another place close by?"

Jenny swallows hard and looks down at the desk. She mumbles something, her hands clenched tight around the edges of the ledger.

"What was that?"

She exhales. "With the kite festival," she begins slowly, "everything is booked up. I'm not even sure the bigger chain hotels down at the beach will have anything available."

Shit. Well. Okay. I didn't know people liked kites that much, but that's—it's fine. That's what I get for my impulsivity, I guess. I shouldn't have jumped on a plane without making some reservations first. I didn't even call Stella to see if it was a good time for me to visit the farm.

But I know myself. I know if I gave it a day, I would have talked myself right out of it. I would have found something else to occupy myself with—a new project, a new task—and in a week, a month, a year, I'd probably still be stuck in this same rut, this endless loop of numb ambivalence.

I frown and glance out one of the big windows that looks over Main Street, the traffic lights wrapped in vibrant green vines with flowers starting to peek open in bloom. Mabel, the stunning and slightly terrifying woman who runs the greenery, must have put them up to welcome spring. The last time I was here, there were wreaths hanging from every front door, garland and lights strung neatly from pole to pole, a row of perfect gingerbread houses wrapped in tinsel and lights guiding you to Lovelight Farms at the very edge of town.

I'm glad people are finally discovering this gem of a town. I only wish it wasn't when I needed it too.

"Any other ideas on where I could stay?"

Maybe I'll check local listings tomorrow morning and see if anyone has a space they're willing to rent. I have no idea how long I plan on being here, but I do know that this feels like my best chance at getting back to myself. At figuring out what's wrong.

Jenny's face brightens for the first time since she came padding down the front steps in a pair of bright blue slippers. "Oh! I could use the phone tree." Her face collapses into a frown almost as quickly. "Shoot. But we're not allowed to use it past seven unless it's a true emergency."

"You have a phone tree?"

She waves her hand above her, like she's calling upon the spirits to explain the mysticism of it all. "It's how we communicate across the town when there's news. I could use it to figure out if anyone has a place for you to stay."

"But you can't use it past seven?"

She shakes her head sadly. "There has been some . . . abuse of the system lately. Gus did a townwide call last Tuesday at ten p.m. to ask if anyone had extra tortillas to spare for taco night at the firehouse. The sheriff almost disbanded the entire system. It was only on account of Caleb stepping in with the curfew rule that the phone tree was salvaged."

"Uh, thank goodness." From the gravity of her tone, it seems like the right response.

She nods. "I'll use it in the morning, do some digging for you. In the meantime, I think you might find some spare room at Lovelight Farms." I'm not sure, but it looks like a smile curls at the edge of her lips. A thoughtful look knits her brows together. "It used to be a hunting retreat, I think."

I remember Stella saying something about that the last time I was in town. I also remember her little cottage at the edge of the pumpkin patch filled to the brim with various odds and ends. At one point, Luka stood in her kitchen with his arms outstretched. He could touch one of the windows and the entry hallway at the same time. I don't want to show up on her doorstep in the middle of the night and ask if I can crash. Especially if she already has Luka there.

"Thanks for that," I say. I have absolutely no intention of driving up to Lovelight tonight. Not until I have a shower, a fresh coat of lipstick, and a serious pep talk. I'm not anxious to see Beckett again. I'm just—

I don't want him to see me and think I'm—that I'm asking for anything. I didn't come here for him.

I've come here for his fields. I want to sit in the tall grass and stare up at the sky and try to find the place within myself that's locked up or rusted over or whatever the hell has been going on with me lately. I want to fix it. I'm tired of feeling like this.

I've come here for a break. I want to sit in the quiet and do nothing. I have seventeen emails in my inbox from right before I left—courtesy of Sway—and I haven't looked at a single one. Anxiety grabs me by the throat every single time I see the little red number on my screen. I turned my phone off the third time I reached for it and buried it at the bottom of my bag. Maybe I'll get a burner while I'm here. Really lean into the whole off-the-radar thing.

I thank Jenny for her time and assure her another four times that everything is fine before slipping out the front door and down the marble steps to my rental parked at the curb. A gust of wind lifts my ponytail and the edge of my coat, bringing with it hints of honeysuckle and jasmine from the flowers twisted around the light pole. I eyeball the back seat as I stand at the driver's-side door.

I've slept in my car before—during long road trips and last-minute ones. Once when I was driving through Colorado, my rental car kicked it in the higher altitudes, and I had to push it halfway off the road and wait until morning, when it was safe for a tow truck to come to get me. I had slept fine in the back seat, only slightly terrified a bear was going to come careening through the windshield.

I'll have to find somewhere slightly private. Somewhere Jenny won't see me. Or the sheriff. Or anyone who might call the sheriff. I don't exactly want to start my trip here with the town gossip mill rolling about Evelyn St. James sleeping in the back seat of her car.

I also don't want a picture of me curled up in the back and using my sweater as a blanket going viral.

I bite my bottom lip. Maybe not such a great idea after all.

I'm still debating my choices when I hear footsteps on the pavement across the street. I glance up at the same moment Beckett glances across, and it's just like that night in the bar, when he elbowed his way through the front door and looked right at me, those damn eyes of his sweeping across my face and down my shoulders. A glance like a touch, a fingertip at the hollow of my throat.

He's frozen across the street, half on the curb and half off it. Corduroy jacket. Open flannel beneath. Dark jeans and heavy work boots. He has a box from Ms. Beatrice's bakery in his left hand, plain white with a thin piece of string in a pretty little bow on top. I focus there instead of his face, and watch as his hand tightens around the box.

I could laugh. He looks like every decadent thing I've ever indulged in. Flannel and scruff and a box of baked goods in his hand.

It makes sense that I'd run into him like this—an abandoned street with just us and the flower petals, my back breaking under the strain of all my exhaustion. It's like this with Beckett and me, I'm starting to figure out. We keep hurtling into each other.

"Don't tell Layla" is the first thing he says to me. His voice is a low rumble, as rough as I remember. I bite my lip against a smile, and his eyes roll up to the sky like he's frustrated with himself before slanting them right back to me. He steps the rest of the way off the curb and strolls across the street.

I look at the box in his hand. "Only if you share."

He huffs and clutches the box tighter. "I don't think so."

"You are not in a position to negotiate."

"We'll see."

I press up on my tiptoes and try to get a peek through the thin plastic on top. "What does Ms. Beatrice make better than Layla anyway?"

He looks supremely uncomfortable at being caught. Or maybe that's just the surprise of seeing his one-night stand suddenly appear, again, in the place he lives.

I wince. "Sorry, never mind." I rub at the headache that's starting to form between my eyebrows. "Listen, I should have—"

"Shortbread cookies," he tells me. He stops about three feet away from me and studies my rental. His eyes dart over my shoulder to the bed-and-breakfast, and then back to the car. He zeroes in on me with that singular intensity he always seems to carry, whether he's licking a line of salt from my wrist or changing the tire on a tractor.

I swallow hard. Neither of those images help with the sharp pulse of heat low in my belly, a single forceful beat.

Beckett looks good.

He's always looked good.

"She's been making them for me since I was a kid. Layla's don't come close." His eyes narrow into slits. "If you tell her I said that, I'll deny it."

I give him a solemn nod while fighting my grin. "All right."

He nods. "Good." He considers my car again. I wonder if Jenny is watching from behind her desk and if this constitutes a phone tree emergency. I saw how this town handled Stella and Luka together. I'd bet this rental car that they were the subject of several phone tree discussions. Beckett raps his knuckles once against the hatchback. "You're in town?"

I nod. "Yep."

"Stella didn't tell me you were coming."

"It would have been difficult for her to," I say quietly—so much for easing into it—"since I didn't know I was coming until this morning."

"You got a thing close by?"

By *thing*, I assume he means a profile or small business highlight. I do not, and I don't especially want to get into my recent issues out here on the street. I certainly don't want to get into them with Beckett, of all people. He already thinks my job is stupid, and I don't want him thinking I came here as an elaborate excuse to see him.

I didn't.

I shake my head and rub my hands over the outsides of my arms, wishing I packed a jacket that was a little bit thicker. I forgot March on the East Coast is just starting to creep out of winter, the mornings and evenings carrying a whisper of it still. I pull my thin wool coat a little tighter around me and rock back on my heels. Beckett's eyes narrow, but he doesn't say anything, the box in his hand creaking in protest at the way he's gripping it.

"You need help with your bags?"

"What?"

"Your bags," he says again, nodding toward the bed-and-breakfast. "You need help bringing them in?"

"Oh, no. Um—" If Jenny is watching right now, she is getting a master class in awkward and uncomfortable interactions. I hitch my thumb over my shoulder. "Jenny is full for the night. Apparently there is a kite festival down at the beach."

Beckett's brow furrows into a heavy line of confusion. "Kite festival? They have festivals for kites?"

I snicker. I thought the exact same thing. "Yeah, apparently."

"So what are you going to do?"

"What?"

He heaves another deep breath to the sky, his exhale a cloud of white that the wind carries away. I am exhausting him.

"Are you gonna stay down by the beach?" Inglewild is about a twenty-five-minute drive from the coast, a long stretch of highway between here and there. More farmland, some outlet shopping, and a custard stand that I've had several recurring dreams about.

"I was—" I cannot tell him I planned on sleeping in my car in the alley behind the café. I look for an alternative, appropriate explanation of my plan. A plan that does not exist. "I was going to figure something out."

He considers me quietly. I still can't get over how different he is here compared to the man I met in Maine. He had been loose and comfortable, quiet but charming. His smiles had been easy and frequent. Here, now, standing a perfect three feet apart on the sidewalk, the streetlights and the moon paint him in shadows. He seems stiff—frozen and uncomfortable. He's got a frown on every line of his face, from the set of his eyebrows to the downward tilt of his full lips.

I wonder how much of that is my fault.

"You don't have a plan."

My chin falls to my chest and I keep my gaze on his boots. He's got a bit of mud clinging to one, right at the toe. I think of him out in the fields, hat on backward and sleeves rolled to his elbows. It loosens something inside of me and lets me be a little honest. I press out a sigh.

"This trip wasn't . . . planned. I came here on a whim. Josie, my assistant, she asked me the last place I was happy and—I don't know." I shrug, feeling silly and small out here on the street with a man who probably never gave me a second thought.

"It was here," he offers.

It's not a question. I blink up at him, and my shoulders slip from my ears when I see the way his face has softened, a lightness to those sea-glass eyes of his that I haven't seen since there was a bottle of tequila on the table.

"It was here," I confirm.

His lips tilt up at the corners. Just the slightest bit. I wouldn't have noticed if we weren't standing directly below a streetlight. I cock my head at the change in his expression, immediately curious.

"What's that look for?"

He shakes his head and switches his box of shortbread cookies to his right hand. "Nothing, just something my dad said tonight." He holds his hand out, palm up. "C'mon."

I stare at his hand like he uncurled his fingers and revealed a tiny baby cobra in there. "C'mon, what?"

He jerks his head behind him and I can barely make out the bed of his truck parked at the corner. "I have three extra bedrooms. You can crash in one until you figure out what you're doing."

That seems like a . . . monumentally bad idea. The last time I was here, we could barely look at each other. I think the longest amount of time we spent together—just the two of us—was that morning at the bakehouse where he told that stupid joke about the strawberry fields. We didn't talk much beyond that. He commented on the weather. I asked him some questions about the trees. He considered me quietly while he slowly ate his zucchini bread, flipping his fork around and offering me a bite, nudging the plate across the table with the back of his hand.

That was probably twenty minutes of peaceful coexistence. I'm not sure shacking up for the immediate future is good for either of us.

"I don't know." I shift on my feet and curl into myself further when the wind picks up again. Beckett's frown deepens. "Won't that be awkward?"

"Doesn't have to be," he mutters. "It's a big cabin. And we're both mature adults."

I raise both eyebrows at him, remembering how he showed up at this same bed-and-breakfast a couple of months ago and basically accused me of being a flake with a stupid job. He flinches and scrubs his hand against the back of his head. "At least I think we can both be mature adults," he amends.

I huff a laugh through my nose but make no move to take his hand. After another moment of indecision, he pulls it back, curling those long fingers around the edges of the box. The cardboard gives slightly under his grip, like it's barely hanging on. That poor box.

"We could start over if you want," he offers. He swallows, and I watch as frustration tightens everything on his face—the strain in his sharp jaw, the tilt of his lips. He really is handsome, even when he's making a face at me like someone stuck a lemon in his mouth. "We could—if you wanted, we could pretend this is the first time we're meeting."

"And you're inviting me to your house on an isolated stretch of farmland? Okay, serial killer."

A smile twitches at his lips. "Yeah, you're probably right."

Not to mention I'm not sure I could forget Beckett if I tried. There's no pretending between us, not anymore.

I avert my gaze back to the flower vines twisted around the light pole. Green and white and yellow and the palest purple I've ever seen. I want to touch each bloom and feel the softness, press my nose into the petals. When I was a kid running through the woods behind my parents' house, I used to pluck honeysuckle blossoms from the bushes, tear the stems, and lick at the nectar. Pure sticky sweetness, petals in my hair. Mud on my knees and hands and everywhere in between.

It would be convenient to stay on the farm. I know Beckett's house at the edge of the property is bigger than Stella's. I saw it once while I was exploring during my last trip. The large stone chimney, the wraparound front porch. It's a gorgeous house. Stella said his place had been the lodging quarters for whatever hunting retreat Lovelight used to be. I could stay in one of his spare rooms tonight and see what the phone tree turns up tomorrow.

With his schedule, we probably wouldn't even see each other.

I look to Beckett, my gaze snagging on the jut of his collarbone, barely visible through the opening of his shirt. I remember sinking my teeth into exactly that spot, tracing my thumb over the marks I left behind.

I drag my eyes back to his. "You sure it's all right?"

A beat of silence pulses between us. He doesn't look away. "I am. You?"

I think about it for a second and then slowly nod my head. It feels like a bad idea, but I'm fresh out of options.

The wind whistles through the old picket fence that lines the gardens by the road. A lock of hair falls over his forehead, and he smooths it back with his palm. I glance at the box in his hand.

"Are you going to share the cookies?"

He turns on his heel and heads toward his truck. "Absolutely not."

5

BECKETT

I HAVE LOST my damn mind.

There's no other explanation for it.

I didn't see her when I first stepped out of the back entrance of the café, a box of cookies tucked under my arm and my mind still in my parents' driveway. My dad hadn't brought up his accident in close to ten years. Certainly not what happened after. I was so caught up in trying to untangle that particular knot, I didn't notice her until I was stepping off the curb, heading to my truck down the street.

It was her hair first, the wind lifting it and swinging it over her shoulder. Jet black and curling at the ends. Everything else followed. The cut of her cheekbones and the soft swell of her bottom lip caught between her teeth as she stared a hole in the side of the unfamiliar car.

Seeing her standing there in a coat that was far too thin, a second shy of shivering right out of her boots, it felt like grabbing an exposed wire. I did that once when I was replacing the bulbs that wind their way through the fields at the farm. It zipped right up my arm, a sharp and brilliant surge.

It took me a second to catch my breath.

"You are an absolute fucking idiot, Beckett Porter." I shove another cookie in my mouth with a huff and watch the headlights behind me rise and fall as we turn in to the farm. The butter and sugar is doing absolutely nothing for me. I glance out the passenger-side window as I rumble past Stella's cottage on the edge of the pumpkin patch, relieved when I see her windows are dark. The last thing I need is Stella and Luka with a pair of binoculars riling up the phone tree.

Pretend this is the first time we're meeting. What a dumb fucking thing to say. Like I can forget the way she looked tangled in the sheets. A smile that tasted like lime and salt.

My foot edges on the gas and I grunt. Stupid. I have no idea why I invited Evelyn—the same woman who left me without a word in a hotel room—to stay indefinitely. My house is big, sure, but not that big.

I turn down the winding dirt road that leads to my cabin, the way marked by flickering solar lanterns. I installed them last month when Luka got lost trying to cut across the fields from my place to Stella's after one too many beers. Stella called a half an hour after he left, asking where he went. I found him wandering in the southeast fields by the carrots.

I pull into the driveway and cut the engine, watching as three little furry heads appear in the window, one after another. I can't help smiling despite the tension twisting my neck. It's nice to have something to come home to, even if they tear my furniture to shit.

Evelyn is busy wrestling an oversized duffle from the back seat of her car as I climb out of the truck. "You need help?"

She shakes her head and grabs a rolling suitcase as well. I try not to read too much into it. If she wants to have a little ambiguity about what she's doing here and for how long, that's fine. I feel like I have at least one person in my life withholding information at any given time. What's another?

Three cats jostle for my attention as soon as I open the door, and I scoop them into my arms, letting them crawl up my jacket to settle across my shoulders. They're still tiny, not having grown much since we found them curled up in the corner of the barn. Comet, Cupid, Vixen. It was a little on the nose when I named them, but it felt appropriate for a family of cats that lives on a Christmas tree farm. I glance around the open living room and spot Prancer stretched out in front of the fireplace, her head resting on the stone. She opens one eye and lazily bats her paw in the air, as enthusiastic a hello as I ever get from her. Good to see she found her way home after this morning's joyride on the tractor.

The door shuts behind me, and I watch Evelyn place her bags by the door, stepping hesitantly into the space. All four cats stop what they're doing and stare at her like she's just tossed a handful of their kibble up in the air like confetti.

She blinks, her dark eyes wide.

"This is—" She looks around the room. A smile loosens every bit of her body when Prancer decides she's not a threat, does a full body stretch, and promptly falls right back to sleep. She looks at me. "This is not what I expected."

Feeling sheepish, I glance around the space and try to see what's unexpected about it. It's fairly simple in terms of furniture and decor. Big, oversized secondhand couches, worn and well loved, a couple of blankets thrown over the back. The kittens went through a clawing phase, and I'd rather not have stuffing spilling over me every time I sit down. A dark red rug beneath to keep the floors warm in the winter. Shelves on either side of the fireplace, haphazardly stacked with books. A giant canvas between—a field of wildflowers painted by Nova, red and yellow and pale, pale pink.

My coffee mug from this morning is still sitting on the edge of the table, and I grab it on my way into the kitchen, sliding the leftovers from dinner into the fridge.

"You want something to eat?"

I barely catch her soft no in response, her feet carrying her over to one of the big windows that looks out over the fields. In the morning, sunlight fills this whole space until it's fit to burst, the hills rolling out behind the house in a patchwork quilt of green and gold. Right now, darkness cloaks everything beyond the wooden porch. Instead of rows and rows of sturdy green trees, I only see Evelyn's reflection. Fingertips at her lips, and high cheekbones. Big brown eyes. I stare a second too long, something scratching at my throat.

I swallow around it.

"I'll show you your room." I snap the refrigerator door closed and collect all the scattered pieces of myself. It's one night, maybe, and then she'll be on her way. Off to the next adventure, the next exciting thing. I'm a stopping point. I'm *barely* a stopping point. One she never even wanted to have.

I need to remember that.

I slip out of the kitchen and down the hallway that leads to the bedrooms. The house is all one level, the upstairs a giant unrenovated storage space with ancient floorboards that creak beneath the slightest pressure. Nessa uses it for dance rehearsal sometimes when her usual studio is rented or occupied. I thought she was going to come right through the ceiling the last time she was here, the gentle pitter-patter of her feet interrupted by booming shakes as she practiced jump after jump. The cats had not been thrilled.

I push open the door to the first room on the left and flick on the light with my elbow, grabbing Comet from her place on my neck just for something to do with my hands. I rub her head with my knuckles and poke my head into the attached bath to make sure Nova or Harper haven't left a heap of wet towels clumped in the corner. All of the bedrooms have an attached bathroom. It's a remnant, I think, from when this oversized house used to be a lodge.

It's no wonder it went out of business. The only things I've seen to hunt around here are a couple of squirrels and a wayward deer. A fox that Stella's named Guinevere.

"Are you running a bed-and-breakfast on the side?"

Evelyn collapses onto the bed with a happy little sigh, and I immediately avert my gaze to the trunk full of extra sheets and blankets at the foot of the bed.

"Some days, it feels like it," I mutter. If one of my sisters isn't here crashing in a spare room, it's Layla, working too late at the bakery and too damn tired to drive herself home. Or Luka, saying he needs guy time and pretending he's actually going to stay the entire night instead of wandering back to Stella's before midnight. Or Charlie, Stella's half brother, snoring so loud the rafters shake with it.

"Blankets are in the trunk," I tell her. I grab Vixen from the back of my neck, where she's valiantly trying to climb to the top of my head. Cupid leaps from me to the bed and kneads her little tiny pink paws into the pillow. Evelyn reaches out a hand and smooths her palm down the kitten's back. "Spare towels in the bathroom. You're welcome to anything you find."

I feel awkward, uncomfortable, kicked out of orbit and floundering to find my way back. I clear my throat twice. "I'll be up and out early, but help yourself to whatever you need."

"I won't be in your space long," she says quietly. "Jenny is supposed to ring the phone tree tomorrow. Find me a place to stay."

A lot of good that will do. The phone tree is easily the most useless thing in this town. I ignore the flip in my stomach and the spike of protest that flares in response. I'm confused by the reaction. I have no reason to want her to stay any longer than she needs to, but I've always been a bit out of my mind where Evelyn is concerned.

"All right" is what I settle on, collecting the cats in my arms and turning to leave. I'm afraid of what I'll do if I stay in this bedroom a second longer. If I took two steps forward, my knees would knock into hers. I could place my hand next to her hip and lean over her, pin her down to the mattress with my hips. She's nothing but temptation splayed out on the bed like that, windswept and warm.

I picked this bedroom for a reason. It's the very farthest from mine, on the opposite side of the house.

"Beckett?"

I glance up from where I've been trying to untangle Vixen's claws from my sleeve cuff and focus on Evelyn in the wedge of moonlight that filters in through the window. She looks tired, her hair beginning to slip from her ponytail, her white button-down wrinkled from travel, one of the sleeves half rolled and the other caught at her elbow. She is deliciously unraveled, a little blurred around the edges, and I only want to mess her up a little bit more.

She gazes up at me, and I shove the urge away.

"Thank you," she says, voice whisper soft.

I breathe in deep through my nose. "It's no problem."

It won't be. She'll stay here, she'll find what she needs, and she'll be on her way. It'll be fine.

I'll be fine.

6

BECKETT

DAWN BRINGS WITH it a pounding headache and a storm cloud of foreboding. I take back what I said last night.

It is a problem.

I am not fine.

I didn't sleep for shit. I jolted awake at every floorboard creak, every scratch of a tree branch against a window, every single sound the house made as it settled around me. When I finally did drift to sleep, it was to dreams of Evelyn standing in front of that window in the living room, the moonlight on her bare skin, those dimples at the base of her spine tempting me. I dreamt of my hands smoothing around her hips and my lips trailing up the column of her neck.

I wake up frustrated, desire pounding through my bloodstream. I groan and drag myself out of bed and force myself into the coldest shower I can manage. The last thing Evelyn needs is me thinking about her like that while she's working through something.

I curse as I pull on my jeans. I somehow manage to stub my toe on the edge of the dresser and the table in the hallway. I burn my hand on the coffeepot and fall down the bottom two porch steps when I'm leaving the house.

The woman has made a damn mess of me.

She said this trip wasn't planned, and I have no idea what that means in terms of how long she's staying or what she's planning on doing now that she's here. She said something about—something about remembering how to be happy, her lips turned down at the corners, her eyes somewhere on the ground by our boots. It was like she was embarrassed about it, her voice catching in the wind and drifting away from both of us.

Has she not been happy? It's hard to imagine Evelyn feeling anything other than absolute joy. Filled to the brim with—fucking sunshine and butterflies. The last time she was here, she had a permanent grin on her face, her laugh loud and bright as it slipped through the trees. But that's the thing about happiness, I guess. You can show whatever you want to the world and not feel a lick of it inside yourself.

"But I'm not new anymore."

"You've been working here for two days."

Voices carry around the edge of the barn, a low grumble in response before a heavy sigh of exasperation. I turn the corner just as Jeremy pushes a hand through his hair, hip cocked against the side of the tractor. I'm glad to see he's wearing boots today, even if they look like something out of a magazine. "Beckett said the *newbie* shovels rocks. I'm not the newbie anymore."

"One day of farmwork doesn't remove the *newbie* title." I clap him on the shoulder and he jumps about ten feet in the air. "You're the newbie until someone else comes along." I hand him the shovel and he groans. "Not much left to do today."

Barney chuckles and runs both hands over his balding head. "Plenty left to do today. Young hotshot over here can't shovel for shit."

"These arms were made for love, baby. Not labor."

Barney and I exchange a look. I bite the inside of my cheek so hard it almost bleeds.

"Good to know." I grab another one of the shovels and nod toward the fields. "C'mon. I'll help you."

A little mindless physical work will be good for me. The tractor engine kicks up, and I catch a flash of white bounding across the field toward us as Prancer settles into her spot right in front of the wheel and shoots a thinly veiled look of disgust in my direction. She never did come to her usual spot on my bed last night, probably busy carving death threats into my couch upholstery for daring to bring another woman into her home.

Barney rubs her head and we're off. The work is slow-moving, especially with Jeremy shoveling at the rate of a small baby bird, his arms limp at his sides and his grip all wrong. I roll my eyes and lose myself in the work, my mind drifting with each repetitive movement.

Push. Dig. Dump. Did she sleep last night? Push. Dig. Dump. Did I wake her this morning when I fumbled my coffee mug onto the kitchen floor? Push. Dig. Dump. How long is she staying? Push. Dig. Dump. Why isn't she happy? Push. Dip. Dump. How can I help?

Push. Dip. Dump.

Does she want me to help?

Harper calls it my hero complex. She says I fix other people's problems to avoid my own, and she's probably right about that. I don't like to see anyone struggle.

I especially don't like the look I saw on Evelyn's face last night, the self-doubt mixed with hesitation.

"All right, boss." Barney is giving me a concerned look, the tractor at a standstill, his arm slung over the back of the seat. I glance down at the field and the hole I've apparently been digging behind the left tire.

"Think you've got a morning meeting to get to," Barney says. He nods in the direction of Stella's office, a steady stream of smoke pumping out of the chimney. The sun is already well above the horizon, the sky a bright and brilliant blue. Jeremy is flat on his back, chest heaving, his shovel about twenty feet behind him. I think he managed two rocks today.

"Aren't you on the basketball team?" I call over to him.

He lifts a limp hand into the air. "I ride the bench, bro. I just do it for the ladies."

We have our partner meetings on alternating Wednesday mornings. An attempt, I think, from Stella to be more transparent after she had hid some of the business details from us last year. Layla usually brings some sort of baked good, and my stomach gives a happy rumble at the reminder. I glance down with a grimace at my T-shirt, covered in dirt and sweat.

Layla mirrors the same grimace as soon as I swing into the tiny office, haphazard stacks of paper on every flat surface. Stella likes to say she has a system, but I think she's full of shit. I snap a picture on my phone and send it to Luka. He'll probably break into hives as soon as he sees it.

"Why do you look like you crawled your way over here?" Layla pulls her sweater over her nose and kicks out the seat next to her until there's a healthy four feet of distance between my seat and . . . everything else.

Stella frowns at her. "It's not that bad," she says. I take a step farther into the room, and she sucks in a sharp breath. "Oh my god, Beckett. Is that blood?"

It is, and I have no idea how it got on the sleeve of my shirt. I ignore them both and collapse into the chair, the legs giving a protesting squeak at my weight. I'm pretty sure Stella found these chairs on the side of the road and decided to bring them home with her. I peer into the tin sitting on top of a stack of invoices.

"Is this carrot cake?"

Layla plucks a muffin from the top and hands it to me. She pauses, considers, and then hands me another. I narrow my eyes at her. It's not like her to willingly offer extras.

"What's going on with you?" I ask, suspicious.

"What's going on with you, *Children of the Corn*?" She fires right back.

I debate hiding it from them, but they'll know soon enough. Especially since Evelyn's rental car is currently parked in my driveway, and farm gossip is more efficient than the town phone tree. I'm honestly surprised Stella doesn't already know. I take a giant bite of carrot cake and kick my legs out. "Evelyn is here."

I get two blank stares in response. Layla smooths her hands down the bright red skirt she has on, thermal black tights beneath. "Care to repeat what you just said?"

I swallow and reach for the coffee Stella has waiting for me on the edge of the desk. "Evelyn is here."

"In Inglewild?"

In my spare bed. Wrapped in sheets that have tiny roses on them. In less than half a second, my brain takes some creative liberties with that, imagining her stretched out naked beneath the blankets, one long leg kicked out. I clear my throat.

"At my house," I say slowly. I drag each word out and watch as Stella's eyes widen. She exchanges a look with Layla. Layla collapses into her chair and raises both eyebrows. Stella's nose twitches and her shoulder kicks up to her ear before it settles again.

"Cut that shit out," I grumble, finishing the first muffin and moving on to the next. "I know you're talking about me."

"We didn't say anything."

"Might as well have."

"All right, let's take a step back." Stella steeples her hands in front of her face. With her behind her desk and Layla and I in the two chairs in front of it, it feels like every single time I was ever called to the principal's office. My phone buzzes on the arm of the chair. I glance at it and spot a text from Luka.

LUKA: Hurricane Stella.

LUKA: Is that carrot cake?

"Stop texting my boyfriend and pay attention."

I breathe out slowly through my nose and try for a subject change. I glance at Layla. "Didn't you have dinner with Jacob last night?"

She makes a face. "I broke up with Jacob two weeks ago. I went on a date with a guy I met through an app." She waves her hand between us and fixes me with a look that says she knows exactly what I'm doing. "Don't try to distract me. I'm not letting the Evelyn thing go."

"Aren't we supposed to be going over this quarter's numbers today?"

"Nice try," Stella adds. "We can discuss this first and move on to reporting after. I also want to talk about why you have Jeremy Roughman doing manual labor out in the fields. But first, how did Evelyn get to your house?"

"She took a flight, I'd imagine. And then rented a car."

Stella is not impressed. "Beckett."

"I ran into her in town last night," I explain. I leave out the part where I ran into her leaving the café, a box of contraband cookies tucked under my arm. I don't know what Layla would do if she found out I'm sneaking baked goods from Ms. Beatrice on the side, but it probably wouldn't be pretty. I like my face the way it is. "The bed-and-breakfast was full, and she didn't have anywhere else to stay."

Layla gives me a critical look, one eyebrow notched high on her forehead. "So you invited her to stay with you?"

"I did."

"For how long?"

I shrug and pick at the wrapper on my second muffin. It has chocolate chips in it, like Layla somehow knew I'd need the extra strength today. "I have no idea. She said something about this trip not being planned." I leave out the part where she talked about Lovelight being the last place she was happy. That feels private, and I don't want to share things that belong to her. "Jenny is ringing the phone tree today to find her someplace to stay longer term, I think."

I ignore the thrum of discomfort that settles in my shoulders at that. It feels the same as when there's too much noise around me, my teeth clenching down around it. I don't like the idea of her anywhere else, and I'm well aware that makes me a fucking idiot. A glutton for punishment, probably. She made her intentions very clear as far as our relationship is concerned. I can't imagine being roommates with her one-night stand was in her plan when she decided to come here.

She could have texted me though. Given me a heads-up. Did she think she wouldn't have to see me? Is that what she was hoping for? I frown.

Stella and Layla busy themselves with another silent conversation while I focus on eating the rest of my breakfast. I drink my coffee and try to put everything back in order within myself. My brain keeps skipping to Evelyn collapsing backward onto the bed in the spare room, one of the pillows tumbling down by her legs. Comet nudging under her chin with her nose. It's been playing on repeat in my mind all morning, and it leaves me feeling like I've been kicked down a hill in a barrel. That exposed wire thing again, my hair standing on end.

"Beck?" Stella's looking at me, face etched with worry and her palms cupped gently around her mug. There's a pine tree air freshener hanging from her desk light, and she knocks it with her elbow when she ducks her head to get a better look at me. "Are you okay?"

"I'm fine."

I am. I'm fine. Evelyn in my space isn't anything I can't handle. If being here is going to help her figure out her next steps or whatever it is that she's doing, then I can suck it up. It'll probably be like last time, where we circle each other and then settle. Share a baked good and move on.

This doesn't have to mean anything.

Layla plucks another muffin out of the tin and hands it to me.

"Here," she says. "You look like you need it."

7

EVELYN

IT'S SO QUIET on the other end of the phone, I check several times to see if Josie accidentally hung up on me. Silence is not what I expected when I delivered the news. In fact, I was bracing myself for the opposite. Extended obnoxious laughter. A cackle or two. A screaming shriek.

"Josie?"

"You're staying at his house?" Her voice is pitched low, and for once, I can't hear a single thing in the background. Josie is constant motion, often sounding like she's at a train station instead of at her house. Right now she sounds like she's in a closet.

"Yeah, I'm staying at his house." He left a key next to the coffee machine this morning. A note with surprisingly neat handwriting with the code to the garage door.

"Does he"—she breathes out a shaky exhale—"does he only have one bed?"

"What?" I give the waitress at the café a small smile, nodding my thanks when she places my latte carefully on the table in front of me. She takes a step back but keeps looking at me, an overly bright smile on her young face. I know this look. I've seen it a thousand times before. I give her a little wave and turn slightly in my seat, lowering my voice. "What are you talking about? No, he has at least two beds that I know of."

Probably more. I wasn't kidding when I said he could run a bed-and-breakfast on the side. The inside of his cabin is huge. Surprisingly comfortable. An entire collection of throw blankets and cozy-looking pillows in his living room.

Josie continues to breathe heavily into the phone. "What does he wear to sleep in? Is it sweatpants? Are they gray?"

"Are you drunk?"

"Please just answer the question, Evie."

"I have no idea what he wears to bed," I answer as quietly as possible, conscious of the fact that I'm sitting smack-dab in the middle of a café in a town that loves to gossip. I peek over my shoulder at the table behind me—two of Inglewild's firefighters on what looks like their third plate of cinnamon rolls. "I didn't kick in his door to look, Josie."

"Maybe you should have," she hisses. "Okay, but seriously though—"

I sigh in relief.

"—I need you to tell me in excruciating detail: What is Mr. Beckett looking like these days? You never did share a picture and you were annoyingly vague. Does he have scruff?"

"What has gotten into you?"

"This whole situation is bananas, and I'm trying to capitalize on the benefits. Have you at least snooped through all of his belongings like a reasonable human being?"

"I have not, though I haven't ruled it out for this evening."

I did notice a couple of things. What looked like a celestial map taped to the front of the fridge, a circle drawn in red over a cluster of little specks with a date and time scrawled above. The corner of the living room with four oversized, soft-looking cat beds, a tiny blanket on each. Five different types of ground coffee on the kitchen counter, all half used and the bags neatly rolled shut.

It wasn't what I expected.

Though to be fair, I didn't let myself expect anything out of Beckett. Besides my game of picturing him in random places, perplexed by mint green succulent vases and fruit arrangements, I hardly let myself consider him at all. Remembering is a slippery slope into wanting, and I've built too much for myself to get distracted by a gorgeous man with tattoos and very large hands.

I suppose that doesn't matter much now though. I'm one big ball of distraction.

"Have you checked your accounts yet?"

A spike of anxiety turns my palms hot. "No. How bad is it?"

I don't think I've ever gone more than four hours without posting, a compulsion to always be one step ahead. Josie hums, and I hear the click of a mouse as she does something on her computer. "Not bad. You are causing quite the stir though. I saw a couple blogs asking where you were. You have a whole 'Where in the World Is Evelyn St. James?' thing going for you right now."

"I'm sure Sway is pleased."

"As much as they can be with their internet darling on lockdown." She makes an interested sound under her breath, another couple of clicks. "I meant to tell you, I'm sorting through some of your inboxes while you're out. It looks like Sway has been screening some messages. Do you plan on posting at all while you're there, or is it a full blackout?"

"I haven't decided yet." This is supposed to be a step back from work. I'm not sure scrolling through my accounts and posting random content is going to help with the perspective I want to find. I don't want to do anything until it feels good again.

But I have found myself itching to swipe open my camera. It's a reflex, a habit formed over close to a decade of sharing my life with millions of strangers. I wanted to snap a picture when I opened the bedroom door this morning, all four cats sitting in a line, staring up at me with their tiny heads tilted in quiet consideration. When I stepped off the front porch, the sun a brilliant, beautiful orange in the sky, everything glowing at the edges. When I wandered down the narrow alley on my way here, floral vines crisscrossed back and forth between the buildings, a canopy of blossoming flowers and drifting petals. The scent of honeysuckle tickling my nose.

"You don't have to do anything at all," Josie tells me over the phone. "You're on a break for a reason. I don't even remember the last time you took a true vacation."

"I know." I smooth my thumb over the edge of the cup. "But maybe it would help if I tried just telling stories again. That's how we started all of this, isn't it?"

No pressure. No expectations. Just me talking to people. Listening again.

"I don't think it would hurt," she offers. "But please give yourself a break. Drink a latte." She pauses for a second. "Find out if the man owns gray sweatpants."

A laugh bursts out of me, and half of the people in the café turn to look. This feels normal, the attention from strangers. When I was younger, it was exciting. I remember the first time someone recognized me in public. I was at the grocery store examining oranges, and a young woman with bright blue hair came up to me and asked if I was Evelyn St. James. She saw my video about the Bagby Hot Springs and took a trip with her friends. I remember being overwhelmed. Flattered. Exceedingly delighted.

Now though, the attention feels a bit like sun-warmed skin just shy of a burn. A hot prickle of awareness and an itch that doesn't feel right to scratch. My eyes snag on my waitress in the corner, huddled together with a tableful of teenagers. Their gazes scatter as soon I make eye contact, and I bite my bottom lip against a smile. I give them a little wave and they collapse into furious whispers. One brave girl with thick black glasses and her hair in braids waves back.

The bell above the door jingles, and Jenny slips in, one of the flower petals from outside caught in her hair. I raise my hand to get her attention and start to shift my collection of plates around. I couldn't decide what to order, so I got one of everything in the case. I might have to get up for another sausage-and-cream-cheese biscuit.

I wedge the phone between my shoulder and ear and move a bear claw to the corner of the table. I consider it briefly and then take a bite. I've never met a pastry I didn't love. "Gotta go, Jo."

"I expect a picture in my inbox later."

I snort a laugh. If I sent her a picture of Beckett, she'd be on the next flight to Maryland. "Sure, sure. Love you."

"You too."

Jenny raises both eyebrows as she slides into the seat across from me. I hand her a plate with a cranberry scone, and she gives a happy little wiggle in her chair. "Boyfriend missing you?"

My lips twitch at the thinly veiled fish for gossip. At least two heads tilt in our direction that I can see. I need to remember that there's always someone listening in this town.

"Life partner," I explain, and Jenny eyeballs me as she breaks her scone in half. I don't bother explaining. "Did you call around?"

She nods. "Haven't been able to find anything, but it's early. I'm sure something will turn up today." She drags the tip of her finger along the edge of her plate, blond hair half covering her face. She reminds me of my mom. Same lines by her eyes, same gentle smile.

Same inability to hide her duplicitous intentions.

"Did you happen to find a place to stay last night? I feel so terrible about what happened."

I grin and tear off some cinnamon roll. The icing clings to my thumb. It tastes like sugar and small-town gossip. "I'm sure you saw the whole thing from behind your desk, Jennifer Davis. Did you really call the phone tree this morning, or are you scheming?"

She blinks twice, slow and steady. She then proceeds to stuff the rest of the scone into her mouth. "I don't know what you're talking about."

I drop my chin in my hand. "Mm-hmm."

"I told you—"

"The kite festival, yeah." I haven't seen a single person in this town with a kite.

"I'll keep checking," she mumbles around a mouthful of dense pastry and dried cranberry. I offer her the glass of water at my elbow, concerned about the compulsive way she keeps swallowing. She takes it with a shaky hand and downs the whole thing in two gulps. "You never know what might turn up."

"Sure."

"Betsey might have a lead on a studio apartment, but I think it's above the mechanic station. Probably smells like oil."

"Probably."

"And I know the McGivenses sometimes rent out their spare bedroom, but I think they're hosting an . . . exchange student."

"Makes sense." It doesn't make any sense.

"I'll keep you updated though!" She slips from her seat and takes a step backward, closer to the door. If I thought everyone was looking before, it's nothing compared to the intense, avid attention we are attracting now. Two of the employees peer out from the kitchen, watching the exchange. I think Gus, one of the firefighters, is recording the whole thing on his phone. Jenny laughs—a bright, unnatural thing. "Okay, bye!"

Her ponytail has hardly disappeared from view when a small but sturdy shadow appears over my shoulder.

"That woman is full of shit," says Ms. Beatrice, her voice always softer and sweeter than I expect it to be. I heard rumors of her around town before I met her the first time. Things like "Remember not to look her directly in the eye" and "Do you think she'll make anyone cry today?"

So when I walked into the café and saw a small woman in a floral apron with her long hair pulled up in a loose gray bun, I was surprised.

Then I saw her throw an empty can of coffee at the sheriff and things made a little more sense.

"Yeah, I know." I sigh. I think about Beckett standing in the doorway of his spare bedroom last night, his body all rigid lines, with a frown twisted across his lips. He had looked about seven seconds away from climbing out the window. "I guess I'll have to poke around myself. See if there is anywhere else to stay."

The last thing I want to do is make Beckett uncomfortable in his own home.

"How long are you here for?"

"I'm not sure yet."

Ms. Beatrice hums, hands flexing on the chair. She doesn't wear any jewelry, but she does have a tiny tattoo of a songbird on the back of her hand just above her wrist. I nod at it.

"That's beautiful." Delicate lines, a touch of red on outstretched wings. It looks like it's about to fly up her arm and rest in the crook of her elbow.

She glances at it once, a smile flirting at her lips. "Nova did it."

"Nova?"

"Beckett's youngest sister." I blink. I didn't even know he had sisters. "I told her I wanted BOSS across both knuckles, but we settled on this instead."

"Well—" I search for the right words. She would look pretty bad-ass with knuckle tattoos, and the look on her face says she knows it. "Maybe you can convince her in the future."

She nods, but doesn't budge an inch. I raise an eyebrow. "Is there something I can help you with?"

A slow smile creeps across her face.

"Since you're asking . . ."

MS. BEATRICE WANTS an Instagram page.

She saw one of my posts featuring a coffee shop in North Carolina— rows and rows of coffee beans behind the counter and colorful ribbon hanging from the ceiling. Walking into that little shop had been like stepping inside a rainbow, Bob Marley coming from the speakers and sprinkles in my latte.

"That thing had over two hundred thousand comments," she says from the side of my table, shoving her phone in my face. "And the beans looked cheap."

I don't know what constitutes a cheap bean, but I indulge her. We snap a couple pictures of her behind the counter—a fierce look on her face in every single one—and set up her details. If the rainbow shop had an opposite, Ms. B's would be it. But there's a certain charm to it nonetheless. I apply a moody filter and smile at the result—a fierce woman holding a plate of scones, a steaming coffeepot at her elbow. She looks like something out of *Goodfellas*. Maybe she should get those knuckle tattoos after all.

"You know you can't use this account to publicly shame people, right?"

A secret smile. "No promises."

Gus and Monty corner me after that, asking if I can swing by the firehouse and help them with a video. Intrigued and amused, I can't help but trail after them to the open bay doors, music spilling out from the back office. I proceed to watch them choreograph a surprisingly involved dance to Jennifer Lopez. Afterward, Monty explains with panting breaths that they're trying to raise money for a new ambulance.

"And you're doing that through . . . dance?" Kirstyn would be delighted.

Monty winks at me, forehead dewy with sweat. "Gotta give the people what they want."

I spot Mabel at the door to the fire station, arms crossed over her chest and a smile ticking up the corners of her mouth. She's busy looking at Gus like he's one of Ms. Beatrice's lattes.

"Evelyn," she calls. She drags her attention away from Gus wiping the sweat from his brow with the hem of his T-shirt and blinks at me, a little bit dazed. "I need some help with my website. Do you mind stopping by the greenhouse for a sec?"

The day continues like that. As soon as I finish up with one person, another appears with a question or a task or—a banner for the farmers market that needs hanging across the fountain in the center of town. I don't know if it's small-town life or just Inglewild's own brand of welcome, but I'm pulled wonderfully and perfectly out of my head for the entire day. No anxiety clawing at my throat, no pit in my belly. I don't wonder once if this is where I'm supposed to be, if I could be doing something better or different.

I'm just here, leaning over a stone fountain with a bit of twine held between my teeth.

"How's it look?" I ask Alex, who is apparently in charge of banner hanging in addition to owning the bookshop. He gives me a thumbs-up from the edge of the fountain, glasses slipping down his nose.

I step off the ladder and tilt my head back to read the bold looping letters hand-stenciled across the canvas.

WELCOME SPRING

Right below it in a smaller font:

SEASONS CHANGE AND SO DO WE

I stretch my arms wide to the side and wiggle my fingers back and forth.

So do we.

I PULL INTO Beckett's driveway and sit in my car for a moment, staring at his house. It suits him, this big cabin at the edge of the field. Faded wood shingles warped by weather and time. An ancient-looking tree to the left, its branches reaching out over the roof. A wide porch that wraps around, a couple of rocking chairs next to the front door. A single wide window. A light on in the corner of the living room.

I laugh a little as I let myself through the front door, a bottle of wine wedged under my arm and a family of cats appearing at my feet. They weave through my legs as I drop my bag next to a worn wooden table flaked with red paint, an old baseball cap on top. I rub my thumb over the edge of the brim and let my eyes trail over the walls, taking in everything I didn't see last night.

I study the collection of family photos, all different sizes in mismatched frames. My gaze snags on one in particular. Beckett with three stunning women who can only be his sisters, two sharing a laugh while Beckett and a woman with honey blond hair give the camera a long-suffering look. I grin as I stare at it and imagine the sound he makes when he's frustrated. The sigh caught in the back of his throat.

My eyes drift to the canvas painting hanging in the middle of all the pictures, the same colors and broad paint strokes as the one above the mantel. A big golden sun hanging lazy and full in the sky.

The cats follow me to the spare room and make a nest out of my T-shirts as I change into an oversized sweater, worn leggings, and thick socks that I pull up to just below my knees. If Beckett is home, he's being quiet about it. I can't hear anything besides the soft patter of tiny paws, the rustle of cotton and flannel.

One of the cats nudges her head against my thigh, and I scratch under her chin.

"Where's your dad, hm?"

His kitchen is as neat as the rest of his house. I resist the urge to go snooping, instead taking in everything I can see from the counter that stretches out into the center of the space. An open bill, a scattering of loose change right next to it. Books stacked on the shelf, pages dog-eared. A couple of coasters out of place on the coffee table.

I collect a glass from one of the cabinets, an old jam jar with bits of the label still clinging to the edges in pieces. I rub my thumb over the faded grapes and shoulder open the door, shuffling onto the back porch, where there's a couple of wide comfortable-looking chairs.

The crickets begin their evening song as I shut the door quietly behind me, a call-and-response of chirps across the wide yard. I didn't notice last night, but Beckett has a small greenhouse at the very edge, right before the trees begin to cluster into woodland. I can see the shapes of leaves through the fogged windows, some stacked boxes, and a long bench down the center. A table in the back with terra-cotta balanced in stacks. I wonder what he grows in there, if he likes to spend his evenings with the flowers after spending all day with the trees.

The dwindling light moves across the porch, and I pour myself a glass of wine. I sip carefully and hold myself too still, waiting for the creak of the front door, boots on hardwood. But after an hour of watching the sun sink in the sky, it becomes apparent that Beckett isn't coming home anytime soon. I fall back in the chair with a sigh, the thought oddly disappointing. Is he avoiding his house? Or is he somewhere else? With someone else?

I frown and curl my legs beneath me in the chair and watch the colors change across the sky. Cotton candy pink. Vibrant red. A deep, indulgent violet. I sit on the porch and I wait.

But as night begins to edge across the yard and a yawn works my jaw open wide, I decide to call it. I collect my jam jar and the bottle by my feet and retreat inside, tidying up some of the things on the counter before shuffling down the hall to the spare room.

I close the door behind me. I'll talk with Beckett tomorrow.

8

EVELYN

BECKETT IS AVOIDING me.

Three days and I haven't seen a single glimpse of him. I know he's been coming and going. There's always fresh coffee in the pot and a handwritten note right next to it listing out what leftovers are in the fridge. I don't know how he manages to be so quiet about it, but I don't catch him once. Not even when I attempt to stay up late on the third night, determined to talk with him.

Instead I fall asleep on the couch, two of the cats purring on my lap. I wake up around midnight with a blanket draped over me and a fresh glass of water on the coffee table.

It's infuriating.

"Where is Beckett hiding?" I ask Layla, my palms pressing pastry dough into the countertop. I've been spending my days with Layla and Stella, helping out where I can. Neither of them looked surprised to see me when I first appeared in Stella's office, so at the very least, Beckett told them I was here.

Or the phone tree did.

Layla hums and continues piping intricate lines of icing across a cookie. She leans back, rotates it once, and then bends to continue. "Aren't you staying at his house?"

"I am, but he's not." Layla makes another contemplative sound under her breath. I press my knuckles into a stubborn bit of dough. "Or he's the quietest man alive."

"He is pretty quiet," Layla offers. "Once I went three whole weeks without hearing him say a single word. Just grunts." She straightens, fixes her face in a frown, and grunts from somewhere deep in her chest. It's a pretty good impression of Beckett. "He's probably trying to give you space. He's like that."

"I'd prefer if he wasn't avoiding his own home."

"You could try telling him that."

I would. If I ever saw him. "I haven't seen him in three days."

Layla gives me a look over her tray of cookies, a streak of bright blue frosting on her chin. "He works here, doesn't he? Go find him."

My forearms and shoulders are sore by the time I decide to leave the bakehouse. I took all of my frustration out on the dough, and I think I rolled out enough piecrust to blanket the entire acreage of the farm and then some.

I trudge my way through the fields, letting my palms pass over the bristly branches of the Christmas trees. The farm is no less magical now than it was during the holiday season, the trees so dense out in the fields that I can't see the buildings or the narrow road beyond it. It's just me and the evergreens, the sun high in the sky. I breathe in deep through my nose and smile.

Balsam. Cedar. Fresh-cut grass and apple blossoms.

I don't find Beckett out with the trees or along the fence that divides the land into neat quadrants, so I change direction and head to the barn instead. I pass a couple of farmhands I recognize from my last trip and give them a wave, then I see a man passing by with what looks like a basket full of radishes. I shield my eyes against the sun with my hand.

"Have you seen Beckett?"

The man nods and points to a smaller barn behind the one they use for holiday decorations, the door propped open with a discarded tractor wheel. *Finally.* I let the full weight of my frustration guide my way over to the shed, and I slip through the door, half expecting him to bolt as soon as he sees me. It would be poetic, in a way, for Beckett to run from me this time.

But he doesn't run. He doesn't hear me at all. I step through the door into the small space flooded with afternoon light and almost face-plant into the wheelbarrow in front of me.

Beckett stands shirtless in the middle of the room, both arms braced above him as he winds a thick coil of rope around and around two parallel pegs. I watch the ink on his arms shift and flex with every rotation of his hands, the constellations and planets on his left arm a beautiful compliment to the flowers and vines on his right.

The smooth skin of his back is unmarked, his spine a strong column flanked with lean muscle. His body is conditioned by work, hardened and cut by days spent under the sun and in the fields. I remember pressing my fingers into that warm skin, how his hips pressed down into me, pinning me beneath him.

I swallow hard as he drops his arms and rolls his shoulders back with a sigh. He reaches for a T-shirt thrown over the edge of a large metal shelf, and I clear my throat, shift my eyes away from the span of his firm shoulders.

"So this is where you've been hiding."

Beckett startles and knocks his head on a low-hanging basket of garden tools. I get a glimpse of toned stomach as he turns and pulls his shirt down to cover himself. The reminder that I've been in bed with this man is like a string looping us together. It pulls taut and I sway forward farther into his space.

He rubs his knuckles behind his ear, his sweat-damp hair sticking up every which way. On one of the shelves is his hat, a faded black snap-back with an Orioles logo, worn at the edges. There's a red mark across his forehead from where it must have been pressing into his skin. I stare at it as he looks at me with lowered lashes, a sheepish look turning his cheeks pink.

That body with that face.

I never stood a chance in that bar all those months ago.

I straighten my spine, gather my frustration close, and hold on to it tightly with both hands. "Have you been sleeping in the barn?" It snaps out of me quick as a whip. Apparently, I'm more annoyed about it than I thought.

"No," he answers. His deep voice is even and calm, but he doesn't look me in the eye. "I've been sleeping at the house."

"When?" I shoot back.

"At night."

I set my hands on my hips. His eyes narrow, studying the stack of spare tires behind me like it's the most interesting thing he's ever seen.

"Beckett."

His eyes reluctantly crawl back to mine.

"I've been getting in late. I've been"—he hesitates, so clearly looking for an excuse I have to fight not to roll my eyes—"I've got a project."

"A project."

He shifts on his feet like a man with something to hide. "Yes."

"Is that project avoiding me?"

"No." He draws out the word like it has a thousand vowels at the end of it, gazing over my shoulder at the open door with naked longing. I bet he's fantasizing about running right out into the hills. "It's—well, it's complicated."

This conversation is ridiculous. "Try me."

He opens his mouth and nothing comes out. I don't think I've ever seen someone at such a loss for words. "It's a duck," he finally manages.

A group of farmhands walk past the open door, their laughter carrying into the small space. I blink at Beckett and he stares right back. Is he serious? "A what?"

"I'm trying to figure out where I can put a duck," he mumbles. His words are tucked under his breath, and I have to strain to hear what he's saying.

"And you can only do that in the middle of the night?"

"Ah, I don't—" He lets his arms fall by his sides. I focus on the vine tattoo that curls from his wrist and around his broad forearm, all the way to his elbow. There are small white flowers on it, a new addition since the last time I saw him. "I thought you'd prefer it that way."

"You thought I'd prefer you sneaking around?"

He nods.

"When did I give you that impression?"

He doesn't say anything in response, hands clenching at his sides. I sigh and press two fingers against the ever-present headache between my eyes.

"I've been trying to talk to you," I explain. "I found a rental in Rehoboth. I can be out of your place in two days, once it becomes available."

It'll be a pain to drive back and forth from the coast, but it's better than—whatever this is.

His face crumples in confusion. "You're leaving?"

I don't understand why he cares, considering he's seen me for a combined twenty-eight minutes since I've arrived, and he's—hiding in storage sheds, apparently. I nod and slip my hands into my back pockets, rocking on my heels.

He considers me quietly. Here in the muted light, his eyes look moss green. Dark and deep. "Did you find your happy, then?"

"What?"

He takes a step forward and reaches for a towel, wiping his hands on it with quick, practiced movements. His whole face is angled lines, a frown twisting everything down. "The first night you were here, you said something about looking for your happy. Did you find it?"

I'm surprised he remembers, but I guess I shouldn't be. Beckett has always been good with the details.

"Bits of it." Gus and Monty dancing at the fire station. A sausage-

and-cream-cheese biscuit. The smell of fresh blooming jasmine at Mabel's greenhouse.

Handwritten notes next to the coffee machine.

He gives me a critical look. "You don't sound sure of it."

"Because I'm not," I say. I still don't have answers to the questions buzzing in the back of my head. I still don't have a solution to my burnout problem. "But I'm not going to have you sneaking around your own house while I figure my stuff out." I shrug one shoulder. "The place in Delaware is fine."

Beckett tosses his towel on the metal shelf and props his hands on his hips. I know he's not doing it on purpose, but his arms flex with the movement, his inked biceps straining at the sleeves of his T-shirt. I have no idea what he was doing that caused him to sweat so much, but I'd like to pen a thank-you note.

"Stay here," he says in his gruff voice—his bossy voice, a voice that's used to getting what it wants out here on the farm. His hand rubs at his jaw, his fingertips fanned out under his left eye. He looks tired. "Stay at the house. I'll stop—"

"Avoiding me? Being weird?" I think for a second, vocalizing a suspicion. "Sleeping in your greenhouse?"

"I haven't been sleeping in my greenhouse."

Okay, well. He's been doing those other things.

"I won't stay here if it's like this," I tell him quietly, the fight draining out of me. "I didn't come here to mess with your life. I wanted a little perspective, and this seemed like the best place for it."

Now I'm not so sure. I've been topsy-turvy since I set foot in Inglewild.

"Stay," he says again, and he nods toward the open door. Some of the apprehension melts out of his eyes. There's a softness there, a bit of understanding. For a second, he's that man from Maine again. The one that tangled his fingers in my hair and pressed his lips so sweetly to mine. But then he blinks and the recognition is gone.

He grabs his hat off the shelf.

"I've gotta wrap up a few things, and then I'll come up to the house. I won't be"—a smile twitches at the corners of his lips—"I won't be weird."

TRUE TO HIS word, Beckett appears about an hour later. I hear the roll of gravel in the driveway and the heavy stomp of boots up the porch steps before he swings through the front door, a guarded look on his face when he spots me sitting at his kitchen table. I rest my chin in my hand and watch as he toes his boots off and places them carefully next to mine.

"I'm making soup," he tells me.

He says it like he expects a fight.

"Okay."

He takes two slow steps down the hallway, closer to the kitchen. "It's Maryland crab."

"That sounds nice."

He eyeballs me as he opens the fridge, one arm braced on the door, palm flat against the freezer. I try not to notice the stretch of his T-shirt. "You're not allergic to shellfish, are you?"

It's strange that I know what this man sounds like when he comes and the shape his fingertips leave on my hips, but when it comes to the simple things—allergies, coffee-to-creamer ratio, sock folding preference—we're both flailing in the dark.

A different kind of intimacy, I suppose.

"I'm not allergic to shellfish."

"Good." He ducks his head down into the fridge and begins to pull things out—tomatoes, onions, chicken stock, two containers of crab meat, a stalk of celery—and stacks them on the counter. He drops a cutting board, a knife, and an onion in front of me.

"Can you cut this?"

I nod and let our silence fill the space between us. A pot sizzles on the stove. My knife snicks against the cutting board. Beckett mutters under his breath about "piss-poor" celery quality.

"For the record," I offer, in between chops, "you're being a little weird."

A smile quirks on his mouth and his eyes cut to mine. It feels like a peace offering, like a step in the right direction.

"For the record, I'm not trying to be."

WE FIND OUR rhythm.

Beckett spends his days on the farm and I spend my days in town, wandering in and out of shops, watching tourists get ice cream, helping Ms. Beatrice curate content for her 137 passionate followers. I disconnect my email and all my social accounts and let myself breathe . . . for the first time in a long time.

No plan. No schedule.

Just me and whatever strikes my interest for the day, whether it's helping reshelve new paperbacks at the bookstore or learning how to clean the espresso machine at the café. I hold myself to absolutely no productivity standards. I let myself be.

In the evenings, I find my way back to Beckett's cabin and wait for him at his kitchen table, an abandoned book of crossword puzzles I've claimed as my own at my elbow. He declares what he's making as soon as he sees me, and silently hands me a cutting board or a mixing bowl or a potato peeler to help. Every day is exactly the same, and there's a comfort in that. In the way his smiles slowly get a touch wider. In the low rumble of his voice over the hiss of the frying pan.

We sit at his table, and we eat our meal, and I wash our dishes after.

It's nice, if not a little confusing.

Tonight, I decide to upset the rhythm.

I'm waiting on the back porch with two steaming bowls, nestled in the chair I'm starting to think of as my own, when I hear him pull up in the driveway. The front porch stairs creak, the third one from the top making a sound of protest as he clambers his way up. The door shuts behind him, and his steps stutter to an abrupt stop in the hallway.

A hesitant voice. "Evelyn?"

"Out here."

I listen as he moves around the house, a comfort in the sounds of him settling. Water from the faucet. His jacket being hung on the hook. The screen creaks open and I tilt my head back.

Standing there like that, fingers curled loose around the neck of a beer bottle, face angled down toward mine—a bit of dirt on his brow and on the back of his hand—he looks like every flicker of a warm thought I've had in the past six months.

A soft and steady glow burning under my skin.

"You made dinner?" He leans over slightly to get a look at my bowl. I nod toward the empty seat next to me and the dish that's waiting for him on the table in between.

"Mm-hmm," I hum. "One of my mom's curry recipes. I hope you like spice."

His eyes flare into something heated and sharp. A recollection, a shared memory. His mouth below my ear and his big palm at my thigh. I watch as he tucks it away, settling his face into something flat.

He might not be in that tiny shed anymore, but he's still hiding from me.

"You're in my seat," he tells me.

I take a long pull from my jam jar wineglass and hold eye contact. I have no intention of moving. Just like the crossword puzzle book and the extra soft towel I have hanging in the spare bathroom, I've claimed these things as mine. He'll have to fight me to get them back.

He snorts a laugh and moves around me to collapse in the chair to my left. He lets out a groan as he does, his long body stretching out in a lazy curve, one leg kicked wide. He drops his head on the back of the chair and reaches for his bowl, looking at me with a hazy sort of softness.

"Thanks for this," he rasps. "It's nice to come home to dinner."

"You should feel honored," I tell him, forking a bite of food into my mouth. "I've made this dinner for exactly two other people."

It's rare that I get to cook, rarer still that I cook my family recipes for anyone. I keep them all in a well-loved notebook in the apartment I never use. The book is too precious for me to lose while traveling, filled with my mom's handwriting and my Nani's too. Three generations of cooking together—adjusting spices for the perfect blend. Beckett didn't have a lot of what I needed, but I improvised.

His eyes narrow. "Who?"

I swallow and reach for my glass. "What do you mean?"

"Who did you make this for?"

"Josie," I offer slowly. I think for a second. "Josie's mom."

He relaxes into his chair and grabs his bowl, poking around at the rice. "Thank you," he mutters again, barely looking at me.

"It's no problem." I keep watching him, at the way his jaw works when he takes a bite. "It's the least I can do."

I had offered to pay him rent on my fifth night here. Beckett had given me a look so affronted I didn't bother bringing it up again.

We eat in silence, and I let myself wonder if this is what he does every night after a long day in the fields. Sunsets on the back porch in his socks. His flannel sleeves rolled up and a beer at his elbow. I have the sudden, confusing urge to smooth his hair back from his forehead. Get up from this chair and go to his, slide onto his lap, and tuck my head under his chin.

That was the problem, I think, in that little room in Maine. It was way too easy to imagine being with Beck. To want more.

I clear my throat and decide to tackle the reason for this little meal. "I don't know for sure how long I plan to stay."

He looks up at me, eyebrows raised. "Okay."

"Probably a couple of weeks, I think." That should be enough time for me to get my head on straight. If it's not—well, I'll cross that bridge when I get to it.

He rolls his head back to look out over the trees. "That's fine."

"You sure you don't mind?"

He shakes his head, fingers flexing on his fork. "Not if you keep making chicken like this."

I hesitate before my next question. I feel like an idiot for asking, but I don't want any surprises. It's something I should have asked sooner, honestly. "There isn't anyone that would be upset about me staying here?"

He turns to look at me again. "Who would be upset about it? Stella and Layla obviously know you're here." He spears another piece of chicken. "Didn't tell them why though."

That's good, because I don't even know the answer to that. I only know that it feels good to sit on this comfy chair on his back porch with my knees tucked to my chest. "I'm asking if you're seeing anyone, Beckett. And if this will complicate things for you."

"Oh." A brush of color dances over his cheeks, the same exact shade as the sun melting into the horizon. "No."

No. That's it. That's all he says. He tips his beer to his mouth and swallows heavily. One, two, three gulps in a row.

"What's your plan for tomorrow?"

All right, then.

"I don't have one," I answer honestly. I stretch out my legs and flex my feet back and forth. Back and forth. I squint my eye and touch my toe to the very top of the greenhouse. "I thought it was pretty apparent I don't have any sort of plan."

"You've always got a plan," he tells me. "Even when it feels like you don't."

That's fair. I've had a plan since I was sixteen years old. The YouTube channel, then college, then a program at Pratt. I deviated slightly when my dream of working at a big-name publication didn't work out and decided to make my own platform instead. I've been pursuing that ever since.

Not letting myself breathe since.

"New territory, I guess," I say, forcing my voice to be light and ignoring the swarm of unease that settles every time I think about work, "for someone who posts cute pictures all day."

He makes a sound under his breath. A frustrated huff. I drop my foot down to the porch and look at him.

"Stop doing that," he finally says.

"What?"

"Making yourself seem smaller than you are." He doesn't bother to elaborate. His hand finds his beer bottle again, and he taps his thumb there once. He heaves out a gusting sigh. "What are you doing here, Evelyn?"

"I missed the trees," I tell him.

"Try again."

"You're right. I missed Layla's peppermint hot chocolate."

"More believable." He turns in his seat until he can fix me with a gaze that offers no room for teasing remarks. It demands the truth and all of it. Right now. "What are you doing here?"

I reach for the wine bottle by my feet and pour myself a glass that redefines the term *heavy pour*.

"I don't know. I just know that I felt stuck, and this was the first place that popped into my head when I thought about taking a break. I think I'm looking for"—I think about standing in the middle of the field, pine trees all around me—"I think I'm reevaluating. To see if what I'm doing is still the right fit."

I watch the tree branches lift with the breeze, tiny green buds starting to appear. Everything will be in bloom soon, the fields bursting with color. I smile. I bet it looks just like the lights on a Christmas tree.

"I wanted to be a journalist, you know? I thought I'd work for

National Geographic or maybe the *New York Times*. Something amazing." The confession trips off my tongue easily enough, loosened by wine and the smell of fresh earth. Spring rain and dirt. "I wanted to travel so badly. See all the places from those features. I got into the media studies program at Pratt, and I thought I'd made it. I was so sure I'd be able to land a good job after graduation. But I didn't. I kept going to interviews with my portfolio, and it was always the same. Too whimsical. Too lighthearted." I shrug and remember one painful interview in which a woman with a high collar flicked her eyes up and down my arms and told me I didn't have the right *look* for on-camera work. "Too brown."

Beckett shifts in his seat, the wood creaking under his weight, but I don't look at him. I can't.

"I went home to lick my wounds, and my parents were having trouble with their shop. They own a boutique in Portland. They sell— all sorts of stuff, really. All locally sourced and produced. I had a YouTube channel with a decent following that I played around with. But I made some videos for my parents, and it just . . . took off. The rest is history."

It all snowballed from there. Traffic increased for the store. My accounts began to attract attention. I started bopping around my old neighborhood, talking to people. Asking about their businesses and what they were doing. Their passions. Their interests. Just everyday people doing incredible things.

I don't know when I stopped. Or why.

I glance at Beckett out of the corner of my eye when he doesn't say anything. "I know you think it's stupid, but social media helps me connect. It's like having a conversation on a massive scale. I really am trying to help people."

He looks startled. "What?"

"I'm not just posting pictures all day. There's a strategy behind it. Planning." A never-ending cycle of content. A crushing desire for more, more, more. Unsolicited opinions and criticism.

"I know that." He's looking at me like he doesn't understand the words coming out of my mouth. Like I just jumped out of this chair and slapped a chicken suit on and started doing the Macarena. "I don't think what you do is stupid."

I blink at him. "Yes, you do."

"No, I don't."

"Yes, you do. You said so."

"When?"

"When I was staying here in November. When I was here to evaluate the farm." When he figured out who I really was and looked at me like I wasn't worth his time.

He frowns. "I never said anything about your job being stupid."

"Yes, you did."

"Evelyn. No, I didn't." He drags his palm down his face. "How could I think your job is stupid? Look what it did for us. For the town."

"Oh." All right, then. I have no response to that.

I stare out at the yard and try to remember the specifics of that conversation. Beckett interrupts with a question.

"Where are you looking?"

"For what?" I want to thumb between his eyebrows until that line disappears. He spends too much time frowning.

"For your happy. Where do you think you'll find it?"

"I don't know." I curl my hand around my glass until the condensation tickles my palm. I'm busy thinking about my answer when he finds one for me.

"'Cause I think it's still in there somewhere." He gestures in my general direction with his bottle. "You wouldn't glow like that if it wasn't."

He finishes his drink and places it down by his feet and then tilts his head to look back out at the fields like what he said didn't slam me right in the chest. "It's okay if it takes you some time to find it again. And it's okay if you find it, just to lose a bit of it here and there.

That's the beauty of it, yeah? It comes and goes. Not every day is a happy one, and it shouldn't be. It's in the trying, I think."

I clear the cobwebs out of my throat. "Trying to be happy?"

"No." He shakes his head once. "That doesn't work. Trying to be happy is like—it's like telling a flower to bloom." He crosses his ankles and drags his palm against his stubble. "You can't make yourself be happy. But you can be open to it. You can trust yourself enough to feel it when you stumble on it."

I stare at him. Stare and stare and stare.

"You're not what I expected, Beckett Porter." Not now. Not the last time I saw him. And not that hazy evening in Maine when he walked in a door like he'd been looking for me forever.

One of the cats wanders out from the house and jumps into Beckett's lap, settling on his thigh with a wide yawn. He drops a heavy hand over her back and smooths it gently down over soft fur. His smile is almost shy when he looks at me.

"Right back at you."

9

BECKETT

I WAKE UP facedown in my bed, two cats burrowed between my shoulder blades and my phone vibrating on the nightstand. I groan and fight not to fling the damn thing right out the window. I was having a dream about Evelyn and those socks she was wearing on the back porch—the ones that go all the way up to her knees. In my dream, she was only wearing those socks, a coy smile on her dark red lips.

I'm a creature of habit, and I can feel myself making new habits with Evelyn in my space. I'm used to having her here now—I like it, even. I like hearing her move around on the other side of the house in the middle of the night, a muffled curse under her breath when she runs into something in the dark. I like listening to her talk to the cats, arguments with Prancer about who has a right to the big fluffy scarf she loops around her neck. I like her shoes in the hallway and her bag on one of the hooks by the door. Her tube of lipstick on the kitchen counter and her hair ties forgotten on the edge of the sink.

I roll over in bed, and Comet and Vixen voice their protest, then I find another place in the blankets to curl up. I dig the heels of my palms into my eyes until I see spots.

I shouldn't *like* anything.

I certainly shouldn't like dreaming about her. Pretty sure that crosses some sort of line in the tremulous friend truce we've slowly pieced together.

But my brain hasn't gotten the memo. Every night is a free-for-all of vivid fantasies. Evelyn in the giant tub, bubbles sliding down her neck. Evelyn in the kitchen, bent over my countertop. Evelyn up against the bookshelf by the fireplace, her hands curling around the edges.

My phone vibrates again and I blindly slap around my nightstand. Predawn light flirts with the edges of my window in a shadow of gray.

> NESSA: You're needed at trivia this week.

> NESSA: I don't want to hear a single complaint or excuse.

> NESSA: One of the categories is botany.

I frown at my phone.

> BECKETT: What are you doing up so early?

> BECKETT: And no.

My family has a trivia team for the bar's monthly competition. They're scary competitive about it. Harper almost threw a chair through the front window when she got a question wrong about Boyz II Men.

> NESSA: Early rehearsal before work.

> NESSA: You have seventy-two hours to come to terms with this reality. Harper can't make it.

I rack my brain for an appropriate excuse.

> BECKETT: I'm not registered.

I know for a fact all team members need to be registered at the start of the trivia season. Caleb had to intervene in a dispute last year when Gus and Monty pulled Luka in for the Bruce Willis category without any clearance.

I sit up in bed and swing my legs over the edge, the floorboards cold beneath my feet. It's been unseasonably chilly this March. I glance at the window and then back down to my phone when it buzzes again.

> **NESSA:** Oh, sweet brother of mine.

> **NESSA:** We register you every year for exactly this reason.

> **NESSA:** Now is your time to shine.

> **NESSA:** The category is BOTANY.

> **BECKETT:** Our father is also a farmer.

> **NESSA:** See you this weekend.

I don't bother with a response. I know if I don't show up to trivia, Nessa will appear at my house—probably with Harper—and physically drag me there kicking and screaming. It's happened before and it'll likely happen again.

I don't like going to trivia. I don't like spending my time in a crowded room that smells like beer and hot wings, a television on in every corner and an old record player that anyone can change whenever they want. For some insane reason, Jesse loves playing ABBA. It's overwhelming, and at least seven people try to talk to me every time.

I go through the motions of getting ready for the day, the edges of my dream clinging to my thoughts. In my dream, I had been tracing the gentle slope between Evelyn's shoulder and neck. I shuffle down the hallway while pulling my flannel over my shoulders and indulge. Would she still taste like citrus if I pressed my tongue to her skin? Would she still hiccup my name?

The clink of the coffeepot distracts me, a warm glow of light coming from the kitchen.

Evelyn stands with her back to me at the counter, Prancer nuzzling her head into her shin. Evelyn hums and pets her hand down the cat's back, whispering something with a laugh as Prancer pushes harder into her. I glance at the countertop. Two mugs sitting out, steaming with coffee.

My heart gives a heavy thump in my chest.

"Morning," I say, and Evelyn turns to glance at me over her shoulder, hair swinging around her face. With her eyes still heavy and a yawn making her nose scrunch, she's better than any dream I could ever come up with. Soft. Sleepy.

Perfect.

"Morning," she says back, voice a little scratchy at the edges. I remember it gets like that when she first wakes up, body lazy beneath the sheets. I clear my throat and continue fastening my shirt, her gaze stuck on where my hands work at my buttons, the thin strip of bare skin that is exposed. I feel the touch of her eyes like a fingertip on my skin, starting below my collarbones and teasing slowly down. A pulse of heat pounds once at the base of my spine.

"What're you doing up?" I make myself ask. My voice sounds like I've swallowed a bag of rocks.

Her tongue swipes at her bottom lip as she turns her back and grabs the two mugs from the countertop. I wish she would keep staring at me, wish she would press her hands beneath this flannel and dig her nails into my skin.

She hands me a mug, her fingertips brushing mine as I curl my hand around warm ceramic.

"I'm coming with you today." She brings her mug to her lips. "I'd like to see what you do. Would that be all right?"

I nod. She could tell me to put on a hot dog costume and do the merengue down the front steps, and I'd probably agree.

"Yeah, that's all right."

"YOU'RE SURE?" I ask for what feels like the eighty-seventh time since we left the cabin twenty minutes ago. She gives me a look over her shovel like she's been counting too, entirely unamused.

"Why do you think I can't handle manual labor?"

I scratch the back of my head roughly, squinting out over the fields. The transplants will be here soon for planting, and we'll be all hands on deck for Dig Day. I prefer to dig by hand (*like a lunatic*, as Layla likes to say) and of course, Stella has made it into a thing. Music, snacks, a bunch of people who are, frankly, unhelpful with the whole process. Caleb might be a good deputy, but he digs the most lopsided holes I've ever seen in my life.

But it makes Stella happy, so Dig Day it is.

We're doing spacing today, marking the distance between each tree. It'll be easier for people to dig if everything is already placed where it should be. I learned that the hard way when Charlie thought it would be "cool" to make his own "private forest" in the last field we did. I now have several clumps of trees growing way too close to one another, throwing off the balance of the whole thing.

"Just tell me what you need me to do," Evelyn commands, and my brain immediately offers several detailed suggestions. She snaps her fingers in front of my face. "Instruction, farmer boy."

I hesitate and her eyes narrow into slits. I forgot how demanding she can be.

I forgot how much I like it.

"You don't think a woman can do what a man does?" If looks could kill, I'd be six feet under.

"No," I reply, amused. "A woman can do what a man does and make it look easy."

Her eyes narrow further. "Don't pander to me."

"I'm not." I laugh and a reluctant smile blooms on her pretty lips. "My sister could kick my ass. All of my sisters could kick my ass. I'm not ashamed to say it. They used to beat up the kids that made fun of me at school."

Poor Brian Hargraves never saw Nessa coming. One second, he was lobbing kernels of corn at the back of my head as I walked toward the bus and the next, Nessa had speared him to the ground like she was an MMA fighter.

The smile wobbles on Evelyn's face. "Kids made fun of you at school?"

Having trouble talking to other people combined with working on a farm made me an easy target. It was never anything too malicious. Easy enough to block out.

And everyone stopped talking shit when I suddenly grew six inches my junior year, my body bulking up from early mornings at the produce farm.

I clear my throat and nod toward the field of dirt stretched out behind us. Soon enough, it will be dotted with small bundles of green, the youngest trees we've ever had. They'll grow here for five years before they'll be ready for their homes in front of fireplaces and in large windows, decorated with tinsel and lights.

"Dig a shallow hole every six steps." I glance at her long legs and consider. She points her toe like a runway model, and I swallow around another laugh. I swear I've never laughed so much in my life. "Five and a half steps."

"See?" She hefts the shovel up and over her shoulder. "That wasn't so hard, was it?"

She takes off toward the far side of the field, ponytail swinging behind her. I watch as she stops at the very edge, digs her shovel into the earth, and neatly tosses it to the side. Five and half steps forward. Again.

I don't know what it says about me that I'm getting turned on by a woman shoveling dirt. Probably nothing good.

"Oh, sweet." Jeremy suddenly appears at my shoulder, and whatever trace of arousal is tugging at me dissipates immediately. I clench my teeth. "There's someone new? I don't have to shovel rocks anymore. Excellent."

He holds up his fist for me to pound, and I stare at him.

"You shoveled rocks for two days."

And only because he told me he strained his wrist the third morning. He complained enough that I ripped the shovel right out of his hands.

"Two days too long, bro."

I hand him my shovel and point in the opposite direction of where Evelyn is working. The last thing she needs is Jeremy being . . . Jeremy around her. He squints at her in the distance, her spine curved over the shovel. She presses her boot to the blade, pivots down, and lifts with her shoulder. I make a pained sound under my breath.

"Shit, dude. Oh my god. Ohmigod." Jeremy bobbles the tool in his hands. "Is that—holy shit, bro—is that Evelyn St. James?"

I don't even know how he can tell who she is from this far away. She's wearing thick athletic pants that mold to her curves like a second skin and an oversized white T-shirt. A sweatshirt overtop with a stitched outline of Half Dome on the bottom edge. She couldn't be more inconspicuous if she tried.

Though the pants certainly leave an impression. I'm sure they'll have a starring role in my dreams tonight. I want to smooth my palms over the shiny material, tug the waistband with my teeth.

"What the hell is she doing here? Oh my god." Jeremy bends at the waist and presses his palms to his knees. "Do you think she'll do a video with me? Oh my god."

"What is that sound you're making?" It's a wheezing noise, high-pitched and irregular. "Do you need water?"

"I need my cell phone," he pants, reaching into his jeans pocket and then his coat. When he can't find what he's looking for, he turns panicked eyes my way. "Dude, my phone isn't here."

"Do you normally bring your phone out here with you?"

He nods slowly. "Gotta feed the 'Gram, you know?"

I don't know. I have no idea what he's talking about.

"Early-morning lighting is dope. The honeys have been lighting up the DMs since I started working here. You might actually be on to something. Is that why all the women in town lose their shit when you roll up?"

"No one loses their shit."

If anything, I get a lot of stares and a few whispers, but that's probably because I don't bother showing up to anything. Nessa's invitation to trivia feels like a burr caught in my shoe.

"Sure, dude. Whatever you say." He slaps me on the back and turns to head to the lot where his mom's car is parked. "I'll be right back. Gotta get my phone."

I grab him by the scruff of his neck before he can go too far and push him in the opposite direction of Evelyn. "Start here instead. You can get your phone after."

He pouts at me. "Your sense of responsibility is super inspiring and all, but—"

I shake my head. "Dig your holes, and then you're spending the morning with Stella in her office."

He perks up at that. "Yeah?"

Yeah. Stella doesn't think all the manual labor is conducive to shaping him into an upstanding young adult. Or something. She wants him to spend time in the office with her, see how we run things from the business side. *You probably don't even talk to him, do you?*

Not if I can help it, I told her.

I point out into the distance. "Off you go."

He gives me a petulant look. "I see how it is. Put the woman and the minor to work while you kick back. I see you, boss man." He splits his fingers and points at his eyes and then mine.

This fucking kid.

Jeremy drags himself to his corner of the field and I spare a glance in Evelyn's direction. I watch as she swipes the back of her arm across her brow, her hands curling around the bottom of her sweatshirt and lifting. I see a flash of brown skin, the top edge of those tight pants.

I pick up the discarded shovel and turn to the southeast corner.

"DID YOUR PARENTS teach you how to plant?"

Sal's laugh booms out of him, his hands busy plucking green beans from the stem as he answers Evelyn's question. "No. Absolutely not. My dad is a mechanic and my mother kills everything she touches. I don't let her anywhere near my houseplants when she visits."

I grunt and jerk at a plant too roughly, a couple of leaves coming with the green beans. It's been like this all day. Evelyn has been uncovering the life story of everyone she meets, charming them with her smiles and her laugh until they're putty in her hands. She spotted Jeremy across the field during digging this morning and waved. Ten minutes later, and the sly little shit was belly laughing with her, neither of them digging a single hole. Barney came rumbling up with his tractor, and after a five-minute conversation was blushing and inviting her to poker night.

She is happy laughter and easy smiles. Genuine interest and affection that leaves you feeling like you're floating with the clouds. That's the magic of Evelyn, I guess. She shines so bright she casts everyone around her in that same glow.

I want to feel that light too. But all I've gotten is hesitant smiles and a carefully maintained bit of space between us.

Evelyn glances at the collection of leaves and beans strangled in my hands. She's got dirt up to her elbows and on the curve of her jaw, hair falling out of her smooth ponytail.

She looks beautiful.

"Everything all right?" she says.

I give in to temptation and reach out my hand, thumbing at a stubborn streak of mud just under her chin. Everything would be all right if I could stop my brain for a half a second, remind myself that she's not here to stay. She sent that message clearly enough the last two times she disappeared from my life without a word. Evelyn is like a spring storm. She appears without warning, makes everything around her bloom, and then leaves with the wind.

But I can't keep myself from touching her. I fan my fingers out against the side of her jaw, and she sways into me, stumbling closer. I want to press my thumb to her chin and guide her mouth open. I want to curl my hand around the back of her neck and pull her into me. I want to feel that heat bloom deep in my chest as I lower my mouth down on hers.

Instead, I settle for this. Slow, careful touches against her warm skin. I slip my thumb down the line of her throat and rub gently at the stubborn streak of dirt, back and forth. Her skin is so soft, it's like touching silk. She swallows and I drag my eyes to hers. We stare at each other for the length of one shared inhale, my hand touching her throat. I wonder if she's thinking about my hands on her skin in that hotel room. If she's remembering too.

A deep breath rattles in my chest, and I drop my hand to my side.

Sal throws his hand up in the air, a *tsk* under his breath. He continues to move down the line of plants without looking up once. "Don't mind him. He's always like that."

Evelyn's eyes slant toward me, a secret in the smile that curls at her lips. Finally, a smile just for me. "Not always," she mutters, mischief with a touch of heat. I remember another time my thumb was at her throat, her legs hugging my hips and her palms tracing my shoulder blades. I shift on my feet.

"You still need my help?" I call over to Sal, breaking our eye contact and dumping the beans into a bucket. I need distance. Some space to control . . . whatever it is that's pressing down on my chest every time I so much as glance at Evelyn. Touching her, feeling her skin under mine. It isn't going to lead anywhere good for me.

I watch the top of Sal's hat as he continues to bob down the neat line of bright green, smack-dab in the middle of the field. "I'm good. Not much left to do today."

I brush my palms on my jeans, two twin streaks of dirt. Evelyn follows after Sal, hands working in the leaves. I grind the heel of my boot down in the dirt and trace the curve of her spine with my eyes. "You wanna stay here or come back with me?"

I take off my hat and scrub my hand over the back of my head, making a mess of my hair. *Come back with me* pounds a beat in my skull and presses sharp right behind my eyes. If I could pull that thought out of my head and bury it under these beans, I would.

"I'll stay. I think I'm finding some happy out here." She looks at her hands with a grin, the dirt caked over her knuckles. Her eyes find mine and her smile tips wider. "Out here in the weeds."

I TAKE THE longest, coldest shower of my life.

Watching her in the fields today was torture. She fits here, with her boots in the dirt and her hand shading her eyes against the rising sun, calling out to me over the wide stretch of land. She fits on my back porch with her legs curled under her, chin on her knee, asking seventeen questions a minute.

Evelyn is not here for you, I tell myself as I stand beneath the stream of cold water. I close my eyes and ignore the pull of wanting—the rising warmth in my chest that's a whole lot more dangerous than any feelings of lust. *She came here for something that isn't you.*

She probably fits everywhere she goes. That's the magic of Evelyn.

She can find a comfortable nook for herself in every coffee shop, food stand, and hole-in-the-wall she visits.

Me, meanwhile—I fit here. Only here. On this stretch of land where I can go entire days without talking to a single person.

My phone begins to buzz on the counter by the sink, and I groan, knocking my head against the shower wall. I have plans to disappear into the greenhouse tonight, lose myself in trimming and planting until the image of Evelyn laughing next to the tractor fades out of my mind. Until I can look at her and not . . . not *want* so damn much.

I slam my hand on the shower handle, and it gives an answering croak of protest. If I'm not careful, this house will be in pieces by the time Evelyn decides to leave. That thought doesn't do anything to ease my dark mood, and when I finally manage to answer the phone, I'm thoroughly agitated, a shiver working over my body from the icy water.

"What?"

A beat of silence. "Is that how you answer the phone for your sister?"

I hang up the phone and slam it down on my dresser. It immediately starts ringing again. I suck in a deep breath through my nose as I pull on my clothes and answer on the third ring.

"Hi, Nessa. What can I do for you?"

She hums. "That's better." I hear the low melody of a piano in the background. She must be at the studio. "You never answered my text about trivia."

I grunt and continue to not answer her about trivia. I grab a T-shirt from the top drawer of my dresser, an old faded one with an angry badger stretched across the chest. Luka's mom is head of the PTA at the high school, and I buy a shirt every year. I'm afraid of what might happen if I don't.

"What's going on with Harper?" I deflect, wrestling myself into my jeans. I jam my knee into my dresser and curse under my breath.

"We're not talking about Harper. We're talking about trivia."

I ignore her. "What's going on with Harper?"

There's a lengthy pause. "I don't know what you mean."

"She's been quiet at dinner, and now she's not going to trivia."

"She hasn't been feeling well lately," she answers in a rush. The music in the background cuts out abruptly. "Woman things."

"Nessa."

"What?"

"You can't just say *woman things* to get me to stop asking questions. When has that ever worked?" I slam my dresser drawer shut, frustrated with this conversation. Myself. The universe. "What's going on with Harper?"

"Okay, well," she breathes out a heavy sigh. "You can't get mad."

I look up at the ceiling and beg for patience. I'm already mad. So it's not a lie when I say, "I won't get mad."

"You can't do anything about it."

"I won't do anything about it," I grit out from between clenched teeth.

"Really? Because the last time you said that—"

"Vanessa."

She pauses and I pull my shirt over my head. "She was seeing Carter again," she says slowly, dragging out each word with reluctance. A hot flash of anger immediately grabs me by the throat. "And he broke things off with her over the weekend."

I knew it. I fucking *knew it*. Every single time Harper has had that look on her face, it's been because of one man. A stupid fuckboy with blond highlights and a fucking puka shell necklace. "What did he say to her?"

Nessa sighs. "I don't—"

I make a frustrated sound into the phone.

"He told her she's only fling material," she whispers, like if she says it quietly, I won't turn into a giant ball of rage. Too late for that. "He said that she's a lot of fun, but that's it."

I take a deep breath in. Let it out slowly. I tap the speaker button and pull up my text messages.

"I already keyed his car twice, but I'm pretty sure Dane is onto me." Nessa hesitates. "What are you doing?"

"I'm texting," I say.

"Who are you texting?"

"Luka."

"You guys cannot do that thing you do where you hide in the bushes in camouflage and jump out with baseball bats. You could give him a heart attack, and Dane told you he'd arrest you if you do it again." She makes an amused sound under her breath that she does her best to hide. "I don't have the bail money for you this month."

I brace my hands on the edge of the dresser and flex my fingers twice. She's right. Dane did threaten to arrest us after the last time.

And I'm pretty sure we used the last of Stella's face paint.

"Okay." I tap out of my text messages. It would take too long for Luka to get here anyway.

"Okay? That's it?"

"Mm-hmm," I hum. Comet and Vixen poke their heads into my room, see the look on my face, and quickly scamper away.

"What are you planning?"

"Nothing." I keep my voice carefully neutral. I'm planning on going down to the bar and slamming Carter's face into a basket of French fries fifteen times in a row. Then I'll have a burger with a beer and come home. Maybe I'll get one of those veggie sandwiches Evelyn seems to like so much.

"Okay." She blows out a deep breath. "Okay. I don't believe you. But okay."

"Okay," I parrot back, looking for my car keys. I could have sworn I left them on top of my dresser. I stomp out of the bedroom, almost mowing down Evelyn on my way into the kitchen. She grabs at my arms to keep herself upright, a startled sound spilling out of her.

"Shit, I'm sorry."

"It's okay," she says, her nose against my neck. I slip the hand not holding my phone from between her shoulder blades to the small of her back, palm dragging down her spine as I make sure she's steady. I suck in a sharp breath when my fingers graze bare skin. Her shirt must have gotten caught between us.

She answers with a shaky sigh, fingertips digging just slightly into my skin. Her nose nudges up, the brush of her lips just below my ear. My entire body goes rigid.

"Beckett Porter, do you have a *woman over*?" Vanessa's voice shrieks through the phone directly into my ear.

"Gotta go, Ness."

"Do not hang up, you—"

I hang up the phone and slip it into my pocket, leaning back and looking down at Evelyn plastered against my front. She's cleaned the dirt off her face, and all that's left is a rosy glow from a day spent outside, her hair curling at the edges. I thumb a strand behind her ear.

That's twice today I haven't been able to keep my hands off her. I feel trapped between holding her at a safe distance and tugging her closer. A pendulum swinging endlessly back and forth.

I step back and clear my throat. I scoop my keys off the kitchen counter and try to scoop some of the feelings playing Plinko inside of my chest back where they belong.

"Going somewhere?"

"Yep." My lips pop the last letter of the word, irritation slithering through me when I think about Carter. That fucking idiot. I frown and glance at the two chairs on the back porch, our dinner plans never discussed but a new habit, all the same. "Want a veggie sandwich while I'm out?"

"You get mad about veggie sandwiches, huh?" She digs her finger into the line between my eyebrows, and I cuff her wrist with my hand. She's so small, my fingers easily overlap. "What's got that look on your face?"

"Someone was a dick to my sister," I explain. I let our hands drop between us, indulging and swinging our arms back and forth once. Her skin is so *soft*. "I'm going to go take care of it."

Evelyn blinks at me. Without a second of hesitation, she reaches for the discarded sweatshirt slung over one of the dining room chairs. She pulls it over her head, arms punching through the sleeves, her hands lifting her long ponytail to pull it from the collar.

"What are you doing?" I ask, a little mesmerized and a lot distracted by all that hair.

She slips her feet back into the shoes she kicked off right at the end of the hallway and gestures toward the door with a nod.

"You think I'm going to let you go alone?" She shakes her head decisively. "I want that veggie sandwich. I'm coming with you."

10

EVELYN

ANGRY BECKETT IS . . . an experience.

Tense forearms, a deep groove in the center of his forehead. Hard eyes and his mouth in a flat, severe line. He keeps taking deep breaths during the drive into town, letting them out slow. His hands flex on the steering wheel and he mutters something about "bleach-blond sonofabitch" under his breath.

Frankly, it's working for me.

Not that there's much Beckett does that doesn't work for me.

Watching him in the fields this morning was like a glass of water set just out of reach. The flex and release of his arms as he thrust his shovel down. The spread of his shoulders and the strong line of his jaw. It didn't help that I know what his body looks like under all of those clothes. The way his hard chest tapers down into narrow hips, the stacked muscle across his abdomen that I definitely sunk my teeth into during our time together.

"Where are we going?"

His truck slows as we hit the edge of town, a painted wooden sign welcoming us to downtown Inglewild. It makes me smile every time I see it. The difference between downtown and the rest of it must be two square blocks. Beckett turns left at the firehouse and rumbles down the street, his gaze focused out the front windshield. I feel like maybe I should turn on some guided meditation, calm him down before he finds whoever it is he's looking for.

"Beckett," I try again. "Where are we going?"

I'm starting to think his plan is to drive his truck right through someone's living room.

"The bar," he answers. Two words. Nothing more. I watch his jaw flex and pop.

"Who is at the bar?"

"Carter Dempsey."

I nod like that name means anything to me. "And what are you going to do to Carter Dempsey?"

Beckett smooths his hand over the gear stick and slows us to a stop. In a series of practiced movements, he maneuvers his behemoth of a truck into one of the parking spots along the main road. Never in my life have I been so turned on by parallel parking. Beckett shifts into Park and levels a look right at me.

"I'm going to kill him."

Okay, well. That is probably not a great idea. He kicks open his door and strides across the street like he's off to happily murder someone. I struggle to get my seat belt unbuckled and follow after him with quick steps, jogging to catch up with his furious walking.

"Did you want to get ice cream instead?"

He shoulders his way through the wide wooden doorway, keeping the door open with his palm so I can slip in beneath his arm. "No."

"They had a new flavor a couple of days ago."

Chocolate waffle cone with little bits of Butterfinger mixed in. Layla and I got three cones in a row. He grunts at me and heads toward the long counter that stretches across the middle of the space. It's dark, even during midday, and no one is standing behind the bar, the place empty except for a man slouched in a booth in the corner. He raises a hand in greeting as Beck stomps his way to a stool, kicking out the one next to him in what I assume is an invitation.

"Jesse working today?"

"No, it's Carter," the man in the corner answers. "Though I don't know where he disappeared to."

I trail after Beckett to the old mahogany bar, cataloging the ornate tin detail layered across the ceiling. If Carter has a lick of sense, he'll disappear out the back of the bar. I take a seat next to Beckett, and he pulls me closer with his foot between the bottom rungs of the stool and hands me a paper menu.

I curl my fingers around it and stare at him. "Will we be eating before or after you commit a crime?"

A smile barely touches his lips. "After."

"I imagine that might be difficult with blood on your hands."

His lip quirks up farther and he nods toward the bathroom. "They have soap."

All right, then. I glance down at the menu, one edge ripped clean off. "What would you recommend?"

Sea-green eyes slant in my direction. "Thought you'd like the eggplant thing."

I hum and tilt my head as I look at the description printed beneath. "You're right. But I'm getting French fries." I refuse to eat a side salad after a full day of manual labor. Or, you know, ever.

"Okay."

He keeps his boot below my stool as we wait, his gaze not wavering from the small half door that leads to the kitchen. His knee bumps into my leg every couple of minutes, and it's nice, despite the tension he's holding in his shoulders. It's nice sharing a space. It was nice spending all day out in the fields with him. It was nice coming back to the house with the teakettle on the stove and muffins from the bakehouse in a pretty green box on the kitchen island. The cats lounging across the furniture and Beckett's boots discarded at the door. It was nice seeing him come down the hall, hair still wet from a shower, jeans low on his hips, his eyes lighting up at the sight of me.

It was nice being pressed against him, his skin warm and his breath a gentle puff against my ear.

I've always felt a pull toward Beck. That's no secret. But it's worse now. Deeper. I like spending time with him, seeing the bits of him he does his best to hide. His routines and his order and begrudging commitment to a family of orphaned cats. His loyalty and his quiet caretaking.

I like *him*.

The longer I'm here, the easier it is to ignore everything else. I don't know if that's a good thing or a bad thing yet.

After ten minutes without an appearance from the mysterious Carter, Beckett sighs and stands from his stool, uncurling his big body from his hunched-over position. I hear him mutter something about "useless fuckwad" under his breath again. He rounds the edge of the bar. "You want a beer?"

"Cider, if they have it."

He squints down at the tap handles. I smile as he bends slightly closer to the labels, his head tilting in confusion.

"Do you need glasses?"

He wraps his hand around one of the taps, tipping a glass beneath and filling it with amber bubbles. He doesn't answer me.

"Because it looks like, perhaps, you might need glasses."

I think about him in a pair of thick black frames slipping low on his nose as he sits in the big leather chair by his fireplace, one of the cats on his lap and a book on his knee. My whole body breaks out in goose bumps.

"I have a pair I wear sometimes, but only for reading," he mutters. He grabs another glass for himself and pours a beer. He glances over my shoulder at the man in the corner. "You need anything, Pete?"

"Tequila on the rocks, young man."

Beckett nods and grabs a bottle off the back shelf. A slow curl of heat unfurls at the base of my spine as Beckett lines up a glass, forearm flexing. The last time I had tequila, Beckett had licked a line of salt from the inside of my wrist and then knotted his fingers in my hair, urged my head back until he could taste it off my tongue.

He glances up at me as he pours, eyes knowing.

I try to smile around the lump lodged in my throat. "This is familiar." My voice comes out in a gritty whisper.

It's as close as we've ever come to talking about that weekend. He nods and slides the glass of tequila down the bar. "I'm not bringing it to you, Pete," he calls over his shoulder.

The old man in the corner chuckles. "Figured as much. Seems you've got your hands full as it is."

Beckett moves around the bar with his beer, his steps slow. His chest brushes against my shoulders as he slips behind me. I feel every single place our bodies touch. When he sits, he's closer than before, his boot back on the bottom rung of my chair. He tugs once, the metal screeching as it drags across the floor. Pete muffles a laugh in the sleeve of his coat as he collects his glass, returning to his secluded spot in the corner of the bar. I turn my face to Beckett and watch as his tongue wets his bottom lip.

"Haven't had tequila since," he tells me, and I don't think we're talking about alcohol. The lick of heat sparking along my skin turns into an inferno. I spread my legs slightly on the stool until I can press my knee to the side of his thigh. I let myself look at him, delighting in all the details I can collect when I'm this close. I tuck them into my palm like secrets. The barely there freckles dusted under his left eye. The straight line of his nose, a little dip in the center of it. The curl of hair behind his ear.

"Neither have I," I say. A whisper. A confession.

I watch the strong line of his throat as he swallows. "Did you—"

He doesn't finish his question. The door behind the bar swings open, and a man slightly shorter than Beckett strolls out. He's wearing a Guns N' Roses T-shirt that's ripped at the bottom and light wash jeans, an armful of clean glasses balanced against his chest. His bleach-blond hair falls into his face as he ducks through the door, a washcloth tucked through his belt loop. He's kind of cute in an unassuming sort of way. He'd probably be cuter if I didn't have Beckett sitting right next to me, hands curling into fists.

This must be Carter, then.

He hesitates as soon as his gaze lands on Beckett, his eyes cutting to the exit and back to the hulking man about to take two fistfuls out of the bar top.

"Beckett," he says, wariness in his voice and with good reason. The warmth that was creeping into Beckett's expression while we waited is gone now, and his jaw looks tight enough to snap. "I see you helped yourself."

He nods at the drinks in front of us. Beckett doesn't say anything. Carter shifts on his feet. He actually does have a puka shell necklace on. I thought maybe Beckett had been exaggerating.

"Did you need anything else?"

Beckett remains silent.

Carter sighs. "You just gonna sit there?"

Beckett reaches for his beer and takes a long sip, gaze not budging an inch. Impatient, Carter's face twists into something unkind. He doesn't look cute at all anymore. He looks petty and childish, his dyed hair turning to a faded green in the lights overhead.

"Did Harper tell—"

"Don't say her name," Beckett interrupts. A shiver licks up my spine. I've never heard that tone of voice out of his mouth before, a warning in every syllable.

Carter bristles. "Well, if she's running her mouth like a—"

Beckett's hand snaps out, quick as lightning. He grabs the collar of Carter's shirt and pulls him over the bar until the other man is practically dangling there, hands braced on the edge to keep himself from falling face-first into the bar top.

"Like a what?"

Carter sputters.

"Go on, finish your sentence." When Carter doesn't say anything in response, Beckett releases him. He goes stumbling to the other side of the bar, his back hitting the edge of a table holding his tray of clean glasses. They rattle on impact.

"I know it's been a minute since we last talked, but let me make it very clear for you. If I hear another word out of your mouth about my sister, I will break every bone in your body." Beckett doesn't drop eye contact, not for a second, his voice deceptively calm for the threat living in each word. "Don't talk about her. Don't look at her. Don't even think about her. If I find out you've contacted her with any more of your bullshit, I'll make what happens next look like an accident. Do you understand me?"

He picks up the menu I placed next to my drink. He glances at it once. Carter edges closer to the door that leads to the back.

"I want a burger. She'll have the eggplant sandwich." He tosses the menu over the bar and gives Carter a dismissive look. "Don't forget the fries."

WE TAKE OUR food to go.

Beckett is quiet but relaxed on the way home, fingers drumming on the center console. I turn the dial until I find a classic rock station, static bursting between Fleetwood Mac. I roll down my window and untangle my ponytail, the wind picking up the ends of my hair until it's a hurricane around my face. I can smell the sun and sweat of the day and a touch of my shampoo, the sweet hint of springtime rain in the fields we're whipping past. Everything is green and gold and bright, bright blue. I laugh and scoop my hair away from my face with my palm and watch as Beckett presses down harder on the gas, a grin tipping at his lips. It lights up his whole face, that smile—the lines by his eyes deepening, his bottom lip a bit crooked.

I release my hair again and close my eyes. I feel like I'm floating, flying. A gentle snip to one of the strings tied tight around my lungs, Beckett's low laugh whispering through the cab of the truck.

Happiness.

The feeling holds as we settle into our usual seats on the back porch of the house. Cupid joins us briefly before scampering off to the greenhouse. I point at it with a fry as I watch her disappear inside.

"What do you grow in there?"

He shrugs, legs crossed at the ankle and half a burger in his hand. "Flowers, mostly. The climate isn't good for them without a little protection, so I built the greenhouse."

"What sorts of flowers?"

He stretches his shoulders and reaches for one of my fries. His knuckles bump up against the back of my hand, and I almost tip the whole container onto my lap. "Orchids, mostly. I'm experimenting with some poinsettias for next winter, but we'll see." He chews a fry in consideration. "I might set the duck up in there."

"There you go with the duck again. What duck?"

"I told you about the duck." He did, but I thought he was full of it. "We found an abandoned duck on the farm. The town vet hasn't been able to find a home for him yet."

"Is it a baby duck?"

He nods. I sink down an inch farther in my seat and shove a fry into my mouth, picturing him sitting in that chair with a baby duck in his shirt pocket.

It's devastating.

"Did you always want to be a farmer?"

I can't help it with the questions. Josie tells me I have a *curious spirit* when she's feeling generous. *Nosy* when she's annoyed by it. With Beckett, I feel like I've only ever gotten crumbs. I want to crack him right open and examine every tiny detail.

He looks uncomfortable with the attention though, shifting around in his chair.

"You don't have to—"

"No, I'm fine." He grabs a handful of fries and settles back in his seat with a sigh, knees splayed wide, dusk beginning to creep through the trees. Everything is a deep indigo tonight, the branches of the trees forming a canopy of midnight blue over the backyard. It feels like we're in the pages of a fairy tale. Beckett glances at me out of the corner of his eye, a brush of pink on the tips of his ears. He looks so bashful and hesitant it steals the air right out of my lungs.

The prince. Or maybe the damsel in need of rescuing. I haven't quite decided yet.

"Don't laugh, okay?"

"I won't," I say emphatically. I'd never laugh at Beckett. Not ever.

He considers that, rolling his words around in his head as he squints out at the fields. "I wanted to be"—he laughs a little bit, his palm on the back of his head—"I wanted to be an astronaut."

I think about the map of the sky he has taped on the front of his refrigerator, times and dates of celestial events scribbled in the margins. A book of the moon phases on the very top of his shelf.

"I think most kids want to be an astronaut for at least half their childhood. I guess I was just checking off that box. My mom got me a space suit for my eighth birthday, and I don't think I took it off for an entire year." I imagine a tiny Beckett in a space suit with a helmet too big, his blue-green eyes smiling through the visor, and my heart squeezes in my chest. "I thought I could work at NASA. Do research or something. I don't know. I just wanted to look at the stars."

"You could have." Stella told me Beckett built all of the sprinkler systems on the farm, a new design she's been trying to get him to patent. He would have made an excellent engineer if that's what he wanted to do. "Why didn't you?"

"My dad worked at the main produce supplier for the state. Parson's. It's a couple of towns over." I know the place he's talking about. I've driven past it on my way in and out of Inglewild. It's a massive farm. Rows and rows of produce as far as you can see. "He had an accident. He fell from a ladder and he, uh—he was paralyzed from the waist down."

I suck in a sharp breath. "Beckett, I'm so sorry."

"Nothing for you to be sorry about." He settles down farther in his seat with a grunt. "My mom didn't work at the time. She went to cosmetology school to get her license once my dad was in a better spot. It took him a bit of time to—to deal with everything." He rubs his fingers against his jaw absently, remembering. "The Parson family was really good about it though. They paid all the medical bills, helped our family out however they could. They let me come on and paid me the same salary as my dad, even though I'm pretty sure I was useless the first couple of seasons."

I stare at Beckett. "You took your dad's place at the farm?"

He nods. "Yeah, when I was fifteen. I've been farming ever since."

Beckett must see the look on my face, because his whole body softens, a thoughtful look on his handsome face. "Nah, don't look at me like that. It's all right."

"You were just a kid," I manage around a throat that's too tight. A pressure burning behind my eyes. I think about that little boy in a space suit looking up at the stars. "You had a dream."

"Found a new one," he answers, smile kicking up the corners of his mouth. He leans back in his chair and tilts his face to the night sky, the stars beginning to wake. "And I got to keep the stars with me."

I OVERSLEEP THE next morning, my body sore from my shoulders all the way down to my calves. Muscles I never even knew existed protest as I pull myself out of bed and shuffle down the hall to the kitchen. Comet and Cupid trail after me, Vixen waiting patiently next to an empty mug by the coffeemaker.

There's a note too, a plain piece of paper with a scribbled map. I stare at it, trying to make sense of the figures Beckett drew. I'm assuming the penciled outline of a house with a cat on top is his cabin, a path marked in a neat line around several farm landmarks.

The big oak tree that splits at the trunk. The pumpkin patch by

Stella's house. The fields we were working in yesterday. All of it leads to a big X in the corner. He's written *Some happy* in tiny block letters right next to it.

I grin.

"DID YOU FIND out about the sweatpants—yes or no?"

That's how Josie answers the phone as I begin my treasure hunt across the farm. I snort a laugh. "I did not."

She breathes out a sigh, long and gusting. "What are you even doing out there?"

Going on a scavenger hunt for bits of happiness, apparently. I round the pumpkin patch and refer back to my map. Beckett has drawn a little dotted line that crosses the next field in a zigzag pattern. I take three big steps to the left and then tilt to the right. I look down at my boots and notice this field is marshier than the last, a somewhat solid stretch of ground moving at a crisscross right through the center of it. I smile.

"I'm figuring it out," I answer. I am, I think. If I'm not out in the field with Beckett, I'm somewhere else in town. I've had a steady stream of consulting requests since I arrived, and I've accepted payment in the form of lattes and secondhand books. It's working out well for me.

I don't feel the same suffocating pressure when I'm helping someone else. I'm not stuck in my head, trapped in an endless cycle of overanalyzing every detail. It's slower, more relaxed.

I like it.

"I noticed you posted the other day."

Just a short video. A mash-up of clips from my wandering around town. A half-eaten croissant on a chipped plate. Flower petals drifting through the air. Dane staring at Matty over the counter at the pizza shop like he hung the damn moon. Sandra McGivens belly laughing on the sidewalk.

Bits and pieces of a normal, extraordinary day. Just like I used to.

"Also, Kirstyn called. You owe me a raise for not ending that conversation with a string of expletives. She wanted to know if you've looked at any of her emails."

"I haven't." The longer I stay away from my inbox, the clearer it is to me that I need to end my relationship with Sway. I don't think I can ever sit through a meeting about the Okeechobee Music Festival again. I've known it for a while now. The time away has made that decision easier to make. "I think we're going to be done with Sway," I tell Josie.

Her relief reaches through the phone. "Thank god. Can I be the one to end it? I'll do it right now."

"No," I laugh. "I'll set up a meeting for when I get back."

"Which is when?"

I stop in the middle of the muddy field I'm walking through and look up at the rolling hills lined with trees. I can just make out the sounds of a rumbling tractor in the distance, the figures of people working in the field. I wonder if Barney is needling Beckett. If Prancer is on her throne at the back of the tractor.

I don't feel ready to leave this place yet. For the first time in a long time, I'm content standing still.

"I don't know," I reply faintly. "I still don't know."

"That's all right," Josie assures me. "I'm actually glad you called. I wanted to talk to you about something I saw in your inbox."

I start walking again. "Yeah?"

"Remember how I told you Sway was screening your messages?"

Not exactly unexpected, as that was a big reason why I signed up for their services. I wanted someone else to sort through for potential. I was also tired of the trolls and the comments and the never-ending criticism. "I do."

"I've been sifting through to see if there's anything interesting, and I have a few new places for you to check out, when you're ready for that. But what really caught my attention was a guy named Theo from the American Small Business Coalition. Has he reached out to you before?"

I rack my brain. "I don't think so."

"He's been pretty persistent. Said he tried to call through Sway and wasn't able to leave a message. Anyway, he thinks you'd be a good fit for a new initiative they're launching. I think you should give him a call."

"Like a partnership thing?"

"Not exactly. I think it's a position within their organization."

That would be a new direction. I never went back to exploring traditional jobs after my string of horrible interviews right out of school. I always liked being my own boss too much.

"I'll think about it. Send me his contact information."

"Sure. As soon as you send me a picture of your hot landlord."

I snort a laugh and continue carefully wandering my way across the muddy field. "He's not my landlord."

"Interesting part of the sentence to contradict," Josie replies. "I gotta go. I'm meeting my mom for a run."

I glance at my watch. It can't be much later than six in the morning on the West Coast. But Josie has always been an early riser. "Godspeed."

I tuck my phone into my pocket and continue following the map, snickering at Beckett's doodles. I laugh at a collection of wavy lines scribbled on the paper, supposed to be a cluster of bushes right before a dip in the landscape hides everything from view. I crest another small hill and then I see it. Exactly what Beckett intended for me to find.

A field of wildflowers rolling out from the base of the hill in a patchwork quilt of color. Blue and purple and a smattering of rich gold, the sight of it so quietly beautiful that I don't hesitate to walk right to the middle of it all and lie flat on my back. They must have bloomed to life during the last string of warm days, still standing tall despite the cold. Resilient. Stunning.

Flower petals tickle my cheek, and I close my eyes with a sigh. A quiet, perfect miracle hidden behind the hills.

Some happy, Beckett had written.

I curl my fingers around the edge of the paper and hold it tightly to my chest.

I LIE IN the field until my stomach starts to grumble, a reminder that I've been here for most of the morning. I'm grateful for the extra sweater I slipped over my head before I left the house, the earth cold at my back and the wind brisk enough this morning for my breath to be visible in tiny puffs of white above me. Beckett told me the weather will break soon and that winter is being a little stubborn this year.

Not the only stubborn thing, he had mumbled, a significant look cast in my direction.

I sigh and watch the stems around me dance in the breeze. Flat on the ground like this, it's just me and the blooms, the sky a perfect cloudless blue above me, endless in every direction. I sit up with a groan and dip my nose into a cluster of aster at my hip. They smell like moss, the grass after rain. I pass my palms over the petals as I leave and decide I'll bring Beckett with me the next time I come. I want him to sit in the patch of foxgloves and see if they bring out the blue in his eyes.

I take a different, meandering path to the cabin, arcing back in the opposite direction from the way I came. Beckett had scribbled a half-moon shape in the top corner of his rudimentary map, and I find the pond he must have been referencing easily enough. It's not very large, but it does have a dock extending over the water with a rowboat tied at the end. The little dinghy bobs up and down gently as the water laps at the legs of the aged wood, and I smile, imagining Beckett trying to cram his body in the tiny thing. The rope is frayed at the edges, the boat painted a dark midnight blue.

Trees arch up over the water, a canopy of tangled branches and bright green leaves. Sunlight dances through where it can, painting the still water beneath in stripes of gold. I see a tire swing on the other end of the pond barely skimming the water, a thick rope wrapped three times around the sturdy branch of an old oak. When I was a kid, I used to climb the biggest tree in my parents' backyard all the way to the top. I'd sit perched there with a book until the sun began to set, a chill making me shudder with the leaves. My dad had offered to build me a treehouse a million times, but I liked climbing too much. I liked the challenge, the scrapes it left on my palms. It always felt like I was keeping a piece of nature with me. Proof that I could do anything I wanted.

Feeling nostalgic, I wander to the trunk of a thick maple, wide branches stretching out over the water, a natural ladder of misshapen knobs and divots in the bark. I reach for the branch closest and curl my hands around it, leveraging my body up and pressing my foot to the base. Muscle memory kicks in as I place my hands and feet in all the right places, the ache in my muscles disappearing as my body warms. I press and pull until I can swing my leg over a branch, holding my body steady about halfway up. From here, the pond looks bigger, the still water a mirror image of the braches above. I gaze down at my wiggly reflection and rest my chin on my knee.

I don't know if it's the sliver of my childhood or the field of flowers or Beckett's hand-drawn map or my time away from everything I thought was important, but I feel the wayward pieces of myself sliding into place. It's not quite there yet, not the perfect fit, but isn't that what Beckett said that night on the back porch? Some of it comes, some of it goes. It's about the trying. Settling into the happy when you find it, being okay when you don't. Feeling all the misshapen bits and pieces and where they fit together. The delightful ordinary blank space in between.

I finally feel like I'm trying.

I lower my body carefully along the branch until my arms and legs are hanging free, my cheek pressed against the rough bark. I'll have imprints on my face, I'm sure, but like this, when I close my eyes, I'm weightless. Nothing bothers me. Not the cold wind twisting through the trees and tickling at the small of my back. Not the dig of a stick against my thigh. Not the endless buzzing of thoughts in the back of my mind. It's just me and the gentle rustle of the branches, the water lapping at the edge of the boat below, and the call of birds as they hop from tree to tree. It's a perfect moment.

Until I tilt to the side, and I fall.

11

BECKETT

"YOU THINK THIS cold snap will end soon?"

I'm starting to get worried. We don't usually see these types of temperatures this late into March. The afternoons have been warm enough, but the mornings and nights are downright frigid. I checked the temperature before I left the house this morning. It was barely breaking thirty degrees.

"Has to," Barney replies, frowning down at his boots, hands on his hips. "'Cause I refuse to do any replanting of the produce we've already put in the ground this year."

It wouldn't be the worst thing in the world to have a low-yield crop this spring. We don't rely on it as our main source of income. But I'd hate to see all those crops go to waste after we poured so much effort into those fields, and any business is good business for our fledgling farm.

I was actually starting to look forward to bell peppers.

"Where's the kid?"

I scratch at my eyebrow. "With Layla this morning. She was showing him how to stock inventory."

Meaning she's making him lug the giant sacks of flour and sugar that she picks up at the wholesaler into the bakehouse. Stella gets on me for forcing manual labor, but I'm pretty sure Jeremy will come crawling back to the fields after an afternoon with Layla. She runs her kitchens like one would a pit crew, but with frosting and pastel sprinkles.

Barney gives me a sly look. "And the girl?"

"The girl's name is Evelyn," I mutter. And she's not a girl. She's a woman wrapped in temptation, topped with an eager, honest sincerity that makes my chest feel hollow. Spending time with her, getting to know her—I only like her more. Which is a problem, when she plans to leave without a backward glance in a couple of weeks.

Hopefully, right now, she's sitting in a big field of flowers. I picture her there, her hands cupped loosely around a blossoming Queen Anne's lace, the white blooms bright against her dark skin. I picture myself there with her, my nose in her neck, her skin sweeter than the flowers around us. Her laugh free and warm.

I sigh and dig the palm of my hand into my shoulder and try to ease out some of the tension. I swear I've turned into the tin man since she started sleeping in my house. A bunch of rattling cans, looking around for where the hell my heart got off to. "She's somewhere around here, I'm sure."

Barney straightens suddenly, his hand shielding his eyes against the sun. "Closer than you think, yeah?"

The smile on his face wilts and then falls off completely. I follow his gaze to a hunched figure stumbling over the hill. The rattle in my chest turns to a roar as Evelyn pauses at the very top of it. There's no mistaking her dark hair or her long legs as she sways in place, arms curled tight around herself. I'm already striding forward when Barney mutters a curse under his breath.

Something is wrong.

"Is she okay?"

"Get the Gator," I call over my shoulder, picking up my pace to a jog as Evelyn stumbles to her knees and then collapses to her side. I lose sight of her in the tall grass, and my heart seizes, a numb feeling creeping up over my legs. When I was twelve years old, I bet another boy in my class I could clear one of the fences at the produce farm with a single jump. I remember running at the lopsided thing full tilt, the brambles from the bushes scraping at my bare legs. I remember the weightless feeling of propelling my body up and then the clip of my shoe against the fence. I smacked into the ground with a sickening thud, the wind knocked clean out of me. I stayed there flat on my back and tried desperately to suck in air, everything spinning around me.

It's like that now as I race to the top of the hill and find Evelyn curled up on her side in the grass. Her wet hair is plastered to her face, her clothes soaked and clinging to her skin. Whatever jacket she was wearing has long been discarded, and her body tucks tighter, knees to her chest, as she tries to conserve any warmth she has left.

Fuck, it's barely above freezing out here and she's soaking wet.

"Evie," I breathe, hands hovering over her before I turn her on her back. She blinks up at me with dazed eyes, teeth clenched tight around the shivers racking her body. I curl my palm around the nape of her neck and the sound she makes splinters right through my chest.

"Hey," she says, her voice a rasp. She tries to smile, but all she manages is a grimace instead. "I f-f-f-fell into the p-p-pond."

"What the fuck were you doing?" I ask, aware that I'm yelling for no reason. But I can't stop myself, not when her breathing isn't quite right and she can barely keep her eyes open.

I glance over my shoulder as I cup my hands above her elbows, her skin so goddamned cold I curse under my breath. I slip my fingers away and fumble with my jacket, ripping it off my arms and tucking it around her. Not that it'll do her much good with her clothes soaking wet. But she clutches it to her chest like a lifeline and buries her nose in the collar.

"Come here," I tell her, hands shaking. I tuck one beneath her shoulders and the other under her knees and lift her against me. Water slips down my arms, and I adjust my jacket tighter around her. She groans the second her cheek presses against my neck, and I suck in a sharp breath through my teeth.

She's freezing.

"W-w-was finding so-some hap-p-p-y," she whispers into my neck, hands draped loosely over my shoulders. I slip my palm under her wet shirt until the material bunches at my wrist, rubbing hard at the small of her back. I want to rip the sun right out of the sky and urge it into her skin, smooth my palms over every inch of her until she's glowing with it.

"How'd that work out for you?" I breathe against her forehead, watching as Barney finally appears on the Gator. He's driving the thing like a madman, taking the turn around the fence like a bat out of hell. I start to head in his direction, careful to keep Evelyn close.

She snorts a laugh into my skin that sounds like a whimper, her nose pressed tight to my throat. "C-c-could have been bet-t-t-er. Thanks."

Barney hits the brakes, his eyes wide in his tan face, and a cloud of dust rises around us. He takes one look at Evelyn in my arms, and his mouth flattens into a thin line.

"How long has it been?"

I clamber into the front seat with Evelyn and wrap myself around her. Over my dead body am I laying her in the back seat. "Don't know," I tell him. I nose into her wet hair and trace my palm over her stomach, trying to pour all of my heat into her. Her hand curls around my wrist, and she holds me there, squeezing once.

"W-walked from the p-pond," she answers with another rolling shiver as Barney takes off with a rumble, heading toward my cabin. I plant my boot on the floor of the small truck and hold on. The pond is easily half a mile from where we are now, and who knows how long it took her walking like this. "My ph-phone was in my po-po-pocket."

"You said you were taking a break, right? You don't need it." I can't believe she's thinking about her phone when she can barely string two words together. A hot flare of frustration knocks behind my eyes, followed by bone-deep panic.

She's too damn cold.

"W-w-why I didn't c-c-call you," she explains, tilting her head back to narrow her eyes at me. Her hand squeezes my wrist again. "G-grumpy."

Damn right I'm grumpy. I'm also terrified. Fucking furious with myself.

Barney comes to a screeching halt in front of my cabin, and I immediately climb out, my hand protectively cupping Evelyn's head, her face still tucked in the crook of my neck. Every brush of her ice-cold skin against mine is like a warning drum beating inside my skull. *Get her inside. Get her warm.*

"No hot water," Barney calls, his face lined with worry. "If you get her in the shower or tub, it might warm her up too quick." He taps once over his chest. Over his heart. "Blankets. Loads of 'em."

At my questioning glance, he shrugs. "Fell into the bay in December helping my brother tie up crab pots. When the coast guard fished me out, that's what they said." He puts the Gator into gear and eases off the brake. "I'm gonna head toward the main office. Let Stella know and get everything sorted. I'll give Gus a ring and have him come over as soon as he can." He gives me a stern look. "Take care of our girl."

Our girl. Another piece of me breaks off, something for Evelyn to hold in the palm of her pretty hand.

He goes rumbling toward the farm, and I take the steps two at a time, bursting through the front door. Evelyn shivers violently against my chest, her breath small puffs against my neck. The cats scramble around my feet as I move down the hallway, heading straight for the fireplace. I set her down carefully on the oversized armchair in front of it, dragging it closer with my hands braced on both sides.

She frowns at me as I back away, stumbling to the stack of firewood on the mantel. I feel like I'm all thumbs, my movements uncoordinated and clumsy. I've been lighting fires since I was a kid, but it takes me three tries to light the damn match, my hands shaking the whole time. I toss the flame behind the grate and breathe out slowly as it catches and spreads, kindling curling at the edges. Out of the corner of my eye, I see her try to stand up and my teeth clench in an audible snap.

"Sit the fuck down."

"B-b-ut the couch. I'm all wet."

"Evie, I swear to god. I don't give a shit about the couch." I rip one of the blankets off the other one and throw it on the hardwood at her feet, the fire beginning to snap behind me. My gaze drags up her huddled body on the very edge of the armchair, from her waterlogged boots to her dripping sweater.

"Take off your clothes," I bark, before stomping my way through the cabin to my bedroom.

I wish I could be softer, more comforting, but my body feels pulled tight, everything a second away from collapse. I can't stop replaying the moment she appeared over the hill, the way her body swayed and then fell out of view. Like a flower wilting on the vine. I can't stop seeing the way she pulled into herself as I turned her over, hands grasping at nothing.

I ball up the comforter from my bed and stalk toward the living room. Evelyn is standing again, her back to me as she fumbles with her clothes in front of the fireplace. All she's managed to do is kick off her shoes, her shaking hands attempting to loosen the button on her soaking wet jeans.

She looks at me over her shoulder, a faintly pleading look that evaporates all of my anger and replaces it with a tender ache. "Beck, I c-c-can't—"

"It's all right." I toss the comforter with the other blanket and curl myself around her back, gently moving her hands to her sides. Her wet sweater soaks my shirt as I slip the button of her jeans free, my knuckles brushing against the soft skin of her stomach as I work at the zipper. I jerk the heavy material over her hips, and she makes a small noise, a thin exhale from her nose. Goose bumps appear on her skin as I work the wet jeans down and off her legs.

"Sorry," I mutter, my hand around the back of her knee as I try to help her step out of them. My thumb traces absently over delicate skin. She's still so cold.

Something that sounds like a laugh garbles out of her, her hands cupping her elbows and her chin pressed to her chest. "Nothing you h-haven't seen be-f-fore."

I clench my jaw. "Doesn't mean it's an open invitation," I tell her, my voice gruff with frustration. I'm too focused on the circles beneath her eyes and the pale blue tint of her lips to notice anything else—the sticky cold that her skin is coated with, her clothes stiff and unyielding. I get to my feet and lift the hem of her shirt, guiding it over her head. I'm careful not to tangle her hair when her whole body gives a tremendous shake, the shirt thrown to the floor with a heavy plop. I smooth my palms down her sides in a vigorous rub and she shivers.

She's nothing but thin cotton and bare skin in front of me, her shoulder blades curved like folded wings as she hunches forward. I reach for the comforter and wrap it around her front, hesitating for half a second before grabbing my sweatshirt and pulling it off. I tug at my T-shirt too, leaving my chest and torso bare. Evelyn looks at me, dark eyes heavy and exhausted.

"That's n-n-nice," she murmurs around another ferocious tremble, her chin and the curve of her lips barely visible above her blanket cocoon. It would be cute if I wasn't so damn worried, her dark hair still a wet clump on her forehead.

I duck into the comforter with her, my arms slipping around her stomach and guiding her to me until her bare back rests snug against my chest. I suck in a sharp breath when every frozen inch of her presses against me, her hands moving from the blanket to clutch at my arms instead.

I need seventeen more blankets. One of those hot water bottle things my mom used to put in our beds when we were kids.

"W-warm." Her exhale is a sigh of relief. It's three shuffling steps to the couch that isn't covered in soaking wet clothes. When I collapse into it, I make sure to keep Evelyn near me, guiding her body above mine until she's sitting sideways, her legs tucked over my lap. I wrap my hand around her ankle and squeeze, my thumb rubbing at the jut of her bone.

We sit in silence, the fire growing in the hearth until the room is glowing with it—the crackle of the flames urging me to settle. I can feel the heat licking at my shins, and I angle her body until she's as close as she can be, tucked right against me.

"You called m-me Evie," she says somewhere into my neck, her palm sliding from my wrist to my elbow. She nuzzles closer, greedy for warmth.

"That's your name, isn't it?" I give in to the urge to brush my lips over the shell of her ear, using my fingers at her back to gently comb through the ends of her hair. It's still dripping, and I wrap the edge of the comforter around it, trying to squeeze out some of the extra water. I should have brought her a towel. Made her tea in the kitchen.

"You hav-haven't called me that in a while, is all," she replies, lazy and slow. Her shaking isn't as violent as it was, her jaw finally relaxing from the tight clench of her teeth. I stare down at what I can see of her face, her dark eyelashes fanned against the rise of her cheek.

"I li-like it," she tells me—a statement. She pauses and breathes out a heavy, watery sigh. "I missed it," she adds—a secret.

I move my hand to her back, slowing my touch until my palm rests along the center of her spine. I spread my fingers wide and listen to the sound of her breathing. I match mine to hers.

"I missed it too," I confess.

The chill starts to leave her skin as I continue to hold her, a soft light from the fireplace filling the room. One of the kittens appears at the edge of the couch, her tiny face turned up in concern. Evelyn's body relaxes against mine, and I adjust my grip, nudging at her once with my nose. "Hey. I don't think you should sleep. Talk to me for a few minutes."

She grumbles something under her breath, shifting in my lap until her arm is low around my back and her knee is hugging my side. She's using me as a human pillow, and the thought makes me smile, some of the tension finally slipping from my shoulders.

"About what?" she asks.

"I don't know. What do we usually talk about?"

"I usually ask you a bunch of questions, and you g-grunt at me." She laughs into the bouquet of daisies tattooed on my shoulder, the delicate petals fanning out over my chest. She traces over it gently—the long stems, the thin ribbon inked between them. Her thumb trails to the hollow of my throat, and she leaves it there, nose at my collarbone. I adjust her in my lap.

I can't think when all her skin is pressed to mine. I can hardly breathe.

When I don't offer anything in the way of conversation, she sighs. "Tell me something about the sky."

I tilt my head back against the couch and consider, stretching my legs out beneath the coffee table. "There's a meteor shower at the end of April," I start. Her legs shift, and I'm distracted by the weight of her against me, her bottom lip dragging over my skin. I breathe in slowly.

"I know," she tells me. "I saw it on your f-fridge."

I forgot I put the map there. Usually one of the cats collects it for their nest, and I have to extract it from between stolen shirts and a necktie I've worn twice.

Evelyn's weight becomes heavier against me, her forehead nudging at my chin. I jostle her slightly, my hand sliding across her skin. "Come on, honey. Stay awake with me."

She whines, and it sends a bolt of heat rocketing through my blood. I clear my throat and grapple for something to fill the limited space between us.

"I read online that it's considered a common shower." That's what the article said. *Common.* Like a bunch of dust, rock, and ice left over from the creation of the solar system isn't something incredible. When did we stop marveling at the world around us? When did we stop looking at the stars?

"Meteors come from comets?" she mumbles it into my neck, lazy and slow.

I nod. "Yeah." I slip my hand down to her hip and squeeze once. "Bits of comet, I suppose. When the remnants start to fall through our atmosphere, they catch on fire."

"When you p-put it like that"—she laughs, a slight catch in the sound—"it sounds beautiful."

I smile against her temple. "It is though. It is when you think about it. These things are circling the sky for—god knows how long, really. And then we knock into their way, and they start to fall, lighting up the sky as they go. Think about every kid that looks up to the sky and sees that flash of light. That's magic, isn't it?" Eight years old and standing in my parents' backyard, cornstalks up to my knees, and my pajamas a size too big, the hem of my pants dragging. A flash of light and my heart in my throat. A wish made on a star. "What in the hell is common about that?"

"I TOLD YOU," I say into the phone wedged between my ear and my shoulder. "I'm not going."

I peer out of the kitchen to the living room, where Evelyn is wrapped up in four blankets on the couch, a mug of tea cupped between her hands. The cats have all burrowed in various spots in her cocoon. I can see Vixen by her shoulder, her tail curled gently over the back of Evelyn's neck. With a purely selfish impulse, I'd brought her one of my flannels to wear, and I can make out the rolled sleeve as she brings the mug to her lips, the collar stretched wide over bare skin.

Gus stopped by not too long ago, the ambulance barreling into my driveway. Evelyn had been mortified, hands curled tight to her chest, quietly asking if bringing the behemoth was really necessary. Gus had chuckled and unloaded his bag, gently checking her over.

"It's my work whip," he'd told her, two fingers pressed to the delicate skin on her wrist as he took her pulse. "Next time I'll rent a limousine."

I had made a sound at that. There won't be a next time. We won't ever be revisiting this little trip to the pond again. The next time Evelyn goes there, it'll be 102 and sunny. I'll put her on one of those backpack leashes. Now that the fear is gone, I'm left with nothing but a buzz of frustration. I have to hold myself back from sitting close to her, scooping her up against me. I want to feel the heat thrumming beneath her skin. I want to wrap her in seven more blankets and lock her in this house.

I slam the box of tea bags shut and toss the metal container in the cabinet, making enough noise to wake the dead. I somehow manage not to dislodge the phone cradled on my shoulder.

"Oh, now you're telling me things," Nova snips on the other end of the line. I can imagine her pinched face, the way her hands clench into fists when she's pissed about something. "You've got a woman— a *high-profile social media starlet*, mind you—staying with you for weeks, and you don't say anything to anyone. But now you're telling me. Okay."

"Didn't want to make it a thing," I explain. I also didn't want all of my sisters showing up on my doorstep. I watch as the social media starlet shifts on the couch, her hand petting one of the cats. It's my sisters' own fault if they haven't been paying attention to the phone tree.

"You could have mentioned something at dinner this week."

Evelyn had been at Stella's place when I attended family dinner on Tuesday night. I brought her home a Tupperware container of potato salad, and she ate it for breakfast three days in a row.

"There was nothing to mention."

Nova snorts.

"I have no idea how long she's staying, and you guys get . . . weird."

They get invasive. All of the rooms in this house would have suddenly found themselves occupied by the sisters Porter if I had so much as mentioned Evelyn's name.

"We don't get weird."

I keep my thoughts to myself. It's not worth the argument.

Nova circles back to her original point. "You have to go."

"I absolutely do not have to go." Evelyn's blank expression morphs into curiosity, a question on her brow when she glances over to me. I roll my eyes. "I fixed the Carter thing. Harper can be on your team again."

"Harper doesn't know anything about botany."

"She knows some things." Like plants need sunlight and water to live, but that's probably it.

"Do you not care if we win?"

"Nova." I stir some honey into my mug. "Please believe me when I say that I could not care any less about your chances of winning."

She sucks in a deep breath and pauses. I can hear her devious little mind plotting on the other end of the line. "All right, well—" She sighs, a gust of breath. She's probably sitting cross-legged in her tattoo studio, a sketchpad open on her lap. "I'm sure it will be fine. Mom will be disappointed you aren't there, but you can always visit her another time."

I pinch the bridge of my nose. "Went right for the kill shot, didn't you?"

She snickers. "I play to win the game, big brother."

"I'm hanging up now."

"Tell Evelyn I say hi."

I toss my phone onto the counter with a clatter and shuffle into the living room, kettle in hand. I top off Evelyn's mug and collapse back against the couch with a sigh, and her feet automatically dig under my thigh. They're still cold, and I consider getting back up for a thick pair of my socks. Maybe the ones she stole three days ago that she thinks I don't know about.

She watches me over the top of her mug, blowing gently on her tea. Comet lets out a content purr and jumps onto my lap, twitching her tail at my hip before settling into a furry little heap across my knees.

"What are you avoiding?"

"Hm?" I can't think when she looks like that, my flannel over one shoulder and her bottom lip at the edge of the mug.

"You said you're not going. What won't you be attending?"

I drop my eyes and busy myself with a frayed edge of the blanket. "Trivia night at the bar."

"Did Carter ban you or something?"

I snort. I'd like to see him try. "No."

"It sounds like fun," she says as she takes a sip from her mug, brown eyes fixed on me. Her voice has more of a rasp to it than usual, a huskiness that has me shifting in my seat and remembering what it was like to hear that voice in bed. Now that she has color in her cheeks and I'm less frantic with worry, I find myself considering the stretch of smooth brown skin of her shoulder. How soft she felt with my arms around her. Her nose in my neck and her hands curled around me.

She holds my stare and waits. I pack those thoughts away.

"I don't—" I break off and consider not finishing my sentence. But she prods me with her toes, and I sigh. "I don't like going into town."

"I've gathered that." Another sip. "You go grocery shopping in the middle of the night."

Not the . . . middle of the night. I usually wait until half an hour before the shop closes, when I know they've restocked the strawberry jam and the fudge cookies. The store is almost always empty, and I don't have to talk to anyone over cans of soup.

Social anxiety. Sound sensitivity. Fancy terms for my general discomfort around other people. My parents sent me to a therapist when I was ten years old and overwhelmed by all the noise around me. The worst of it was in school, when I couldn't get the damn noise to . . . stop. All the chatter around me felt like the worst sort of buzz under my skin, settling into a deep ache that pounded like a metronome through every inch of my body.

I couldn't focus. I could barely speak. It was miserable.

"Beckett?"

Evelyn touches the top of my knee lightly, guiding my attention back from the table to her open and eager face. It's the part I like best about her, I think, her curiosity and kindness. Her desire to help where she can, however she can.

When she says something, she really means it.

She frowns at me, and I wish I could swipe at it with my thumb. Make everything a little bit easier for her. Be half as good at this as she is. A shiver slides down the smooth line of her neck, and I reach forward to adjust the blanket higher. I think I've got a heated blanket around here somewhere. An extra quilt or two in my room.

My knuckles brush her throat, and she shivers again, a little shimmy of her shoulders and a clench of her jaw.

"Still cold?"

She shakes her head, a dazed smile kicking up the corners of her mouth. I feel her gaze like a touch on my skin, dancing down my cheek and cupping at my jaw. "I'm okay," she finally says. She wiggles down farther in her blankets. "Is it people?"

I hum, distracted again by her hands around the mug. Her nails are a pale pink. The same color as sand on a beach. A perfectly ripe peach, sitting pretty on a tree branch. "What?"

"You're not exactly a talker, Beck." She grins at me. "Case in point."

I huff a laugh and tuck the edges of the blankets tighter around her. "I don't know how to explain it," I tell her slowly. "I've always had trouble talking to people. I try to avoid large groups if I can."

I'm most comfortable with people I know. Outside, if I can be. Something about seeing the sky above me loosens something deep in my chest and makes everything . . . easier. I don't think so hard about what I have to say. I don't trip over my own thoughts.

"The first time we met," she begins, her eyes squinted in thought, remembering, "you came right up to me and asked me what I was drinking."

The first time ever, I think, that I approached a woman at a bar instead of letting someone come to me. It had felt necessary that I talk to her. A tug, a pull—whatever you want to call it. I saw her sitting there, and I wanted to be sitting right next to her.

"The bar we met in was empty. Do you remember?"

She nods. "There was a baseball game on the TV in the corner. I stopped in because I smelled the French fries from the street." She grins. "The ones that you stole half of."

I did steal half of them, after I was two shots of tequila deep and her hand found my thigh under the table. "I chose that bar because it was the least crowded place on the street." Then I saw Evelyn and I didn't want to go anywhere else. "Plus, everything gets quiet when I look at you."

She gives me one slow blink, lashes fluttering. Her eyes dance between mine, bottom lip caught by her teeth. "Would it help?"

I rub the edge of the blanket again, the worn blue-gray material soft under my touch. "Would what help?"

She tilts her head to the side and reaches over me to set her mug on the side table. Her hair brushes my forearm, and I'm the one shivering.

"If I came with you," she says. I swallow hard and become fascinated with the legs of the coffee table. "Would it help to have a friend with you? At trivia?"

I don't want to be her friend. I want to be more. I want us to be the people we were when we were away from everyone else. I almost say it, biting down on the inside of my cheek to keep the thought to myself.

"I don't know," I answer slowly. Probably not. I'm most comfortable with my family, and even then it's a challenge for me to sit somewhere with so much sound around me. Trivia night is an . . . event. It almost always ends with Dane carting people to the drunk tank at the station. Last time, he had to put Becky Gardener in the back of his cruiser for launching a plate of chicken tenders across the room.

"I'll go with you," she says, just as slowly, "if you want to try."

12

EVELYN

I GRUNT AS I reach for the handle of the bakehouse door, seventeen layers of clothes thick and warm around me. Beckett had glared at me as he forced a sweatshirt over my head in the kitchen this morning—an old green faded thing with a giant badger across the chest.

"Stay away from water today," he ordered, lips tilted downward. I had gone to pull my hair loose from my collar, but he had gotten there first, gathering it up in his fist. He had paused, just for a second, and then released it down my back.

There had been a handful of memories in that second. I could see it in the single flash of darkness in those bright eyes. He remembered, same as I did. His hands in my hair, tilting my head back as he guided me toward a bed with too many pillows. Sticky humidity against my skin. A deep, indulgent moan from me. A shaky exhale pressed right between my breasts from him.

The ribbon of silver bells above the door announces my arrival and successfully disrupts my little daydream.

Layla and Stella glance up from behind the counter, Stella's face twisting in confusion at my marshmallow man layers. It's not even cold today. I can feel a single bead of sweat slipping down my spine.

"Cute sweatshirt," Layla says immediately, a sly grin on her full lips. She has a cake in front of her, white buttercream and hunter green icing. A trail of delicate pale blue forget-me-nots cascades down the side, her hand poised above. She adjusts her grip on the bag and tilts her head to the side. "I like your new farm look. It suits you."

It suits me too, when I'm not sweating half to death. I putter over to the countertop and pick up a broken cookie, Layla's stack of imperfect discards on a tray for anyone to grab.

I'm supposed to be helping her with her weekend orders, but maybe I'll eat all her scraps and call it a day. I feel like I've earned that.

"I saw the ambulance pull in yesterday." Stella wipes her hands off on a towel and steps around the counter. "I was going to stop by if I didn't see you today. Everything okay?"

The ambulance. God. I had never felt like more of an inconvenience than when Gus came rumbling into Beckett's driveway with his red-and-white behemoth. At least he didn't have the lights and sirens going. I'm pretty sure I would have crawled under the bed in the spare room and never come out.

"I'm okay. Beckett took good care of me." With the blankets and his warm skin pressed to mine, his arms tight around me, his chin on my shoulder. I feel another flush of heat that has nothing to do with my layers. He hadn't hesitated at all, instantly scooping me up and holding me close.

Layla snickers down at her cake and makes a practiced flick of her wrist as she pipes a tiny, perfect leaf on the corner. "I'm sure he did."

I give her a look around a mouthful of oatmeal chocolate chip cookie. "Very mature of you."

I finish my cookie and tuck my elbows into my chest, an attempt to pull my arms from the sleeves of my top two layers. The thick material bunches around my biceps, and I make a helpless sound as I attempt to twist out.

Stella takes mercy on me and grips the hem. "I'm glad you were able to get to Beckett. It's a long walk from the pond to the fields."

Even longer when you're soaking wet and shivering so badly you can hardly breathe. I lost my coat somewhere along the way, the thing so heavy with water it felt like seventy-five extra pounds of weight. I'll have to go grab it at some point.

Stella tugs the sweatshirt up and over my head, and I breathe out a sigh of relief. Movement. Oxygen. Sweet, sweet freedom. She drapes the jumble of cotton over a chair. "What were you doing out at the pond anyway? We really only ever use it in the summer."

"Trying," I offer as an explanation that makes absolutely no sense at all. But Stella always seems to read between the lines. The confusion on her face settles into a soft understanding, her hand squeezing at my arm once.

"Everything okay?"

I nod, shrug, and then shake my head. "I don't know." I tuck my hands into the cuffs of my shirt and glance at the picture hanging just behind the counter—Beckett, Layla, and Stella together with a giant pair of scissors, cutting a big red bow in front of the bakehouse. "Do you ever feel like—do you ever want to slow down? Not be responsible for everything all of the time?"

She breaks off a piece of my cookie as she considers her answer. "About six months into owning the farm, I started sleepwalking. Most of the time, I'd wake up somewhere in the house. Going through drawers in the kitchen. Inexplicably taking all my clothes out of the dresser. Rearranging houseplants. Other times I'd wake up in my office, sitting behind my desk." She huffs a laugh. "Once I woke up in the middle of typing an email to a supplier, asking for four times the amount of everything. Beckett would have had enough topsoil for years."

"The office is pretty far from your house." At least in the middle of the night, it is. When one is presumably asleep.

Stella nods. "Yeah. One night I fell in the middle of the field. Sprained my ankle. I had to hop my way home in my pajamas." She shakes her head. "I was covered in dirt, sitting in my kitchen, with my leg propped up on the counter."

I take another nibble of cookie. "Was Luka mad?"

She nods. "Furious. He was upset that I never told him about the sleepwalking. That it had been happening for a while and I never thought to mention it or slow down."

She glances out the window to the trees beyond, a half smile tugging at her lips. "I'm not great at listening to myself. Some days I push myself too hard. Some days we don't get a single customer, and I panic about losing everything. Some days I make up an elaborate story with my best friend and pretend we're in a relationship so a social media influencer likes us more." She gives me a rueful grin. "Some days I'm so tired I can hardly remember my name. And that's what's expected, right? When you own a business. I think—I think we're told that we should embrace the grind. The work. That everything will be worth it in the end. But sometimes we need rest more than we need another thing on our list. And that's okay. I'm learning that's really okay."

I blow out a noisy breath. That's what I'm looking for, I think. A little rest. Something slower. I'm so tired of everything else.

Stella watches me carefully. "It's okay to want different things," she says. "People change. You're allowed to change. Doing less doesn't make you less."

Seasons change and so do we. I wonder if Stella made the banner that hangs in the center of town.

"Nice shirt," Layla calls, a laugh hidden in her voice. I look down at the oversized flannel tied in a knot at my waist and pluck at one of the buttons.

"It's comfortable," I say.

"Mm-hmm."

"It's really soft."

"I'm sure it is."

Not as soft as the look on Beckett's face though, when he helped me slip the material over my shoulders, his knuckles grazing the insides of my arms and then my collarbone. *Mine*, that look had said, possession in the nimble work of his fingers on the buttons. But then he had cleared his throat and looked away, staring at his mug of tea like it held the meaning of life.

I have no idea what he wants from me, if he even wants anything from me at all.

Stella studies me with a knowing look. "Have you talked to him?"

"He knows I have his shirt."

"That isn't what I meant, and you know it."

I haven't. What could I possibly say? *Those nights in Maine were some of the best nights of my life. I want to keep sitting on your back porch.*

Every day we spend together, I only like you more.

I can't. There's still too much to figure out. I'm confused about work and that confusion is bleeding out, jumbling up the rest of me.

Specifically my feelings for a very handsome and very stoic farmer. It feels like it's too soon. Like maybe it's too much. I need to figure myself out first.

Our conversation is interrupted by a knock against the thick glass of the front door. Caleb Alvarez edges the door open and pokes his head through, the rest of his long body lingering on the small porch. Dark hair, bashful grin. Eyes only for Layla.

"You open for business yet?"

Layla waves him in from behind the counter, tongue between her teeth as she finishes piping her flowers. "Always for you, Deputy."

Caleb straightens and slips through the door, a pleased blush high on his tanned cheeks. He gives us a wave and a sheepish smile that causes twin dimples to blink to life in his cheeks. Stella and I sigh in unison. "Told you to call me Caleb," he says to Layla.

"Your cake will be ready in a sec," Layla offers. "Help yourself to a coffee while you wait."

Caleb ducks behind the counter to the coffeepot, and Stella leans closer to me, hiding her mouth with the back of her hand. "This is the third custom cake he's ordered this month," she whispers. "I think he's gained fifteen pounds."

I take in his trim body, legs crossed at the ankles as he leans against the counter and stares at Layla like she's made of sugarplums and fairy dust. Maybe all those calories are going right to his gigantic heart. I grin.

"Has she noticed?"

The smile slips from Stella's face as she shakes her head. "She's so used to men treating her like garbage, I don't think she recognizes when someone has genuine interest in her." She sighs and rubs a fingertip across her eyebrow. "I've got faith in Caleb though."

So do I, if Layla's laugh is any indication. It bursts out of her at something he quietly murmurs over the countertop, an answering grin blooming on his handsome face.

I narrow my eyes. "Does that mean you've got money on Caleb?"

The last time I was here, I stumbled upon a townwide betting pool with odds on Stella and Luka making it official—a surprisingly organized and efficient whiteboard in the back of the firehouse with scribbled names and amounts.

Stella snickers. "Luka does."

I EAT OATMEAL chocolate chip cookies until I have to unbutton my jeans, reclined in the back kitchen across three sacks of sugar. I make a moaning sound as Layla walks by with a tray of brownies, a small square dropped neatly on my chest.

"You're gonna kill me," I groan.

"Death by chocolate." Layla sets the tray on the large metal island in the middle of the room and wipes her palms on her apron. "There are worse ways to go."

I sit up and watch as she cuts the brownies into perfect two-inch squares, her movements graceful and efficient. The whole day I've watched her spin around this bakehouse like a dancer, every single step part of an elaborately choreographed routine.

"You moved to Inglewild when you finished college, right?"

Layla hums and nods, reaching for some plastic wrap at her elbow. "I met Stella our freshman year at Salisbury. I decided to move here on a whim, really. Not much of a plan." She presses the back of her hand across her forehead, fingertips covered in dark chocolate. "I lived with Stella for a while. We shared a tiny apartment above the service station. I'm pretty sure I smelled like oil and grease for six months straight. Beatrice hated it."

"Ms. Beatrice?"

"Ah, yeah. I worked at the café for a while. She taught me everything I know about baked goods."

Huh. I had no idea. I'm guessing Ms. Beatrice kept her shortbread recipe to herself. Layla's eyes narrow in a secret smile, her pink lips curled at the edges. "I know Beckett gets cookies on the side. It amuses me to watch him sneak around."

Her phone begins to rattle across the countertop, and she glances at the screen. "Speak of the devil," she mutters. She reads whatever message pops up and snorts a laugh. "Beckett says he's running late and you should head to trivia with me. He also says we should not, under any circumstances, walk by the fountain in town. You might go careening in."

I roll my eyes. "How long am I going to be teased about this?"

"Oh, a decade or so. Is your phone still in the pond?"

"Probably," I say. I imagine it sitting at the bottom with the silt and the mud, an endless stream of social media alerts pinging like bubbles. The image is oddly satisfying. "What's the likelihood Beckett is avoiding trivia?"

"Depends." Layla hangs up her apron on a peg by the door and rolls out her neck. The amount of things this woman creates in a day is astounding. Peach tarts and warm butter croissants and donuts with fresh vanilla custard inside. She should have her own Food Network show, an entire line of cookware. "Who did he promise? You or Nova?"

"Me."

She smiles. "Then he'll be there."

THE BAR IS crowded when we arrive, several large folding tables filling the space that was empty only a few days ago. There are groups clustered together along each, chairs pushed together, and everyone is dressed in—

"Are those costumes?" There is a man at the far end with his elbows resting on the table, leaves in his hair, his chest wrapped in what looks like brown paper.

Layla nods and waves to someone by the bar. "Yup. One of the rules for trivia is you have to dress to the theme if you're on a team."

I see a pretty young woman standing behind the man with the butcher's paper wearing all yellow, top to bottom. She has fake vines twisting up from her sneakers to her knees. "And tonight's theme is . . . ?"

Layla bends over a couple having a spirited discussion about mozzarella sticks and grabs a flyer off the table. At the top in big bold letters, it reads GARDEN PARTY. I glance back up at the man who must be a tree, and his partner who, I guess, is a . . . sun?

Layla laughs. "The interpretations are always creative. Ah, there's Beckett's family. We can sit with them before it starts, but I want to be out of swinging distance when the questions get going."

I follow after her through the crowd, stepping around someone with actual feathers stuck to a majority of their body. A sparrow? Who knows?

"Swinging distance?"

"It isn't trivia night if a stool doesn't almost go through the window."

"What?" Her statement has me pausing right at the edge of the table we've been working our way toward, five heads with varying degrees of dark blond hair bent close together and whispering. Layla clears her throat, and the man closest to us shoots up in his seat, grin already pulling his mouth wide.

"Laaaaayla," he sings, voice tilting down an octave at the end as he does his best Eric Clapton impersonation. Layla laughs and bends at the waist to kiss him on the cheek. His eyes slant to me and hold, and his grin turns mischievous. He has the same features as Beckett but lighter somehow. Laugh lines deep by his eyes and around his mouth. I don't notice the wheelchair until he pulls back slightly from the table, turning the wheels in my direction with one sure hand. "You must be Evelyn. My son is awfully evasive about you."

"He's evasive about everything," the woman at his elbow mumbles, but she's smiling too, familiar blue-green eyes on her kind face. Everyone at the table is wearing a different version of a flower crown, thick with seeded eucalyptus and magnolia leaves, perfect blooms of bright purple statice woven between. She pats the space across from her with a cat-that-got-the-canary smile. "Come sit with us."

"Try not to sound like such a creep, Ness. Christ," a small woman gripes, a French fry hanging out of her mouth like a cigarette. She gives me a little wave. "I'm Nova. I'm his favorite."

"Favorite headache, maybe," the first woman snaps back. She gives me a quick smile. "I'm Nessa."

"At least I didn't put my foot through his spare bedroom ceiling," Nova grumbles.

Nessa blanches. "Shut up. He still doesn't know about that." She glances at me. "Does he know about that?"

"I have no idea," I reply.

I slip into the empty seat and make a note to check the ceiling in the other two bedrooms when I get to Beckett's. An older woman with streaks of gray in her honey blond hair smiles at me, nudging a pitcher of beer in my direction.

"It's good you got here early," she says. "Now we can talk without interruptions."

THERE ARE PLENTY of interruptions. All in the form of Beckett's family eagerly asking questions over one another.

I've only consumed a quarter of my beer but answered close to 107 questions. Apparently, Beckett has shared nothing with them at their weekly dinners, and they're rabid for information. I'm happy enough to indulge, delighted by the way they banter with one another, love in every single smile and snap and spilled drink. They remind me of nights with my parents and aunties and all of my cousins.

"Which of his tattoos is your favorite?" Nova asks.

This question feels like a trick though.

"Did you do any of them?" I remember Ms. Beatrice mentioned that Nova's an artist.

She nods proudly. "All of them—my first when I was sixteen." She taps the inside of her wrist, where I know Beckett has a small leaf. "I was having trouble finding clients, and Beckett volunteered. He kept volunteering." She laughs.

I think about the art that covers every square inch of his arms, from the backs of his hands to the strong line of his shoulders. I picture a much younger Beckett sitting with his arm outstretched, allowing his little sister to put her mark on his skin, and my heart swells in my chest.

"The galaxy one," I answer, and rub my finger along my triceps. "The one right here. The coloring is gorgeous."

It hides under his T-shirt most of the time, a bright blue streak poking through when his sleeves are slightly rolled or when he's reaching for something above his head. A rich cobalt with streaks of purple, the ink so smooth it's like someone pressed their thumb and dragged it across his skin. Tiny, delicate stars outlined in crisp white.

Nova beams, pleased. "I gave him that for his birthday a couple of years ago. It's my favorite too."

"What's your favorite?" Beckett's deep voice rumbles against my back as a big hand appears over my shoulder and lifts the beer out of my grip. I tilt my head back and watch as he takes a long pull, the strong column of his throat working.

"Hi."

I want to lean my head back until it rests against his hip. I want to tell him I've been thinking about him all day.

He looks tired, a little frustrated. But a small smile quirks his lips when he glances down at me with a raised eyebrow. "Hey. My sisters getting you drunk?"

"Not yet." His mom smiles softly and accepts the kiss he leans over to press to her cheek. "But we've got time. Now sit down and put your flower crown on. Trivia starts in three minutes."

Beckett drops into the seat next to me and dutifully puts on his flower crown without complaint. It dips over one eye, and I push it back on his head until the blooms are resting in his hair. He looks like something out of Greek mythology, unfairly beautiful.

"Damn." Harper pouts. "I was hoping you'd look ridiculous."

Beckett's eyes slant toward her, sitting cross-legged at the end of the table with a piña colada in front of her. "Glad to see you could make it."

She shrugs. "Can't participate." She gestures toward her fair blond hair twisted in a braid, unadorned by a flower crown. "Didn't dress up."

Beckett reaches for the leaves on his head. "You can have—"

"Oh, hey, Jenny! Hold on a sec, I'll be right—" She stands up without finishing her sentence, disappearing into the crowd that surrounds the bar.

Beckett releases a defeated sigh and finishes the rest of my beer.

"You okay?" I ask.

"It's loud," he says with a wince. He reaches for the pitcher in the center of the table and almost topples it when Gus climbs up on the bar top with a megaphone, announcing the start of the games. Beckett shakes his head slightly, a short reactionary movement. Like he's flicking off a fly or trying to keep himself from falling asleep. He secures the pitcher and pours himself another glass. "It'll be fine."

13

EVELYN

IT IS NOT fine.

He barely finishes his beer before a dramatic rise of music begins to pump through the bar. It sounds like something from Lord of the Rings or maybe . . . *Battlestar Galactica*? I have no idea. Whatever it is, Gus slowly rises to the beat from his crouched position on top of the bar, megaphone in hand.

"Let's get ready to triviaaaaaaaa!" he shouts into his speaker, dragging out the last word until he can't breathe. The crowd erupts into raucous cheers.

"Jesus Christ." Beckett sighs next to me.

"All right, everyone. You know the rules. Each team has one runner. You'll write down your answers, and at the end of each round, your runner will bring your submissions to Monty." He points down at the bar, where Monty sits with an official-looking hat and a wide grin. "The sheriff would also like me to remind everyone that the term *runner* does not mean you have to run, and if anyone starts tackling again, that's an immediate end to the night." Gus narrows his eyes and searches the crowd. "You hear that, Mabel, baby? No violence tonight."

"I've never seen trivia like this before," I say in the general direction of the table.

Nova slaps down a sheet of paper that looks like it's embossed at the bottom, a Sharpie between her teeth. "And you never will again. Let's kill these motherfuckers."

Beckett drags his entire hand down his face.

"The first category"—Gus pauses dramatically; the entire bar waits with bated breath—"is botany."

"Not fair!" Someone shouts from the back. "The Porter family has generations of agricultural knowledge on their team!"

Nessa shoots up from her seat next to Nova. "No one questioned you last month about how you know so much about the Spice Girls, Sam. Sit down."

There's a grumble from the opposite end of the room. No one else says a word.

"First question. What type of vascular plant possesses neither seeds nor flowers?"

"Fern," Beckett, his dad, and I all answer the question at exactly the same moment. Beckett looks at me, bewildered.

"How do you know that?"

I shrug and sip at my beer. "I know things."

He opens his mouth to say something else, but Gus cuts in with that damned megaphone. "Second question! Which part of the rhubarb plant is edible?"

"Stalks." Again, Beckett and I answer the question at the same time. He narrows his eyes at me as Nova furiously writes down the answer.

"How did you know that?"

"I told you, I know things." I trace my pointer finger around the rim of my glass. Beckett's eyes flick to it and his gaze sharpens, his jaw flexing.

"It doesn't matter how she knows it, because she's not registered, and she can't participate with answers," Nessa supplies from the other end of the table. She gives me a shrug and a regretful grin. "Sorry. You can give moral support though."

"We should have registered her on the team," Nova says.

"Next time," Nessa agrees.

A warm glow settles in my chest. I didn't realize how much I was hoping they'd like me until just now. Nessa snaps her fingers in front of Beckett's face. He hasn't looked away from me. "Head in the game."

My designation as team moral supporter is needed, because two rounds later, Beckett is miserable, so tense next to me that I'm pretty sure I could break a bottle over his head and he wouldn't notice. He participates only when he's asked, offering one-word answers and clenching his hands into fists during the breaks. He guzzles his beer like it'll disappear if he doesn't down each glass in three gulps. At one point, Nova leans forward with a concerned look and quietly asks him if he needs his earmuffs.

"No," he says, barely audible over the sounds of the bar. His cheeks pinken as he glances at me quickly before blinking away. "M'fine."

I try to engage him when I can, but he's stiff and unyielding next to me, retreating further and further into himself. He doesn't speak unless spoken to and flat-out ignores me more than once. I sigh and glance over my shoulder to the far end of the room, where the bathrooms are. I cuff Beckett's wrist loosely with my hand and attempt to get his attention as he stares blankly at the tabletop. He tilts his head slightly, flower crown tipping to the side. A white daisy brushes against his forehead.

"I'll be right back."

For a second it looks like he might try to stop me. He opens his mouth, and his eyes trip over the planes of my face, considering. But whatever it is, he bottles it right up. His jaw snaps shut. A quick, sharp nod.

I squeeze his wrist again.

I make my way through the raucous crowd, a group of people dressed as birds having a heated argument with ladies in long pastel dresses and sun hats. Layla wasn't joking when she said trivia night is serious business in Inglewild. Both Caleb and Dane are in attendance, sitting at the far end of the bar with a basket of jalapeño poppers between them. Dane has a long-suffering expression on his serious face. Caleb looks like he's holding himself back from participating.

I get sidetracked by Jeremy and his friends as I travel through the tables, their heads bent over their cell phones, a pitcher of soda in the middle of the table. They ask for selfies and tips on lighting, and then I'm shown seventeen video drafts that they're thinking about posting. It's like a social media version of *American Idol*, and I slip away with promises of more tomorrow if they come by the bakery in the morning.

Gus and Monty corner me next, proudly showing me the numbers on their dance video. When I ask them how they plan to follow up such a stunning debut, Gus gets a twinkle in his eye and stands from his stool, scooping me in his big arms and spinning me around the small square of floor space. I laugh loudly and hold myself steady on his shoulders, my heart so light it feels like I could float away.

This is what I was missing. Foundation. Belonging. People and stories and my name tossed out in greeting over half-eaten baskets of greasy French fries. All of my trips—I haven't stayed in a place long enough for anyone to know me. I haven't had Caleb waving at me from across the bar with a jalapeño popper held between thumb and forefinger. Ms. Beatrice screaming in someone's face about the official name of New York's Sixth Avenue while wearing a sun hat and holding a croquet mallet, a wink tossed over her shoulder. A chorus of whistles when I wave to the ladies from the salon.

Stella's words drift back to me. People change. Maybe this is what I need now.

I'm still smiling, breathless, when I finally make it to the bathroom. I stop and stare at myself in the mirror—my cheeks are flushed and a grin makes my face almost unrecognizable. It's been so long since I've felt like this. I touch my fingers to my cheeks and try to memorize it.

"You're doing okay," I tell myself quietly. My smile softens into something lasting, and I let myself feel good about everything that's brought me to exactly this moment. No guilt. No hesitation. Just a bubbling warmth right in the center of me. "You're doing the best you can."

That's enough.

I wash my hands in the sink and edge my way out of the door, a wall of sound slamming into me. Music has somehow joined the mix, shrieks and laughter and someone yelling about a quesadilla over it all. It's chaotic but lovely. A soundtrack of community and love.

I barely manage two steps down the dark hallway before I see him. His big body is tipped up against the wall, one shoulder and his head pressed to it. His arms are crossed and his face is shadowed, but I'd recognize the angles of his body anywhere—in the dark, especially.

"Beckett?"

He looks like he's in pain. Shoulders hunched. A deep frown on his handsome face as I get closer. I reach out to him, and my hand hovers over the slope of his shoulder. I'm not sure if he wants to be touched right now or not.

He makes the decision for me, lifting his head and blinking at me blearily. He curls his hand around my wrist and tugs, a quiet "Oof" slipping from my lips as I stumble into him.

His usual smell is tucked under layers of alcohol and fried food, and his skin is warm where my nose finds his neck. He wraps his arms around my back and holds on tight, clinging to me in the narrow hallway at the back of the bar. My hands slip over his shoulders, and I hold on just as tight, confused and concerned.

"You okay?"

I feel a shudder work its way up his spine, a thin tremor in his hands. He rocks his forehead against my shoulder and grunts, mumbling something under his breath. He sways slightly and I tighten my grip.

"S'loud," he finally mumbles, low and rough in my ear. "Needed a break."

I drag my hands up and down his back in a soothing rhythm. He makes a grateful sigh against me.

"That's all right. What can I do?"

"This is good," he says with another squeeze. "Just wanna listen to you breathe for a second."

I make sure to take a noisy, obnoxious breath on my next inhale, and he softens further, the grip of his arms relaxing slightly but his body becoming heavier on mine. I shuffle back until I'm leaning against the wall, Beckett pressed right up to me.

It is loud in here. I hear Gus clamber on the bar top with his megaphone, a short siren wail that has Beckett flinching against me. I smooth my fingers through his hair, and he lets out a deep, rattling breath. Gus announces last call and last round, and the crowd gives a belligerent groan in response.

"Why did you come?" I ask him quietly, nails scratching lightly. He leans harder against me. "You could have said no."

"Nova asked," Beckett supplies quietly. "Didn't want to disappoint anyone."

I asked too. I wonder how much pressure Beckett puts on himself to be what everyone needs all of the time.

"Not right back," Beckett grumbles into my shirt.

"What?"

"You said you'd be right back," he accuses, leaning back until I can see the lines of his face in the light from the bar. He frowns down at me. "You didn't come right back."

"I got caught up. Everyone wanted—"

"You were laughing," he says, cutting me off abruptly. "Dancing." He swallows hard. "You aren't like that with me."

His hands flex at my hips and he takes a step back, leaving me propped up against the wall. I feel the two inches of space between us like a shove to the chest.

"I smile," I start to say. "Beckett, I laugh with you all the time—"

He shakes his head. "It's not the same. Not like when we were in Maine."

He must have had more to drink than I thought. I glance out at the crowded bar and can barely make out the table we were sitting at—a wide collection of glasses haphazardly stacked next to empty food baskets.

"Sorry," he snips, not sounding sorry in the slightest. His voice is grit and gravel and shades of possession, eyes heated to match. He takes a step forward and props his hand by my side. I am flat against the wall again, Beckett everywhere around me. "I forgot we don't talk about it. I forgot I'm supposed to pretend like I don't know exactly what you taste like."

The image that blinks to life is immediate. Beckett on his knees at the edge of the bed, hand splayed low against my belly to hold me still. His nose at my hip and my thighs pressing at his ears, my foot drumming between his shoulder blades.

My entire body shivers, a forceful pulse pounding once right at the base of my throat.

"Beckett," I say, a little bit dazed. His name lingers in the space between us. We don't talk about it, he's right, but I thought that was what he wanted. "How much have you had to drink?"

"Not enough," he says, his eyes intent on my face. " 'Cause I still think about kissing you all the damn time."

I let that confession press into me, the words ringing in my ears despite the loud noise of the bar. I hold his gaze and blink as he stares right back. He sighs, his hand pushing through his hair.

"I need a beer," he tells me.

I loop my fingers around his wrist. "I think you've had enough." I glance toward the end of the hall and the door with EXIT marked in blinking red letters above. "I'm gonna drive us home. You want to say bye to your family?"

He shakes his head, muttering something about texting them

later. He twists his arm out of my grip and straightens with a stumble. I slip my arm around his waist and his hand finds my shoulder, head tipping until his flower crown brushes my forehead.

"Sorry," he says, his bottom lip at the shell of my ear. His voice is still that rough scratch that I like way too much. "I know I'm being an asshole."

I pat his back through the thick material of his flannel. "Let's just go home."

As soon as we step outside the door into the stillness and silence of a mostly abandoned street, Beckett lets out a heaving, gusting sigh. He sounds like he's just finished a run, lungs burning and legs twitching. Aching, blissful relief.

I keep my arm around his waist, guiding us to his truck parked two blocks over, right behind the café. He's already got his box of shortbread cookies in the passenger seat, and he's careful to place them on his lap when he slips into the car.

It takes me a second to orient myself in the driver's seat, everything feeling a little too big. Beckett snickers as my hands hover over the steering wheel, trying to find a position in the seat that doesn't feel like I'm operating a float in the Macy's Thanksgiving Day Parade.

"What?" I ask. I like him like this. Messy hair. Flower crown. A grin that curves his bottom lip beautifully.

"You make a cute face when you're frustrated," he tells me, letting his head drop onto the seat. "Nose scrunches."

I look over at him in the passenger seat, splayed out as much as he can be in the cab of the truck. His knee is tucked up against the window, and his arms are loose, face relaxed. I put the truck into Drive and ease us out of the space, rumbling down the road that will take us to the farm.

It's nothing but the growl of the engine and the wind licking at the windows as we head back, and Beckett's gentle and easy breathing.

I don't know what to say to him, have no idea how to respond to the things he said in the bar.

'Cause I still think about kissing you all the damn time.

I had no idea. I sneak another glance at him from the corner of my eye, my hands flexing on the wheel.

"I don't like noise," Beckett announces as we maneuver our way out of town. "It was loud tonight. At the bar."

"I know."

Beckett doesn't have a television in his house, doesn't listen to music while he putters away in his greenhouse. He flinches when he enters a room and people are talking too loud, and his head tilting slightly to the side. It's like he's trying to muffle the sound without being obvious about it. He shifts in his seat until his shoulder is pressed to the back of it, his elbow on the center console and his chin in his hand.

"I have earmuffs," he tells me, an earnest expression on his face. I glance at him and then to the road. I want this version of him in my memory always. Cornfields flashing by the windows, magnolia leaves in his hair. Eyes hooded but glowing, his knuckles resting under his chin.

Handing me his secrets like he wants me to hold them for him.

Nova's question at the table makes sense now. "Okay."

We drift into silence again. He rearranges himself until he's staring out the window.

"You're not asking me questions," he mumbles after a few minutes, a little bit petulant, his fist on his knee.

"I thought you didn't like my questions." I swipe at the turn signal with the side of my hand even though there isn't another soul for miles. "Plus, you've been drinking. That's an unfair advantage."

He huffs, a grumble under his breath I don't quite catch. The pause drags on and then he quietly says, "I like your questions."

I bite my lip against a smile. "Okay."

"I know you know more words than that."

I do. I do know more words than that. But the truth is, I'm struggling to restrain myself. This adorable, open version he's showing me right now is—it's a lot for me to handle. I want to pull over onto the shoulder of the road and throw the truck into Park. I want to climb over the console and slip onto his lap. I want to fist my hands in his flannel and guide his mouth to mine, kiss him until he's breathless and then drive him home and tuck him into bed.

All this time he's been wanting me, I've been wanting him too.

"We'll talk tomorrow morning, once you sleep this off."

"About what I said at the bar?"

I nod. "Yeah, about what you said at the bar."

'Cause I still think about kissing you all the damn time.

If he still feels that way in the morning, we'll have a few other things to talk about. I follow the lanterns that lead to his cabin back at the farm and pull into his driveway.

"I meant it," he says.

I take a fortifying breath as I slow the truck to a stop in front of his house, yanking with what feels like my entire body weight to throw it into Park. I turn off the engine, and the rumble cuts out, the cab of the truck filled with the muffled sounds of night lingering outside the window. The chirp of the crickets that hide in his gutters. The creak of the weathervane at the peak of his roof. A loose shutter tapping lightly at the siding.

Beckett doesn't look away from me, the light from the moon casting his face in shadow. Like this, he is only strong angles and smooth lines. His nose. His jaw. The slant of his serious brow. His hand shifts on the top of the console, his fingertips barely brushing at my knuckles.

"Evie," he breathes, his deep voice even deeper than usual. I don't think I've ever liked the sound of my name so much. "I really did mean it."

"I know you did," I whisper. Beckett isn't capable of saying something he doesn't mean. It's one of the things I like best about him. I know he's always telling me the truth.

"I like you," he whispers. His gaze slips down to my lips and holds. "I like you so much."

I need to get out of this truck.

He follows me as I stumble from the truck, my knee hitting the banister at the edge of his porch as I clamber my way up. All of a sudden, it feels like I was the one downing beers at the bar tonight, my hands clumsy as I fumble to find the right key.

"I thought about you all the time," Beckett says from right behind me, his chest brushing my back. A single fingertip traces the top edge of my shirt where it sits against my neck. I drop the keys to the porch.

"I *think* about you all the time," he continues. When I tilt my head to look at him, his hands are clenched in fists at his side. That ridiculous flower crown is still in his hair. "Do you think about me?"

"Beckett."

"Do you?"

I scoop the keys from the weathered wooden planks and shoulder my way through the front door, Beckett trailing after me with slow, careful steps. He does his best to hide a sigh as he toes off his shoes and slips the crown from his head. I watch as he places it carefully on a hook, his finger tracing a pale purple petal. He's an emotional drinker, I tell myself. That's all this is. Our best bet is to call it a night and retire to the two very opposite ends of the house. Maybe we can— maybe we can try this conversation again in the morning.

I doubt very much he'll say anything about it. He'll probably pour his coffee and mumble about making an egg scramble for breakfast. Complain about the quality of store-bought spinach and scrape the wooden spoon on the bottom of the pan with quick, agitated movements.

I just—we can't have this conversation right now. Not when alcohol has made him honest. I want him to *want* to be honest.

I pour a glass of water and set it on the counter, press up on my toes to root around the cabinet. A strong arm appears above me, the smooth skin on the inside of Beckett's arm close enough for me to drag my nose against. I see the edge of bright blue—a galaxy peeking out from beneath the sleeve of his shirt.

"What are you doing?" His voice is low behind me, his warm breath fluttering my hair.

"Getting you some ibuprofen," I say to the thin line drawing of Orion above his elbow, a shield held loose in his fist. Instead of a club above his head, he's holding a cluster of flowers—poppies and posies and a big, stunning sunflower. It's so beautifully Beckett, it makes my chest hurt.

"Evelyn."

"Of course I think about you," I say in a rush. Some secret part of me unlocks, unravels, unspools. I've been thinking about Beckett Porter since I left him in a tiny coastal town all those months ago. I swallow and curl my fingers around the small bottle of pills, pull it down, and hold it close to my chest.

When I turn, he's standing close, both hands anchored on the countertop at my sides. I'm tucked between his arms, close enough to brush my lips along the cluster of flowers on his bicep. My knees knock into his and I lift my chin up.

His eyes study my face, knuckles grazing at my hip where his hands flex and hold. "I like having you here," he says roughly. Another confession.

I try to ease the tension that has us stumbling closer together. "You're not tired of me yet?"

"If you're waiting for me to be tired of you, Evie—" He raises his hand and catches a strand of my hair, curls it around his finger and tugs once. There's an answering pulse low in my belly. "—you're gonna be waiting a long time."

I search his eyes to measure how serious he is. "You're very good at hiding all of this."

"Really?" He looks surprised. "Doesn't feel like it. I feel cracked wide open around you."

I know the feeling. I let out a shaky breath. "We should go to bed."

"We should."

Beckett doesn't move an inch. His tone suggests we should go to bed, but that maybe we should do it together. I squeeze the pill bottle in my hand like it's the only thing keeping me pressed up against this counter. This close, I can smell the outdoors on his skin. Spring wind, a crisp, clean bite. It would be so easy to lean up and taste it on his collarbone. I already know the sound he would make. The way his hands would mold to my hips, his pinky finger slipping down into the waist of my jeans.

"We can—" I close my eyes to resist the temptation. Childish? Probably. But I'm way too close to taking advantage of a tipsy Beckett in his kitchen. "We can talk about it in the morning."

I feel his nose at my temple right before he pushes off the counter and takes a step back. I keep my eyes closed and thrust out the pill bottle. Rough fingertips brush over the back of my hand before he grabs it.

"G'night, Evie." It sounds like he's smiling, but I refuse to look.

"'Night, Beckett."

I hear footsteps down the hallway and the quiet click of a door.

I breathe out slowly.

"I like you too," I whisper to the dark kitchen. "So much."

14

BECKETT

I GLANCE AT the closed bedroom door at the end of the hall for the fifteenth time since I stumbled out of my room, a headache pounding at the base of my skull. Less from the drinking, I think, and more from the wanting.

I was so close to kissing Evelyn last night. At the bar, with her sunshine smile as Gus spun her on the dance floor. In the truck, with her hand curled around the gearshift and her hair falling around her face. In the kitchen, with my hips an inch away from hers, pink lighting up her cheeks.

I wanted to do more than kiss her in the kitchen.

"Shit." I pull my hand away from the skillet and pop my thumb into my mouth. I turn off the burner and glare at her door like I can knock the damn thing down with the force of my thoughts.

We need to talk about last night.

She said she thought about me too. But that could mean a million different things. All I know is I can't deal with this feeling that sits like a stone in my chest every time she walks into a room. I can't see her in my flannel shirt—the bottom two buttons undone and the hem tied at her hip—and not feel something about it. We'll talk about it, and we'll clear the air.

Maybe then I'll be able to breathe without wanting her so damn much.

I see the shuffle of feet in the crack beneath her door.

"Evie!" I bark, impatient. I'm making a scramble, goddamn it. She doesn't need to hide in her room all morning. We've already done the awkward shit together. We don't need to do it again. "I made breakfast!"

The door swings open and she appears, a scowl scrunching her nose. My gaze sweeps down from her shoulders to her long, long legs, and my entire body tightens. She's wearing the damn knee socks again, a creamy white against her dark skin.

"You don't need to yell about it."

And she doesn't need to be temptation incarnate, but we are where we are.

I turn with a grunt and push the eggs around in the pan in an effort to keep my hands occupied. She makes me feel things I have no business feeling. Out of control half the time. Out of my mind the other half. I want to do a thousand different things, starting with my hands in her hair and my mouth on her neck—everything I thought about doing last night when it was just us and the moonlight.

I'm clinging to the rope of my restraint, and I can feel the ends starting to fray. Every look, every touch, every smile she gives me—it unravels a bit more.

"Would you like some breakfast?" I try again, a conscious effort to soften my voice into something gentle. It still sounds like a demand instead of an offer though, and Evelyn snorts a laugh.

"Did you mean what you said last night?" Right to the point, then.

I continue to poke listlessly at the eggs. The edges are starting to brown. I flick off the stovetop and rest the wooden spoon across the pan.

I like you so much.

"I did."

I've thought about her every day since that morning I woke up alone, a storm thundering in from the east, thick gray clouds hanging low over the water. I've thought about the exact sound she makes when my body is over hers, the way her breath hitches and then releases, a breathy sigh around my name. I've thought about her laugh and her smile—prettier than all the wildflowers in the meadow and every star in the sky.

I feel a deep exhale against the cotton of my T-shirt, Evelyn standing at my back. "Are you still drunk?"

I huff a laugh and shake my head. "No."

I wasn't that drunk to begin with. Just loose enough for some of the desire rattling around inside me to slip through. Standing in this kitchen last night, I had swayed right into her space like I've been wanting to. My arms on either side of her hips, my nose at her neck. I wanted to kiss her more than anything. Almost did too.

"Was it the alcohol?"

"That's not how that shit works." Alcohol doesn't make things up, it just pries them loose.

I glance at her over my arm. She's standing close, her feet nudging the back of mine. I could drop my head and press a kiss to her temple if I wanted, prop her up on the countertop and make the rest of this breakfast with her wrapped around me. It's a tempting thought.

She considers me with curious eyes. I get the impression she's looking right inside to the heart of me. "Were you teasing me?"

"Teasing you about what?" I watch her hand as she catches the bottom edge of my T-shirt with two fingers. She rubs the material, considering.

"I like you too, Beckett." She pulls on my shirt until I'm facing her, her hands at my sides. She raps her knuckles against my ribs and my whole body jolts. "You haven't noticed?"

"Too busy liking you back to notice, I guess," I reply faintly, watching the shape of her bottom lip curve into a smile. All of the versions of Evelyn I've gotten to know flicker through my mind like the frames of a filmstrip. Sitting at the bar with her hand on my thigh. Tangled up in bed, bare skin and dark eyes. Laughing across the bakehouse with a plate between us. Curled up in the chair on my back porch, her chin on her knee. Out in the fields making everyone around her glow.

Standing here like this with her face tipped toward mine.

I like every version a little bit more.

Her hands find my arms, fingers tracing over ink. She lingers over a single white blossom, a sensitive spot on the inside of my elbow.

"Okay," she says with a decisive nod.

"Okay, what?"

She ignores my question. Instead, she curls her hand around my neck, tugs me down, and kisses me.

The first time I kissed Evie was under a broken light in a dingy bar, the dull orange glow flickering on and off and on again. I could see it behind my eyes as our mouths moved together, a drumbeat of desire I kept pace with. I feel like I've unpacked the memory of that kiss enough over the last several months for the edges to run smooth, like stones at the bottom of a riverbed. It's nothing but hazy flashes of sensation. Fingertips under my ear. Her cheek brushing mine. The slow, wet slide of heat as I urged her chin down and kissed her more deeply.

Now, here in the bright light of my kitchen, with the window cracked half an inch and coffee brewing in the pot, I feel that memory crack right down the middle.

There's nothing hazy about this kiss.

No sweet introduction. No gentle relearning. Evie scratches her nails up into my hair and tugs, a demand in the way her mouth works at mine. She kisses me like she's hungry for it, like she's been dreaming of me the same way I've been dreaming about her. I smooth both of my hands over her hips and grip tight.

"There you are." She breathes into my mouth. I squeeze again and she lets out a husky chuckle.

"I'm right here," I tell her. I've always been right here. Waiting, it feels like, for Evie to show up and kiss me in the middle of my kitchen. Our kiss tilts into something hotter, wetter, slower in the span of a single stuttered heartbeat. Evie's hands turn demanding as they grip the front of my shirt, strong fistfuls of soft material between her fingers as she pushes me up against the refrigerator. The appliance at my back shudders with the impact, but I'm too occupied with the slide of her tongue along mine, too focused on feeling the soft skin of her back beneath my palms.

I dig my thumb into one of the dimples just above her ass as I lick into her mouth, and she makes my favorite sound—a throaty whimper. I press harder and she pulls her mouth from mine, drops her head against my collarbone and presses that sound into my skin.

I move my hands up her back, impatient as I map the arch of her spine. I drag my hand back and forth over the band of her bra and slip my fingers beneath, snapping it once as I release the elastic against her skin. She nips at my jaw in retribution.

"Be nice," she tells me.

"I can be nice." As a matter of fact, I can think of several nice things I want to do right this second. Her shirt gathers at my wrists as I tuck my fingers under the straps of her bra again, following the line over her shoulders. I curl my hands there and tug, watching her sway farther into me.

"Oh?" Evie's eyes are dark with desire, her mouth kiss-bitten. "Would you like to show me?"

It's like our bodies are frantic to make up for lost time, our mouths diving together as I drag my knuckles across her collarbones, down over the swell of her breasts. I linger there in the space above, her chest heaving, my thumbs tracing where skin meets fabric.

"Still a tease," she says with a nip to my bottom lip. Her nails dig half-moons into my chest through my shirt.

"Still impatient," I reply, caught between wanting to laugh and falling to my knees. Reacquaint myself with every square inch of her.

"I swear to god, if you don't touch me, I'll—"

She doesn't finish her sentence. I cup her in my hands and squeeze, my thumbs dragging slow and sure against the cotton of her bra. I feel it when her breath stutters, a quick rise and fall beneath my touch. I want bare skin. I want more of those sounds. I grip the center of her bra and yank the material down until it's twisted underneath her breasts, watching my hands grip and smooth and pluck beneath her shirt.

"You'll what?" I ask.

"I'll be"—her eyelashes flutter, a half smile curling her lips—"I'll be so mad."

"Hm."

She turns her face and catches my mouth again, my hands working under her shirt. I rub my thumbs across her nipples until she makes the panting sound I like best, her hands gripping at my jaw in silent demand. I wrap one arm low around her waist and hitch her closer. I want her body pressed to mine, her softness everywhere I'm hard. Her nails scratch into my beard and I stumble forward, backing her into the table. I vaguely notice my coffee mug tip over the edge and land on the rug with a muted *thunk*. I'll look at that stain every day and remember exactly this. Evelyn gasping against my lips, her knee hitching high on my hip.

I drop my forehead to her shoulder and brush a kiss there, my hand slipping from her breast to her hip. I squeeze once and try to get myself under control. "We should stop," I mumble. "Talk."

This has always been the easy part—letting the sparks between us catch and burn. It's everything else we need to sort out. I like her body, but I like everything else more. And I don't want her to think this is all I want.

She nods, hands slipping beneath my shirt to scratch at my back. I arch into her and trap her hips with mine, flattening her to the table. "Yeah," she says.

I nose at the collar of her shirt until I can reach the skin where her shoulder meets her neck and suck a lingering kiss there. She's sweet with a touch of salt I know will stay on my tongue for days. I drag my face down her chest until I can catch her nipple between my teeth through the fabric of her shirt.

I can't stop touching her, tasting her.

"Excellent talking." Evelyn breathes around a laugh, her hand at the back of my head, holding me to her. "Very best talk I've ever had."

I drop my forehead between her breasts and press a kiss there. "I want to take you out."

"Okay," she pants, pulling on the hem of my shirt until I relent and tug it over my head. I immediately catch her lips in a kiss again, my hands at her thighs. I urge her up until she's sitting on the table-top, legs wide, her foot curling around my knee. My fingers find the ends of those damn socks, and I trace the thick cotton, a groan in the back of my throat.

"We'll get dinner," I say against her mouth. Her hands squeeze my ass and I thrust against her once. Her head drops back, long dark hair gliding over the tabletop like spilled ink. Christ, but she makes me crazy. Scrambles all my plans until I'm mindless with her. I roll my hips into her and lower my head to watch the way we move to-gether. "I'll bring you flowers."

"Flowers, huh?"

She chases my touch, her hips circling just right. I hum and nod. "Pretty ones. It'll be a date."

Her hands lose their grip on my body, and she drops back to the tabletop with a happy sigh. The heat between us shifts and settles into something softer. I let my fingers play at the outside of her thighs, trace the thin white scar I haven't forgotten. She kicks her feet back and forth and cocks her head to the side, looking at me through half-lidded eyes. She smiles something sweet with her ruby red lips—a little bit of beard burn on her chin and neck.

"I like you, Evie." I straighten her shirt and place a single chaste kiss to the tip of her nose. My heart begins a gallop in my chest. "I like you a lot."

Her smile lights up every damn corner of this room. The shadowed parts of me too, and all the pieces I keep to myself.

"I like you too," she tells me. She kicks me lightly and chews on her bottom lip. "Now put your shirt on, or we'll have sex on this table."

I collapse overtop of her with a groan. She combs her fingers through my hair with a laugh, tugging once at the ends.

"You say that like it's a bad thing," I grumble. I can already picture it. The way the legs of the table would creak and groan. Our clothes moved just enough for friction and heat and blissful relief. I try to adjust myself as delicately as possible, but I still hear her snicker.

"I want that date," she tells me, voice soft. A little bit dreamy. "Maybe this is our do-over. A chance to do things differently."

There's simple honesty there, a thin thread of hope from her heart to mine. I reach for her hand and tangle our fingers together. I'm pretty sure I'd do things any which way with Evelyn, as long as we ended up like this. My chin resting on her chest and a smile on her pretty face.

"Yeah?"

She nods. "Yeah."

15

EVELYN

NOT MUCH CHANGES after our furious make-out in the kitchen.

Despite slamming his body against a kitchen appliance and kissing him like I've been thinking about nothing else, we continue to act as if nothing has changed. We have dinner together on the porch every night. He leaves me notes on the kitchen counter. I steal his socks. We exchange long heated stares over the rims of our coffee mugs in the morning, a perfectly polite three feet of distance between us.

It is both wonderful and exceedingly annoying.

I like Beckett. I like his half smiles and the way his voice deepens and scratches early in the morning, the gentle brush of his fingertips across my shoulder as I slip past him in the kitchen. I like the calendar he keeps taped to the side of his fridge, his family's important dates scribbled in red. I like that he's always taking care of everyone around him, from the cats to his sisters to the pastries Barney demands from atop the tractor.

I like the way he looks at me when he thinks I'm not paying attention. The softness he tries to hide.

I'm looking forward to our date, whenever he decides to follow through on that particular promise.

I'm also looking forward to throwing him down on the nearest flat surface and having my way with him.

I've caught him staring at the kitchen table a couple of times since that morning, his thumb at his bottom lip and a look of deep concentration on his serious face. I've caught myself staring at it too.

My restraint is hanging on by a thread, bolstered only by Beckett's extended time in the greenhouse. He disappears there every free moment he has, mumbling something about making space and clearing clutter. Spring cleaning, he says.

Nothing to do with a duck.

But I've seen four packages arrive this week, and I know the man isn't buying duck food for himself. The smallest box contained a tiny little golfer's hat with a bright red pouf on top that Beckett snatched away as soon as he saw me with it, his cheeks a furious shade of pink.

By Wednesday, I'm a tangled-up mess of tension. I sit at the kitchen table with my legs folded beneath me, my laptop open but my gaze fixed firmly out the window. I catch a glimpse of him every now and again through the fogged glass of the greenhouse, his tall form bowed over something, his hand braced flat on the window, fingers spread wide. I have to turn away and busy myself with emails, lose myself in work in an effort to forget how that hand felt on my skin. How the sun lit up every single line and ridge of his body, his shirt thrown to some corner of the kitchen. The cut of his hips and the trail of hair below his belly button, the thick press of him against the front of his flannel pants.

I put my head down briefly over my computer and tap it there twice.

Beckett is a complication in my plan. My wishy-washy plan that doesn't have a timeline or a clear end point. It would be easier if all I wanted was his body—to fall into bed with him and bury my confusion with the things he makes me feel. But I don't. I want late nights on his back porch and stories about the stars. I want dirt on my hands and that smile on his face, the quiet one that inches up in increments.

Last night he found me on the back porch, tucked in my chair with a blanket wrapped around my shoulders. I had been in a foul mood, annoyed with myself and my inability to just—figure this out. Get it together. Be better. He had watched me quietly with his shoulder propped against the door and asked, "Did you find your happy today?"

I ground my teeth and shook my head. A quick jerk. "No."

He had hummed once, head tilting to look out over the fields. "You want a hug?"

And that had been its own sort of magic, hadn't it? He hadn't tried to fix it. Just . . . asked if he could hold me through it.

I nodded and he wordlessly collapsed in the seat next to me, patting his thigh once. I shuffled over to him and curled up in his arms, my head nestled under his chin, his palm a heavy weight against my back, sweeping from my shoulders to my hip. A gentle pressure. A quiet affirmation.

My job means I travel all the time. This trip to Inglewild is the longest I've stayed in one place since I turned twenty. I've always had an itch under my skin to explore. It still flares to life now and again, but these days, it's tinged with exhaustion. More muscle memory than any sort of compulsion propelling me forward. I don't want to go.

I want to stay.

I direct my attention to my laptop and scan my email for the note from Josie. She sent over the information for Theo yesterday, the guy from the small business group who's been reaching out. I compose a quick message to him about connecting and hit Send, the back door creaking open as I finish.

I glance up at Beckett, dirt covering his hands and in a smudge above his left eyebrow.

"How are the plants today?"

"They're fine." He glances down at his dirty hands and then back at me. There's consideration there, like the only thing keeping him from throwing me onto the table I'm sitting at is the topsoil on his palms. I curl my hands into fists. "Can you be ready to go in an hour?"

"Ready to go?"

He nods. "Yeah. Ready to go out."

I stare at him and wait for an explanation. He doesn't give me one. "Out where, Beckett?"

"On our date," he tells me. A smile starts in his eyes. "You still want to?"

I nod. I absolutely want to. I was starting to think he had forgotten about it. That maybe it was just something he had said in the heat of the moment.

I push back from the kitchen table and stand. "Where are we going?"

His smile spreads until he's biting his bottom lip against the force of it. "Not very far."

"ARE YOU WARM enough?" Beckett asks as we trudge our way through the fields an hour later.

I huff and puff my way up the hill, the second sweatshirt Beckett pulled over my head before we left the house making it difficult to move. I give his T-shirt a pointed look, my lips pressed in a thin line.

"Yes, I'm warm enough." I'm too warm, but every time I try to take this damn sweatshirt off, Beckett looks like he wants to wrestle me right back into it. Which could be fun, but I'd much rather he wrestle me out of it.

He had appeared at my bedroom door at six on the dot with a large greasy paper bag clutched in his hand and a backpack slung over his shoulder. A single perfect white peony held between thumb and forefinger.

"Told you I'd bring you flowers," he said.

I toy with the stem of it now as we wander our way through the fields, the branches of the pine trees catching on my sleeves. It's warmer tonight, the first real spring evening we've had since I arrived. The dark sky blinks to life above us, the moon beginning to rise over the trees. I can see the glow of it, stars scattered behind.

"Not much farther," Beckett tells me.

It better not be. I'm being tortured by the way he looks in those jeans. The crisp white of his T-shirt against his tanned skin.

I bump his shoulder with mine.

"Do you take all the pretty girls out in the fields late at night?"

"Nah." He shakes his head and bumps me back. "Just you."

A flicker of warmth lights in my chest as he slows to a stop at the edge of a field. A clearing rolls out from beneath our boots to the edge of the woods. He looks at me from the corner of his eye and slips the backpack from his shoulder.

"Do you know where we are?"

I spin on my heel slowly, trying to remember. Two giant oak trees overlook both sides of the entrance to the clearing, towering like guards to the forest beyond. I have a hazy memory of standing between them last fall with my arms outstretched, trying to touch both at the same time. Big rust orange leaves almost the size of my hand drifting down around me.

"The trees," I say. "I remember them."

He nods and pulls a blanket from his backpack, letting the edges fly out with one flick of his wrist. It settles on the grass with a quiet *swish*. A bottle of wine comes next, and he uses it to anchor the corner. Two "glasses," one of them my jam jar. The other a chipped coffee mug.

"This is very impressive," I say. He gives me a skeptical glance, but I mean it. The last date I went on was close to a year ago, and the guy took me to a shooting range where his ex still worked. Needless to say, there wasn't a second date.

"You haven't even seen the best part yet."

"I've already seen your dick, Beckett."

He barks out a surprised laugh, shaking his head. In the light of the moon, I can barely make out the little lines that appear next to his eyes with his grin. He grabs the greasy bag by his feet and holds it out to me, letting me peek inside. Cheeseburgers from the café, two over-flowing cups of crispy French fries that are somehow still hot. I moan and reach for one, but he snaps the bag shut before I can, placing it by his feet.

"Hold on a second."

"But . . . French fries."

"They'll still be there when we get back." He starts walking back-ward, closer to the edge of the woods where the twin trees stand. "C'mere."

I laugh. "*C'mere*, what?" But still I follow after him. The moon lights up the constellations tattooed on his skin, the sky dipping down to twist around his arms.

"You haven't had your happy today," he tells me, hands already reaching, stars on his skin and in his eyes and in the sky above.

My heart flip-flops in my chest. "And you're gonna give it to me, huh?"

"Yeah." He smiles, as full and bright as that damn moon. "I'm gonna give it to you."

He's wrong though. I have had my happy today. I'm practically drowning in it—in simple, quiet joy. The warm comfort of a perfect moment with a good man.

I stop right in front of him and he stares down at me. I trace the lines of his face, and I feel like one of those meteors he loves so much. Tearing through the atmosphere, a giant ball of light.

"The last time you were here—" He cups my face with both of his hands and presses a gentle kiss to the tip of my nose, the space between my eyes. Everything in me shivers and melts, and my hands grasp at his elbows. "The last time you were here, I wanted to kiss you under this tree."

"You hid it well," I murmur as I follow his retreat, silently beg-ging for more.

"Nah," he says, his voice a rasp. "You just weren't looking close enough."

And then he kisses me.

And he shows me everything I missed.

"AND THAT ONE?"

I point at a bright cluster of stars with my French fry, my boot knocking his on the blanket. I shift my head on his shoulder, and he follows the direction of my hand, nose brushing my hair briefly as he angles to get a look.

"Cetus," he says around a mouthful of burger. He swallows and tosses the wrapper toward his bag, settling on his elbows with a happy sigh. I follow after him when he tugs once at my belt loop, my back against his chest. "The sea monster. Poseidon sent him to ravage some coastal town when Cassiopeia said she was more beautiful than the sea nymphs."

"That sounds petty."

He hums in agreement and curls his hand around my wrist. He guides my hand slightly to the right so we're both pointing at another cluster of stars. "Ares is right there."

His thumb drags a lingering half circle against my pulse point, and I feel it like a touch between my legs. I shift on the blanket and wiggle closer, my head under his chin. "And that one?"

"That's an airplane, honey."

A laugh slips out of me and I peek up at him. Relaxed, his face tilted toward the sky, a smile curling at the very edges of his mouth. He's loose out here in the fields in a way he isn't anywhere else.

"This is a good date," I tell him quietly. The best I've ever had. "Thanks for bringing me out here."

"Thanks for coming out here." He looks down at me and plucks at the cuff of my sweatshirt. "Properly dressed."

I glance down at the doubled-up material stretched awkwardly across my chest. "Overly dressed, I think."

He makes a sound against me, a deep rumble low in his chest that I feel on my back. His hand slips from my wrist to my elbow, up over my shoulder. Two fingers tuck into the collar and trace along my bare collarbone. My whole body shivers.

"Yeah?" he asks, voice rough.

He catches the edge of my ear between his teeth, and I grin. His first concession to the heat banked between us. I remember how much he liked that the last time we were together—his teeth against my skin, praise whispered with every rough scratch.

I nod. "Mm-hmm."

I shift and shimmy until I can tuck my arms through the sleeves, the movement clumsy. I laugh as the material gets caught around my head, two big hands grabbing and pulling until I can see the field and the sky and the trees again. Beckett looking at me like I hung the damn moon myself.

It's so different from the last time we were together. Different but exactly the same. He still looks at me with a ferocious heat—careful eyes mapping out exactly what he wants to do and where. What touch to give me first. But there's wonder too. Like he can't quite believe I'm here with him, in this place. Affection and amusement and a bubbling warmth deep in my chest.

He blows out a breath and scrubs his palm over the back of his head, watching as I lean back and prop myself up on both hands. I don't think he meant it as a grand seduction, but it feels like one now, those sweatshirts sitting in a clump by his hip. I'm left in nothing but jeans and the threadbare T-shirt I pulled on before we left the house, the wide collar slipping over one shoulder. He catalogs the bare skin it reveals with heavy eyes, his tongue sweeping across his bottom lip when I shift slightly and the shirt droops a little more.

"I want you," I tell him, finally voicing the thought that has been running circles in my head since I first saw him step off the curb in the middle of town. Since I saw him step through the doorway of a dive bar. I don't think I've ever stopped wanting Beckett, not really. I tiptoe my fingers up the delicate ink on his wrist and curl my hand around his forearm. Pull once. "And I think you want me too."

His eyes snap up from where they were burning a path across my bra strap and he gives me that half smile again, somehow better than the full grin that spills out of him like starlight. This smile feels like mine and mine alone. He gives in to my tugging and shifts up to his knees.

"Of course I do," he says, sure and direct, impossibly Beckett. He says it like it's something he's been thinking about too. Maybe since he saw me standing with my hip against a rental car. Maybe since he saw me sitting at a bar with a glass of tequila in front of me. "Wanting you has never been a question."

He maneuvers in front of me until he can grip my ankle, caressing it once with his thumb as he opens my legs wide, making enough space for him to move in between. We're only touching at that one place, his hand on my leg, and already I feel it everywhere. In the small of my back and the tips of my breasts, the arch of my neck and the space between my legs.

His hand squeezes me gently and his palm moves up. The calluses on his hands catch on the rough material of my jeans, a stilted movement that's better in its honesty. Another squeeze at my thigh, thumb dragging along the inseam above my knee. He hesitates there briefly, considering, and then reaches for my hip.

"If we do this again, Evie, there's no running." His eyes are serious, his body held perfectly still between my open legs. "I don't want to wake up alone."

I grip his shirt in my fists, regret slicing across my chest. For the way I left him all those months ago and for the ways I've left him since. I lean up and brush a kiss across his bottom lip. An apology, but a promise too. "You won't."

"All right," he says, and his eyes flash darker, his tongue appearing briefly at a corner of his mouth. His hands flex at my sides, fingertips pressing and guiding. "Lie back, then."

16

EVELYN

I SHAKE MY head and urge Beckett back until he falls with a grunt, my knees clambering up and over to hug his hips. I cup his jaw in my hands as he gazes at me and trace my fingers once over the roughness of his stubble.

"I want you to see the stars," I tell him. Something behind his eyes flares and burns bright. Brighter than anything in the sky. My own private supernova.

He guides me closer to him with his hand at the small of my back and trails small biting kisses up the line of my neck. He sucks hard at a spot just beneath my jaw and then leans back, lingering there with his lips barely brushing mine.

"I'll only be looking at you."

His mouth on mine sends shivers cascading down my arms, both twined tight around his neck as our lips meet and press. We lean back in the same breath and readjust. Something deeper, hotter. He kisses me like he's telling me a thousand secrets, each one something different. *I missed you*, his first kiss says—soft and lingering on my bottom lip. *You're so pretty*, says the next—a sweet, teasing brush. *I want you*, says the last one—a hungry, grasping thing as he licks into my mouth and holds my face against his. *So fucking bad*—his fingertips sinking into my hair.

His hand fists and pulls, a slight hint of roughness that earns a desperate sound low in my throat. I don't think I've ever wanted someone so much. Not even at the bar that first time. I roll my hips down onto his and he pulls his mouth away to suck in a lungful of air. I like that he hasn't stopped me—that he hasn't asked if this is something I want. He can feel it vibrating through me, same as him. Perfectly in tune. I circle my hips again and he exhales a shaky laugh.

"You feel better than I remember," he says.

I grin. "You haven't even seen the best part yet."

He smiles up at me, his grin a little wild. I take back what I thought about his half smiles. This is the one I want to keep. "I've already seen your tits, Evie."

A laugh bursts out of me, muffled by a rough kiss against my lips. It's clumsy, both of us smiling into it. I want him to ask me here, like this. That same question he asks every evening while we sit on his back porch, the sun dipping low in front of us.

Did you find your happy today?

Yes, I would tell him. *I found it right here. With you. Like this.*

I reach for the hem of my shirt and I pull it over my head. His hands immediately slip up my belly, thumbs rubbing in a firm sweep below my breasts. I let my head drop, my hair tickling at the small of my back. It feels so good everywhere he touches. I only want more.

"You cold?"

I shake my head and reach for the clasp of my bra. "Not with your hands on me."

His eyes flare. He likes that answer. The material of my bra falls away, and I'm bare skin in the moonlight. I feel Beckett's deep exhale brush the valley of my breasts, the tip of his nose following after. Big hands bracket my hips and slide up my back—a delicious pressure on both sides of my spine. He curls his hands around my ribs and tugs me closer. "What about my mouth?"

I comb my fingers through his hair and twist, urging him forward. He chuckles at my wordless response and nuzzles into me, pressing deep, sucking kisses below my collarbone and at the top of my ribs. His hands squeeze, and he urges me farther back, holding me suspended at exactly the right angle for his kisses. He barely grazes my chest and instead skips to my shoulder, the line of my neck. Everywhere but where I want them most. I arch my back, tugging at his hair impatiently.

"Beckett," I say on a gasp, his stubble perfectly rough against my chest. He drags his jaw against me and I grind my hips down. One hand leaves my back to cup my breast, fingers pinching at my nipple. I make an incoherent sound and pull at his hair again, demanding relief.

"Just wanted you to get bossy again," he teases, mouth busy at my throat. He dips his tongue there as his fingers pinch and my whole body shivers.

"You could have just asked."

"This is better."

He finally puts his mouth to my breast, and I sigh his name, my hands held tight to the back of his head. He feels so good. Warm and wet and just the right amount of rough. He nips with his teeth, and the stars shake in the sky.

I hate that I decided to wear jeans tonight. I can feel him thick and hard against me, but the friction is dulled by our layers, every roll of our bodies against each other urging my frustration higher. I want to feel his bare skin beneath me, satisfy the ache low in my belly. I feel itchy with need, thrumming with it.

He smooths his palm down my bare back. "Relax," he whispers under my ear. "I'm gonna take care of you."

"You relax," I grumble, frustrated by his half touches. I'm too keyed up for a drawn-out tease. I feel like it's been weeks of foreplay between us. I feel every lingering glance, every restrained touch. I want him hard and fast and filling up every inch of me until I can barely breathe with the pressure of it. He gently lays me on the blanket, and my hair spreads around me, my knees still hugging his hips as I fall flat. I tug on his belt loops with a frown. He thumbs at the edge of my lips with a smile.

"What's this face for?"

"You're teasing me."

"I'm not." He shakes his head and rolls his hips against me, a deep, dirty grind that has his eyelashes fluttering against his cheeks. A lock of hair falls over his forehead, and I press it back with the palm of my hand. A man losing his grip, finally. "I'm trying to go slow," he grits out.

"Also defined as teasing."

He huffs a laugh and leans down until he can lick a hot stripe between my breasts. He moves his head to the left and catches the tip between his teeth, follows it with a deep, sucking pull that has me arching up off the blanket.

"I'm just trying to hold myself together," he says into my skin, his hands batting mine away from his jeans. He quickly finds the button of mine instead, slipping it free and tugging at the zipper, his movements quick and agitated. He jerks the stubborn material down my legs with a grunt—only halfway down before he gives up completely, distracted by the sight of plain white cotton. He groans and tightens his grip on my thighs.

"I had a plan," he says, eyes still fixed on the line of unimpressive cotton at my hips. I wiggle under his stare.

"Oh? Feel free to share it."

"I was going to make you come and then take you home," he says in a low voice, his eyes blazing a path up my body. He fixes me with a hungry look and flexes his hands again. "But I don't think I can."

"You can't make me come?"

He releases my thigh to smack lightly at my ass. Goose bumps erupt on every square inch of my body.

"You know I can, honey."

I feel a sharp pull low in my belly—a string between his words and the desire running hot through my blood. "Did you come up with a new plan?"

He considers, gaze lingering on the two inches of soft, smooth skin between my belly button and the edge of my underwear. I've had his mouth there before, while I was propped up against the edge of a dresser with my hands in his hair. I want that again. I want a million other things too.

"Up," he commands, tapping once at my bare hip. When I lever my body up, he curls his hands in my jeans and tugs, pulling them off with three rough jerks. I'm in nothing but a sensible pair of white cotton briefs while he's still fully dressed, out in the middle of a grove of trees in the dark of night. It has me shivering beneath him, hands clenching in his shirt.

I clutch at it. "Off."

He reaches between his shoulder blades with one hand and pulls it over his head, biceps flexing as he throws it to the blanket. He collapses on top of me, his mouth on mine, his body a delicious, warm pressure holding me down, down, down into the ground. I curl my legs around his hips and lock my ankles at the small of his back, denim rough against the insides of my thighs. His zipper bites into my skin and I flex my legs higher, his chest pressed to my breasts and his inked arms holding me tight. I focus entirely on him—the heat of his body and the hollow ache between my legs.

"Tell me you brought a condom," I plead into his mouth, his thumb and forefinger plucking at my nipple. He shakes his head with a muffled sound of frustration, pushing up on his arms to meet my gaze. He strains there for a second, distracted, before he dips down to brush a kiss on my lips. He lingers and groans, another stolen kiss when I squeeze his hips tighter.

"No," he says, regret etched into every line of his face. I let my hands map the strong line of his shoulders, his broad chest, the muscles stacked down his abdomen. His body is formed by work, colored by the sun and the earth. I've already seen every piece of him, but I find new things to discover. The cluster of freckles at the top of his ribs. The thin line of contrast where tanned skin meets pale, creamy white. The trail of hair that leads down his stomach, under the hem of the jeans riding low on his hips.

"Okay, that's okay," I babble. We don't need a condom. There are plenty of other things we can do. My mind unrolls a list a mile long, and the ache within me pulls deeper. Sharper.

I scratch my nails over his hips and reach for the button of his jeans, sliding my hand beneath when it gives. My knuckles brush warm skin and I wrap my hand around the hard length of him. He closes his eyes, teeth clenched. "I didn't think—" He looks down at me, bewildered and enraptured. Disheveled and delighted. All of my favorite things. "I wasn't expecting this."

"You literally just told me you had a plan." I pump my hand once and he makes a bitten-off groaning sound. I immediately want to hear it again. "You weren't expecting me naked on this blanket?"

He shakes his head and rolls his hips into my touch.

"Do you remember the night we met?"

I stroke him again, and he thrusts into my grip harder, fucking into my hand with another pained, desperate sound from between his teeth. I like that sound so much I do it again. And then again, my thumb swiping at what I can reach.

"You almost fucked me in the back hall of the bar, Beckett." I had wanted him to. Practically begged him for exactly that, if I remember correctly.

His hand catches my wrist and he holds me still, eyes blazing. "You first," he says. His fingers graze the curve of my hip, slide under the waistband of my underwear and squeeze at the bare skin of my ass.

I shake my head and smile at him, my hand still trapped in his pants. I need him so badly I almost hurt with it. All of my ideas scatter and I know what I want. I want us, together. "I'm tested regularly," I tell him. "On birth control. If you wanted—"

His mouth drops to mine in a kiss, softer than it should be with my body bare beneath him and an invitation on the table. He grips my chin and licks into my mouth with a gentle caress, his thumb tracing my jaw to the tender skin below my ear. He rubs there once, a slow swipe.

"I was tested last month," he manages when he pulls away, his palm flat against my neck. He slips it down slightly until it's pressed right in the center of my chest. I loop my hand around his wrist and squeeze. "There hasn't been anyone since you."

My heart thumps an uneven beat beneath the palm of his hand. "Same for me," I confess. I offer him a little bit more. "I haven't wanted anyone else."

Not even close. Not even tempted. Just the memory of Beckett had been more than enough. The ghost of his hands on my skin.

"Is this okay?" I ask, my fingertips tracing back and forth across his skin.

He nods, eyes bright, and his hand slips down my body to join the other, toying with the sides of my underwear. He slips his thumbs beneath and snaps the fabric once, enough to have my hips jump beneath him. He grits out a laugh, and I squeeze with my hand still in his pants.

He stops laughing real quick.

Hands grab and pull, a rush to get the relief we're both craving. He fumbles with his jeans while I try to help, an attempt to kick them off without moving from overtop me.

"If you just—" I pull hard at the material.

"If I what?" He shimmies his hips, and the motion presses his cock right against me. I gasp and edge my legs wider. "You're not helping. You're making it harder."

I snicker. "I'm making something harder."

"Evie," he grunts, still trying to pull his jeans over his hips, distracted as I roll mine beneath him. He pins me down to the blanket with his hand at my hip, palm squeezing tight. "Be good."

I release a slow breath, a smile still on my lips. I'm having trouble keeping still. I press my fingertips over his jaw and rub my palm down his neck. His skin is warm beneath my touch, flushed pink in the low light. "I feel like I've been waiting for you forever," I confess.

His face softens. "I know, honey."

Ignoring the jeans still trapped around his thighs, his hand slips lower, two fingers gliding right where I need him the most. After all the teasing, his firm touch has me halfway there already. He circles them once and I choke out his name. He shifts his hand, presses again, and my nails dig half-moons into his back.

"Fuck, you feel good," he grinds out. I forgot how deep his voice gets when we're doing this. How desperate he sounds.

I nod and grab at his arms, palms smacking lightly at the ink on his skin, trying to urge him closer. His thumb slips beneath cotton, and we both groan when he feels how wet I am.

"Now," I demand. "Right now, please."

He doesn't bother slipping my underwear from my hips, just twists his thumb in the material and pulls it to the side, lining himself up with his other hand and pushing deep. One heavy thrust, all the way in. My legs scramble at his hips and he drops his forehead to my neck, a groan slipping from his chest to mine. I feel deliciously full, overwhelmed in the best possible way.

My memory is nothing compared to the reality of him. Hands flexing at my thighs, forehead rocking against my neck, stubble scraping at my skin. He pulls back, rolls his hips, and pushes inside. A smooth, easy rhythm that I match. He urges his body into me, again and again, pushing me up the blanket with every thrust until my shoulder blades brush cold grass.

"Evelyn," he says into my neck. "Evie. Fuck."

"S'good," I slur on a laugh, champagne bubbles in my chest. He leans up on his knees and tucks a palm to the small of my back, guiding my hips tighter against him. Everything grinds just right, and I'm at the very edge already, teetering.

"I've thought about this," he says, a breathless confession. His hands curl around my hips and hold tight, lifting me up another inch. He looks beautiful like this. A little bit wild, a bead of sweat working its way down his neck. His gaze brushes all the places we're touching and some of the places we're not—my thighs, my hips, the bounce of my bare breasts and the curve of my cheek. "Every single day, I've thought about this. You."

My heart flutters, and I feel like I've got starlight slipping under my skin, hearing he's thought about me just as much as I've thought about him.

"Come on," he says, eyes locking on mine. I watch his face as he drags his hand over the swell of my hip and spreads his fingers wide. His thumb traces down my belly, and then he presses it between my legs. He holds it there—a simple, heavy pressure. Everything in me pulls tighter. A hiccuping breath slips out of me and a cocky grin hitches up the side of his mouth. "Give it to me."

I grin at him and chase his touch, placing my hand over his to move him just the way I like. "Earn it."

His laugh is a rough thing, breathless with the way he's still moving against me. He collapses on one arm and tangles his free hand in my hair. He rolls his hips harder, staying deep.

"I'll take whatever you've got," he tells me. His fingers curl into a fist in my hair, and he kisses me like he doesn't want to do anything else ever again.

Just this.

Me and him.

It sneaks up on me, the bright burst of pleasure. It licks up my spine and I arch beneath him, a laugh caught in the back of my throat. I've never felt like this. Not ever. Stardust, it feels like, right in the center of my chest.

He keeps moving through it—frantic and without his smooth control—and I'm too occupied with the fuzzy lightness in my limbs to do anything but hold on as he chases his pleasure. He shudders and freezes against me, hands grasping, mouth working soundlessly at my neck. Everything settles in soft waves of pulsing warmth, my body perfectly, deliciously worn out.

I blink up at the sky above me, the tree branches dancing in the light breeze. I smooth my palm down his back. Beckett drops his forehead to mine and breathes out my name.

"I hope your plan includes carrying me to the house." I yawn, the back of my hand pressed against my mouth. Every bit of me feels stretched and sated. Lazy. "Because I don't plan on moving."

He leans up on his elbows. His eyes are soft, his touch even softer. He brushes a kiss to the tip of my nose.

"I'm not carrying anything." He collapses at my side, eyes heavy and smile loose. "Let's just lie here. One more minute."

"All right." I yawn again, a shiver racing down my arms. He chases it away with his palm on my skin, urging me closer. "One more minute."

WE LIE THERE much longer than a minute.

Eventually, Beckett bundles me up in my sweatshirt and carries me on his back during our trek to the house, his hands hooked under my knees and his palms rubbing at my thighs. With my arms looped over his shoulders, he makes quick work of it, pointing out different constellations as we go. Andromeda and her chains. Taurus and his mighty horns. A million stars and a million stories. I bury my nose in Beckett's neck and drift to the sound of his rumbling voice.

I startle out of my lull from the sound of his boots against the steps of the porch, his hands adjusting his grip to dig in his pocket for his keys. I begin to slip sideways, and he lets out a muffled curse, placing me carefully on my feet. I yawn and dig my fists into my eyes as he unlocks the door, dragging my fingers through my hair. I snort when several twigs and some blades of grass fall to the porch, remnants from our time in the field.

Maybe this is what happy is supposed to be. A person, a place. A single moment in time. Beckett in the hallway helping me untangle the sweatshirt from around my shoulders. A family of cats jostling for our attention as we trip into the kitchen. Tea in the kettle on the stovetop and two mugs sitting side by side right next to it.

I collapse onto one of the stools lined up at the countertop and watch him move around the kitchen, settling into the warmth expanding in my chest.

"What're you thinking about?" he asks, hands busy with a tin of tea. He passes me the honey before I can ask, and there it is again, that flutter right beneath my ribs.

I shake my head and reach for a spoon. "Nothing," I say. "Just watching you."

He hums like he doesn't believe me, a smile hidden behind the lip of his mug. We sit there at the counter and drink in the calm quiet of the house. We watch the cats bat around a ball of string, and I rest my forehead on his shoulder, his hand finding my thigh, fingers drumming.

A yawn creaks my jaw and Beckett noses at my hair, curling his fingers around my mug before I can drop it. He places it in the sink and comes back to me, bracing himself with his arms on the countertop. I find the galaxy on the inside of his bicep and trace the color.

"Come to bed with me," he says, his voice a rough whisper. I lean into him until my chin is on his shoulder, and the whole top half of my body is resting on his. I could fall asleep, just like this. It would probably be the best sleep of my life.

"I don't think I have another round in me."

Beckett shakes his head and guides me off the stool, directing me toward his room with a gentle pat on my ass.

"Neither do I," he agrees. He drops a kiss to the back of my head and walks us forward, knees bumping against mine. "I want to feel you next to me. Just sleep."

I'm too tired to pretend that's not exactly what I want too. I twist my fingers through his and nod. "Just sleep sounds really nice."

17

BECKETT

I WAKE TO Evelyn sprawled across me, her thigh tossed over my hips and her nose at my shoulder. I smooth my hand down her bare back and watch as she shifts closer, a single beam of morning light dancing down her skin. I chase the light with my touch and her nose scrunches, a huff in her sleep as she rolls and settles again.

I love how she looks beneath my sheets—the gentle curve of her hips and the dip at her waist. The graceful line of her arm across her bare breasts. She looks like a piece of art. Painted with oils and pressed into canvas with rough fingertips. Bold strokes of burnished gold and rich plum and deep forest green.

Despite my insistence that all we'd do is sleep, I woke up before dawn to soft fingers grazing against my stomach, searching kisses in the dark. I had pulled her over me and touched her until she was breathless, hands tugging at my clothes. A lick of heat curls at the base of my spine as I remember the sound she made as I sunk into her. A low moan. Pure unadulterated relief.

Desire pulses hot, and I dig the palms of my hands against my eyes until I see spots. I need to get out of this bed if I have any hope of getting anything done today. I still feel desperate for her, needy for her sounds and touches and body.

For the way she looks at me. For her laugh and smile and careful attention.

I flip back the blankets and slip from the bed, Evie immediately rolling into my space. I drop a kiss between her shoulder blades.

Her hand tangles briefly in my hair, a gentle tug and then a soothing rub with the pads of her fingers against my scalp. A deep, satisfied sound rumbles low in my chest. Evie grins into the pillow.

"Like a cat," she mumbles.

I nudge my head farther into her hand playfully, and she pushes me away. "Pancakes," she says with a sigh. "Bacon." She still hasn't bothered with opening her eyes.

"All right." I trace the swell of her cheek with my thumb. I want to bottle up this moment, her body soft and sweet beneath my sheets, the sounds of the house settling around us. Tree branches scratching at the windows and floorboards yawning in the hallway. "Let's start with coffee and go from there."

I'd make her pancakes and bacon and a fucking all-you-can-eat buffet—anything she wanted—if she told me she wanted to stay. But I push that thought away as quickly as it enters my mind. Bury it deep. It's wishful thinking in the worst of ways. Evie is too big to be contained by a place like Lovelight. Far too bright to be tucked away on a small-town farm. I won't have her lose her shine because—because I can't stand to see her go.

I glance at her smile tucked into my pillow, her fingertips mindlessly tracing lines along my tattoos.

"Meet you in the kitchen," she tells me, already halfway back to sleep, foot twitching out from beneath the flannel blankets. I pull the curtains closed on my way out the door and scoop my discarded pants from the floor, stepping into them as I wander down the hall. The cats ignore me completely, content with their places in the sun beneath the window.

"Nice to see you too."

Comet rolls over, her tiny paw waving briefly in the air.

I busy myself with starting the coffee and setting out the ingredients for pancakes, a deep soreness between my shoulder blades and in the back of my thighs. I have two twin scratch marks at the curve of my ribs—a souvenir from when I pressed my thumb between her legs and her hands curled into fists at my sides.

Sleeping with Evelyn last night probably wasn't the best idea. I'm only falling deeper into this thing between us. I'm afraid that when she leaves this time, she's going to be taking all of the important parts of me with her.

But I'm tired of holding myself back. Tired of pretending I don't want her in every possible way. On my porch and at my table and in my bed. I've never been so greedy for a woman in my entire life.

It's Evie.

I never stood a chance.

I want to talk to her about her day and then fuck her senseless up against the wall. I want to make her grilled cheese and tomato soup and then spread her out on my table.

A light musical ring interrupts my thoughts, and I glance over my shoulder at the table. Evelyn's laptop is open on the corner, a spiral notebook just beneath it. My eyes shift down the hall and back again, and the ringing cuts off abrubtly.

It begins again a moment later.

I know she doesn't have her phone. It's still at the bottom of the pond, likely making a fine home with one of the boat oars Luka dropped in two summers ago. I take a step closer and squint at the screen. A tiny box in the corner tells me Josie is calling. I've heard her name before from Evelyn, friendly affection in her voice.

My hand hovers over the trackpad, and I tap answer before I can talk myself out of it. I'll take a message, hang up, and make us some damn pancakes.

A woman's face instantly appears on the screen. Short black hair. A Metallica sweatshirt. Wide brown eyes that blink and then grow wider.

"Holy shit," says a tinny voice from the speaker.

My reflection appears in the top left side of the screen, arm braced against the edge of the table and hand still hovering over the keyboard. I am . . . not wearing a shirt. Pretty sure you can see Evie's scratch marks across my chest. I push up off the table and stand there like an idiot, hesitantly waving the spatula in greeting.

Did not know this was a video call.

"Um, hello."

Socked feet shuffle down the hallway. Evie appears in the entrance to the kitchen wearing one of my flannels, half buttoned and barely skimming her thighs. She has her knit—I exhale a shaky breath and grab the back of the chair—she has her cable-knit socks pulled to her knees. I'm torn between the desire to burn those fucking things and to have her wear nothing but those, her knees hugging my ears and her hands in my hair.

"Hey," she mumbles, scooting her way over to me and brushing a brief kiss to the underside of my jaw. Her arms curl around my waist, and she hugs me tight. It's the sort of easy affection I've been craving from her, and I can't appreciate it because I'm frozen in front of the camera, staring like a deer in headlights over Evie's head. If the kitchen floor could swallow me whole, that would be great.

I knew I shouldn't have answered the fucking call.

"My, my, my. Look what we have here."

Evie jumps, face snapping toward the computer. My hands grip her hips in silent apology.

"I didn't know it was a video call," I whisper, just for her.

Evelyn blinks. The woman on the screen stares wordlessly at us both and then steeples her fingers together. She taps them lightly, looking like a movie villain. A slow grin starts at the edge of her mouth, until her whole face looks fit to burst with unrestrained glee.

It's terrifying.

"So many things are beginning to make sense," she says with a weird aristocratic accent. Evie sighs and pats once at my chest, tipping her head to look up at me. She has a faint blush on her cheeks, but she has a smile too. Her eyes trail down my torso and land on the thin scratches on my side. The flush on her cheeks trips a shade darker.

"Why don't you go put a shirt on?"

"No need to on my account," comes the voice from the screen.

"I'm gonna go put a shirt on," I say. I place the spatula on the table and make a quick exit, retreating to the safety of my bedroom.

Once the door clicks shut behind me, I pull a flannel from the top drawer without bothering to look at it, taking my time to do up the buttons. It's for the best that I'm not standing awkwardly behind Evie during a phone call with her friend. I'm not trying to make anything difficult for her. I don't want her to feel any pressure, from me or anyone else. She puts enough on herself.

I rub the palm of my hand along the back of my neck, frustrated. With the situation but mostly with myself, at my inability to just—say what I want.

I know what I want.

I glance at the bed—the twisted sheets and the faint indent in the pillow next to mine.

But I know it's selfish to want it.

The door cracks open, and Evie pokes her head around the corner, her hair a tangled mess and falling over her shoulders. She smiles gently at me when she sees me standing in the middle of the room and opens the door farther. She places a coffee mug on the edge of the dresser like we do this every day.

I wish we did.

I clear my throat. "Everything okay?"

She nods and crosses her arms over her chest as she leans against the doorframe, an easy smile on her face. All I can do is stare at the buttons of the shirt she stole, the sides barely covering the swell of her breasts. It would be so easy to hook my finger there, pull her to me and forget the mess in my head.

How long is she staying? What will happen when she goes?

How far gone am I and do I even care?

It would all disappear with my mouth on hers.

Half of me expects her to push the conversation, demand that we talk through everything we cracked wide open last night. But she keeps her eyes on me, gaze warm and honest and kind. There's a faded line pressed from the corner of her eye to the curve of her jaw, a crease from my pillow imprinted on her cheek.

I want her like this every single morning.

"You left your phone on the counter," she tells me, uncrossing her arms and edging farther into the room. "Mabel called and said you're late."

I groan. I forgot I volunteered to help her today. Spring wedding season is chaotic at the greenery, and she's too short to do the arches by herself. I glance down the long line of Evie's body propped up against the dresser and groan again.

I had plans this morning. Pancakes and syrup with the doors to the porch thrown open wide. The sun on her skin and the tempting line of her throat. I rub at my chest and ignore the low flare of disappointment.

She grins and turns, bending at the waist for the third drawer down. I make a helpless sound as the swell of her hips and the curve of her ass are put on display, and she gives me a little shimmy, legs rocking back and forth.

"I'll go with you," she tells me over her shoulder, pulling out a pair of jeans and tossing them in my direction. "I've got to drop off website stuff for her anyway."

"You're still doing that stuff around town?" Social media was the majority of it. But helping Alex stock books on the back shelves too. Taking a turn on the cash register at the hardware store. Christopher had been beside himself, telling anyone who would listen about the celebrity who wanted to work at his store.

She's been sharing her sunshine with anyone who needs some light, even as she struggles herself. She's open and warm and kind, and it's so easy to picture her here. To want her to *stay*.

She hums in affirmation, a balled-up pair of socks soaring through the air and narrowly missing my head. I reach back and grab them off the bed.

She sets her hands on her hips. Bossy in every line of her body. Gorgeous too. "But if we're skipping breakfast here, I'm gonna want bacon on the way."

I ease and settle. We'll figure everything out in time, for better or worse. Worrying about it isn't going to get me anywhere.

"We can do that."

THE BACK PARKING lot of the greenery is full when we arrive, a spike of anxiety making me fidget in my seat. This is not how I wanted to spend my morning with Evelyn. In fact, this is not how I want to spend any morning—ever. I want to go back in time and punch myself in the face for volunteering.

I can feel Evie's eyes on me, watching me carefully as I maneuver the truck into one of the back alleyways. I reluctantly put it into Park, and she slips a piece of bacon out of the foam container on her lap, offering me half.

"They like seeing you, you know."

I bite into the bacon, keeping my gaze firmly locked on the large floral wreath over the door. It usually takes me between five and seven minutes to convince myself to get out of the car. "Who does?"

"Everyone. The town."

I grunt.

"I just—" I turn to look at her, the bright morning light making her skin glow. She has pink on her neck from where my stubble brushed against her, the edge of a hickey peeking out from beneath her shirt. I give in to temptation and reach over, thumbing once at the mark before pulling her collar over it. She turns her head and brushes a kiss along the constellation on the back of my hand. Argo Navis. The mighty ship.

"I don't want you to be lonely," she confesses. "Sitting by yourself in that big house. I hate thinking of you lonely."

She means when she leaves. I slip my hand out of her grip and rub my palm along my thigh. She's busy planning for her exit while I'm still out in the fields with her, my hands on her bare skin and my heart in my throat.

Disappointment punches me in the gut, a cheap shot that steals the air out of my lungs. All morning I've been trying to think of the right words to tell her I want her around, and she's thinking about where she'll go next. I let out a slow breath and reach for the handle of the door.

"All right." I scratch at my nose and push everything into place. Shoulders back, chin up, crumbling walls held up by toothpicks. "Let's go in, then."

She stops me with her hand on my wrist, the foam boxes placed neatly in the back seat. Her thumb rubs once against my skin, and she smiles gently at me. There's a secret there in the set of her mouth. Comfort and a little bit of coercion too. All the best things about Evie.

She rummages around in her bag and emerges with her hand wrapped tight around something, shuffling up on her knees to lean over the center console. She cups my jaw in one hand and reaches for my temple with the other, a small foam earplug held carefully between thumb and forefinger. She gently fits it into place against my ear, thumb smoothing along my jaw as the sound is muffled around me. It's like slipping underwater in the bath, warm water rushing overhead.

She guides my head to the left and fits the other earplug into place. She holds my face when she's done, thumbs brushing under my eyes. She leans forward and drags a gentle kiss across my mouth. *Let me take care of you*, her kiss says.

I want her to. More than anything, I want her to.

"For the sound," she explains, her voice harder to hear but still there. "To make it easier."

I swallow around the words that burn unfamiliar in the back of my throat and settle for squeezing her hand in mine. But I wonder if she knows. If she can read it on my face.

I didn't realize falling in love could be so simple. Bacon in a take-out container and earplugs in the bottom of a handbag.

I make a decision sitting in the front seat of my truck, my thumb across her knuckles. I don't know what we're doing, how long it'll last, when she'll leave again. But I'll take all her pieces while I have her.

I'll take whatever she can give me, for as long as she can.

THE EARPLUGS HELP, but Evelyn helps more.

She keeps her touches light and reassuring against the back of my arm as we twist flowers and vines around the sturdy legs of an arch. Half of the entire town is crammed into Mabel's greenhouse space, bundles of fresh flowers and rolls of chicken wire and dense green foam on every flat surface. Loud conversation and bodies brushing close. I've seen glimpses of Mabel, hurrying between stations, a flurry of activity as she arranges and rearranges and sends people out the door.

"These are beautiful." Evelyn fluffs some baby's breath near the top of the arch and drags a fingertip over the petal of a pale pink peony, the bloom still clustered tight. She's standing on the step stool, and her ass is right above my face. I could bite at the top of her thigh if I wanted to. She turns and looks down at me, a sly smile curving her lips up. I don't bother looking away from her ass.

I reach out a hand and help her down. "They are."

Mabel is incredible at what she does. Her floral business has been slowly expanding over the past couple of years, and this might be her biggest wedding yet. I look at all the arrangements spread out over the greenhouse, Gus standing by the door with what looks like five bouquets balanced in his massive hands, a patient look on his kind face as Mabel talks animatedly in front of him. He nods and jerks his head toward out front, where the ambulance is waiting, back doors propped open.

"I think Gus is trying to drop off flowers at a wedding in an ambulance."

Evelyn hops off the last step of the stool but doesn't drop my hand. I squeeze her fingers with mine, a tiny white bloom stuck to her pinky.

"He might need the ambulance in a second."

I laugh and Evelyn glances up at me, a wide smile on her pretty face. I forget that we're in the middle of town in a crowded greenhouse. I forget that Cindy Croswell is standing three feet behind us, sneaking a peek through a bundle of eucalyptus.

All I know is that I want to kiss Evelyn while she has jasmine caught in her hair, and I've got this feeling in my chest. Like someone kicked me out of an airplane. Total free fall. No parachute.

So I do.

I cup my hand around the back of her neck and tug her into me, a soft *oh* pressed against my mouth and her hands flat against my chest. I keep it chaste and easy, a gentle brush back and forth. A quick nip at her bottom lip. Her hands curl into fists as she sways into me, a light admonishment with the rap of her knuckles on my collarbone.

"Everyone can see," she whispers against my mouth, not moving an inch. The sound is muted by the foam in my ears, but I can hear her all the same. I can also hear Cindy Croswell drop everything she's holding right behind us and go rushing toward the supply closet where Becky Gardener disappeared ten minutes ago.

I bump my nose against hers. "I don't care."

Her smile widens into a grin, her brown eyes shining. This close, I can see flecks of gold in them. She thumbs at my jaw. "Those earplugs made you bold, farmer boy."

I shrug and lean back, carding my hand through the length of her hair. For once, I don't mind the attention. I'm not going to lose a moment with Evelyn just because someone might be watching. Though there is a lot of whispering going on all of a sudden, furtive glances in between ceramic vases and rose gold twinkle lights.

"Ah," I see her point now. Gus and Mabel have abandoned their argument on the sidewalk and are standing with their faces pressed to the window. I wince. Everything in the greenhouse has come to a comical standstill. The whispers start like a hornet's nest a second later. "All right, well. Can't take it back now."

"Do you want to?" she says. I look down at her, the way her smile is slipping from her lips. "Take it back?"

I shake my head. I really don't. I want everyone in this nosy-ass town to know. I'm half tempted to dig my cell out of my pocket and dial the phone tree.

Relieved, Evie takes my hand and squeezes. "Good. Because I think we just went the Inglewild version of viral."

⇜ 18 ⇝

EVELYN

MY BRAND-NEW PHONE rings on the arm of the chair as I sit on the back porch of Beckett's cabin, a mug of tea in my hands and my feet propped up on the railing. It's an unfamiliar number, but I recognize the area code.

I tap Answer as I watch Beckett cross back and forth through the thick glass windows of his little greenhouse, bending at the waist with a watering can held loosely in his fist. I don't know how anyone got this number. I asked Josie for a new one when she ordered me a replacement phone.

"Hello?"

"Inglewild phone tree calling," a vaguely familiar voice chirps out on the other end of the phone. "Beckett and Evelyn were seen making out in the corner of Mabel's today. Pretty sure he would have thrown her to the ground if no one had been around."

I pull the phone away from my ear and glance at the screen. That is a . . . creative interpretation of the sweet but lingering kiss Beckett gave me beneath the flower arch.

"Bailey? Is that you?"

I'm pretty sure Bailey McGivens wasn't even in the greenhouse earlier today. There's a pause, and then her loud and boisterous laugh dances over the line.

"Oh, goodness. What are the odds?" Her laughter tapers off. "I guess you're officially a local now . . . if you've been added to the phone tree."

"I guess so." The thought makes me grin. I have questions about how they got this number though. "We weren't making out."

"Oh, honey. That's a shame." She tuts once. "You should always be making out with that man."

I hang up the phone and kick my legs as I stare out at the rolling hills. I let myself imagine what this would be like. Mornings spent in town and afternoons on the farm, brilliant color spilling out behind the house as the flowers begin to bloom. Calls from the phone tree and cookies from Ms. Beatrice in the dead of night. Beckett's mouth on mine.

I still haven't gotten that itch to move. The pulse that beats in my chest to go somewhere new—chase, discover, find—it's fainter now. Quiet. I don't think it's gone. It's just . . . satisfied, I think.

I glance at my phone, and instead of feeling a swell of anxiety rising like a tide, I just feel . . . nothing. I didn't bother reconnecting any of my social accounts when I set up this new phone. Didn't connect my email either.

I'm starting to let some things go.

I watch Beckett cross behind the windows again—one thing I don't want to let go of.

With Beckett, I'm trying to figure out too much on my own when there's another half to the equation, currently hiding in the greenhouse, tending to his plants. Does he even want me to stay? I stand from my seat and step down from the back porch, following the path laid by oversized flat stones. Comet and Vixen rush ahead of me, hopping from rock to rock to slip through the crack in the door.

Beckett's back is to me, his T-shirt stretched over his shoulders as he works at the table pressed against the length of the rear wall. Almost all of the floor space is occupied by various pots and planters, a long shelf against each floor-to-ceiling window crowded with orchids and petunias and bright red poinsettias, their silky petals open to the setting sun. I duck my nose into a cluster of pink I don't recognize, its scent like the first bite of a crisp apple. Tangy and sharp.

I lean back and find Beckett watching me.

"Phone tree called," I tell him. "We're official."

I regret my choice of words almost immediately. The only thing official about what we're doing is officially avoiding the conversation. Officially stupid about it. I roll my eyes up to the glass panels of the ceiling and back down again. "You know what I mean."

He wipes his hands on a towel, his movements practiced and smooth. "We're officially on everyone's creep radar?" He tosses the towel to the side. "We're officially going to have to start checking the front bushes for neighbors?"

I like that word so much. *We.*

"I don't think you'll find Luka and Stella hiding in your bushes," I say as I lean my hip against the table he's been working at. Three small pots and a packet of seeds. A bright blue watering can and some pruning shears. I tilt my head and glance at his neat handwriting at the bottom lip of terra-cotta. *Lavender.*

"Are we going to talk about what's going on, or are you going to silently poke around my greenhouse until I lose my mind?"

I blink up at him and feel a smile tug at my mouth. I bite down on the inside of my cheek in a show of restraint. "The second option sounds nice, thank you."

He shakes his head and rubs his knuckles over his neck, exasperated. This poor man. I've really put him through the ringer this week. The pond, a kiss . . . sex in a field. I'd feel bad if I didn't know for a fact he loves it. He loves the challenge, the fight, the big tease of it all. He drops his hands and reaches under the table, flicking some hidden switch. A low string of lights twined around the ceiling panels blinks to life, and the whole space glows with a warm hazy light. I catch a reflection of us in the glass to my right, night creeping across the fields outside and cloaking everything in shadow.

I'm captivated by the look of us reflected back in a wavy distortion. Me standing in front of Beckett, his body strong where he's propped up against the table. His tattooed arms spread wide. My ponytail curled over my shoulder.

"There are other options to explore, I think." He steps forward and cages me with the table at my back, his hands finding my hips and lifting me carefully on top. He drags my legs wide and pats once at the outside of my thighs, stepping between them. All of his movements are so easy, so effortless. Like he's been out here planning exactly what he wants to do with me.

"So far, so good," I say.

A smile flirts with the corners of his mouth. He settles the palm of his hand on my neck and traces below my ear. "I like you, Evie." He breathes, and the humid air in the greenhouse turns thicker, warmer. His gaze softens on mine, and everything in his eyes looks a lot more than *like*. My heart pounds in my chest, and I know whatever he feels, I feel it too. "I like you a lot. I want to see where this goes."

"See where this goes," I repeat to him slowly, focused on the fingers of his other hand toying with the hem of my dress. He could be reciting the "Star-Spangled Banner" and I'd probably still have the same stupefied look on my face. He strokes my legs again, thumb curling under the edge of my skirt. I put on a dress before we left the house this morning. I liked the way Beckett swallowed hard when I walked into the kitchen, how his eyes lingered on where the hem brushed my thighs.

He gathers the fabric in his fist and rolls the material up once. I shiver.

"Yeah," he says quietly. "Does that work for you?"

"It's a good start." I want more from him than that. *See where this goes* sounds a little ambivalent for the big feelings bursting the seams of my chest, but it'll do. He flips the skirt of my dress up again, another inch of skin visible. "I like you too, for the record."

I more than like him.

"I'm glad we talked about this," he tells the tops of my knees, a heavy swallow in the strong column of his throat. He leans forward and nudges under my jaw. I obediently lift my chin, and he presses a soft kiss right over my pulse point. He likes that small concession, a rough breath exhaled over my skin, fingers dragging along the outsides of my thighs. I stop his hands at the place where my underwear rises over my hips, my hands curling around his wrists.

"I'm going to want to talk about this more."

"All right."

"Lots of conversations."

His hands flex at my waist, fingers slipping under the band of my underwear. He twists the material and tugs. "As many as you want, honey. We'll keep talking."

"Beckett." I drag my lips across his forehead. I'm taller than him like this, propped up on the table, his big body occupying all the space between my spread legs. "The walls are made out of glass."

He nods and tucks another kiss under my ear. Drags his teeth down my throat and gives me a sharp, biting kiss just above my collarbone. "They are."

"Someone might—" I cut off on a gasp when his meandering path takes a sharp turn, his mouth wet and warm over my breast through the fabric of my dress. He bites once at my nipple and my hands release his wrists to find his hair instead, threading through the thick strands. I jerk his head back roughly, and he makes a soft pleading sound in the back of his throat.

Oh boy.

"Someone might see," I manage. "We should go inside."

I already know how I want him when we get there. Fast. Hard. Against the dresser in his bedroom. Bent over the edge of his bed. Maybe the couch too. I fist my hand in his hair and guide him until I can catch his lips with mine. I let him know everything I'm thinking with my mouth on his, and he groans something desperate into my bottom lip. When he pulls away, his hands are clenching at my legs, head already shaking.

"No one will see," he tells me, voice rusted over with need. "It's just us here—you and me. I want you just like this."

His gaze slants to the side, and he curls his hand under my jaw, guiding my face to follow until I'm looking at our reflections again.

"Can I have you like this?"

I see it then, exactly what he wants. Beckett pressing me into the table with my dress rucked up around my hips, the long line of my legs a streak of copper in the window. I can't see anything beyond the glass now. Just the two of us, globe lights glowing above our heads like fireflies. The one in the corner flickers on, off, and then on again.

"I want you to watch," he tells me.

And then he drops to his knees.

It's strange, watching him in the glass. Everything is a little bit off. I feel his breath against my knee before I see him brush a kiss there. Feel the calloused pads of his fingers before I see him drag my underwear down my legs, wrap them around his fist, and put them in his pocket. I watch myself spread my legs wider before I've even realized I've done it, his head disappearing between my thighs, only the top of his hair visible in our reflection.

"I like this." I breathe out, surprised by the heat surging through my veins. He makes a sound against my inner thigh, and his hands squeeze tight, inked fingers flexing. One palm guides my leg up and over his shoulder, my thigh pressed to his ear.

He watches my face as he puts his mouth against me, his eyes drifting closed in agonized relief with his first slow kiss. I watch him in our reflection as he rolls his tongue over me, a steady pulse that has me scrambling for purchase against the tabletop. A long, thorough drag. A gentle hum of satisfaction.

The watering can goes clattering to the ground. His garden shears too. The lavender is spared, but only because my hands find the low shelf at my back, Beckett's grip steadying my hips. I look away from our reflection, more interested in the reality of it instead. His head bowed over me, one arm banded low over my stomach to hold me in place. The other disappearing below us, the clink of his belt on the concrete floor letting me know exactly what he's doing.

It pulls and pulls and pulls—this feeling—low in my belly where his forearm rests against me, my hips desperately rolling up and into him. Chasing that beautiful feeling that I only ever get with Beckett. His hands and his lips and his deep grumbling groan of relief against me when I gasp his name and arch up, my release stealing the breath from my lungs.

He drags his mouth back and forth along the inside of my thigh, the prick of his beard making my legs jump. He rests his forehead there briefly. "More?" His hand slips low over my belly and his thumb curls down where I'm wet and sensitive. Another jump in my hips that has him grinning into my leg. He taps there once and I almost slip right off the table to the floor. He'll have to collect my pieces in a basket and cart me into the house.

While the idea of Beckett giving me another orgasm on this table with his hands and his mouth is tempting, I want something better. I shake my head and use the hand still in his hair to urge him up. It's a wonder he has any strands left at this point. I rub my fingers against his scalp, and he makes that rumbling sound again, deep in his chest. Like a cat in the sunshine.

"Can I have you like this?" I ask, curling my legs at his hips, the heel of my foot at the small of his back. I want to look at him, watch the way his whole face relaxes as he slips inside me. Relief and desire and . . . something else too. Something that pounds in my chest to the same beat as his. He palms at my thigh, hand flexing, and swallows hard as he gazes down at me.

"You can have me any way you want me, honey." His hand cups the side of my face, cradling my cheek. "You know that."

He drags his thumb over my bottom lip, and I pull it into my mouth. He makes another deep sound, a heavy exhale of breath.

I slip my hands under his shirt and scratch my nails up his chest, back down again when his body falls deeper into mine. I curl my hands in the material of his jeans and push them down over his hips, the button and fly already undone, the band of his briefs pulled low. The thought of him touching himself as he touched and tasted me, it sends heat flooding through my body. A pluck of arousal in all the right places.

"Good," I say with my teeth at the base of his throat, scraping until he shivers and his hips jolt forward, hard where I'm soft. The metal of the table bites into the backs of my thighs, the surface cold against my bare skin. "Because this time I want you to watch."

The hand on my cheek slips into my hair, tilting my head back as his mouth finds mine. It's a rough kiss, possessive, and I hold on to the sides of his torso as he bends me backward over the tabletop. A perfect curve, his hands holding me up. He pulls back and drags his nose along my jaw, dips down and presses a single lingering kiss on my shoulder.

He doesn't say anything as he presses into me, a thick slide of heat that has me shifting my body against the table—trying to take more. Trying to take it all. He watches with his head tipped down between us, a low groan that sounds like my name. I close my eyes and feel him everywhere he's tucked against me. One hand in my hair. The other on my thigh, guiding my leg wider. His deep, panting breaths on the sensitive skin behind my ear. The tiny restless movement of his body against mine when our hips press together, like he wants to move but can't quite yet. Like he needs a moment to collect himself.

He pulls out slightly and pushes back in, a short stilted movement that still, somehow, manages to steal my breath. He curses and does it again, a messy grind on his retreat that rubs against me in all the right places. My hand slips down to his jaw, fingers curling over his rough stubble. I guide his face until he's looking at us on the glass wall to our left.

"Watch," I tell him.

We look like something from a dream. A filthy dream that I've had a million times where I wake up still tangled in the sheets. My heart in my throat and a thin sheen of sweat on my skin, a drumbeat of wanting between my thighs.

My legs are curled high around his hips, my back arched in a delicate bend against the tabletop, anchored with his hand twisted through my hair. His body, strong and tall above me. His jeans caught halfway down his legs. I look at him in our reflection and the storm raging in those green eyes. Banked desire. A wordless promise.

He pulls out slowly. Thrusts back in so hard the entire table shakes. A planter goes crashing to the ground and I cling to him.

And I don't hide a single thing from him as I fall apart.

"EVIE."

I grumble and swat at the warm pressure at my back, a heavy hand at my waist over the thick quilt. Beckett huffs a laugh and his hand squeezes, rubbing over the flank of my thigh and back again. I have marks on my legs from the metal of the table last night, light bruises from when Beckett pulled me from the edge, turned me around, and bent me at the waist. *There*, he said with his mouth at my ear, his hand between my legs. *Now we can both watch.*

I shiver as I remember, and Beckett gives a knowing chuckle above me.

"Why did you wake me up?" I whine into the pillow, pulling the blankets farther over my shoulder and burrowing down. His bed is perfectly warm, his body my own personal space heater.

Except his body is currently fully dressed and outside the covers, a baseball hat pulled backward over his messy blond hair. I blink at him over my shoulder, confused.

"Why are you dressed? Is everything okay?"

His thumb traces over my bottom lip, a half smile on his handsome face. "Everything is fine. Kind of. They delivered our saplings to the wrong farm. Barney and I have to drive to upstate New York and grab them."

"New York?"

He hums in the affirmative.

I blink some more. "Right now?"

He nods. "If we wait for them to do it, it'll be next week. I don't want the trees to dry out."

"Can't have that," I mumble, still half asleep. His smile widens.

"No, we can't."

"How long will you be gone?"

"Not long. We should be back tomorrow night."

I sit up on the bed and rub my hands against my eyes. Prancer lets out a plaintive meow from her place at the edge of the bed, upset by the disruption. I drop my hands and yawn in Beckett's general direction. "I'll come with you."

He shakes his head and shifts forward to brush a kiss across my lips. Soft. Perfect. "Stay here," he says. He hesitates for a second and then curls his hand around my neck, his palm sweeping against sleep-warm skin. "Sleep in my bed while I'm gone, yeah? I'll see you when I get back."

I collapse into the pillows and blankets with a grateful sigh and bury my face in flannel. "You're sure?"

"Yeah, I'm sure." The mattress dips at my waist and warm lips drift across my forehead. "Get some rest."

"Have fun with the trees," I mumble.

The last thing I hear before I drift back to sleep is his rough chuckle, his fingertips combing through my hair.

WHEN I WAKE up again, I'm curled on Beckett's side of the bed clinging to the sleeve of a flannel hanging from the bedpost. I laugh at myself and give in to an indulgent stretch beneath the comforter. There hadn't been a discussion last night as to where I would sleep. We stumbled in from the greenhouse with our clothes rumpled, and I followed Beckett into his bedroom. I draped my body over his, pressed a sleepy kiss to his mouth and fell asleep with his arm slung over my hip.

He grumbled about me hogging the blankets, but I woke up in the middle of the night to Beckett holding most of them close to his chest, his face buried in my hair.

I reach blindly for my phone on the nightstand, squinting at the screen. The house sounds too quiet without Beckett here. I miss the sound of drawers opening in the kitchen, metal spoons and the clink of his coffee mug.

> JOSIE: Text me when you have a second. I've got
> news.

I tap her name and let my phone rest on my chest as it begins to ring. I stretch out my legs with another groan.

"You don't need to sound so smug," Josie says when she answers, catching the tail end of my stretching sounds. I let my body flop back to the bed, my arms above my head. My hand brushes against something soft and cool and I wrap my fingers around it.

A long green stem. A cluster of small blue blooms. Meadow sage, I think it's called.

I hold it under my nose with a smile.

"What's your news?"

"Nuh-uh," Josie admonishes. "You were way too short on our video call. I have things I want to discuss first."

I said maybe two words to Josie the other morning in the kitchen before I slammed the laptop shut. Luckily she had been too gobsmacked by the appearance of Beckett's bare torso to do anything but gape like a fish.

I guess she's collected herself.

"I'd like to start with the tattoo along his collarbone and work my way down."

I laugh. "No."

"I took a quick screenshot, but he moved. It's kind of blurry."

"You . . . what?"

"I'm gonna frame it and put it on my wall."

"No, you're not."

"Does he have flowers on one arm and stars on the other? Because that's pretty devastating."

It is devastating. Lovely and sentimental and sexy as hell too. I curled my hand around the constellation on his forearm last night when he braced his palm on the table next to me. A bull with its horns lowered. Crowns of thick, vibrant greenery twisted around its head. "I'm not going to objectify him."

"Appreciation is not objectification."

I set the flower I've been twirling between my thumb and forefinger on the nightstand and see a Post-it note stuck to his stack of books. Sneaky man. I pick it up and glance at his neat handwriting. *Muffins on top of the oven*, it says. *Be back soon.*

A scribble beneath, something that looks like a . . . cat dozing? His doodles are horrendous.

But I like it better than any saccharine thing he could have written. One hundred percent Beckett. Practical and sweet—care through action. Breakfast waiting on the counter and coffee in the pot.

I place his note next to the flower.

"What's your news?"

"We will circle back to this."

I laugh, a quiet snicker that has one of the cats poking her head up from beneath a mountain of sheets to look at me. She flops down and nudges me once with her paw for the inconvenience. "I have no doubt."

"All right, then. Your news." I hear paperwork in the background and imagine her in the office in the front of her house. The big bay window that looks out over dense green forest, a thin layer of fog in the mornings that rolls against the glass. "Theo gave me a call when he couldn't get through to you."

That's right. The head of the Small Business Coalition. We've talked briefly over email about the position and what it would entail. Small business advising, more or less. Helping people like Ms. Beatrice and Stella get up on their digital feet. I had given him Josie's number in my email reply, letting him know my phone was temporarily out of service. I didn't mention that it was at the bottom of a pond. "Everything okay?"

"Yeah, he was thrilled to hear from you. He said you can expect an email today, but he wanted to follow up by phone too. He wants you to come in for an interview."

My heart beats a little bit faster in my chest. Excited, I think. Hopeful too. Nervous as hell, surprisingly. "Yeah? That's good, right?"

"I'm pretty sure he would have offered me the job on your behalf." I can hear the smile in her voice. "That's how excited he is for you to come in."

I'm flustered, smiling so hard my cheeks hurt. "Do you think— do you think I'm qualified for something like this?"

"Of course you are." Josie's response is quick. No hesitation. "You created your own social following from nothing. An entire content stream that attracts hundreds of thousands in ad revenue. You've helped countless businesses thrive. Developed your own grant that has literally made people's dreams come true. Frankly, I think you're overqualified." She pauses for a second and I hear the tip-tap of her keyboard. "Maybe this Theo guy should work for you," she muses as an afterthought.

I sit up in the bed and stare at the cats cuddled up around me, a stack of Beckett's neatly folded sweaters on a chair in the corner. The job is half remote office work, half traveling to small businesses around the country. Not all that different from what I'm doing now. It would mean I would have some flexibility as to where I stay. I would have options.

Inglewild-shaped options.

Beckett-shaped options.

"Jo Jo," I whisper. "Am I crazy for thinking about this?"

"The job?"

"The job, yeah. Also"—I gather some of my courage—"this place. Inglewild. I think I want to stay."

It's the secret I've been holding in my heart for the last couple of weeks. Nowhere has ever felt like such a perfect fit. It's not just Beckett. It's the friendly call of my name as I walk down the street. It's the same order every Wednesday from Matty's pizza. It's knowing the exact steps to take down the side street and through the park to make it to the café before the morning rush.

Comfort.

Familiarity.

A home.

She sighs, long and slow. I'm grateful she's thinking about it and not blurting out mindless reassurances. But then again, that's Josie.

"You've been struggling for a while now. What you've been doing isn't working for you anymore, and that's okay." I haven't touched my social accounts since my last little video, ignoring all of the comments and tags and posts. I am . . . more than okay with that. "So I think if this new path feels good, then it is good. There's nothing wrong with wanting to stay. When's the last time you wanted to stay somewhere?"

I rack my brain for the last time I felt this content. This settled. I can't think of a single time.

I pick up my flower from the nightstand and twirl it between my fingers. "We'll have a lot to do to tie up loose ends." My mental to-do list appears, gathering items like raindrops in a bucket. I frown, a thought occurring. "We wouldn't work together anymore."

"Like you could get rid of me," she says quietly. Fondly. "Plus, I'd like to remind you that the man has a tattoo just below his collarbone. I'd have questions if you didn't want to stay."

19

BECKETT

"STOP SMILING LIKE that," Barney snaps from the passenger side of the flatbed truck, his arms crossed over his chest and a bagful of snacks from the last gas station resting on his knee. The man has consumed more Honey Buns in forty-eight hours than anyone has a right to. "You look like a maniac."

"I'm not even smiling," I tell him.

Barney sinks farther into his seat, his head against the window. His hand reaches for his plastic-wrapped heart attack. "Might as well be."

The bed of the truck is filled with 183 Douglas fir saplings. I know this because Barney insisted on counting them twice, loudly and in front of the people who mistakenly received our shipment.

"I still think those Lovebright people were up to something," Barney grouches around a mouthful of processed sugar. "I don't trust maple syrup farmers."

I tap my fingers on the steering wheel. It was pure coincidence that our names were so close, though I do have questions for our supplier. I gave him our address three times, and it's printed on the invoice we already paid. "They don't just harvest maple syrup. They have apples too."

"My point remains. I watched a documentary on the underground syrup trade. Apparently there's a whole black market. Gang activity."

I glance at him out of the corner of my eye. "What's gotten into you?"

He mumbles something.

"What?"

He shifts in his seat and gives me a look, debating. I raise both eyebrows in encouragement. We have another three hours left of this drive, and I'm not thrilled about the prospect of listening to Barney hem and haw over there like he's sitting on a seat made out of metal spikes. "I like you better when you're a grumpy ass," he finally says in a rush.

That was not what I expected. "What?"

"You've been humming for six hours," Barney seethes, biting off another giant mouthful. "Are you aware of that?"

I was not aware of that. I had no idea, actually.

"The radio in this thing is broken, and you have been humming the whole time. Six. Hours. Straight." He slouches back down in his seat. "Driving me up a damn wall."

I rub my palm over my jaw and keep quiet. I've had an old Tom Petty song stuck in my head since I left Evie tucked beneath my blankets, the kittens crowded around her, and a flower from the greenhouse woven in her hair. I didn't realize I'd been humming.

"Your dad does the same shit," Barney complains, digging around in his bag of snacks. He pulls out some pretzels and sour watermelon gummies, offering me the latter. I shake my head. Those things make my tongue feel like a wool sweater. "Always humming something."

"Yeah?"

"Mm-hmm. He once did the whole soundtrack to *Grease* for a week straight on a loop. He said it was my punishment for having an opinion."

"What was your opinion?"

"That he shouldn't fuckin' sing."

I manage to restrain myself for twenty-seven seconds. My opening bar to "Summer Nights" is a little shaky, but Barney recognizes it all the same. He lets out a loud bark of laughter and punches me hard, right in the thigh. I tighten my grip on the wheel.

"Not while I'm driving, old man."

"Old man," he repeats to me. "I'd still kick your ass."

I snort a laugh. He probably would. He taught Nova everything she knows about self-defense. He once picked her up early from school and took her to WrestleMania in Baltimore. She tried to suplex me from the top of her bunk bed for close to three months.

We settle back into silence, the rush of wind at the windows and the creak of the truck beneath us. The crinkle of plastic as Barney fishes out another Honey Bun. If I'd remembered my damn cell phone, we'd at least have something to plug into the AV outlet. But I left it sitting in the center of my kitchen table, along with the thermos of coffee I was supposed to bring and all of our paperwork.

It's a good thing Barney keeps duplicates shoved in a coffee-stained folder under the seat. Something about Evie tangled in worn flannel, the curve of her shoulder bare in the sunlight, scrambled my brain before I even left the house.

"You know when his musical inclinations were at their worst?"

I grunt and change lanes, my mind still fixed on the way she stretched and rolled into me, not even all the way awake. A smile on her face and her hands reaching for me like she couldn't bear to let me go. "December 1994. When you lost seven poker games in a row and you owed my dad ten thousand dollars and a boat you don't own?"

"I can't believe he still tells that story," Barney snorts. "No, smart-ass. The week he met your mom. He was moon-eyed, working in the fields, and bellowing Springsteen at the top of his damn lungs."

I shift in the seat. Clear my throat twice. "Sounds like you're trying to make a point."

Barney takes another bite of Honey Bun. "Imagine that."

BY THE TIME we unload the trees and I return the truck to the large garage for service vehicles, I am tired down to my bones. I have aches in muscles I didn't even know existed, and my ears are ringing from the loud rumble of the truck. I want a sandwich the size of my head, a cold beer, and Evelyn.

I want to kiss the skin between her shoulder and neck, that little spot under her ear that makes her hum. I want to hear about her day and if she found any happy. Fall into bed with her and sleep for the next six days under seven layers of blankets. I want bare skin and husky laughter. More sandwiches.

My boots crunch on gravel as I wander up the walkway to the cabin, a twist in my stomach when I don't see any light spilling from the windows. I can usually see Evelyn moving around the kitchen from the path, lounging on the couch with a book and the cats. I like seeing remnants of her spilled out across my hallway when I first walk in the door. Her scarf looped over the hook on the wall. Her boot knocked on its side by mine.

But the house is dark tonight, everything cast in shadow beyond the window. I stop on the bottom step of the porch and breathe in deep through my nose. The daffodils in the garden have started to peek through the mulch, a glimpse of bright green that looks gray in the darkness. They'll be in full bloom soon, the other flowers not far behind. Black-eyed Susans and tulips. Pink and gold and yellow so pale it almost looks white, tumbling out of the front flower beds.

I continue up the stairs and ignore the anxiety sinking like a stone in my gut. I've had this feeling before. This twisting, painful thing that clasps against my throat and squeezes. Maybe she's on the back porch or maybe she's with Layla at the bakehouse. She's been helping Stella digitize some of her records. Maybe she's still at the office.

But I know as soon as I swing open the door. It's too quiet, too still. I glance at the dark hallway and the empty hook next to mine where she usually keeps her jacket.

She isn't here.

It's exactly the same as that morning in Maine. I'm standing in the place she used to be, and I'm not sure where she's gone off to.

And I'm not sure if she'll bother coming back.

I knew this would happen. It's why I told her I wanted to *see where this goes* when I really wanted to say, *Stay here with me. Hold my hand on the back porch. I'll hold yours too.*

I've been waiting for the other shoe to drop since she pressed up on her toes in my kitchen and grabbed me by the back of my neck and kissed me like she damn well meant it.

I close the door behind me. I swallow and drop my keys on the table. I pull off my jacket and hang it on the hook. I go through the motions of coming home while a thin and trembling tension continues to twist in my chest, winding around and around. Like a piano being tuned, the strings vibrating with pressure. "Evelyn?"

No answer. One of the cats appears on top of the couch, a discarded sock draped over her body. I rub her tiny forehead with my knuckles and reach for it, a faded green pair that Evie had stolen from me.

"She isn't here, is she?"

Vixen offers me a meow and then scampers off, back to the huddle of kittens at the edge of the fireplace. I see that Prancer has grown her little nest, an old necktie between her paws where she lounges with the rest of them. A scrap of paper and a kitchen towel.

I scrub both hands through my hair and glance down the dark hall, then to the table where my cell phone and coffee mug sit untouched in the middle.

I could go down the hallway and check her room, see if her suitcase is gone. Her laptop and the stack of papers she kept on the nightstand under a book. That's what I did the first time she left. I wandered around that little room and looked for any clues. A note, maybe. A slip with her phone number scribbled down. All I found was a pile of loose change and a receipt from the tiny bar we were in. A button and a pen cap.

The second time, I was in the bakehouse. I sat at the corner table with two cups of coffee and a cinnamon roll I had no intention of eating. I waited while telling myself that I wasn't waiting at all. I picked at the edge of that damn cinnamon roll until the whole thing was gone.

If Layla thought it was odd that I was sitting at the window seat with two mugs of coffee for the duration of her morning rush, she never said a word about it. Turns out Evelyn left that morning. I hadn't even warranted a casual goodbye on her list. No text. Nothing.

The solution, this time, is a simple one.

I won't go down the hallway to check. I won't look for signs or signals or whatever the fuck else. I need to realize that sometimes a shooting star isn't magic at all. Sometimes it's just a bunch of space dust burning through the atmosphere.

Sometimes you don't get a wish.

Evie is always going to be leaving. And I'm always going to be the one standing here, wondering where she went.

Third time's the fucking charm, I guess.

"Stupid," I mutter. My muscles vibrate with the urge to throw, snap, break. I want to flip the table. Smash the glass vase holding a bouquet of wildflowers against the wall. I rub my palms down over my face until I see spots.

And then I go to the fridge and I make a sandwich.

"BECKETT?"

I ignore the call from the far end of the field and continue digging.

Push. Dig. Dump.

I've been out in the fields for an hour, and the sun still hasn't inched above the horizon. I couldn't sleep, and this seemed like the best use of my time. The sky is filled with the dull gray light that comes just before dawn, the sky deciding how it wants to wake up for the day. Thick clouds have hidden the stars, and it looks like they might hide the sun today too.

Good.

"What the hell are you doing?" Luka demands from halfway across the field.

What the hell are you doing? I want to snipe back. These are my fields, after all. But I'm not in the sixth grade anymore, and Luka is damned persistent when he wants to be, trudging his way toward me with a mug of coffee in each hand. I ignore him and drive the shovel down again.

Push. Dig. Dump.

"I'm digging."

I'm digging because the second I sat on the edge of my bed and reached for my sweatpants, I remembered her fingertips at my shoulder blades, her body twisted in worn flannel, and her face in my pillow. I got up to go to the kitchen and heard her laughter bouncing against the countertops. Pictured her chopping tomatoes with her hair tucked behind her ear.

I'm seeing Evie in every single empty space, and planting these saplings felt like the logical thing to do. I've got a hurricane inside my chest, and the pull and stretch of my muscles is the only thing keeping it contained. I bite my teeth around it—clench my jaw so hard it hurts.

"I can see that," Luka mutters, eyes firmly on the hole at my feet. "But why are you digging at four in the morning?"

I don't say a thing.

Push. Dig. Dump.

"Beck, what's going on?" He sighs.

I grunt. "I'm digging a hole—"

"I can see that."

"—for your body."

He snorts a laugh into his coffee mug. "That's nice."

I drive the shovel into a fresh piece of earth and rest my elbow against it, my thumb swiping at my eyebrow. "How'd you even know I was out here?"

"The cameras," Luka offers. Stella installed cameras over the winter when someone was vandalizing the farm. It turns out the town librarian, Will Hewett, really wanted an alpaca farm and decided that destroying ours was the best way to accomplish that particular goal. *Idiot.*

"Stella got a notification about a madman loading saplings into his truck and driving them out into the field." He takes a loud, obnoxious sip of coffee. "Which is weird because Dig Day is in a couple of days. It is also not scheduled for four in the morning."

"Decided to get a head start," I say as casually as I can manage, peering over the handle of my shovel at the hole I've been working on. It's way too deep for a sapling, but I'm committed now. I place the shovel to the side and reach for one of the bundles from the wheelbarrow. I loosen it from the travel-safe container they arrived in and transfer it carefully to its new home.

It drops to the bottom, the top branches not even visible.

I sigh.

"That's quite the hole," Luka says.

I pinch the bridge of my nose.

"Will it"—he tilts his head to the side and takes another slurp of coffee—"will it grow up out of the ground, you think?" He mimes some complicated gesture with his hand, like a rocket launching. "Like a pineapple plant. Have you seen one of those?"

I have. I sincerely doubt this will look anything like that.

I reach into the hole and pull the tree out, shoveling some of the dirt back in with my arm. Luka taps my shoulder and holds a cup of coffee in front of my face.

"Hold on a second. I brought you coffee."

"I don't want coffee," I say, contradicting myself by immediately grabbing the mug out of his hands. Luka's mom always makes sure Stella has the good stuff stocked for when she and all of Luka's aunts randomly descend upon her cottage. Last time, they brought biscotti too.

I collapse on my ass in the dirt and take a sip out of the mug. It has a tiny fox on it, a chip on the handle. Luka stares at me with one hand on his hip. For the first time, I notice he's wearing one of Stella's old sweatshirts, the sleeves too short on his long arms.

"What's going on with you?" he asks.

"What do you mean?"

He makes an exasperated sound in the back of his throat, the hair on the left side of his head sticking straight up in a riot of curls. Stella must have kicked him out of bed to come check on me. The thought lifts my spirits, oddly enough. "Oh, my bad. You're right. This is totally normal. We always have conversations before the sun is up." He rolls his eyes and kicks at my boot with his. "Why are you out here planting trees? Where is Evelyn?"

Probably in some boutique hotel in a bright and shiny city, charming everyone she meets. Glowing like the fucking sun.

She's not here. That's the only part that matters.

"I don't know."

I hate that I don't know.

Luka's eyebrows flatten into a line of confusion. "Isn't she staying with you?"

"She was," I say. "Now she's not."

I avert my eyes to the line of trees I've managed to plant this morning—a somewhat chaotic row of small green bundles. In five to seven years, this whole field will be filled with whispering branches and thick evergreen.

I wonder if I'll still be sitting here.

"What do you mean she's not?"

"I mean her rental car isn't in the driveway, and her stuff isn't in my house." Maybe. I think. There's a part of me that's rolling my eyes at my assumptions, but the much bigger part of me is just trying to protect what I can. "She left."

I don't know if Luka wants me to draw him a map or what, but it feels pretty straightforward. I can see her reasoning. She was staying with me while she figured her stuff out. She figured it out. She left.

That's it.

Luka makes another small sound under his breath, his eyes squinted in concentration. I want to roll into the hole I dug until he decides to leave me alone.

"You know how I met Stella, right?"

I roll my eyes to the sky and drape my arms over my knees. I guess he's staying.

"I know how you met Stella." I've heard the story enough over the past couple years. She fell down the steps of a hardware store and smacked right into Luka. They then proceeded to pretend they weren't hopelessly in love with each other for close to a decade. I fix my gaze on the trees swaying in the distance and clench my jaw. "You can skip this whole thing."

"Skip what?"

"Whatever hopeful platitudes are about to spill out of your mouth." Luka loves a good motivational speech. "I don't want to hear it."

Luka huffs a laugh and goes quiet. Another gust of wind rolls over the field, and all the branches lift and dance. It'll be harder not to think of Evie this time, but it'll pass. Maybe in a month or two I won't see her in every damn corner of this place. I just need—I need to remember how to be on my own, I think. Me and the cats.

And that damn duck I said I wasn't going to adopt.

"I almost told her." Luka considers the ground with a frown, relenting after a lengthy pause and sitting in the dirt across from me. He rummages around in his sweatshirt pocket and emerges with his fist clenched around a roll of cookies. He opens it with his teeth and offers me one. "Way back," he explains. "At the start. I almost told her how I felt."

I begrudgingly take a cookie. Another when I realize they're chocolate hazelnut and Luka intends to launch into his best encouraging speech despite my protest. "Could have saved yourself about seven years, I bet."

"Could have," Luka agrees. "She was getting out of a cab in the city. I was waiting for her on the curb, and she sort of—she got stuck, I think. Getting out of the car. Her bag or something was twisted around the seat belt. She tried to step out of the cab, and her bag yanked her right back in. She laughed so hard she snorted." He smiles at the memory, his eyes a little bit glassy. "She was so beautiful I couldn't stand it. My heart felt like it was right here." He taps his throat and then between his eyes. Pops out a cookie and shoves it in his mouth.

"Why didn't you? Say anything?" I'm annoyed with myself for asking.

He shrugs. "Because we had a good thing going, and I didn't want to rock the boat with a difficult conversation." His brown eyes narrow on me, and he bites into a cookie so hard it snaps in two. "Does that sound familiar?" he asks around a mouthful.

It does. I'm not going to argue with him about the particulars. I've actively avoided having a conversation with Evelyn. Absolutely. Sure, some of it has been fear. But a big part—the biggest part—has been—

"I don't want to tie her here," I confess with a deep, heaving sigh. "I don't want her to feel obligated." To my feelings. To me.

"You think she would?" A little line appears between Luka's brows.

Maybe. I sigh and rub the palm of my hand across my forehead. "What the hell is the point of being honest with her if she's just going to leave anyway?" That's the heart of it. It all comes down to me fumbling my way around a tiny bed-and-breakfast in the late summer heat, looking for scraps of her affection. Why the hell would I crack myself open just for her to look at everything inside and decide it's not enough? So I can feel this same twist in my gut every time she leaves without a word? Continue to lose pieces of myself until I'm a collection of ragged edges? No, thank you. "She already left. She's left three times now."

"Phones exist, you know. You could call her."

I take another long drink from my coffee mug. If Stella is watching us on the cameras right now, she's probably wondering why the hell her boyfriend and her lead farmer are having a picnic in a field full of holes.

At four eighteen in the morning.

"I tried calling her," I explain. While sitting on the edge of my bed with a wilting blue flower in the palm of my hand. I dialed her number three times and listened to a generic voicemail message. I typed out seven different text messages before I settled on a simple Where did you go? I wanted to send another. *Why did you go?* "She didn't answer."

"That's it? You're gonna give up? Relationship over?" He snaps his fingers. "Just like that."

"What else am I supposed to do?"

I'm a realistic man. I know where I belong and where I don't. I set my expectations and act accordingly. Going around with fanciful ideas in my head about things I can't have has never served me well.

This thing with Evie—it isn't any different.

My empty house is proof of that.

"Listen, man." I blow out a breath, and some of the coffee from my mug spills over the edge and drips onto my knuckles. I ignore it. "I appreciate what you're trying to do, and I—I know I said I didn't need the pep talk, but it was"—I tilt my head back and forth—"it was fine."

Luka sputters out a laugh, and I push to standing, an ache in my back and in the center of my chest. I rub my palm there and hand Luka my empty mug, grab the handle of my shovel and squint out at the fields. I have over a hundred trees left to plant, and it looks like rain. The anticipation of it hangs heavy in the sky, clouds thick over a blanket of stars. It occurs to me that it's rained every time Evelyn has left, and it almost makes me laugh.

Even the sky is sad to see her go. Weather to match my mood.

Luka stands with a grumble and drops both mugs into the wheelbarrow with a clang. His sleeve of cookies too. He grabs the extra shovel I brought and stares at me with both eyebrows raised, a determined clench to his jaw. "I have one more thing to say to you."

"All right." I glance longingly at the too-deep hole and wonder if I'll fit inside.

Luka squares his shoulders. "I don't think you should give up. Not yet. I don't know where she is, but I've seen the two of you together. I've seen the way she looks at you. And Beckett . . . When have you ever given up on anything? You built tiny tents over saplings to protect them from the rain last winter. You monitored soil saturation levels in the middle of a hurricane. You showed up for Stella when she first had the idea for this place." His voice cracks at the edges. "You walked away from a secure job with good pay to help her get on her feet here, with no guarantee. You adopted a duck—"

"I didn't adopt the duck."

"You adopted a duck you found in the barn. Four cats too. You smuggle in cookies because you're afraid of hurting Layla's feelings. And I know you were the one who drove two states up the coast to get her the fancy butter she wanted when all the local suppliers were giving her the cold shoulder. You aren't a guy who gives up, and you aren't a guy who doesn't care. So please stop pretending you're either of those things."

I stare at Luka. He stares at me. I clear my throat. "That was, uh . . . That was more than one thing."

"It was," he says, winded and worked up. His cheeks are red, his mouth set in a firm line. He shifts on his feet and points at the marked spots in the field with the blade of the shovel. He stabs at the air with it once. "I'm going to go dig some holes now."

"That's fine."

I think he expected me to fight him on it. I'm still a little shocked from his speech. Those piano strings in my chest vibrate under the strain, all of my notes out of tune.

"You remember what you said to me when I showed up at your house? After that fight with Stella?"

Right before they got together, Luka appeared on my doorstep, his sweatshirt on inside out and a look on his face like someone stole all of his cookies and his last slice of pizza too. He sat on my couch wrapped in three blankets and stared blankly into my fireplace for close to five hours. *I just need a second*, he had said. *Just a few minutes*.

"I told you to stop being an idiot," I say reluctantly. "Tell her how you feel."

Luka raises both eyebrows. "Stop being an idiot," he tells me. A smile twists his mouth to the side. "Tell her how you feel."

STELLA APPEARS NOT too long after, a sweatshirt down to her knees and a shovel dragging listlessly behind her. She looks like she just went seven rounds with her mattress and lost every single one. She brushes a kiss to Luka's cheek, wraps her arms around my middle in a hug, and then tows her way over to the far end of the field and proceeds to dig the slowest, sloppiest holes known to mankind. Luka lasts three minutes before he trudges his way over to help.

Just as a few fat raindrops decide to fall from the sky, Layla arrives wearing rubber boots and a bright blue knit beanie. She walks right up to me and squeezes tight, her head under my chin. I get a mouthful of puffball.

"I didn't have time to make zucchini bread," she says. She squeezes harder and I let out a wheeze. "I'm sorry."

I blink down at her head and give her a gentle squeeze back. Really, I'm trying to encourage her to let go. Rolling out all those piecrusts has made her scary strong. "That's all right."

"I'll make some this afternoon."

"Okay."

She hoists the shovel I didn't see her bring over her shoulder and joins Luka and Stella, her hat bouncing the entire way. I see headlights flash in the distance, and I frown.

"What's going on?" I shout over to my trio of unexpected assistants. A raindrop lands on my nose and slides down.

Stella is leaning back on Luka's chest, her head tipped against his shoulder. Her eyes are barely open, and for a second I think she's asleep. "The phone tree," she yells back, her call echoing out over the empty field. "We moved Dig Day up."

Another pair of headlights appears in the distance, two beams of light cast down the dirt road that leads to the farm. I watch them for a second and swallow hard. Those piano strings relax, just a bit.

"Why?"

I can see the look Stella is giving me from all the way over here. One delicately raised eyebrow, her lips in a flat line. Layla scoffs and Luka shakes his head.

"If you're digging, we're all digging," she yells. The heat in her statement is lessened slightly by a giant yawn, right in the middle. She shivers and Luka presses a kiss to the back of her head, his forearm anchored across her collarbone. "That's what partners do."

20

EVELYN

I HATE THIS place.

I hate this place. I hate this car. And I hate this stupid back road that my GPS told me would be the more scenic route. I hate that I thought a more scenic route sounded nice, and I didn't just take the highway. I could have been back by now.

Or, at the very least, I could be drinking a milkshake on my way back.

On the highway.

I stare out at a field of dead grass and kick my flat tire. There is not a single scenic thing about this stretch of poorly maintained road or the abandoned gas station thirty feet away, a family of crows staring blankly at me from their perch on the boarded-up storefront. I'm getting faint Hitchcock vibes, and I press two fingers between my eyebrows, silently willing some positive vibes instead. It feels like I've had a string of cosmic bad luck since I left the American Small Business Coalition offices in Durham. I try not to read into it.

Spilled coffee. Missed turn. Another missed turn. Lost signal. And now this. A flat tire.

At least the rental has a spare. I only need to . . . remember how to change a tire.

My mom had been big on this stuff in high school. Replacing old rusted-out pipes beneath the sink and changing the oil in the car. She said it was important for me to learn how to be my own hero.

You won't ever need to ask a boy, she had told me, grease up to her elbows and across her forehead, a grin on her face as she released the jack. Her laugh had been proud and bright in our tiny garage, crinkles in the dark skin around her eyes. Her arm warm around my shoulders as our minivan rocked in place. *Self-sufficient women raise self-sufficient women*, she had said.

She'd be scowling at me now though if she could see me staring at the tire propped up against the wheel well.

I put my hand over my eyes and glance down the long winding road I've pulled to the side of. I can't hear a single engine rumbling in the distance. I check my phone again and note the lack of bars in the top-right corner.

"All right, well . . ." Maybe it'll come back to me through muscle memory. I certainly have nothing better to do at the moment.

I lug the heavy jack out of the trunk of the car and set it by my bum tire and get to work. This, at least, I remember. I pour all of my frustration into turning the stubborn lug nuts, a groaning sound coming from each one as I hold the metal steady in my palm and crank.

Despite my string of bad luck since leaving their offices, my interview with the Small Business Coalition went well. Really well. Theo had been warm and welcoming—a little bit awkward—offering me coffee and a trayful of small Danishes as soon as I arrived, the covered dish balanced precariously on the edge of an overcrowded desk.

"A lot of your content features food," he had said, adjusting his glasses with his knuckles. "I was hoping to woo you to our side with sugar."

He didn't need to woo me with sugar or coffee or anything else. He had launched into his pitch immediately, his quiet voice coming to life with excitement at the list of small businesses on their roster. His office had been cluttered, stuffy, a small window above his desk that overlooked a narrow alley and a brick wall. There was hardly any natural light or extra space, only one chair across from his desk, a dated phone with a tangled cord wedged next to the Danish tray.

I loved it immediately. All of it. The half-empty mug on the bookshelf by the door and the stack of papers that ruffled every time he moved in his squeaky desk chair. His space looked like hard work and enthusiasm, ideas spilling out of every corner. I found myself examining the pictures hanging in clusters along the wall as he talked, a mismatched timeline of people and places in Technicolor. A food stand at a small park. A storefront with a red-and-blue awning, large looping letters on the window. A smaller picture, right beneath, of him and a handsome man, their hands clasped together and a little girl clinging to their knees.

"You'll get fancier offers, I'm sure," he told me. I couldn't help but think of Sway—the fruit art in the water and all of the odds and ends that don't matter at all. "But I don't think you'll find work that makes you happier than this."

Happier. Of all the words he could have chosen.

He hadn't needed to say more than that.

The details on the position had been like icing on my fulfillment cake. Working with small businesses, helping them establish their digital channels—this new position is exactly what I've been doing but better. More time building relationships. Stronger resources to support initiatives. And an entire Rolodex of small business owners across the country just trying to figure it all out.

Countless stories to tell.

And support for me. Rest when I want it.

I had been humming with excitement when I left the interview, bursting at the seams with a feeling I thought was gone forever. I walked to my car and dialed Beckett's number, picturing him sitting on the back porch, one of the cats on his knee and his hand curled around a beer, socked feet crossed at the ankles and his long legs stretched out. I imagined what his face might look like when I told him the news, the way his eyebrows would lift. That quiet smile in the lines by his eyes and the dimple in his cheek.

But he didn't answer.

I turn the wrench with a grunt and loosen the last lug nut, a bead of sweat sliding down between my shoulder blades. I drop the wrench to the concrete, and one of the crows launches itself off the top of the gas station in a flurry of ruffled feathers. I frown at his friends and then down at my flat tire.

"So far, so good," I mutter.

It comes back to me in pieces as I work. My mom's voice in my ear, instructing me how to crank the jack, how to hold myself away from the car, how to pull the tire off and gently push the new one on. A thrill of satisfaction runs through me as I move through each step until I secure the new wheel and tighten the last of the lug nuts. I roll the popped tire to the trunk and lower the jack again, and the car releases a groaning, heaving sigh.

Maybe I should have changed a tire sooner. The pride burning in my chest has me short of breath, a fierce burst of energy that zips through my entire body. I stand there with my hands covered in grease and my arms burning from the effort.

I feel fantastic.

I almost laugh when I hear the growl of a car engine behind me, a bright red truck tearing down the back road. It slows to a stop by my side, and an old man with a faded baseball cap pokes his head out the window, his tanned arm hanging over the door. He looks at all the tools scattered across the ground and gives me a quizzical look.

"You need any help?"

I shake my head. I don't. For the first time in a long time, I'm not left wanting for a single thing. I am firmly here in this moment. Not planning for what's next, not thinking about all the things I'm missing out on by standing still. Everything is exactly where it should be.

I give him a grin that he mirrors with a bewildered twitch of his lips. A strange lady standing outside a boarded-up gas station with grease on her face, smiling at nothing.

"I'm good, thanks."

I CALL JOSIE from a rental shop exactly halfway between Durham and Inglewild, a foam cup of coffee in my hand and a stale donut cradled in my arm.

"He offered you the job?"

I glance through the window at the service center, my little blue car receiving a proper tire replacement. I'm impatient to get on the road, another couple of hours left of driving before I'm back at Lovelight. Beckett still hasn't answered his phone, and I don't know what to do with that.

I put a note on the kitchen table when I left, my own attempt at a doodle at the bottom. *I had to leave on short notice*, I wrote. *An interview!!! We can celebrate with burgers when I get back.*

I hesitated beneath that, my hand hovering over the scrap of paper. *Talk soon* felt incomplete. *Miss you* felt silly. I stared at that piece of scrap paper and chewed on my bottom lip, clueless as to how to sign the damn thing.

In the end, I settled for a tiny heart with lopsided edges, a circle of tulips curling at the bottom.

"Informally," I reply to Josie, nibbling at the edge of my Boston cream donut. It pales in comparison to Layla's flaky, buttery dough, and a punch of longing hits me right in the chest. What I wouldn't give to be sitting in her café right now, my boots propped up on the seat across from me and Beckett leaning heavily into my side, his scruff catching in my hair and his fingers toying with the sleeve of my shirt. I sigh. "He said he'd send me an offer letter in the next couple of days."

"That's good, right?"

I nod. "Yeah. Yeah, it's good."

"Then why do you sound weird?"

"A lot to do," I mutter, peering out the window again to check on my car. There's a guy in coveralls half tucked beneath it, another mechanic approaching. I wish I had taken the replacement they offered. It's ridiculous to feel a sense of camaraderie with a car. "A lot of details to sort out."

Josie hums. "Like if you're staying in Inglewild or not?"

"Hopefully, that won't be one of the details that needs sorting." Once I talk to Beckett. Once he answers his damn phone.

I'd like to stay. Not at his house, of course. A new place, maybe somewhere in town. Somewhere I can step off the porch and press my toes into wet grass. Flowers in the garden. Lots of windows.

"I'll have to fly to California," I tell her. "I need to close out the contract with Sway. Sort out a couple other projects." Collect the rest of my things from my barely used apartment. Probably visit that empanada shop.

"I'll fly down and meet you."

"You don't need to do that."

"And miss your breakup with Sway? I don't think so." She snickers on the other end of the phone, and I hear the creak of a screen door opening.

"I'm proud of you, you know." Her voice is quiet, a smile in every syllable. "I know you haven't been feeling like yourself, but you're—you're getting there. And I'm proud of you."

I blink at the pressure behind my eyes. I'm proud of myself too.

A conversation whispers back to me. Worn flannel tucked around my shoulders and that old porch chair rough beneath my palms. Borrowed socks on my feet and Beckett in the chair right next to me.

"I'm trying."

BY THE TIME I make it to Inglewild and the single dirt road that leads to Lovelight, the sun is setting over the farm, the big red barn by the road turning a faded rust in the dwindling light. Relief blossoms in my chest, warmth radiating all the way out to where my hands grip the wheel. Two days, and I missed this place. Missed the wide-open space and Beckett in the spot right next to me. The cats and the trees and the lightness I feel as the road changes from dirt to gravel, my car rumbling along.

It feels like coming home.

The house is dark when I pull into the driveway, but Beckett's truck is in its usual spot, a dull glow from the greenhouse in the backyard letting me know where he is. I smile as I slip from my car and leave my things for later. I'm eager to see Beckett, to wrap my arms around his waist and squeeze.

I skip from rock to rock down the stone pathway that hugs the side of the house, counting the wooden signs in the garden as I go. More herbs than blooms on this side of the house. Basil. Thyme. Mint and rosemary. I wonder if he'll make that chicken soup again. If he'll taste like sage when I sit sideways in his lap and press my mouth to his.

I see him as soon as I turn the corner, his head bowed over a shelf of plants near the front. Messy hair. Strong arms. Sleeves rolled to his elbows. He looks like one of those old statues—the ones that sit lonely in the middle of bustling city squares, their crisp edges worn down by time. My smile falters and I trip over a tree root sticking out along the path. The ones that look so sad.

I'm quiet as I lean up again the frame of the glass door, my fingers itching with the need to smooth my palms over those tight shoulders. Press my face in the space between until he releases a deep, relieved breath. I want to make it go away, whatever it is.

"Hey," I tip my head to the door and watch as his entire body goes rigid, half bent over a pot of fledgling poinsettias. He's frozen where he is, my arrival clearly unexpected. Unwelcome, by the looks of it. A cascade of nerves flutter in my belly and I pause. "What're you up to?"

It's so good to see you, I want to say. *Two days and I missed you like crazy.*

He straightens out of his crouched position and sets his watering can to the side, his movements slow and hesitant. It's like he's forgotten where he is, what he's supposed to be doing. He glances at me slowly, a thin tremble of confusion twisting at his lips.

"I'm finishing up a few things," he tells me, voice rough. He wipes his palms down the front of his jeans, clenches them into fists, and shoves them into his pockets. "What are you doing here?"

"I'm staying here, aren't I?" I laugh. He doesn't. The smile slips right off my face. My heart jumps to my throat, and everything in my body tightens. "Is everything all right?" He remains quiet. The space between us feels like a chasm. "Did something happen with the trees?"

"No." He shakes his head and glances out one of the big windows. The sky glows behind him, a bright and fierce orange. One last burst of brilliant color. "No, nothing happened with the trees."

"Your family okay?"

He nods.

"All right, good." I glance over my shoulder at the back porch, the two chairs that look like they're a little bit farther apart than the last time we sat in them. "Why are you out here so late?"

Why is the house dark?

Why won't you look at me?

Why haven't you kissed me yet?

"Evelyn," he sighs, exhausted. He drags his gaze up from the floor to blink at me slowly. "What are we doing?"

Evelyn. I feel that like a pinch. A tiny prick to my heart. He hasn't called me by my full name in weeks.

"Well," I rub my fingertips over my heart and urge myself to settle, "right now, it sounds like you have something to say to me."

"That's not what I meant."

"I know that's not what you meant." I sigh. Maybe I should go back to the car, do a lap around the farm, and we can try this again.

I had been so excited to see him, so relieved to be back in this place. And he's treating me like my arrival is the worst thing that could have happened. "What's going on? Why are you upset?"

"I'm not upset."

"Beckett. You can barely look at me." His jaw clenches and impatience grabs me by the throat. "If you have something to say, I wish you'd just—"

"What are you doing here, Evie?" he asks in a rush. I take a half step forward and he takes two steps back, his hands gripping the metal frame of the shelf he's backed into like he needs the anchor to keep himself grounded. In all this frantic motion, he's sure to keep his body away from mine. We don't touch anywhere, and I feel that absence like a hand to my chest, demanding distance. His eyes search mine, desperate and a little bit hurt. "What's your plan? Are you coming or are you going?"

"What are you talking about? I thought I was coming home." His face crumples and I have no idea what's going on. "Do you want me to leave? I don't understand."

He pushes off the shelf, but I reach out and grip his T-shirt in both hands, hauling him close. "No. No, you explain what the hell you're talking about. Right now, Beckett."

"You left."

"Yes." I left for two days. I came right back. I bought him a stupid gas station T-shirt and a koozie for his beer.

He curls his hands around my wrists and squeezes gently, urging me to let go of his shirt. I do, and he takes three steps across the small space, his back against the same table he propped me up on two nights ago. I can barely make out the shape of the man who pressed a kiss to my neck and tangled a flower in my hair.

"You didn't bother to tell me," he says. "I thought you left for good."

"I left a note." Right in the middle of the table. Next to a thermos of coffee and a stack of mail.

"There was no note."

"But I left one." I think about the scribbles at the bottom of the page, how I agonized over what to write. Guess that didn't matter. "I drew flowers on it. Tulips."

He doesn't move an inch, not even a flex of his fingers at his side. "There wasn't a note on the table when I got home. There wasn't anything."

A lead weight sinks in my chest.

"I left all of my stuff in the spare bedroom."

"I didn't check."

"Well, maybe you should have," I snap. All he had to do was crack open the door to see my laundry thrown all over the place.

"I didn't want to see an empty room." His response thunders out of him, a fist against the table. "I didn't want to look at the place you were and find you gone."

"You think I could just leave?"

He shrugs, and I know exactly what he's going to say the moment before he says it.

"You've never had trouble leaving," he accuses, and I feel the words like a slice against my skin. "Leaving me," he says, a little bit softer.

That was before, I want to tell him. *Before I stood in your kitchen and watched you make pancakes. Before I sat on your back porch and listened to you talk about the stars. Before you trusted me with all of your smiles. Before you let me know you.*

Before I fell in love with you.

"We didn't know each other then," I say. "That morning in Maine . . . I had an early flight, and I didn't want to wake you."

It's not a good excuse, but it is the truth. He shakes his head, and I know he doesn't believe me. I think I've left more bruises on Beckett's heart than he's shown me.

"You'll leave again," he adds. I hurt him before, and I'm paying for it now. He doesn't trust me to stay. Not when I've left before. He looks exhausted, completely spent. Dark circles under his eyes and a strain in the lines of his body that I haven't seen since that night at the bar when everything was too loud around him.

"You're gonna keep leaving, Evie." His face twists in naked longing. "Why wouldn't you?"

Oh, I think quietly. *There it is.*

"Then ask me to stay." The words are out of my mouth before I can consider them. They hold in the space between us, impatient. Pleading.

His eyes meet mine and he shakes his head once. "I can't."

"Why not?"

He swallows hard, a catch in the strong line of his throat. He stares at me for a long time. So long, I think he won't answer the question.

"I dreamt about you," he says, his voice rough. He looks embarrassed to say such a lovely thing. "After those two nights in Maine, I dreamt about you all of the time. When we ran into each other again that night on the street, I thought I had fallen asleep for a second. You were so beautiful." He swallows again and looks down at his boots, gathering himself. He looks at me, eyes bright. "Having you here has felt like that. A dream. But I think we both know it has to end, yeah? You've got a great big life outside this tiny town, and that's okay. That's the best thing, really. You glow like—you glow like the fucking sun, and you shouldn't bottle that up here. You shouldn't waste your light. I thought I could be happy with whatever pieces of you I got. I thought it would be enough. But then you left, and I realized it—it won't be. You'll take a piece of me every time you go until I've got nothing left. I can't keep standing here and watching you walk away from me."

But I'll bring your pieces back, I want to say. *I'll bring them back and give you some of mine too.*

Silence rings between us, a faint buzzing in my ears.

"How long have you been thinking about this?" I say.

He looks so tired, propped up against the table. He drags his palm over his face. "What?"

264 • B.K. BORISON
264 • B.K. BORISON

"How long have you been expecting me to leave? After our date?" I swallow hard and will the hum in my blood to settle. "After we had sex?"

He's too still over by the windows, the shadows twisting around his ankles and cloaking him in darkness. He shrugs and averts his eyes to the floor.

"I don't know what you want me to say here, Evie." He rubs his palm against the back of his neck. "I'm just—I'm just trying to hold on to what I can. Do you understand?"

I shake my head, a pressure behind my eyes. "I don't understand."

His hands fall limply by his sides. "I don't know a better way to explain it to you."

I take a step closer. "If I had waited for you to get back . . . if you saw my note . . . would you have believed me when I told you I was coming back?"

He doesn't say a word. He sighs and closes his eyes tight and then meets my gaze. I see the answer in the lines of his face. In the sad, sad blue-green of his eyes.

"Why can't you believe me?" I ask, my voice cracking at the edges "I want to be here."

With you. With everyone else. Where I can breathe and rest and think. Where I can be whoever I want to be.

His mouth opens and closes. I wait for him to say something, anything. But he doesn't. He snaps his mouth shut and looks at a spot over my shoulder.

"That's it, then?" I say.

He glances at the empty pot on the table, the seed packets next to it. Everywhere, it seems, except at me. He sighs and scrubs his hand against the back of his head. A small shrug.

"You can—you can stay as long as you want. You're always welcome here. I just think—I think maybe we should go back to the way things were before. I complicated it and I'm sorry about that."

Like it would be that simple to untangle all the feelings in my chest. Like I could sit down in the seat next to him on that porch and not love him with all of my heart.

"You're sorry." I don't bother phrasing it as a question. He's sorry for how he complicated things. My chest cracks right open.

He hesitates, and then, "Yes."

All of the fight drains right out of me. He thinks I'll be giving something up by staying, not getting everything I've ever wanted. The flame of hope that was burning bright in my chest as I drove from Durham flickers. Embers, really, cooling in the circle of ash that's taken up residence in the open space between my lungs. Every breath burns.

"Beckett Porter," I sigh out his name and blink too quickly. I don't want to cry. Not here. Not right now. "Are you letting me down easy?"

I hate the way my voice wobbles at the edges. He notices and his eyes snap to mine. I watch his fingers flex, the small oak leaf on the inside of his wrist dancing as his arm turns.

He huffs a laugh, but it doesn't sound amused at all. It sounds sad, a thousand unspoken things tucked into a single sound.

"No, honey." He watches me with those serious eyes, looking for all the world like he's trying to memorize the curves of my face. His mouth twitches to the side. Not quite a smile, not quite a frown. Something resigned, right in between. "I'm letting myself down hard."

I stare at him for a long time, memorizing him right back. I don't think Beckett ever thought we'd have a happy ending.

It makes me sad that he's been waiting this entire time for me to disappoint him. I take a deep breath and watch his hands clench and unclench at his sides. Like he wants to reach for me but doesn't trust himself to.

Time to start fixing that.

"I need to do some things," I finally tell him, voice uneven. This isn't how I thought this conversation would go, but it doesn't change my plans. Not really. "I'll be back. I'm not asking you to wait for me or to believe me. I'm just . . . I guess I'm just letting you know. I'm coming back."

I press up on my toes and brush a gentle kiss to his lips before he can answer. I don't want him to have a chance to tell me no. So I tell him I'll see him soon and squeeze his hand in mine. I leave him standing in the greenhouse, with the flowers and the herbs and the spilled soil on the table.

My body moves without my mind needing to check in. I go to the spare room and pack up my things. I fight with the door of my car and toss my suitcase in the trunk. I stomp up the stairs and leave the stupid gas station T-shirt and koozie sitting by his door.

I gather all of the parts of me that are unraveling and hold them tight in my shaking fist, two deep breaths and my hands on the steering wheel. I stare at the house and exhale slowly.

I back out of the driveway and rumble down the little road that leads to town.

21

BECKETT

I STARE AT the duck.

The duck stares at me.

One of the kittens meows from behind the makeshift fence I've made in the kitchen. Not that it would stop them if they truly wanted to get out. I still have no idea how Prancer manages to leave the house every morning for her tractor rides. I've looked over every square inch of the perimeter and can't figure out where she's leaving from, short of opening the front door herself.

I sigh and glance at the cat family waiting patiently behind some chicken wire. They came running as soon as I elbowed my way through the front door with our new addition. It's the first time they've acknowledged my existence since Evelyn left two nights ago. They haven't forgiven me yet for letting her slip away.

I haven't quite forgiven myself either.

I found her note crumpled and half torn in Prancers' bed by the couch next to a hair tie and an empty tube of ChapStick. I stared at that little piece of paper for a long time, the flowers scribbled along the bottom edge, the three exclamation points.

It doesn't matter that she left a note. It doesn't matter that she had every intention of coming back. Keeping all her light for myself still feels like the worst kind of selfish. I won't do it.

I tell myself that, anyway. And I put the note in the drawer next to my bed. Next to the damn dried-up blue flower and a crumpled receipt.

I sigh and scoop the duckling up in my hands, bigger already than the last time I saw him. Dr. Colson had called this morning and let me know there was no place for him at the local wildlife center. It likely had been too long anyway for the little guy to make a successful transition back to the wild.

He hadn't needed to say much more than that.

I didn't want the little duck to be alone.

"All right, everyone"—I shoot a stern glance at the cats lined up in a row behind the makeshift wall—"we're going to be on our best behavior, yeah? No nibbles or anything teeth adjacent." I swear Prancer frowns at me, a pout on her tiny furry face.

I sit down on the floor and carefully—slowly—extend my hands. With Dr. Colson's recommendation in mind, I keep one hand hovering over the top of the ball of yellow fluff in my palm, ready to protect him if I need to. But all four cats seem calm enough to meet their new housemate, faces turned up in interest.

The duck pokes his head out from between my outstretched fingers, a tiny *chirrup* of greeting.

Prancer stares in avid concentration and then meows in response. She rises from her prone position on the floor and nudges gently at my hand, her pink velvet nose brushing my thumb and then the duckling. She meows again and the three kittens echo in kind. The duckling offers the beginning of a quack.

All right. That seems . . . good.

Duck and cats continue investigating each other, and I hear my front door swing open. For a split second, a flare of hope seizes in my chest. But then I hear Stella and Layla bickering about cinnamon rolls, and my heart tumbles, disappointment pounding out a slow beat.

I looked at Evelyn and told her I wouldn't settle for the pieces of her. It's how I feel, but I wish I said it in a better way. Softer, maybe. I can still see her face as the words tripped off my tongue. The way her whole body flinched, her hands clasped tight together. Her eyelashes against her cheek. A single sharp inhale.

Regret is a funny thing. Self-preservation too. I've been swinging wildly between the two and reached for my phone more times than I can count. But I can't quite make myself dial her number, my thumb hovering over the screen.

Stella and Layla stumble to a stop at the edge of my kitchen. I don't bother looking up.

"Christ," Layla breathes. "It's worse than I thought."

I watch as Comet nudges once at the duck with her head, a happy purr tucked between them. The duck flaps his little wings against my hand. I'll have to name him now. It's settled. "I thought I locked my door."

"I have a key," Layla says mildly.

"I took your key away three months ago when you broke in and stole all of my Pop-Tarts."

"Like I'd eat store-bought Pop-Tarts." Layla is offended. "That wasn't me."

Stella raises her hand. "That was Charlie. He'll buy you a new box." She pauses for a second and drops to her knees next to me, holding her hand out toward the kittens. "Beckett, why are you sitting on the floor?"

Interesting question from a woman who just told me her half brother broke into my house and ate all my processed sugar. I ignore it. I'm too tired for the details.

"I'm introducing them to each other."

"All right." She blinks at me. "How long have you been doing this?"

"Sitting on the floor?"

"Yes."

Layla busies herself with something on the counter. I hear the sound of foil crinkling, my drawers opening as she looks for silverware. Vixen is more interested in whatever she brought than her new family member and goes trotting off, winding herself between Layla's ankles.

I glance at the clock. "I've only been sitting here for ten minutes. Why?"

Stella looks relieved. "Okay, good."

"Why?"

"Because Sal told us he saw you on your back in the middle of the Santa barn yesterday for three hours," Layla interrupts. She holds out a plate with a single blueberry muffin on it—a perfect buttery crumble on top.

I frown. I hadn't realized I'd been there that long. "I was checking the roof for holes. Some of the farmhands have noticed leaks."

And then I fell asleep, flat on my back in the middle of the Santa barn. I woke up tired and disoriented, a hollow ache in the pit of my stomach.

Missing Evelyn is like missing the bottom step on a flight of stairs. I keep expecting her to be where she's not.

It's that expectation, I think, that's the worst of it. I step into the kitchen and expect to see her sitting at the counter doing her crossword. I walk past the back door and peek out the window, looking for her long legs curled beneath her on the back porch. I check for her coat on the peg next to mine. Her boots tossed beneath the entryway table. I leave a space in the fridge for where she likes to put her coffee, right next to the iced tea.

I'm missing all the pieces of her.

I want them back.

Layla sits down on my other side with her own plate of muffins and extends one to Stella. I bring the duck closer to my chest—behind the protection of the fence—and deposit him carefully in my lap. He gives a happy quack, wanders in a circle, and then falls into a little clump of yellow fur on my thigh.

"Evelyn texted us," Layla offers, like that single sentence doesn't steal all the breath out of my lungs. I take a bite of muffin to keep myself from saying something stupid. *When?* I want to ask. *Did she sound half as sad as I am?* "She wanted us to check in on you."

That's something, I guess. I pluck a dried blueberry off the top of the muffin. I checked her social media profiles the other day, desperate for a glimpse. She hasn't posted anything in weeks. Nothing since a picture of her flat on her back in the wildflower field, the shot angled to get only the top of her face. Smiling eyes lit up by the sun, her long hair spread around her head like a halo, flower petals twisted between the strands.

I stared at that picture for a long time.

"I'm fine," I say. I want to ask more about Evelyn, but I can't bring myself to say her name.

Stella sighs. "You can't sit here all day." She looks like she wants to walk out, get the wheelbarrow, and dump me into it. "Come over to the house. Luka will make you gnocchi."

He'll also probably sigh his way through the meal, muttering under his breath the entire time. "No, thanks." I take another bite of muffin and ignore the silent conversation happening on either side of me. I can feel their eyes like little lasers. "I'm going to my parents' house later. I'm fixing the porch."

What I'm doing is avoiding my problems. Getting out of this house that still has the ghost of her laugh and her smile and her big brown eyes everywhere I look.

"Well . . ." Layla stretches out her legs on the floor of my kitchen and frowns down at her socked feet. She must have toed her boots off at the door. She drops her head against my shoulder just as Stella curls her hand around my arm, right above my elbow. She squeezes affectionately. "We'll sit with you until you have to go."

I let out a shaky exhale and watch the cats bat around an old

272 • B.K. BORISON

cardboard box, something they must have pulled out of the recycling bin. Stella crosses her ankles and Layla lets out a yawn. The three of us sit there in silence, huddled on the floor.

Partners in all the best ways.

"Does the duck have a name?" Stella eventually asks.

"Hm?"

"The duck," she says. "He needs a name."

He does. The three of us consider it.

"How about Pickles?" Layla offers. She peers over my shoulder at the duck fast asleep against my knee. "He kind of looks like a Pickles."

"In what way does he look like a Pickles?"

"The little mark on his head sort of looks like one, don't you think?" She glances at me, and her eyes widen at the look on my face. "All right. Not Pickles."

"Eggbert?" Stella suggests.

I make a noise low in my throat. I haven't forgotten that Stella wanted to name Prancer *Raccoon*.

"James Pond?" Layla adds.

"Squeak?" Stella fires back.

I ignore them both. "I like Otis."

My dad used to play Otis Redding in the morning while we were getting ready for school. He would blast it from the speakers in the living room. Turn it up loud enough that we'd hear it all the way in our bedrooms. It was the very first artist Nessa ever danced to. He still plays "These Arms of Mine" for my mom every Wednesday night after he thinks we've all left. She sits across his lap and he hums in her ear, a slow turn around the driveway with nothing but the porch lights on.

"I like that name," Stella says.

Layla nods into my shoulder. "Yeah, me too."

I rub my knuckle over the little guy's head. "Otis it is, then."

჻

I BRING OTIS with me to my parents' house and set him up in a small box on the front porch while I get to work unloading the wood from the back of my truck. The house and the gardens behind it are still and quiet, the narrow windows on either side of the front door reflecting the afternoon sun. A single beam of light cascades through, dust motes dancing in golden waves.

It's strange being here when no one else is. I'm used to the front door being cracked open, my sisters spilling out into the front yard. Loud laughter and the smell of something on the stove. My dad pleading with Nova for a full back tattoo.

But I planned this specifically for the silence. I'll fix the ramp, secure the railing, and be on my way without having to talk to anyone. It's the perfect plan.

"You building me a new deck?"

I drop all the wood gathered in my arms as my dad wheels around the side of the house, a grin on his face. I press a closed fist to my pounding heart and frown down at my supplies scattered at my feet. "What the hell, Dad?"

He laughs. "When are you going to realize I'm always around, kiddo?"

"Never, apparently," I grumble. He meets me at the back of the truck and leans forward in his chair, levering a piece of wood I've dropped up into his arms. He stacks it neatly next to my toolbox and gives me an amused look.

I narrow my eyes at him. "What are you doing here?"

"I live here," he responds with a chuckle.

I roll my eyes to the sky. "Why are you home? I thought you were working."

About seven years ago, my dad took on a different job at the produce farm. Now he works in the front office, helping manage shipments and agreements with local markets and grocery chains. He also occasionally steals the tractor when Roger Parson leaves the keys lying around.

"I took today off."

"For what?"

"Are you my keeper now?" Another rough, amused chuckle tumbles out of his barrel chest. "What are you doing at my house in the middle of the day? With enough supplies to build your own Unabomber den, mind you."

I glance at the haphazard stack of wood. The handsaw I borrowed from the farm. "It's not that much," I hedge.

"It's enough." He looks up at me in that way he has. Eyes squinted, one eyebrow slightly higher than the other, his lips in a thin line but tilted up at the edges—like he's got some private joke. Every time he looks at me like that, I feel like I'm seven years old again—lying to him about what happened to the window in the back shed, my baseball bat hidden in one of the shrubs. His hand reaches for my arm, and he squeezes there once, the same exact place Stella had, not two hours ago. "You doing okay?"

"I'm fine," I say, not quite lying.

Because I am. I'm fine. Everything is—everything is fine. I wish everyone would stop asking me that. I just need a few hours to not think about Evie. To not replay that last conversation and see her arms curled around herself, her eyes blinking too fast.

I'm tired of seeing her every time I close my eyes. I'm tired of missing her when she's barely been gone at all.

I blow out a breath and brush my hands off on my knees. "I just want to fix your ramp."

My dad searches my face. "You want help?"

It's a fight not to clench my teeth. I really don't. I school my features into something nice and neutral instead, organizing some of the tools by my feet. I begin to gather some of the wood, my body grateful for the task. "If you want."

"What do you want?"

I pause with my arms full of two-by-fours. "What?"

"What do you want?" He rubs his fingertips over his bottom lip in thought. "If someone held a gun to your head right now and asked you what you want, what would you say?"

"Uh . . ." I look over my shoulder to make sure one of my sister's isn't standing nearby with a phone in their hand. He seems way too serious for a question about porch assistance. "I want someone to not be holding a gun to my head over a porch railing."

My dad is not amused. "Beckett."

"What? This is—" A weird conversation. "What are you asking me?"

"You're always letting us do what we want," my dad says after a lengthy pause. "When have you ever done what you want?"

"Like what?"

"Trivia," he says immediately. He holds up his finger. "We all know you didn't want to go, and you went anyway."

"Because Nova and Nessa asked me to." And sometimes I need to be dragged out of the house, or I'll never leave it. I can acknowledge that about myself.

He flicks up another finger and digs his phone out of his pocket, tapping around and then reading from the screen. "January sixteenth. We all ordered pizza, and you ate the one with mushrooms even though you don't like mushrooms."

It was the only option and I had been hungry.

"Do you have a list on your phone?"

He ignores me and scrolls down. "December twenty-eighth. You drove your sister to three separate grocery stores so she could find Nutella."

I kick at a piece of wood. "She said she wanted it."

He drops his phone to his lap and looks at me. "You were about to let me help you with the damned ramp when you don't want me to."

"It's not a big deal," I counter. I can see the point he's trying to make. He's about as subtle as a brick through a window. "There's nothing wrong with me doing things to help other people. Mushrooms aren't that bad."

My dad's face turns into a thundercloud. "They're terrible if they're not what you want."

I shrug. "Not really."

"Fine." The word comes out of his mouth like a gunshot. "I have two more for you."

I sigh and roll out my shoulders. "Let's hear them, then." It'll likely be something about the chicken coop I made in Harper's backyard that still doesn't have chickens, or the time I was Nessa's stand-in dance partner for a week. I lasted two days.

"You let your teenage sister put tattoos all over your arms, just to help her out." He swallows hard. "You dropped out of high school to support this family. You worked yourself to the bone."

And I'd do it again. All of it. No hesitation.

I love the tattoos on my arms. Each one is a piece of my family—a piece of me. It feels like armor when I need it most and comfort when I need that too. I love looking at the leaf on my wrist and tracing the wobbly edges, remembering the way Nova's whole face lit up when I agreed to let her try.

And the farming thing. That wasn't even a choice. Of course I was going to step up. It was the easiest decision I have ever made, that day in the kitchen. The Parsons had come to visit my dad once he got home from the hospital, and the idea came to me like lightning in a summer storm. I had been itching for something to do—some way to help—and taking my dad's place was the best way to do it. The *only* way to do it.

"Because I love you," I say, stubborn. I don't see anything wrong with the things he's listed. "Because I love all of you."

"I'm starting to think I made a mistake, then," my dad says quietly, his entire face lined with regret. He blinks quickly and clears his throat, never looking anywhere but right at me. "When I taught you how to love."

Something in my chest fractures. Worse than when Evelyn walked out my greenhouse door. "What?"

"If you think love means having to sacrifice bits of yourself to make someone else happy," he explains. "If you're afraid to ask after what you want. Maybe I did something wrong."

"I'm not—" My voice cuts out, my throat closing around the words. I look down at the ground, at the edge of my boots. Mud-splattered from my time in the fields. I clench both my fists. "That's not what I'm doing."

It's *not*. I love helping my family. Helping people is my—Christ—Nessa would say helping people is my love language. It's how I show them I care. Actions have always been easier for me than words.

"Did you ask Evelyn to stay?"

I shake my head. "That has nothing to do with this."

"Did you?"

I wish I had already started on the porch. It would be helpful to have a hammer in my hands. Pour all the restless energy twisting through my chest into the lift and pound of work.

"I didn't," I grit out. "Because she wouldn't be happy here. Because she'd leave again."

Because I can't be the reason she gives anything up. She'd hate me and I'd hate myself.

"Aren't those her decisions to make?" When I open my mouth to respond, my dad talks louder, steamrolling right over me. "How the hell is she supposed to know you want her here if you never even ask her to stay?"

I close my mouth.

Blink.

Blink again.

"Sometimes love is greedy, kiddo." My dad sets his mouth in a firm line. "Sometimes it's a little bit selfish too. You think it's never crossed my mind that your mom deserves something better than the life we carved out for ourselves here? It has. A million times. A million and one. But I'm holding on to her with both hands. I'm trusting her to make her own choices. To choose me."

He looks right at me, a smile hooking at the sides of his mouth. He bends at the waist and grabs a piece of wood. He flips it over his shoulder and begins making his way to the ramp.

"Be selfish, Beckett. Just this once."

22

EVELYN

"WHAT DID HE say?"

I glance up at Josie from my collection of folded leggings—a frankly alarming amount of comfort wear that towers next to one of my moving boxes. "When?"

"When you left."

He hadn't said a thing. He'd stood in the entrance of the greenhouse with his arm braced against the door and watched me quietly move around his house. I only allowed myself a single look back, right before I walked out the front door. He had his back to me by then, both hands anchored in his hair.

I can't keep standing here and watching you walk away from me.

I topple the whole stack into the box. "He didn't say anything."

"Has he said anything since?"

I glance at my phone and then shake my head. It's been radio silent.

Not that I expected anything different.

It's been two days, and the only update I've received on Beckett is a banal text from Stella. A simple He's okay that she didn't choose to elaborate on, along with a picture of a baby duck with a cookie by his webbed feet. *Otis* written in icing on top.

Though I suppose that was an update in and of itself.

"I need you two to communicate," Josie offers from the other side of the room, holding up a shot glass from . . . I have no idea, honestly. She rummages around above my microwave and finds a bottle of whiskey that is so old it's accumulated a layer of dust. I think the cap is fused to the bottle. "The miscommunication here is . . ." She trails off, grumbling under her breath.

"What?"

"It's extremely frustrating for me as a bystander in this relationship of yours."

She shuffles her way back over to me around a minefield of moving boxes and . . . more leggings . . . the bottle wedged under her arm. She collapses in front of me and hands me the shot glass, working at the cap with her teeth. She spits it toward the windows when it's off.

"It's not a miscommunication," I reply. It's Beckett thinking there's no possible way I could find my happy on his farm. It's him making a decision for the both of us out of a misplaced sense of . . . something. "It's a lot of little mistakes piling up into one big one." I sigh.

I see it every time I close my eyes. Beckett and the way his entire body went rigid when I walked into his space. The resignation on his face, like it was what he'd expected the entire time.

Josie fiddles with the bottle. "Did you ever tell him you wanted to stay?"

"What?"

"You know. 'Beckett, I want your gigantic heart and your smoking hot body. I'm staying.'"

I open my mouth and then close it.

Josie continues. "You were very communicative with me about your plans." She sniffs at the open bottle and makes a face. "What was his reaction when you told him about the new job?"

"He doesn't know about that," I mumble.

Josie makes a sound, exasperated. The bottle in her hand almost goes flying across the room. "So it is a miscommunication thing."

"Yeah." I rub my fingertips against my forehead. "Yeah, it might be a miscommunication thing." I think about our late nights on the porch, talking about everything under the sun. Everything, apparently, except our plans for the future. The things I was working toward and the things he was afraid of. I think we were both happy enough to exist in the little bubble we made for ourselves. We didn't want to test it with any real pressure.

See where this goes.

God, we've both been so *stupid*.

But I've shown him, haven't I? Trivia with his family and my name written on the registration sheet for next time. Afternoons spent in town and evenings spent with him. I've been putting down roots this whole time, carefully cultivating each one to be something lasting and true. Hasn't he seen that? Hasn't he realized?

Josie pours the amber liquid into the shot glass and I frown at it. "What do you want me to do with this?"

She raises both eyebrows. "Drink it."

"I'm not twenty-two anymore." Taking a shot physically hurts me these days.

"We need to commemorate this new chapter of your life and solve the giant mess the two of you have made." She takes the shot out of my hand, sips half of it, and almost spits it right in my face. She swallows it down with effort, her fingertips at her lips. "Oh my god."

"I told you."

"You did not tell me."

"I thought my refusal might say enough."

"All right, change of plans." She scoops up her phone and scrolls and taps—and taps some more. "I ordered us two bottles of wine and a pizza."

"That was very efficient."

"Modern technology, baby. We cannot shepherd you into the great unknown without grease, fried cheese, and carbohydrates." She wiggles her phone and places it to the side. "All right. Let's talk through your plan with the farmer man."

It's a loose plan at best. I want him to see that it's not just him I'm going back for, but everything else too. I think he needs to see that I mean it.

"Well, I'm going back." I always planned on going back.

Josie nods.

"And I have that little house I'm renting. It's weird that it suddenly became available, but whatever."

It's not weird. I know for a fact it's been empty since before I came to town. Gus told me so when I called him to put down my deposit over the phone. Apparently, he wanted to try his hand at flipping houses—in addition to the trivia night emceeing and firehouse dancing. A man of many strange talents. Unfortunately for him, there were no other houses to flip within Inglewild's town limits, and that dream came to an abrupt halt.

"And I'll"—this is where the plan gets murky—"I'll go to the farm. I'll show him that even though I left, I always planned on coming back." I'll bring burgers and fries in a brown paper bag. Maybe I'll wait until the sun sets so the stars are bright in the sky. "If he doesn't want to see me, that'll be okay."

It'll be heartbreaking, but I won't leave.

"I'll stay in the house and I'll visit if he'll have me. I'll bring him the cookies he likes. I'll keep showing up. I'll stay." I breathe in a shaky breath through my nose. "I'll tell him I love him. That I love the town too. That I went there looking for one thing, and found a bunch of other things instead. The best things."

Happiness and freedom and belonging and community and . . . shortbread cookies in the dead of night. Weird trivia. Layla's buttercream frosting.

"I think you could have saved yourself some trouble and told him all of this earlier, but"—she reaches for my hand with hers—"it's a good plan."

"Yeah?"

"I mean, you could text him and tell him you're coming back, but I like the drama of this."

"I did tell him I'd see him soon. When I left."

"You did?"

"Yeah. I told him I was coming back."

I don't think he believed me though. We keep missing each other. Every time we collide, something is slightly off. We smack into each other and go ricocheting into space, a million miles between us. One of those meteors.

A misalignment, maybe?

A missed opportunity, certainly.

Hopefully I can fix that.

Josie taps her fingers along the open bottle of liquor and keeps her gaze on me. She looks like she's considering another taste, previous experience be damned. I guess the wine she ordered is taking too long.

"Either way," she tells me, "I'm here for it."

"I'LL FINISH OUT whatever contract work I'm on the hook for, but after that, I'll be exploring other opportunities."

I stare out at a conference room full of blank faces. For some inexplicable reason, they called the entire organization in here for this meeting. I see Kirstyn in the corner openly weeping with her face hidden in a patterned handkerchief. She has a tiny cup of espresso at her elbow and a miniature cucumber sandwich. There's no bass coming from the speaker in the center of the room this time, thank god.

Though I bet Josie is dying to break out a tiny violin.

"I'm so appreciative of everything your team has done for me," I tack on lamely when I get no response. "I've, uh, I've really enjoyed working with all of you."

Josie snorts, and I drive the heel of my boot into her Converse beneath the table.

I wonder what Beckett is doing right now. If he's out in the fields or at the bakehouse stealing snacks from the front case when he thinks Layla isn't looking. He doesn't know it, but she puts the oatmeal chocolate chip cookies in the bottom right just for him, half-hidden behind the lemon bars so he has a chance to grab one after his morning list is done.

I picture him there, leaning against the counter. Flannel rolled to his elbows and hat backward. The slightest curl to the ends of his hair behind his ears.

This time, Josie has to step on my foot.

I glance at her, and she raises both eyebrows expectantly.

Ah, that's right. A roomful of people.

I glance sheepishly at Leon, sitting at the head of the table with both palms flat on the wood. He looks lost and a little desperate, his dark brown eyes resigned behind his horn-rimmed glasses.

"What was that?" I say.

"I asked if there is anything we can do to convince you to stay on," says Leon.

"Not unless you grow some scruff, adopt one hundred cats, get full-sleeve tattoos, and develop a six-pack," Josie mutters under her breath.

I bite the inside of my cheek to keep myself from laughing. "I don't think so." I gather the small stack of papers laid out in front of me. Notes from Josie with tiny handwritten scribbles at the bottom telling me to *Stay strong* and *Do the damn thing*. Oddly motivational, when it came down to it. "Thank you again, for everything."

Now I just want empanadas.

And a plane ride to Maryland.

We all file out of the room in a slow slog, hindered by two people at the front too busy on their phones to watch where they're going. I'm surrounded by people with hunched shoulders and drawn faces, actively avoiding eye contact. One guy wipes at his cheeks with the back of his hand. Someone wanders into the kitchen and turns off the pink neon light above the refrigerator. THERE'S NO PLACE LIKE SWAY stutters and then blinks out, the kitchen oddly cold without the fluorescent glowing light.

It all seems a bit much.

Josie leans into me as we walk toward the elevator. "That was nicely done."

I glance back over my shoulder at Kirstyn sitting at the edge of the long table in the center of the room, her forehead flat against the surface. I frown. "It didn't feel very nice."

Josie shrugs and jams the elevator button. She does it again when it doesn't light up right away. They're going to have to replace the damn thing when she's through with it. "Sometimes the right thing for one person isn't the nice thing for someone else." She turns to me and gives me a grin. "Hey, do we have any pizza left over from last night?"

We do. Barely. I'd much rather walk across the street and devour the entire menu of empanadas. The elevator finally arrives, and Josie storms the doors, muttering something about pizza with croquetas on top while digging for her phone in her bag. I step in behind her and pivot on my foot, then trace my eyes over the ferns on the wallpaper. Beckett would hate it. *Too green*, he would say. *The coloring is all wrong.* I can practically hear his voice in my ear, telling me the difference between vascular plants and . . . nonvascular plants. What kind of sunlight they need. The perfect soil consistency.

I'm so lost in my little Beckett bubble that I almost don't notice it.

A few things happen at once.

My phone begins to go wild in my pocket. Josie whispers a quiet "Oh my god" that gains volume as she repeats it over and over again. Several people stand up at the long coworking table, and—the most jarring—I see Beckett's face suddenly appear in the conference room, ten times larger than usual on the screen that's dropped from the ceiling.

I slam my hand against the elevator door to hold it open, a dip in my belly. It feels like this elevator just dropped all the way to the basement, and I'm along for the ride.

Josie reaches for my arm and squeezes. "Evie."

I take a step out and then another. I watch Beckett's mouth move silently through the industrial glass window. He looks—god—he looks good. Two days, and I feel like some of the details have already dimmed. How did I go weeks before? How did I go months?

How did I ever slip out of his bed to begin with?

"What is—"

Josie trails after me, her gaze stuck on her phone. "Your mentions are going absolutely insane," she says.

I watch through the window as Beckett's eyes crinkle slightly at the corners, a barely there smile on his handsome face. I can hear the muted rumble of his voice, the low tones of him speaking on camera, but I can't make out any of the words he's saying. "Why is there a video of Beckett playing in the conference room?"

Josie's head snaps up and her eyes narrow. "I guess it's hit the blogs already. He must have posted it while we were in that meeting."

We watch together as the video ends and then starts up again. It looks like—it looks like he posted a video online. It's hard to tell with all of the people in the conference room standing in front of the screen, watching. None of this makes any sense. Beckett's coffee maker is a single-switch machine from what I'm sure is 1986. He doesn't have any streaming services. And as far as I'm aware, Beckett also doesn't have a single social media account.

Josie loops her arm through mine and drags me across the office space, back to the conference room. She comes to an abrupt halt right outside the door, watches the screen, and seems to time her entrance with whatever Beckett is saying in the video.

When the video loops again, she shoves me once—hard—between my shoulder blades. I catch myself on the edge of the table and watch.

It's an awkward shot. The camera angle is a little off, leaving him lopsided in the center of the screen. One of his fingers is slightly covering the camera, a halo of obstruction in the top corner. But it only makes it better, the imperfection of it.

"Hey," he begins, a fierce frown on his face. A laugh immediately bursts out of me. Leave it to Beckett to make that one syllable sound so damn reluctant. Sharp edges. A grumble. His voice is so deep through the speakers in the corners of the room that I can almost feel it right at the back of my neck. The way it rolls out of him, the tingle of my skin when he's pressed all the way against me. "I know this is—well, I think this is sort of the coward's way of doing this. Saying what I'm gonna say to you through a screen. But it felt—it felt appropriate to do it like this. To be uncomfortable."

I watch as he swallows and looks up, over the camera. I can see trees behind him, and I imagine him out there in the fields, dirt on the palms of his hands. "I haven't been doing that with you, have I? Going out of my way." His eyes snap to the screen. "We've been sitting on my back porch for weeks, Evie. Just watching the sun move. We've been doing things how I've wanted to do them."

Me too, I want to tell him. *I haven't wanted to be anywhere else but on that porch with you.*

He lets out a deep gusting sigh, and his mouth curls at the edges, just a touch. Regret, it looks like. "So I thought—I don't know. I guess I thought making you one of these things would be a start at saying sorry for the way I left things. The last time we were together, I told you I couldn't keep watching you walk away. You told me to ask you to stay, and I didn't. I was having trouble with the possibility that you'd want to. I thought, 'How could someone like Evie want to be here? With me?'" He pauses and his hand drifts over his heart. My own pounds in response. "I've kept so much from you."

Hope lights up every inch of me, my heart in my throat. I ignore everyone else in the room and take a step closer to the screen, looking at those blue-green eyes, somehow the same color as the sky above him and the trees behind him.

"So this is—I'm asking you to stay this time," he rasps. "I'm trying to do it right. Come home, honey. Stay with me for a bit. I'll make you those muffins you like and won't say a damn thing about you stealing my socks. We'll sit on the porch and I'll tell you about the stars.

I'll bring you flowers every day." He scratches behind his ear and shifts his phone, a rustle of fabric against the speaker.

"I'm sorry I didn't say this next part." He gives the camera a grin, knuckles against his jaw. "I want you to stay with me. You can leave when you have to. So long as you come back when you're done."

I hold on to the back of the chair in front of me, my hands gripping the top edge until my knuckles turn white. I wish I were standing in front of him. I wish I could trace those lines by his eyes and step between his feet, press my palm to his neck, and guide his mouth to mine.

He blinks, and his gaze trips somewhere else, another lingering pause. His eyes swing to the phone with a brush of color across his cheeks, a slow-curling bashful grin that inches under my ribcage. "All right, well, that's it, I guess." He shrugs, a little unsure. "I know you came back here because you were looking for your happy. But, Evie, you gave me mine while you were looking for yours, and I think it's only fair if I try to return the favor. I'll be, uh"—he swallows around his words, looking, I know, for the right ones—"I'll be here. You know where to find me." He stares at the phone like he wishes it were me instead. "Bye."

The video cuts off with a fumble, his movements unpracticed, his frowning face the last thing I see before the video loops back to him standing beneath the sun.

I stay there in that tiny conference room, and I watch it again. Again and again and again. I feel the eyes of the other people in the room as they watch me for a reaction. I'm pretty sure a couple of them have their cameras out.

But I don't care.

I see only Beckett and the dark shadows under his eyes that tell me he hasn't been sleeping much, the way the sunlight catches in his hair and makes it seem lighter—a halo of gold around him. I catalog the lines of his face and the way the ones by his eyes deepen when he says, "Come home, honey."

I feel those words melt over me.

I tighten my grip on my bag as a smile begins to bloom across my lips. Like the wildflowers in that field at the edge of the farm, my face tilted toward the sun.

On my way.

"For the record—" Josie appears at my side with her phone clasped loosely in her palm. It hangs down by her side buzzing away as her chin finds my shoulder. She ignores it and instead sighs happily as ten-foot Beckett scratches once under his jaw. "I like his plan better."

23

BECKETT

I'M HAVING REGRETS.

Not for what I said, but for—

"Dude, you made me *cry*."

I grunt and ignore Gus, and throw a box of pasta into my cart. For whatever reason, I decided today is the day to break my unspoken only-shop-at-night rule. An attempt, probably, at integrating myself into town like Evie was always encouraging me to do.

Evie, who I haven't heard a word from since I posted that video almost twelve hours ago.

I've heard from the rest of the continental United States though. A bunch of other countries as well. My phone has been buzzing non-stop since I decided to stand out in the middle of the fields like a jackass, recording a message for Evelyn I'm not sure she'll even see.

I wanted to do something outside my comfort zone. I wanted Evelyn to see that video and realize that I'm—I'm going to try. I wandered to the place with the towering oak trees just because it made me feel better—to stand there between them and remember the way Evie looked in the moonlight. With her hair tangled across the blanket and stars in her eyes.

It took me a couple of tries to get it right. I had to stop thinking so much about it, close my eyes, and pretend like she was standing right in front of me. Wind in her hair, ruby red lips, the sun making her brown skin glow. It was easy when I went about it like that.

I didn't bother watching it before I posted it, and still haven't quite mustered up the courage to watch it. I had to ask Stella if I did anything weird. She had shaken her head wordlessly with her eyes full of tears. Not exactly a confidence boost. I have no explanation for the thousands of new followers on my account featuring exactly one video. Or the hundreds of thousands of comments that are both confounding and terrifying in their abject passion and enthusiasm.

I throw another box of pasta into my cart. Gus trails me down the aisle.

"It was poetic. Just—" He makes some sort of gesture with his hand that I cannot interpret. His finger and thumb pinched together and . . . I have no idea. I don't want to know, frankly. "Who knew you were so eloquent under all that grunting?"

I fight the urge to grunt in response and steer my cart around the edge of the aisle. Gus leaves me for candy and beer while I debate the strawberry jam on the endcap. Evelyn liked it, and I ran out three days before she left. I grab a jar and place it gently next to a carton of orange juice and three packs of Fudge Stripes cookies. I stare at it there in my cart like the sad sack I've turned into.

A little hope never hurt anyone, I reason.

Though that hope is quickly circling the drain as the silence stretches between us.

Maybe she didn't see the video? I find that hard to believe, considering her profession and the fact that every other living person in the universe has watched it at least three times.

Maybe she did see it and dropped her phone in another stagnant body of water. Or maybe she saw it and commented on the post. I haven't figured out how to see if she did or not, and I'm too embarrassed to ask Nova for help.

Maybe she watched my video and hopped on the next plane she could.

Or maybe she saw it and laughed, pocketed her phone, and went about her business.

"All good?"

I blink away from the coffee creamers I've stalled in front of and glance at Sheriff Jones standing next to me. It's weird seeing him out of uniform, almost unrecognizable in an old Orioles T-shirt and dark jeans. "What?"

"For about seven minutes, you've been staring at the dairy section like it's done you personal harm." He chews around a toothpick. "Would you like to file a formal complaint?"

"No. I'm—" Tired. Losing hope. Uncomfortable that a woman in Cincinnati called me her cat daddy garden himbo in the comments section of a video meant for exactly one woman. I have no idea what that means, but it doesn't sound good. "Fine."

Dane makes a huffing sound. "You've looked better."

I pick up a bottle of peppermint mocha creamer and eyeball it. Not so sure this should still be on the shelves in April. I put it back and grab a carton of half and half instead. "Thank you?"

It's really a wonder that I prefer shopping when the place is empty.

Dane picks up my discarded bottle of peppermint mocha and places it in his basket. When I stare at him a little too long because of it, he raises both eyebrows at me. "You got something against seasonal creamer?"

I shrug. "When it's the wrong season . . . yes."

Dane picks up the bottle and checks the expiration date on the bottom. Whatever he sees must be reassuring, because he drops it back into his collection. "Matty likes it," he tells me.

Wonderful. I couldn't care any less.

I move past Dane to the checkout line and the blissful silence beyond. I don't want to stand here and shoot the shit a second longer.

I'm tired of people talking to me. I'm tired of people asking me if I'm okay. I am tired of the unsolicited advice. At this point, I'm even tired of Layla dropping her baskets of baked goods on my front porch every morning. The heaps of pity muffins sitting on my kitchen table are starting to make me feel a little pathetic.

"I heard Gus rented out his house," Dane calls down the aisle. I turn and find him poking around in the butter section. Behind him, I see one of the kids from the preschool attempt to scale a balloon display. Roma, I think her name is. "The yellow one, right behind Matty's."

A sigh rattles out of me from somewhere deep in my chest. I know the place. "You mean the one with the porch roof he fell through?"

Dane snorts. "That's the one."

There had been a lot of confusion that day, wondering who should drive the ambulance when the town paramedic was lying in a heap of broken wood in the front yard.

"All the paperwork was signed a couple of days ago," Dane adds. "That's what I hear anyway."

"From the phone tree?"

"From the phone tree."

I take another step closer to the exit. "That's good."

"Heard the new tenant is moving in today, actually."

I don't care. I make my best approximation of a vaguely interested sound and keep walking.

"Maybe you should stop by." Dane's voice carries down the aisle. When I turn to look at him, he's examining a container of cream cheese. His frown deepens and his eyebrows collapse into a straight line across his brow. "What do you think *buffalo-style whipped cream cheese* tastes like?"

I'm more interested in why he wants me to stop by the little house with daisies in the backyard. "Someone new in town, huh?"

I'm the last person anyone would want on the welcome committee. A flare of hope flickers to life in my chest, along with a healthy dose of suspicion. Dane throws the cream cheese in his basket, right next to the creamer.

"Yep." He pops the last letter of the word.

"And I should stop by?"

Dane gives me a look. "Are you having trouble hearing, Beckett?" But his eyes are smiling, a twitch at his mouth that is as close to a grin as Sheriff Dane Jones gets. "Yes, I think you should stop by."

EXCEPT THERE ISN'T anyone at the house.

No car in the driveway, no moving truck at the curb. No one answers the door when I knock. I feel ridiculous standing there listening to the grasshoppers chirp in the long grass at my back, my boots shuffling across the new front porch that is . . . actually really nice. I'm glad Gus didn't destroy this part of the house in his quest to become a home renovation expert.

I dig the heel of my hand against the base of my neck. I feel like an idiot standing on the front porch of a random house in the early-afternoon sunshine. I sigh and wander to my truck, wondering what in the hell Dane was talking about at the grocery store. I drive to the farm with a tightness in my throat and an open pack of Fudge Stripes cookies in my lap, the windows all the way down and the ghost of Evie's laugh slipping along the seats. She had been so beautiful that day, with the wind in her hair, chin tilted up and back. I wanted to kiss every mark on her skin. Every scar, every nick, every line that appeared with her smile.

I've perfected a rhythm over the last couple of days. I wake up. I don't allow myself to linger in bed for more than a few minutes. I shuffle into the kitchen for coffee without glancing at a single thing. And then I trudge out to the fields and let my body take over for my mind. It's the only place I can bear missing her—where there's enough open space for all my yearning to come tumbling out of my chest. In the house, I feel stuck. I stare at the empty chair next to me, and the longing steals my breath.

I've planted more in the past week than I think I have during my entire tenure at Lovelight Farms. We'll have bell peppers for the next 750 years.

I grab the groceries and stomp my way up the stairs, ignoring the aluminum tray of . . . something on the top step. I think Layla is convinced sugar highs will see me through this difficult time. I hesitate with my key in the door and then lean back to snatch it up, balancing it on top of everything else. I get a whiff of cinnamon, the bottom of the tray still warm.

She might not be wrong.

Four cats greet me at the door, a chorus of quacking from the small fenced-in area in the kitchen. Otis and the kittens have taken well to each other, Prancer adopting the little guy as one of her own. My evenings are spent watching four cats trying to teach a duck how to meow, nudging their little felt mice at his webbed feet and then rubbing their heads against his downy fluff. Maybe I should put that on the stupid video app.

I put my groceries away in a haze. It only takes a few minutes for the silence to feel oppressive instead of comforting, pressing down on my shoulders until it's a ringing in my ears. I've never once had trouble with quiet, but now I feel my jaw clenching in the stillness of the house. I got too used to the sounds of her here with me—whispered fights with Prancer over scarf ownership, the clink of her mug on the countertop.

This whole house is bathed in memories of her, and I can't breathe because of it.

So I slip on my boots and step out the front door, half of my groceries still left in disarray on the countertop. My chest loosens as soon as my feet are on the ground outside, the tightness slipping away with fresh air and sunlight. I make my way through the tall grass, and I watch the trees sway in the breeze. Spring has arrived in earnest after its lengthy delay, the flowers and their bloom with it. Black-eyed Susans with their yellow petals opening to the sun. Bright purple monkshood in thick clusters at the base of the oak trees. Scarlet bee balm and early blue violets.

I'm so busy carefully stepping around tiny bright orange poppies bursting from the ground in licks of color that I almost don't notice it at first. I categorize it as background noise—a habit of life on a farm where there's always someone doing something.

Except everyone is already home for the day, and we finished the fieldwork hours ago.

I tilt my head up and shadow my face with my hand. I catch a figure at the very edge of the field. Tall. Legs for miles. The back of her wrist pressed against her forehead.

My heart does something complicated in my chest. A nosedive or a—a free fall. I can't really focus on anything other than—

Evelyn. Standing in the middle of my field with a shovel, wearing a pair of loose faded jeans and her hair pulled into a ponytail. For a second, I think I'm hallucinating. A sugar-induced fantasy. Dreaming again, maybe. But then she straightens, tosses the shovel over her shoulder, and yells at me.

"Do you know how long I've been out here shoveling rocks?"

I'm frozen, my boots planted in the ground, one foot in front of the other, caught midstride. There's a feeling in my chest that's overwhelming, staggering, the burst of it brighter than the flowers at my feet and the sun at my back. I bite a corner of my mouth against my grin.

She's looking at me like I've kept her waiting. A tilt to her brow like she's pissed about it too.

"Why are you shoveling rocks?" I call back. I keep my feet moving forward, helpless not to. I stop about an arm's length away from her, my eyes unsure what to focus on first. Her messy hair, a sheen of sweat across her forehead. Dirt up to her elbows and in a line across her white T-shirt. She looks like she's been personally kissed by the sun, all that skin just . . . shining.

I've missed her so *much.*

"Newbie does rock duty, right?"

I clear my throat and ignore the implication of what she's saying. "You've been talking to Jeremy?"

"Jeremy has been talking to me," she amends, her voice that low rasp I love. "Everyone has a lot of ideas."

"Ideas about what?"

"For me to tell you how I love you," she says simply, like she's not driving that shovel in the center of my chest and breaking my ribcage right open for all her sunlight to come pouring through. A smile starts in her eyes, nudging at her bottom lip until she's standing there and grinning at me, looking like every happy thought I've ever had. I take a step closer, and she tilts her head to keep her eyes on mine. "Josie's suggestion involved fireworks."

"Don't need fireworks," I grit out, my voice rough and tight. My hands ache to hold her. "Just need you."

"I told you I was coming back," she says. There is a perfect three inches of space between us, and I want to pull her closer, feel her tucked against my chest. She inclines her head and considers me. "But I didn't say it enough, and I know you appreciate action over words. I'll prove it to you. I'm here. I'm staying here. You didn't have to ask."

"I did though." I give in to temptation and drag my pinky along the side of her hand. All of her fingers twitch on the handle of the shovel. "I needed to ask. Because words are important too. You deserve that from me. I'm working on it."

She smiles at me, gentle and shy and unbearably beautiful. "Okay."

I nod. "All right."

"I did love your video," she tells me. A whisper—a secret—a flush in her cheeks that deepens as I uncurl her fingers one by one. "Who knew you'd be the TikTok sensation between us, farmer boy?"

I tangle our fingers together and grip her hand in mine. "I missed you," I say. "I missed you so much. I feel like I've been missing you the whole time I've known you." I swallow hard. "Loving you too."

"Well, you don't have to miss me anymore," she says, her voice soft. A gust of wind comes to catch the words off her lips and twist them away. She squeezes my hand, and I halve the space between us, my boots against hers. "We're going to have to work on that." At the confusion twisting my mouth, she clarifies. "When I told you I was coming back. You didn't believe me."

"I didn't."

I don't remember hearing that promise, to be honest. I was too focused on the look on her face when I told her I wouldn't settle for pieces. That what she was willing to give me wasn't enough.

"If this is going to work, you need to trust what I feel for you, okay? I won't ever lie to you."

Her brown eyes search mine and I nod. "I'm working on that too. I promise."

"Good." She tilts her head to the side, considering me. The sun shines on her skin, and her hair clings to her neck. "I got a new job, you know. Down in Durham."

The subject change leaves me grasping. I blink at her, confused. "Durham?"

I don't care if it's in Antarctica. I'll buy a parka and learn how to speak penguin.

She squeezes my hand again, a deep press of her thumb in the center of my hand. The same way I do when everything around me is too loud and I need to calm down. "That's where I went. The offices are headquartered in Durham, but the job is remote. I need a change and this feels—this feels right. Finally."

"Yeah?"

"Yeah." She tucks some hair behind her ear. "You know, when I first got here, I had no idea why I picked this place. But I think somewhere in my head or my heart I knew this is where I needed to be. I need something slower, Beckett. Something deeper. A place where I can catch my breath and find my footing." She holds my hand tight. "I need to be here. I want to be here."

"Good." I need her here too. Want her here just as much.

"I've got something else to say to you."

"Let's hear it, honey."

I can't imagine anything better than the words she's already given me.

"It's a request, actually." Her smile is coy, that blush deeper, her body moving farther into mine. She curls her free hand around the nape of my neck, fingertips sifting into my hair.

"Anything you want."

She presses up on her toes until her nose brushes mine. Until everything but her is a little bit blurry around the edges. Her mouth hovers there, hardly a centimeter away. I want to kiss her so bad, my hands shake with it. She brushes her mouth over mine, and I taste the bite of her smile.

"Ask me," she whispers.

I don't need her to say anything else. It feels like we've been slowly making our way to this exact spot since I stepped through the doorway of a bar all those months ago.

"Honey . . ." I cup her face in my hands and smooth my thumbs across her cheeks. I drop a kiss to the tip of her nose, the little dip at the corner of her mouth. I close my eyes and exhale. "Did you find your happy today?"

I feel her grin when she kisses me.

"Yes," she whispers into my mouth. "I did."

❧ EPILOGUE ❧

EVELYN

A Year Later

April

"EVIE." HE MOUTHS my name between my bare shoulder blades—a smile tucked into my skin. "Wake up."

I groan and burrow farther into the pillow beneath my head, ignoring the handsome idiot braced above me. My flight from El Paso was delayed twice, and I didn't pull into our driveway until after midnight, Beckett asleep in the chair by the fireplace. He had a book open on his chest and a bouquet of fresh flowers at his elbow, his own tradition for when I get home from trips. He tells me he likes to see me walk through the door. That his favorite thing is to wrap his arms around my waist and nudge his nose under my ear, a quiet "I missed you" pressed into my skin.

Words and action, together.

I beat him to it this time, slipping onto his lap and brushing the words against his lips. He had woken up in increments, his sleepy eyes hazy but his hands sure on my hips.

Now though. Now he's not letting me sleep.

"It's time to wake up," he says again, with a gentle bump of his nose behind my ear. I let out another groan, louder this time, and shimmy forward beneath my mountain of blankets to nip at his wrist with my teeth.

"No."

A grunt trips out of him from somewhere deep in his chest, his body going lax and pliant against mine. I'm pressed down farther into the mattress, his hips pinning me through the comforter and two blankets he insists on sleeping with.

"That had probably the opposite effect you were going for, honey," he tells me, his voice a gruff promise. He scrapes his teeth along my neck with intention, another press and roll of his body over mine.

I grin into the pillow. "Not if my goal is to stay in this bed with you."

Poor Gus had a tenant in that cute little house for only two months before I broke my lease and moved all of my belongings into Beckett's cabin. I was tired of pretending I wanted to be anywhere else except on his back porch—jam jar in hand and my feet tucked under his leg.

Our chairs are much closer together these days.

Beckett's hand peels back the blanket over my shoulders as he drops lingering, indulgent kisses on my neck. His palm presses beneath me until he finds my bare breast and squeezes gently. I gasp into my pillow and turn under him.

Messy hair. Warm skin. A soft smile that's prettier than the moonlight streaming in through the window.

"Hey," he says to me, his hand still cupped around me. His fingers pluck at my nipple and my back arches.

I stretch my arms above my head, and he watches their journey with interest. I twist my hands around the slats on the headboard, and he makes a pained sound, low in his chest. I grin. "Hi."

"You should put some clothes on," he says, his other hand at my hip, squeezing and stroking and contradicting his statement.

"Yeah?"

He nods but doesn't move his hands. He traces the soft skin between my breasts and his eyes trip down to watch the answering catch in my breath. "Yeah," he answers.

"You sure about that?"

His head tips to the side, and his tongue appears at the corner of his mouth as he indulges himself in another stroke of my soft skin. I trace my fingers over the full swell of his bottom lip, and we both shudder out a groan when he catches my thumb in his mouth and bites at the pad once. He pushes himself up on his knees, a strain of fabric at the front of his sweatpants.

He takes his hands off me and pats my hip. "You're dangerous."

I sit up to follow him and brush a kiss across the warm skin of his shoulder. "You started it."

He catches my chin in his hand and guides my face to his. He kisses me slow and deep until I'm leaning into him, my naked skin tucked against his.

"I'll finish it too," he says against my mouth. "After we watch the sky for a bit."

That's right. His meteor shower. The date has been taped to the front of the fridge for months, circled in bright red.

I drop my forehead to his collarbone, and he combs his fingers through my hair. "We don't have to," he says quietly after a second of me rubbing my knuckles against my eyes. He brushes a kiss across my forehead. "If you're tired."

"No, I want to." He's been so excited. Another yawn twists through my body, and I shiver into him. "But I'm going to wear your sweatshirt."

He hums. "That's fine, honey."

I'm clumsy as I dress myself, mismatched socks and an old pair of sweatpants, one of Beckett's sweatshirts dwarfing my frame as I tug it over my head. I push the hood out of my face and catch him staring, leaning against the door.

"What?" I push my hair out of my face. He's looking at me like I'm everything he's ever wanted. Everything he'll ever want.

I know the feeling.

"Nothing." He holds out his hand and tilts his head toward the door. "C'mere."

"*C'mere*, what?" I laugh, but my hand is already in his.

I'm reminded of another night, the two of us under the same stars. Together we slip down the dark hallway and through the front door, our boots quiet in the wet grass. It's a clear night, the stars so bright it's like I can reach out and touch them—a collection of diamonds in a sea of black. I tip my face up toward the night sky and watch as we walk, waiting for a flare of light.

Beckett's hand cups my cheek, and he guides my face down until I'm looking at him instead of the stars. He shakes his head once. "Not yet."

I frown at him. "Aren't we supposed to be watching a meteor shower?"

His thumb rubs behind my ear as he tugs me forward, beckoning me to walk some more. I make a disgruntled sound under my breath, and he does his best to hide his smile. "Not yet."

"I can see the sky just fine right here."

"Not much farther."

I know where we're going as soon as we crest the second hill, the path to this stretch of field a well-worn route in my mind. We haven't gone a week since I moved in without visiting. Picnic lunches and late-night drinks on a threadbare blanket. Bare skin in the moonlight, Beckett's mouth hot against mine.

I shiver again, and Beckett gives me a look over his shoulder, one eyebrow jumping up in interest.

"Eyes on the road," I tell him, and he snickers in front of me, fingers threading through mine. We walk and walk and walk until finally we get to the clearing with the two giant trees, their branches curved up and out like they're welcoming the sky into their massive swaying arms.

Beckett tugs me forward and places me in front of him. He curls both arms around my shoulders and rests his palm flat over my heart.

"Watch," he instructs, and we tilt our heads back together, eyes fixed on the stars.

The sky remains still as we stand there together, the rustle of the trees and our gentle breathing the only sounds in the night. I feel like my eyes are as wide as they can possibly get, unwilling to miss a single thing. Beckett's hand squeezes at my wrist, the other dipping into the collar of his sweatshirt to press against warm skin.

"Watch," he says again, a whisper. I feel his smile at my ear, and just like that—magic.

I see something streak across the sky so quickly I almost miss it. A burst of light and a bright flare of gold followed by green, like a spark bursting into flame. My breath hitches and Beckett's grip on me tightens.

I watch as another appears. And then another. Another—a cascade of light dancing across the sky above us.

"Ask me," Beckett says suddenly, his voice low in my ear.

I tip my head until I can see his face, a backdrop of a billion stars haloed behind his head. Another meteor flares in the night sky above him, and I make my wish on that one, exactly like this, wrapped up in Beckett with my hands clinging tight.

I look at him looking at me out here in the field where he kissed me like it was the very first time. I shake my head, my hair catching and pulling at his shirt. "I don't need to."

Because I feel it every time he brings me a mug of tea on the porch or slips a thick pair of his socks over my cold feet. In every handwritten note and pot of coffee and touch against my bare skin in the stillness of night. In the drives we take along the dirt road that leads to the farm, all the windows down and my hair in the wind. In every familiar face we pass on the way into town, a call of my name and a happy wave, Beckett's hand warm and comforting in mine.

In the tiny tattoo of a lime on the inside of my forearm—the very same place he licked a line of salt from my skin the first night we met. A birthday present that made him laugh so hard he fell out of his chair.

In the tattoo of some poorly drawn tulips, just above his heart.

I don't ask because I don't need to.
He found his happy in me.
Like I found mine in him.
In us.
In this.

❧ BONUS CHAPTER ❧

THIS BONUS CHAPTER is Beckett's perspective of Evelyn's return from a work trip and features some new houseguests.

BECKETT

IN RETROSPECT, I probably should have given Evelyn a heads-up.

But she was in Durham for work, then she flew to see her parents in Portland, and decisions had to be made while she was gone. I don't particularly like talking on the phone, and if I did, I don't know how I could have explained it so that she—

"Beckett!" Evelyn's voice punches through the open kitchen door and across the backyard. I glance down at the duck in the front pocket of my flannel and then at the cat winding through my legs. Her flight must have gotten in early. I thought I had more time.

Well. Can't do much about it now.

I scratch at the soft downy fluff on top of Otis's head. "Yeah?"

I hear some muffled cursing followed by a few happy clucks from the family of chickens that has made our kitchen their temporary home, and then Evie appears in the doorway. Her hair is in a long braid over her shoulder, and she's wearing one of my shirts, a pale blue button-down that she's tucked into the front of her black jeans. She looks tired from all her traveling, but she also looks fucking beautiful, even with the frown that's twisting her lips. Something in my chest slots back into place, and I take the first deep breath I've managed in days. She's exactly where she's supposed to be, standing on our back porch. Looking right at me.

Holding a chicken.

"Why the hell is our kitchen full of chickens?"

"Is it?"

Evelyn sighs, a smile that she does her best to beat into submission flirting with the corners of her mouth. She gives me a look, all lowered brows with a cute little wrinkle in her nose. If she's trying to be intimidating, she's doing a shit job.

"Beckett."

I shrug my shoulders and make my way over to her, a tug right in the center of my chest. She watches me with those whiskey eyes as I trudge up the steps, her face tilting towards mine when my feet find the ledge below the porch. She's all smooth skin in the orange glow of the porch light, sea salt and jasmine and my favorite freckle, right on her bottom lip. I nudge her chin with my nose and press a kiss to it because I missed it. I missed her. I missed her bare feet tucked between my legs in our bed and her hair in my face when we wake up. I missed her grumbling at the coffee machine and the notes she leaves on the fridge, taped down on every side so one of the cats doesn't run off with them.

"Missed you," I tell her, because she deserves the words, and there was a time when we weren't so good at sharing what's in our heads and in our hearts. Her reluctant smile grows. "M'glad you're home," I add.

She narrows her eyes. "You're sucking up."

"Nah." I drag my hand through my hair. "It's true. I'm a mess without you here."

She huffs. "You know what's a mess? Our kitchen." She holds up the chicken in her hands in silent explanation. Delilah—a beautiful Rhode Island Red that is far too skinny thanks to the negligence of her last owner—blinks at me and cocks her head. Evie tucks her back to her chest. "Our kitchen is a mess because there are six chickens in there."

My eyes dart over her head to where I've set up a makeshift pen. There should be eight chickens in there.

"Are you sure?"

"Am I sure, what? That there are chickens destroying the rug I bought a month ago? Yes, Beckett. I'm sure."

"I can fix it," I tell her. "Or I'll buy you a new one. Whatever you want."

"Beckett." She sighs again. She leans to the side and gently drops Delilah onto the porch. We both watch as the chicken struts happily into the kitchen to join her sisters. Otis quacks in my pocket and I scoop him out, letting him follow. He's taken well to the addition of new feathered friends. Evie gives me a look. "We've talked about this."

"I know," I mutter.

After I adopted the four cats and the duck, another duck appeared. Zelma is technically the last animal I adopted, but there's been a steady stream of temporary houseguests since then. A little dog someone found in the dumpster behind Matty's. A three-legged fox that got trapped in one of the broken fences at the edge of the property. A baby lamb that was rejected by her mom. And a really sweet goose that liked visiting the back porch for some stale bread crusts.

And now Delilah the chicken and her seven sisters.

"I was going to have them out of here before you got home."

Evelyn hums, her fingertips walking up my chest. It's distracting and she knows it. "Do you often take in animals while I'm traveling?"

I shrug. "Not really, no. It just happens like that sometimes."

A laugh slips out of her and settles beneath my rib cage. She leans forward and drops her face into my neck. She sighs, and her whole body relaxes. Mine does too. I cup my hand around the back of her neck and breathe her in. Fuck, I missed her.

"Good trip?" I ask.

She nods, nose nudging against my throat, and her hands clench the front of my shirt. "Yeah. It was. I missed home, though."

Home. There it is. The word that sends satisfaction thrumming through every inch of me. I never thought this home would be enough to keep Evie, but she keeps coming back to me here. She keeps giving me the pieces of her no one else gets to see, and I keep holding on to them tight, giving her pieces of myself right back.

She presses a kiss against the hollow of my throat, and I slip my hand over her shoulders and down her back to the curve of her ass. I squeeze there once, her warm husky chuckle a different sort of satisfaction. I climb the steps so I'm standing on the porch with her, eager to hold more of her. She rests her chin against my chest and looks up at me, her arms circling my waist.

"I'd say you could have me in the kitchen, but it's currently occupied by your feathered children."

I lick my bottom lip. "The greenhouse is available."

"There're no animals in there?"

I glance over my shoulder. There is probably at least one cat in there. I make a face, and Evelyn laughs.

She leans back against the porch railing and arches an eyebrow at me. "What's the story with the chickens?"

"They were found abandoned on a farm over in Delaware. Justin, the animal rescue guy down on the coast, he gave me a call when he found them."

Her lips twitch. "You've built quite a reputation for yourself, haven't you?"

I nod and then shrug. The pet rescue stuff wasn't intentional. It's just sort of . . . happened . . . over the last couple of years. I can't see an animal in need and not do something about it. And before Evelyn was here, it was nice to have some company in this big house.

"I know we can't keep them," I tell her quietly. "I'm trying to get Layla to build a coop behind the bakehouse. I figured she could use the eggs."

Evelyn's smile grows. "And how is that working out for you?"

It's not going well, if I'm being honest. Layla caught me dropping a roll of chicken wire outside her back door and had a few things to say about it. But I'm confident I can convince her.

Maybe I'll have Caleb hold a chicken. I'm sure that'll change her mind.

"It's . . . going," I manage.

Evelyn watches me carefully in the fading light. I don't think I'll ever get tired of her like this. Socked feet crossed at the ankles, and her arms propped up against the rail of the porch. Fireflies dancing in the fields behind her, and stars starting to wink to life in the sky up above.

This whole big, wide world, and I somehow managed to find her in it.

"I'm glad you're home," I tell her again, the words slipping out.

Her smile is a soft, gentle thing. "I am too." She rubs her lips together. "Kiss me again, and I'll let you keep the chickens for another few days."

I halve the space between us and reach for her hips, spreading my fingers wide and letting my thumbs dip under the sides of her oversized shirt. I trace the warm skin of her belly, and her breath catches.

"Can I earn a week if it's a really good kiss?"

She hums, eyes closed and waiting. "We'll have to see, won't we?"

I smile. This woman drives me halfway out of my mind, and I wouldn't have it any other way. I step between her legs until the small of her back is pressed against the rail of the porch, smoke and sunscreen and salt on her skin. I let my mouth hover over hers, our noses brushing.

And then a cow moos from behind the greenhouse.

Evelyn's body goes rigid against mine. I drop my forehead against her shoulder with a sigh.

"Beckett Porter, was that a cow?"

ACKNOWLEDGMENTS

My first thank-you, as always, goes to you. I've been blown away by the kindness and generosity of complete strangers. There aren't words to explain what it means to me. Thank you for giving my book some of your time. It means the world. I read every comment, every tag, every caption, and every review. From the very bottom of my very full heart, thank you. I hope this book was the hug you needed.

Sam: Thank you for taking every word-vomit email I sent you and turning it into something beautiful. You made my cover dreams come true, despite probably hating me for a solid couple of days in December.

Annie: Every book starts and ends with you. Thanks for making me better, for answering all twelve thousand of my panicked text messages, and for distracting me with things I shouldn't be looking at while writing a book. Let's do this forever.

Sarah: Getting to share this with you has been the best thing. Talking to you about characters and books and headcanons will always be my favorite. Love you forever.

Eliza: You are the best hype woman a girl could ask for. I'm lucky to be your sister.

E: You give me my happy every single day. I love you.

Ro: You made this one tough, kiddo. Thanks for going back to taking naps as I wrote the second half of this book. I'm so proud to be your mom, but also maybe sleep more.

I couldn't do any of this without all of you.

Keep reading for an excerpt from the next novel in the
Lovelight series

MIXED SIGNALS

LAYLA

"YOU'RE NOT WHAT I expected."

That's a bold statement coming from the man slouched in the seat across from me. He picked me up forty-five minutes late, berated the waitstaff as soon as we got here, took two shots of—and I quote—*the cheapest bourbon available*, and then promptly ordered a steak without bothering to ask what I would like.

"Oh?" I indulge his attempt at conversation. It's possible that he's not as bad as he seems. I'm not sure how, but I've seen stranger things happen. Like the guy who picked me up for dinner in a horse and buggy. "How so?"

I cut my dessert into four perfectly portioned bites and try to make my face do something that resembles vague interest. He burps into his closed fist and I abandon the effort.

"Prettier," he tells me. His eyes dip down to my neckline and hold. "I had no idea you were hiding all that." He twirls his fork in my general direction. "Your profile picture doesn't do you justice."

Gross. I shovel another bite of passion fruit and coconut into my mouth.

"Probably all the baking you do, right? Those sweet treats make you thick in all the right places."

I don't even know where to start. "Yes, I own a bakery."

I own a little bakeshop tucked in the middle of a Christmas tree farm about forty miles west of here. I'm also part owner of the farm. I spend my days mixing and plating and rolling and wrapping inside of an old tractor shed that my business partner Stella and I converted into a bakery as soon as she bought the place. Big floor-to-ceiling glass windows. Old oak floors. Walls lined by cozy booths with throw pillows and blankets. It's my very favorite place in the world.

Every day I flick on the lights and set the tables and feel like I'm living inside a snow globe. Even in the middle of the summer when the humidity is so thick it feels like I'm walking through Jell-O, the sticky heat making my hair curl. I love it. Working at Lovelight Farms is the best part of my day, and being able to go to work with my two best friends is icing on the proverbial cake.

Stella manages business operations, and Beckett keeps everything growing and thriving as head of farming. They're the kindest, loveliest people—and in relationships with equally kind, lovely, beautiful people. I'm so happy they're happy, even if their so-cute-I-want-to-die relationships make me want to tip over an entire row of mini cakes in a fit of jealousy.

They have the sort of romances that dreams are made of. While I'm here with . . . Bryce.

I didn't even recognize him when he pulled up in front of my house. Our tiny tucked-away town is hard to find on a good day, and most people bypass Inglewild completely on the way to the shore. When his car pulled up in my driveway, I thought Bryce sent a Lyft driver to pick me up for the evening. But then he rolled down the window, yelled, "Hey, Layla!" and I stupidly got in the passenger seat.

I should have ended it right there. I know better. He had a hamster bobblehead on his dash, for god's sake. I'm lucky I wasn't murdered.

The entire drive to the coast, I stared hard at his face. I could have sworn his profile picture was of a tall brunet, and yet . . .

He drags his hand through his bottle-dyed blond hair.

And yet.

He probably thinks he looks charming sitting there like that, all lazy and loose in his seat, his knuckles beneath his chin. Unlucky for him, I'm more sexually attracted to the warm rum butter sauce on my cake at this point.

I sigh and glance over his shoulder at the bar, trying to catch the eye of our beleaguered waitress. We'd shared a commiserate look earlier when he stared too long at the hem of her skirt. I'm pretty sure it's why she brought me this slice of boozy passion fruit cake that I did not order.

I grasp for a subject change. "You said you work in Ellicott City?"

He nods, shoveling another bite of steak into his stupid, smug mouth. He chews with his mouth open and doesn't bother finishing before he replies, bits of food flying out with his answer. I want plexiglass between us. A ten-foot wall. "Yeah. That's where my dad's law offices are."

"And you work with him?"

"I just said that, didn't I?"

All right, then. We lapse into another uncomfortable silence. He stabs at his steak, and I drag the tip of my fork through a thick layer of whipped cream. He told me he owned the law firm, organizing pro bono work across the mid-Atlantic region. Po-tay-to, po-tah-to, I guess. I sigh and cut another piece of cake.

"Where are you from?" he asks.

The depths of hell. Sent to destroy men who lie on the internet and are mean to those in the service industry.

"Annapolis," I say instead. I am so tempted to get up from my seat, walk between the tables, and step into the ocean. It sounds infinitely more appealing than another moment with Bryce.

This is the third first date I've been on this month, and I am tired. Tired of men who are entitled, small-minded, and generally disappointing. What spirit did I disrespect to curse myself with bad date after bad date? I pay my taxes. I don't leave my popcorn bucket stuffed under the seat at the movie theater. I obey traffic laws and donate to that one charity for three-legged goats that Beckett quite literally never shuts up about.

Why can't I find a single human being that I connect with? My standards are not impossibly high. I want someone who makes me laugh. Who cares about what I do and what I say and what I think. I want to sit on the couch with someone in blissful, perfect, comfortable silence—pizza on the coffee table and my feet tucked under their thigh. I want someone to hand me the recipe section of the local paper while they read the headlines. I want to share all of my small, silly, silent moments.

I want someone to give me butterflies.

I stare at Bryce, who lied about everything but his name, and watch as he picks at something in his teeth with his thumbnail.

Maybe that someone doesn't exist.

"Did you go to college?"

There is no curiosity in his question, just a smug satisfaction and a callous condescension. A familiar insecurity pricks at the back of my mind, a twist in my stomach that pulls tight.

"I went to Salisbury."

He laughs like I've made a joke and then reaches across the table with his fork for a bite of my cake. I don't slap his hand away, but it's a near thing. To me, dessert is *sacred*. "Ah, the party school. That makes sense."

I clench my teeth so hard I'm surprised my molars don't crack right in half. "What does?"

"Bakers don't need to go to serious schools, do they? It doesn't matter where you went or what you did. You probably could have gotten a degree from circus school and been just fine baking your little treats all day."

Circus school.

Little treats.

Oh my god.

It takes me a second to collect my bearings. When I do reply, my voice is quiet fury laced with exhaustion. I am so *tired*.

"I graduated with honors with a dual degree in mathematics and engineering." Not that it should matter. "I'm a baker and a small business owner, and I bet I do more in an hour than you do in a day."

He scoffs.

I set my fork down on the table. This evening just rocketed to the top of my Worst Dates Ever list, and the competition is robust. I can't believe I put on my green dress for this. What a freaking waste. "I think you should go grab the check."

He holds up both hands, his eyes wide. "Whoa, don't be so sensitive. I didn't mean to offend."

I ignore him and slip another bite of coconut into my mouth. This rum sauce really is life-changing. Maybe after we wrap up here, I'll sneak back into the kitchen and sweet-talk the chef into sharing his recipe. I bet he's better company than bampot Bryce.

He makes no move to get the check, as requested. I whip the napkin off my lap and drop it on the table. "That's fine. I'll go settle the bill at the bar."

He rolls his eyes. "I was getting to it. You don't have to be so rude."

All right. I'm the rude one. Okay.

I push my chair back and head toward the bar at the edge of the surf. I don't usually come this far out for a date, but Bryce had been insistent about trying a new tiki bar right on the coast. Low-hanging string lights. A couple of fires burning in large round pits. The tide rolls in behind bottles stacked on old wine barrels. Bartenders move back and forth behind a small rowboat that's been flipped over and converted into bench seating.

It would be a romantic spot if my date was not a complete and total asshole.

Our waitress, Celia, waits behind the bar with her lips in a thin line, her eyes kind and understanding. She hands me the bill before I can even ask.

"Did the dessert help, at least?" she asks.

I snort a laugh and flip open the bill. "It was the best part of my evening."

"I can get you another one," she offers. When I shake my head, she makes a short contemplative sound. "I wasn't going to say anything, but that guy is a jerk. You can do better."

"Yeah, you're not wrong." Unfortunately for me, I haven't seen much better on any of the dating websites I pay unseemly monthly membership fees for. Bryce is pretty par for the course. "Any ideas on where to look?"

Her gaze trips over my shoulder as she pulls a thick evergreen rag out of her back pocket and shines the rim of a tumbler. Her face morphs into something glassy, appreciative, and she tilts her head behind me. "That looks like a good place to start."

Photo by Marlayna Demond

B.K. BORISON lives in Baltimore with her sweet husband, vivacious toddler, and giant dog. She started writing in the margins of books when she was in middle school and hasn't stopped.

CONNECT ONLINE

BKBorison.com
AuthorBKBorison
AuthorBKBorison